WOODWINDS
Fundamental Performance Techniques

WOOD

GENE A. SAUCIER

WINDS

Fundamental
Performance Techniques

SCHIRMER BOOKS

A Division of Macmillan Publishing Co., Inc.

NEW YORK

Collier Macmillan Publishers

LONDON

Copyright © 1981 by Schirmer Books
A Division of Macmillan Publishing Co., Inc.

All rights reserved. No part of this book may be reproduced or transmitted in any form or by any means, electronic or mechanical, including photocopying, recording, or by any information storage and retrieval system, without permission in writing from the Publisher.

Schirmer Books
A Division of Macmillan Publishing Co., Inc.
866 Third Avenue, New York, N. Y. 10022

Collier Macmillan Canada, Ltd.

Library of Congress Catalog Card Number: 80-5223

Printed in the United States of America

printing number
1   2   3   4   5   6   7   8   9   10

Library of Congress Cataloging in Publication Data

Saucier, Gene Allen.
    Woodwinds.

    Includes index.
    1.   Woodwind instruments—Instruction and study.   I.   Title.
MT339.5.S3   788′.05′0712   80-5223
ISBN 0-02-872300-7

To my wife, Joan

Contents

Preface and Acknowledgments   xi

PART I
General Aspects of Woodwind Study

1 TEACHING RESOURCES AND CURRENT PRACTICE   3

Personal Experience and Observation   3
Group vs. Individual Instruction   3

2 FUNDAMENTALS OF TONE PRODUCTION   7

Primary Factors   7
Embouchure   7
Breath Support   8
  Single Reeds   11
  Double Reeds   14
  The Flute   17
Study Questions: Chapters 1 and 2   23

PART II
Fundamental Techniques and Supplemental Aids

3 THE FLUTE   27

Instrument Assembly and Care   29
Instrument Angle and Hand Position   31
Tone Production   33
  Embouchure   33
  Breath Support   39
  Tonguing   41
Fingering   44
  Trills   48
  Frequently Used Special Fingerings   54
Study Questions   57
Teaching Aids   60

vii

viii Contents

Flute Literature 60
 Selected List of Graded Solos 60
 *Class Methods for the Public School Instrumental
 Music Program* 63
 Individual Methods and Supplemental Studies 64
 Recordings of Flute Literature 65

4 THE OBOE 69

Instrument Assembly and Care 70
Instrument Angle and Hand Position 71
Tone Production 74
 Embouchure 74
 Breath Support 78
 Tonguing 81
Fingering 82
 Trills 86
 Frequently Used Special Fingerings 91
Study Questions 94
Teaching Aids 96
Oboe Literature 97
 Selected List of Graded Solos 97
 Class Methods 99
 Individual Methods and Supplemental Studies 99
 Recordings of Oboe Literature 100

5 THE CLARINET 103

Instrument Assembly and Care 105
Instrument Angle and Hand Position 106
Tone Production 109
 Embouchure 109
 Breath Support 112
 Tonguing 113
Fingering 116
 Trills 120
 Frequently Used Special Fingerings 125
Study Questions 130
Teaching Aids 132
Clarinet Literature 133
 Selected List of Graded Solos 133
 Class Methods 134
 Individual Methods and Supplemental Studies 135
 Recordings of Clarinet Literature 136

THE LOWER CLARINETS 139

Individual Suitability 139

Embouchure Modifications   140
 E-flat Alto Clarinet   140
 Bass and Contrabass Clarinets   140
Recommended Study Material   141
 Beginning Students   141
 Transfer Students   142
 Additional Supplements for Alto and
 Bass Clarinets   143

6   THE BASSOON   145

Instrument Assembly and Care   147
Instrument Angle and Hand Position   148
Tone Production   148
 Embouchure   148
 Breath Support   151
 Tonguing   153
Fingering   153
 The Bassoon Key System   153
 Trills   160
 Frequently Used Special Fingerings   166
Study Questions   170
Teaching Aids   173
Bassoon Literature   174
 Selected List of Graded Solos   174
 Class Methods   175
 Individual Methods and Supplemental Studies   176
 Recordings of Bassoon Literature   176

7   THE SAXOPHONE   179

Instrument Assembly and Care   180
Instrument Angle and Hand Position   181
Tone Production   183
 Embouchure   183
 Breath Support   185
 Tonguing   187
Fingering   188
 Trills   192
 Frequently Used Special Fingerings   196
Study Questions   199
Teaching Aids   201
Saxophone Literature   202
 Selected List of Graded Solos   202
 Class Methods   203
 Individual Methods and Supplemental Studies   203
 Recordings of Saxophone Literature   204

The Lower Saxophones 207

B-flat Tenor Saxophone 207
E-flat Baritone Saxophone 208
Recommended Study Material 208

PART III
Secondary Factors

8 Mouthpieces and Single Reeds: Selection and Care 211

Mouthpieces 212
   Selection 212
   Care 213
Single Reeds 213
   Selection 213
   Care 219

9 Double Reeds: Selection and Care 221

Selection 221
Care 224
Source References for Reed Making and Adjusting 224
   Oboe 224
   Bassoon 224

10 Vibrato 225

Defining Vibrato 225
Types of Vibrato 227
   Involuntary Vibrato 227
   Voluntary Vibrato 227
Choice of Vibrato 227
Developing Jaw Vibrato 228
Developing Diaphragmatic Vibrato 231

Index 235

Preface and Acknowledgments

This book has been written to serve as a primer for the instrumental music education student in training and to assist the instrumental music teacher in the field. Its design is such that it can be—and is recommended to be—used concurrently with a class instrument method. For obvious reasons class methods—such as Harry I. Phillips's *Play Now* (Silver Burdett, 1969) or Douglas and Weber's *Belwin Band Builder* (Belwin-Mills, 1953)—cannot cover in the scope of one text both reading materials and detailed aspects of woodwind pedagogy, nor should they attempt to do so.

Although many books have been written covering performing techniques and teaching methods for woodwind instruments, it is the writer's judgment that there is still a need for a text that achieves the following:

1. fits into a one or, ideally, two semester course for the instrumental music teacher in training,
2. is concise, to the point, relatively free of overly technical terms, and designed to aid the teacher in the field,
3. correlates visual and aural teaching aids as much as possible, and
4. emphasizes tone production as the primary factor, with all related factors as secondary.

Additional aims will be to place greater emphasis on visual aids and present original as well as "tried and true" ideas. Where necessary, older concepts will be redefined in order to achieve greater clarity and accuracy.

The author is especially grateful to Ms. Gayle Brownlee, Dr. Robert Jordan, Ms. Sue Reuter, Mr. Pat Simmons, and Dr. Gilbert Sommers for their generous help with the task of proofreading, and last but not least, my wife, Joan, and my son, Allen, for their patience and support. A very special note of appreciation is due the following artist-teachers whose collective knowledge of the solo literature proved invaluable: Ms. Judith Genovese, Ms. Janet Ratay, Dr. Dan Ross, and Mrs. Nancy Vinson. The author is also indebted to Mrs. Aurelia Hartenberger and Mrs. Vinson for their sensitive criticisms and helpful suggestions regarding flute pedagogy. Additionally, the author wishes to thank Mr. William C. Martin, photographer extraordinaire, for his endless patience and support. A final word of acknowledgment is made to Mr. Ken Stuart, Ms. Abbie Meyer, Mr. Michael Sander, and Mr. Fred Sard for their genuine encouragement and consummate professional guidance in refining the final draft of this text.

GENE A. SAUCIER

General Aspects of Woodwind Study

PART I

Part I of this text consists of two chapters. Chapter 1 is devoted to two topics that the author feels are of key importance to the reader. First there is a discussion of *teaching resources* that the instrumental music teacher may utilize. The second topic involves current methods of presenting minor instrument study on the college level. The pros and cons of each method of presentation are weighed in light of both academic and practical needs.

Chapter 2 is an in-depth discussion of the primary factors that must be taken into account if an effective and successful study of tone production is to be accomplished. *Embouchure* and *breath support,* the primary determinants in tone production in all wind instruments, are discussed first as singular aspects. Breath support, the less visual of the two primary factors, is subsequently discussed in light of the natural woodwind categories, namely, single reeds, double reeds, and flute.

Additional discussions of recommended embouchure formats with pictorial visual aids have been reserved for Part II, where a chapter has been assigned to each of the major woodwind instruments.

In the final analysis a beautiful musical performance is predicated first on the rendering of a beautiful tone.

Teaching Resources and Current Practice

1

There are two primary sources which instrumental music teachers draw upon and utilize in their teaching. On the one hand, there is the individual's personal, applied performance experience. On the other, there is the analytical observation and deduction of another's applied performance experience and subsequent recommendations. In the former instance an instrumental music teacher utilizes personal insights gained from his or her actual performance experience—experience which generally involves major and minor instrument study. Of equal importance is the second instance, wherein the instrumental music teacher utilizes performance practices recommended by a recognized authority.

The experienced and successful teacher will be quick to note that the use of both of these sources is necessary for competent and meaningful instrumental teaching. Each has its own unique validity, but it is the utilization of both that ultimately brings about excellence in teaching. In fact we may say that one tends to compliment the other.

Personal Experience and Observation

Currently, instrumental music education majors are provided with either of two teaching approaches when they begin their minor instrument study on the college level. Some larger schools of music offer minor instrument courses on a "one-to-one" basis, just as they do with applied music performance majors (where the ratio is customarily one teacher to one student, meeting one or one-half hour per week). Other schools—especially those with smaller music departments—often use the "mixed-class" approach for minor instrument course offerings, meeting two or three days per week. Although economics may certainly play a role in determining which approach will be used, it is by no means the sole determining factor. Some music educators advocate minor instrument study on a class basis for purely academic and educational reasons; others recommend the one-to-one approach for similar reasons. Some music departments use both approaches. Thus, the use of these approaches will vary from one institution to another.

The author, speaking from a purely academic point of view, recommends the "mixed-class" approach for the study of minor instruments on the college level. (Major instrument study on the undergraduate level is indeed another matter, as is applied group study on the graduate level.) The reasons for advocating the mixed-group approach center on such key words as *repetition, contrast, time,* and

Group vs. Individual Instruction

3

the *experiential aspect*. While class instruction may permit three meetings per week, the private lesson is in practice quite often limited to one per week. Class instruction also affords each student the opportunity to compare, through aural and visual contrasts, the woodwind instruments with each other, as well as the differences and similarities that inevitably occur from individual to individual. (Such an experience is precisely what the teacher in training will be most likely to encounter upon leaving college and initiating a first beginners' band program.)

Another strong point in favor of class instruction centers on the experiential aspect. It is through the circumstance of group performance that the student teacher can personally experience the applied value of certain performance and teaching techniques, techniques which he will in the future impose in like manner (through class instruction) on his own students. This is not to say that an instrumental teacher in the field cannot effectively evaluate or utilize another's proposed teaching technique simply because he has not personally executed and demonstrated a certain performance practice. (The value of using another's applied teaching experience has been fully acknowledged above.) It is to say, however, that if one has been required to perform on minor instruments with others, one then may experience a personal aspect and a very personal appreciation of the instruments that can come about only through such group performance. For example, the student teacher who participates in regular class meetings is presented such advantages as the following:

1. He has the opportunity to acquaint himself with practical class methods and visually and aurally work through them—methods which he will in turn use in the field.
2. He is provided with, in addition to the assumed content of the class course, an indispensable opportunity to practice ear training with regard to developing aural awareness of pitch, timbre, and tone production.
3. The student is required to listen, make judgments, evaluations, and adjustments on a regular basis—often as part of a one-hour-per-day, three-days-per-week routine.
4. It becomes possible to make first-hand visual and aural observations regarding the necessity to alter general recommendations to fit the individual when deviations are needed! In a mixed group, individuals will inevitably vary in their physical makeup. It is within the group setting that certain standard recommended concepts—such as the flexed offset embouchure for bassoonists —can be dealt with openly for the mutual benefit of all class participants. In some cases, such as an excessive, unaccommodating "cupid's bow" in an aspiring flutist, it has to be frankly acknowledged that certain individuals should not be started on the flute.[1] It is through the class experience that both minor and major exceptions to general rules may be viewed openly, and subsequently dealt with in an appropriate manner.

1. An unaccommodating cupid's bow occurs when one's upper lip has a tab dipping downward toward the lower lip which is straight and unaccommodating. The net result of an extreme unaccommodating cupid's bow is that two apertures tend to form when the student tries to flex his lips to make the desired flute embouchure.

The repetition of such musical activity in group study—with the varied aural and visual observations which can be gained therefrom—amply reveals its distinct advantages and value. It is for these reasons —academic reasons—that class instruction in minor instrument study is advocated for the instrumental music education major.

Fundamentals of Tone Production

2

If the message of this book was to be embodied in one concept, that would be: tone production. In the final analysis a beautiful musical performance is predicated first on the rendering of a beautiful tone. There are of course many other factors involved, but a beautiful tone is the first requisite. Thus a study of tone production is indispensable to woodwind students.

There are two primary factors that must be taken into account in the study of tone production: *embouchure* and *breath support.* The remaining factors (reeds, mouthpieces, etc.) may be considered secondary—although certainly important—and will be discussed later.

After gripping an instrument with the hands, the next thing a woodwind performer does is "grip" the mouthpiece with his mouth. Musicians use the term *embouchure* to refer to the manner in which the mouthpiece is gripped. A literal translation of the French *emboucher* would be "in-mouth" or "to put to the mouth" (*bouche* meaning "mouth"). History indicates that many early wind instruments were "in-mouthed," so to speak. Today only the single- and double-reed instruments of the orchestra or band require that the mouthpiece be placed into the mouth; the expression "out-mouth" would be more accurate in describing the embouchure of the flutist today.

The key point to remember, however, is the aforementioned phrase: "the manner in which the mouthpiece is gripped." How the mouthpiece is gripped or the embouchure formed is a major determinant in the making of a tone on wind instruments. The *type of embouchure* is sometimes a matter of dissension among teachers.

Often a teacher is prone to teach students the embouchure which he himself employs on his major instrument. As for those wind instruments on which he does not perform in public, he usually feels compelled to choose a recommended approach advocated by an authority on that particular instrument. These viewpoints are certainly understandable, but not necessarily appropriate to every individual case. The essential point to remember about types of embouchure is that while there is considerably more unanimity among woodwind performers and teachers today than in the past, there always will be exceptions to the general rule. To illustrate this point: The members of one woodwind class were asked to examine five different texts and compare the recommendations of each author regarding bassoon embouchure. In each case the author advised an embouchure best described as flexed and offset (that is, with the lower jaw pulled back considerably behind the resting point of the

*Primary
Factors*

Embouchure

7

upper teeth and lips, while the surrounding lip muscles appear flexed and smooth—not loose and bunched up, so to speak). Next, the class was required to watch and observe closely a professional bassoonist in a major orchestra appearing weekly over national television. This bassoonist did *not* employ the flexed, offset grip generally recommended by many fine bassoonists. It appeared that his grip tended to be more even or parallel, that is, the upper and lower lips appeared to rest at approximately the same point, equidistant from the wired end of the reed. The point here is that while there is a generally recommended embouchure format that works best for most students and professionals, there are and will continue to be exceptions due to individual differences in physical makeup. (It should also be pointed out that the aesthetic factor may account for certain exceptions.)

Where a seemingly radical embouchure is successfully employed, it is safe to assume that the performer does so for some physical reason—perhaps an acute malocclusion. In such a case several other factors have in all probability been altered to fit his particular needs. For example, the vamp or makeup of the reed, its strength, and the particular mouthpiece facing are all among the variable factors that can be modified to suit an individual.

While there is a basic embouchure format for each woodwind instrument that is recommended above and beyond all others, the student in training and the teacher in the field should be aware that the biggest problem they may be confronted with will be determining *if, when,* and *how* the basic format should be changed. Knowing about the most generally accepted and recommended embouchure type is one thing. Knowing when it is applicable and when it is not is indeed another matter. Additionally, the matter of developing an effective embouchure may occasionally rest with external factors, such as appropriate mouthpiece and reed fitting.

The subject of tone production and related aspects will be discussed in more detail in subsequent chapters devoted separately to each woodwind instrument. Additionally, recommended embouchure formats (with picture illustrations) and deviations from the basic approach will be discussed in these chapters.

Breath Support

The second major determinant in tone production is *breath support.* Considering first things first, a wind performer may be observed to do the following: (1) grip the instrument with his hands, (2) grip the vibratory source—mouthpiece, double reed, or tone hole—with his mouth, and (3) blow a stream of air into the instrument via the vibratory source. Although embouchure and breath support are major determinants, it should be mentioned that how the performer grips the instrument and the resulting *angle* at which it is held in relation to the body can affect tone production. Generally speaking, the matter of instrument angle is self-adjusting. However, some students—particularly those doing minor instrument study who display a carry-over of inveterate habits acquired in their major instrument work—must be constructively criti-

Ch. 2/Fundamentals of Tone Production

9

cized and advised to experiment with instrument angle in order to discover which position is best for them.

Breath support may not appear to pose as much of a problem as does the development of embouchure. Yet if it is left to chance or unattended it can become a major remedial problem for the developing student. It should be remembered that with woodwind instruments embouchure can be viewed visually and is thus more accessible to specific criticism. However, breath support—like diaphragmatic vibrato—is "covered" or hidden from the eye. It is one's *aural* acuteness that plays a major role in the establishment of effective breath support.

Some authors have gone into considerable analysis of the mechanics of so-called "proper breathing." Some even go so far as to define types of breathing. Although it is difficult if not impossible to forget certain things that one has read, it is this writer's intention to dismiss much of what has been written on the subject of "proper breathing." It would be well for the reader to note at this point that the following material on breath support is based primarily on extensive applied performing experience as well as observation.

The content of this material will be twofold in nature, centering largely on an accurate explanation for the benefit of the teacher in training, and the presentation of simple but effective approaches toward mastery of breath support that are more immediately accessible to the young beginner.

To teach proper breath support effectively to students, it is best to present the subject as simply as possible, avoiding all unnecessary complexities. Breath support is really a matter of *breath pressure* (amount or degree), *breath consistency* (continuity of air flow), and last, *application* (as related to each woodwind instrument).

Many students fail to produce a full, resonant, and centered tone simply because they do not use an appropriate *amount of breath pressure.* They take the course of least resistance, exerting only enough breath pressure to produce a tone—rather than enough for a *full* tone. The student who uses a minimal amount of breath pressure may be said to "play at half-mast." Not only does his tone quality suffer, but he cultivates an aural habit of accepting an inferior, less beautiful sound. While it is impossible to prescribe exactly the degree of air pressure that is best used for a woodwind instrument, it is by no means impossible to describe it adequately. A full tone may be characterized by its inherent capacity to make the listener sense that it is controlled, stable, and well placed.

A very simple experiment can do much toward solving the problem of how much breath pressure should be used to attain a full resonant tone. Have the student sustain a "bell tone," and then tell him to experiment with his breath pressure. (For this experiment open tones—throat tones —should be avoided; tones calling for long fingerings are best for young performers.) More specifically, have him exert considerable breath pressure—until he feels his lower abdomen expand or flex against his belt— and then have him use less, exerting only enough air pressure to activate the vibratory source and produce a mere tone. By experimenting with extremes—too much or too little pressure—the student can discover both aurally and physically how to calibrate air pressure and experience a well-placed full tone. It should be noted that this experiment, based on the principle of contrast, can create aural guidelines concerning timbre (a result of tone production) where heretofore none may have existed. Additionally, the performer who develops a full tone is the one who will be able to manage dynamic markings in a truly musical manner.

The reader may have noted that no mention has been made of *how* one should breathe in order to achieve proper breath support. It is this writer's judgment that an explanation of the physiology of breathing involving such technical terms as "clavicular," "costal," or "diaphragmatic" breathing has its merits, but for the young beginner such a discussion would be inappropriate. In the case of the wind instrumentalist, it is far more important to be able to explain *breathing habits used when playing a wind instrument* than it is to dwell on the mechanics of *just breathing*—a singular act. Consequently, key questions—such as: (1) How much air is to be inhaled? (2) How is the air to be expelled? and (3) Considering deviation of air flow, how would one contrast the problems of a bassoonist with those of a clarinetist?—must be considered in light of playing a particular wind instrument. These and similar questions simply do not fall in the same category as the technical explanation of "how one breathes." Comment regarding the *how* of breathing— a natural action—will be limited, simplified, and general at this point. In the subsequent chapters on each woodwind instrument, the above three items and related questions will be considered in more detail.

For the most part, woodwind performers inhale through the mouth. The amount of air taken in may vary depending on the instrument, the individual, and the passage to be executed. An oboist, for example, may occasionally complain of not being able to get rid of the air fast enough, while a flutist (especially if young) might experience the opposite feeling of expelling the air too fast. The analysis of either case is relatively simple, and with a minimum of constructive criticism each problem can be alleviated. In the instance of the oboist, the small *preset aperture* of the double reed limits air flow, often causing an excessive backlog of air pressure for young players who have not yet learned how to cope with the problem. Student oboists must be informed that (1) on certain occasions the amount of air to be taken in should vary according to the length of the musical phrase, and (2) it is necessary to develop skill in rephrasing a melody with breath marks so that the melodic line is always musically tasteful and at the same time practical from the standpoint of execution. In the case of the student flutist who "never seems to have enough air supply," it is usually a matter of an undeveloped aperture that is most often too large, thus allowing the air to escape too fast.

Should the teacher feel the need to explain how one should inhale prior to producing a full tone, it would be best in the beginning to use a simple approach. Have the student recall how he inhales when he takes a deep breath and then ducks his head under water. Next, have him simulate and experience this action. In all probability he will take a deep, full breath, and more air will be inhaled than will be needed. Be that as it may, this simple approach can be used effectively with students, and the cumbersome verbal task of defining and pinpointing specific areas of the respiratory system that "should be used" is eliminated.

Ch. 2/Fundamentals of Tone Production

Continuity of air flow is involved in expelling the air. Depending upon the instrument and musical circumstance, air flow may be even and consistent or it may reflect a deliberate increase or decrease in pressure. Just as the amount of air to be taken in may vary—for reasons previously stated—so may the rate and manner of air release vary. It is difficult if not impossible to make a general rule regarding air flow that would apply equally to all of the woodwinds. A general rule would be very helpful, but in this case exceptions and qualifications are imperative.

If the woodwinds are divided into the categories single reeds, double reeds, and the flute, subjects like embouchure and breath support can be discussed in more detail with fewer qualifications.

SINGLE REEDS

Let us consider the single reeds first. Here, continuity of air flow is more often kept at an even rate of pressure. Deviations from this general rule may be noted, however. Certain musical passages may require a sudden burst or increase of air supply. For example, in the second and fifth measures from the end of Marc Delmas's "Fantaisie Italienne," the climactic high G-sharp and G-natural may be executed more readily by many clarinetists by extending the lower jaw slightly forward and up and simultaneously adding a burst of air to each note. (Accurate pitch may be controlled in this case through the use of alternate fingerings.)

Copyright © 1921 by Andrieu Frères, Paris, France. Copyright assigned 1940 to Alfred Music Co., Inc., New York, N.Y. International copyright secured. Printed in U.S.A. Used by permission.

FIGURE 1.
Excerpt from "Fantaisie Italienne" (for B-flat clarinet and piano)—Marc Delmas

The same performance technique can be used in "Three Pieces for Clarinet" (Gene Saucier) in the third movement where another climactic point centers on the high A, marked triple-*forte*.

Copyright © 1966 by G. Schirmer, Inc. International copyright secured. Printed in U.S.A. Used by permission.

FIGURE 2.
"Curiosity," Excerpt from "Three Pieces for Clarinet" (unaccompanied) —Gene Saucier

These examples are of course exceptions, and should be so noted. In developing elementary players and training student instrumental teachers, the general rule regarding air flow in single reeds warrants first consideration. Deviations such as those aforementioned properly fall in the domain of the advanced performer; to completely explore them does not fall within the scope of this text. However, reference to such deviations at this time can be helpful from an adacemic standpoint as the reader looks to the future.

There are various effective approaches that may be used by single-reed students to achieve a consistent and even flow of air. The most common one used with beginners is the study of long tones. But the study of sustained tones at the elementary level often involves multiple tasks such as (1) learning to read new notes, (2) counting time, (3) trying to remember a recommended embouchure format, and (4) working to develop an initial sense of tone quality. It is no wonder that the distinguished performer and teacher, E. C. Moore, would advocate the following in his valuable offering, *The Flute and Its Daily Routine:*

Under no consideration show the student notes at the first couple of lessons or until the correct blowing and position habits are formed. The beginner will always learn faster and more accurately by concentrating his faculties upon a minimum of things at first.[1]

Truer words were never spoken! The study of long tones may be found in practically all elementary methods and in many master texts for woodwinds. If, however, a beginner is to attain maximum effectiveness from the study of sustained tones, discretion should be used where multiple tasks are presented simultaneously.

This writer has found that the following simple exercise for long tones can be used very effectively with both young and older beginners. I have named this practice routine the "3-and-3 Exercise." It is discussed here in terms of the B-flat clarinet. After the student has acquired some skill with preliminary mouthpiece exercises (for embouchure formation), have him assemble his instrument, grip it, and depress all the fingers of the left hand. This fingering on the clarinet will produce its middle C (concert B-flat). On the E-flat alto saxophone this fingering—without the octave key depressed—will produce its G above middle C (concert B-flat). Next, have him *try* to sustain a full clear tone. This may well require trial-and-error repetition; of course, the initial sounds will more often fall short of being full and clear. However, when the student's tone is at its clearest point, have him slowly lift three fingers one by one, and then return to C by lowering them consecutively. Next, have him begin on C again and depress three fingers of his right hand consecutively. During all this he should try to carry the same full sound initiated on C up the musical line and down again. Within a few moments most students will be able to add four fingers and subsequently play the F major scale one octave. It is important to note that:

1. No music is used.
2. No tonguing is allowed.
3. The simplicity of lifting and adding fingers consecutively allows for maximum concentration on the tonal line and quality and the development of a regulated flow of air pressure.

1. *The Flute and Its Daily Routine* (Kenosha, Wis.: G. Leblanc Co., 1953). Reprinted by permission.

The "3-and-3" exercise (for beginning clarinet students)

Variations in the above step-by-step format should be left to the discretion of the teacher. Older beginners may read the exercises. Young beginners should follow E. C. Moore's advice and read nothing—simply move their fingers consecutively up and down and listen. Some instruction books require beginning clarinetists to start on "open G." Nothing could be more awkward or cumbersome than to try to hold the clarinet with only one thumb and a partially developed embouchure, and then attempt to produce a tone, much less a full tone. It is much easier for any student to grip the instrument with a few fingers when taking the initial steps to produce a tone reinforced by a regulated and even flow of air.

Remedial Work with Older Students

Thus far, only elementary and older beginners have been considered. Since many teachers are compelled to do remedial work involving basic fundamentals, some comment should be made regarding students in this category. An intermediate or advanced student who has not mastered continuity of air flow *can* improve and master tonal continuity within a reasonably short period of time. All that is required is serious application on the student's part, and at least one-third of the lesson time devoted to (1) an initial presentation of the 3-and-3 exercise in order to establish concept and objectives, (2) long tones and slurred twelfths, and (3) the application of the 3-and-3 principle while playing the easiest beginning scales. Next, the 3-and-3 concept should be applied to more difficult scale lines, and finally to scales in thirds and other disjunct lines. It is recommended that the single-reed student doing remedial work to develop a beautiful tonal line or regulated air flow practice all three of the above-mentioned exercises. While the student may intellectually grasp the significance of the graduated steps between exercises 1 and 3 very rapidly, the matter of application requires a slow, methodical, step-by-step approach for best results. Additionally, mastery of exercise 3 is actually a culmination of exercises 1 and 2.

Imagery And Visual Aids

It should be noted that the application of the 3-and-3 principle can be greatly facilitated by using one's imagination and visual faculty. When the older remedial student has conquered this routine and is ready for complete scale lines, have him imagine that he is playing a long sustained tone and then execute the scale pattern. To make the matter more vivid, use graphic illustrations such as the following:

The 3-and-3 principle applied to scale lines

Sustain the first note. While experiencing the feeling of a full tone, try to retain this mental image as you execute the entire scale line.

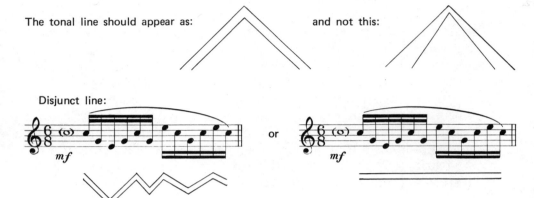

The 3-and-3 principle applied to disjunct lines

Sustain the first note and try to retain the "feeling" or image of a full tone as you execute the entire disjunct musical line.

DOUBLE REEDS

In considering breath support and continuity of air flow in double-reed instruments, it becomes necessary to depart from the general rule for single-reed instruments, in which air flow is more often kept at an even rate of speed or pressure. It should be pointed out, however, that the elementary oboist or bassoonist may follow the general rule and indeed use it very effectively *until he begins to extend his range into the upper register.* The matter becomes acutely apparent on the bassoon within the span of the first octave of the F major scale. On the oboe, however, it is not until the upper second octave tones (C above middle C to high C) are produced that it becomes evident.

Once the double-reed student has mastered breath pressure and air flow in the lower register he is ready for work in the upper register. It then becomes necessary to employ a different approach. The following phrase from a former teacher, James Thornton, has proved one of the most effective performance guides this writer has found for bassoonists wishing to develop an even tonal line: "Less fingers means more air."

Although this short phrase captures the main point of departure between single reeds and double reeds in the matter of breath pressure, there is one additional point that warrants consideration. It has already been stated that effective tone production is actually the result of (1) embouchure, (2) breath support, and (3) related factors such as reeds, mouthpieces, etc. This writer has found that with the bassoon it is often necessary for young beginners and teachers in training to be reminded that as the air pressure and flow increase, the embouchure may need an increase in muscular tension. While single-reed performers tend to use the same degree of muscular flex in the embouchure and the same rate of air flow, the bassoonist may be observed to increase embouchure tension in the upper register and relax lip tension in the lower. Although this may be true from a purely technical view for the oboist, it is best to simply advise him that while the respiratory system should always be responsive to register changes, the embouchure should remain basically the same insofar as lip tension is concerned. The margin of difference between the size of the bassoon's vibratory source and that of an oboe is such that the slightest alteration in lip tension on an oboe reed is prone to produce an acute pitch change instantly. This is not to say that there are no deviations such as those pointed out in the discussions on single reeds and the bassoon; but such deviations are strictly for the advanced oboe performer.

A final point that can be most effective in developing an even tonal line on double reeds centers on graphic illustrations which can help in understanding the inherent behavior of the oboe and bassoon insofar as their "natural tonal line" is concerned. If a bassoonist played the following musical line with no increase in air pressure, the resulting sound could be portrayed visually as follows.

Natural tonal line for bassoon

The top notes will not be as full as the bottom notes because of the natural acoustic behavior proper to the bassoon. If, however, the student will listen attentively, he can apply the "less fingers means more air" technique to produce a tonal line that is even from top to bottom. Some students may tend to overblow in the lower register, and it will be necessary to advise them to start the tonal line with less air pressure in order to achieve a balanced *mezzo-forte* line from low F up to the second F. The tonal line will appear as follows when the air supply is increased ascending, decreased descending, and managed overall with the appropriate embouchure:

Desired tonal line for bassoon

When an oboist is ready for work in the upper register, there is an excellent exercise that will enable him to develop effective embouchure stability and appropriate air pressure. This octave exercise reveals immediately how important it is to use increased air pressure for the oboe's top register rather than over gripping high notes with the embouchure and causing them to be sharp, pinched, and narrow in sound.

Octave exercise and desired tonal line for oboe

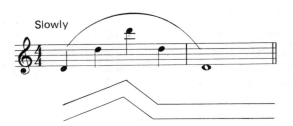

Inform the oboe student that the second- and especially the third-octave D are produced with an increase in air pressure. His embouchure or grip on the reed should remain essentially the same. As with all of the exercises designed to develop tonal quality and tonal line, this exercise should be practiced with slurred phrasing marks. Exercises such as those previously outlined for single reeds and bassoon can also be used; however, this three-octave exercise should be presented as soon as possible. Many developing oboists seem to develop a fear of high notes, such as high D through high F. This can be prevented before such unnecessary concern can flower through attentive study.

If the three-octave exercise is played without an appropriate increase in air flow, the resulting sound may be depicted as illustrated below.

A pinched tonal line on the oboe

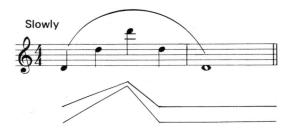

In this instance the top D sounds pinched, narrow, and (usually) sharp in pitch. All of this is caused by an increase in the muscular tension of the lips in executing high notes; this is called "pinching" by woodwind teachers. The first object of the octave exercise is to provide a concise practice routine that can help the student quickly learn to adjust his breath pressure as needed in the higher register. Ultimately the final object is to develop the ability to produce a tonal line that in character is even from the lowest to the highest note.

A final point to be considered centers on the relationship between increased air supply and dynamics. The reader should be reminded that the increase in breath pressure in double reeds involves a fluctuation in air flow essential to attaining an even tonal line at a *mezzo-forte* level throughout the tessitura of the instrument. However, in order to achieve a truly consistent *mezzo-forte* level of sound throughout the practical range of the double-reed instruments, performers must also be cognizant of other aspects of their instruments' natural behavior. Bassoons produce a larger sound at the lower end of their range and a smaller sound at the upper end. This is especially noticeable when playing the F major scale over one octave (see page 15). The natural oboe line behaves similarly, but not to the same extent; it is in its third octave that the oboe tends to produce a small, narrow sound.

Therefore, the three-octave exercise is much more valuable if it is *understood* and *mastered*. After the double-reed performer has reached a

Ch. 2/Fundamentals of Tone Production

point at which he can execute a tonal line that is even from top to bottom, advanced work on shadings and dynamics will be much easier; the player will be in command over the natural acoustical behavior of the instrument rather than subject to it.

For the double-reed student who has been advised to do remedial work on breath support, the most effective exercises will center on the aforementioned studies—not on sustained tones, which for double reeds are often more effective in embouchure study.

THE FLUTE

By now it may be observed that although breath support is a common denominator of woodwind instruments, *how* the breath is used is indeed a matter that varies. The flute is no exception in being another exception; it is indeed unique among the woodwinds for many reasons. In so far as the utilization of breath is concerned, it should be noted that the last control center for air flow is the flutist's embouchure—not, as with the other woodwinds, a preset mouthpiece and reed or a preset double reed. Additionally, the flute has no register key or octave vents to facilitate large interval breaks or accommodate the change from one octave to another.[2] Although no attempt will be made here to exhaust the total meaning of these points, it is necessary to acknowledge them and present at least a cursory consideration.

The goal in developing proper embouchure and breath support is the same for all wind instruments: the homogeneous functioning of embouchure and breath support—and related items such as reeds, etc.—leading to the achievement of beautiful tone production. In the case of the flute, the relationship between embouchure and air flow is further intensified due to (1) an additional controlling point (aperture) for air flow having to be *developed and managed by the flutist* and (2) the special acoustical makeup of the flute (without octave, register, or breaker keys) imposing additional problems and tasks. For example, *the flutist must develop a method whereby he can negotiate register changes without the aid of an octave key.* At the same time he—like all instrumentalists—is obligated to produce a beautiful tonal line. How is the flutist to accomplish these tasks, and what role do breath pressure and air flow play in these matters?

First of all, we might ask if there is a general rule regarding air flow for flute such as the one for single reeds. In a broad, general sense the answer would be in the affirmative, but such a "yes" in the flute's case is not as easily explained as with single reeds. The matter of how breath pressure is regulated on the flute is considerably more involved. Unlike any other woodwind player, the flutist can and must vary the size of his aperture according to the register in which he is playing. In the very low register, he actually changes the size of the air stream by enlarging the aperture. The aperture of the flute embouchure may appear as follows in the low, middle, and high registers:

---

2. A possible exception is the flute's first-finger key (left hand), used to sound middle D. However, in no way does the flute have mechanical advantages comparable to the clarinet's twelfth key, the bassoon's breaker keys, or the oboe's octave vents.

FIGURE 3.
Flute embouchure aperture for different registers

In all probability the amount of air focused over the tone hole is affected by such changes in aperture, but to what extent is not known. What is known—and of utmost importance to the reader—is that the professional flutist always strives to produce adequate breath pressure in all registers of the flute. Additionally, it would appear that a progressively wider air stream is needed as the flutist plays a descending scale to the lowest note. Conversely, a smaller, more and more thread-like air stream is produced as the flutist ascends to the highest register. Depending upon the individual, the intensity of breath pressure may tend to feel the same in the middle register from G above middle C to the third F above middle C. However, in the extreme ranges most flutists will agree that the intensity of breath pressure varies.

Just as instrument angle is self-adjusting for many single-reed students, breath pressure and aperture size tend to become self-adjusting for many flutists. The beginner will quickly learn that he must decrease his breath pressure and air flow in his first attempts at playing the lowest four or five tones on the flute. If he doesn't decrease it at this early stage, the low tones will sound not as written but usually an octave higher. With practice and time, after the embouchure and aperture are developed, the young flutist should have the ability to increase his breath pressure in the lowest register without "splitting" or overblowing of notes, and at the same time eliminate the excessive waste of air flow in the upper register which makes the higher tones sound breathy. When these basic physical adjustments do not occur as the performer develops, supervised guidance becomes all the more essential for the student.

If the natural tonal line of the flute were to be graphically illustrated, it would appear approximately as follows:

Natural tonal line for flute

It is truly an uneven line. Note that the bottom tones are depicted as small in size, the notes from second-line G through high D are somewhat similar, and the tones above high D tend to become larger—that is, louder in sound and often breathy in character. Ideally, the line should be even throughout, and the serious flutist will work to accomplish this aim. (See top of page 19.)

It is perfectly normal for the beginning and even the intermediate flutist to produce an uneven tonal line. No one would expect an intermediate trumpet student to produce the upper register tones in the second and third octave range even with perfectly natural breath control and support, for the development of embouchure is a much slower pro-

Ch. 2/Fundamentals of Tone Production

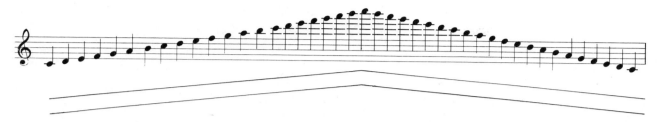

Recommended tonal line for flute

cess with brass than with single-reed instruments. Such is the case with the development of a flutist's breath support, aperture, and tonal line. It takes considerable time and effort to master the task of beautiful tone production.

The following comments and exercises can be of immense help to the young flutist. First, remember to expect and allow the beginner to play with an uneven tonal line for a much longer period of time than the single-reed student. After he has completed his first embouchure exercises with the head joint only, have him practice the 3-and-3 exercise. For example, have him play the following without music, moving the fingers consecutively in an even and rhythmic manner:

The 3-and-3 routine for flute

Again attention should be called to the simplicity of the above exercise. It involves consecutive finger movement, slurred phrasing, and the avoidance of tonguing; the student should not be confronted with notation at first. After notation is introduced, simple quarter-note or eighth-note variations of the melodic line may be sketched by the teacher for use in further study of tonal line, as in the two examples below.

Head-Joint Interval Exercise for Flute

As the student progresses into the upper register he should be introduced to (1) the "head-joint interval exercise" and (2) beginning octave studies. The head-joint interval exercise involves working on breath support and embouchure simultaneously, due to the nature of the flute. Briefly, the primary objective of this exercise is to develop a *manual in-*

terval mechanism. In accomplishing this task, however, it would be well to remember that the *principle of contrast* can be used very effectively with the student to achieve the desired aim.

Have the flutist take the head joint and close up the end with his right hand. Next, have him produce a sustained tone. The resulting tone, A, will be pitched at about 440 vibrations per second. He should "center" or "place" the tone so that it is as clear, rich, and free of excessive hiss as possible. While he is sustaining the A, have him deliberately increase the air flow with a burst of breath pressure, and literally overblow the A to produce the twelfth above (high E). The E will pop out, with its volume considerably louder than the A.

Next, have the student repeat the exercise, except this time have him slowly extend his lower jaw forward while sustaining the A. *There should be no increase in the breath pressure.* As for the aperture of the embouchure, it can be utilized in two ways; this will vary with the individual. First, one may advise the student to extend the lower jaw forward and make no change in the size of the aperture. On the other hand, some teachers may prefer to have him, while extending his jaw, flex the aperture of the embouchure by telling him, for example, to imagine that he is spitting a grapefruit seed when sustaining the A and a grape seed when reaching for the high E. The essential point to remember here (regardless of whether you advocate two movements—jaw and aperture—or just the single movement of the jaw) is that *there should be no increase in air supply.*

By executing the head-joint interval exercise utilizing two methods which stand in direct contrast to one another, the young flutist's perception can be greatly increased. On the one hand the high E is produced by literally overblowing, and the volume is always loud. On the other, the high E is produced with a slight forward movement of the lower jaw (and a minute flexing of the aperture in many cases), and the resulting high E can be played at any volume level. The major point of difference between the two methods becomes self-evident to most students. If the student were to develop the habit of literally overblowing to produce all octaves and large intervals, he could never play softly in the upper register. Thus the second method of approach is the one to be mastered. But it is doing both methods—even though one is not recommended for continual use—that allows the student to establish clear guidelines where heretofore none existed. This is an instance of the value of employing the principle of contrast—one too often overlooked—in applied teaching; used in a discerning manner it can serve as a valuable teaching aid.

PERFORMANCE OF HEAD-JOINT INTERVAL EXERCISE

1. Using the head joint only, cover the open end and sustain a full, clear, and rich tone. It will be pitched approximately at A = 440. Keep the tone straight; do not permit it to waver.

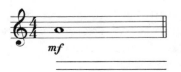

Ch. 2/Fundamentals of Tone Production   21

2. Next, while sustaining the A, deliberately overblow the twelfth above (high E) by using an immediate burst of air supply. The top note will always sound louder than the lower note *when overblown.*

3. Sustain the A again; this time do not overblow, but rather extend the lower jaw forward until the high E is produced with perfect ease.

   Repeat steps 1, 2, and 3 until complete control is developed over step 3.

4. Repeat the exercise as illustrated here. Remember to extend the jaw for the slur to high E, and draw it back for the slur down to A. Use no increase of breath pressure.

It is the marked contrast that exists between steps 2 and 3 that more often proves to be very effective in teaching this fundamental technique. Mastery of the head-joint interval exercise has a threefold benefit: (1) The primary objective of developing a workable octave mechanism can be achieved, (2) it allows one to play with contrasting dynamics in the upper register, and (3) clear guidelines regarding breath pressure can be established with relative ease!

In addition to the head-joint interval exercise for flute, octave exercises can be very valuable in developing flexibility. For younger students the octave intervals should center on the middle range. This author has had excellent success with sixth-grade students playing all octaves within a period of one school year. This of course will vary with the individual. The exercise at the top of page 22 is designed for initial study of octave intervals with elementary students.

Note that these exercises are not centered on the extreme low or high tones. The object is to work gradually into the extreme registers. After this exercise can be executed with reasonable control, the student

Initial octave studies

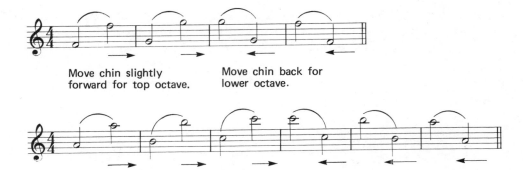

should then be advised to apply the principles and techniques of these interval exercises to more advanced studies such as the one below.

Additional octave studies

It will help in many cases to have students "think" a smaller aperture as the chin moves forward to produce the octave above. Some students produce ascending octaves by squeezing the lips only, never using any jaw movement. This author recommends emphasis on jaw movement first, since squeezing of the lips seems to come about naturally and sometimes to the detriment of certain students. It is the delicate fusion of these two movements—jaw and aperture—that facilitates interval flexibility. Utilizing one resource only is like operating at "half-mast" and those students using only the muscular flex of the aperture to play various intervals will inevitably tire more quickly.

Caution the student not to overblow the top octaves excessively here. Breath pressure can and should remain essentially the same throughout this exercise. Exceptions might be the top F-sharp, which is difficult to produce on certain student-line flutes without an increase in breath pressure. Also, the lowest three notes (E, E-flat, and D) will almost inevitably be produced with less breath pressure by younger students. These exceptions can be expected, and pose no major problems.

In presenting an exercise such as this to first- or second-year students, it should be remembered that they cannot be expected to execute it with a "finished" sound. At this stage it is sufficient to develop flexibility and maneuverability, upon which "finish" can subsequently be applied.

For more advanced work in the development of breath support and embouchure, these octave studies may be extended to the extreme ranges of the flute. Such advanced work, however, does not fall within

Ch. 2/Fundamentals of Tone Production

the scope of this text. Addditionally, the general rules regarding breath pressure and aperture must be altered to accommodate the extreme upper register.

EXCEPTIONS.   One additional point should be noted regarding initial steps in executing the head-joint interval exercise. Observation has revealed that some students—particularly student teachers—should be advised to practice the exercise in reverse order! In these exceptional, occasional cases, the student actually starts out with the jaw in a natural forward position. Consequently, the margin for additional movement forward is curtailed, and the student finds himself at an impasse. In such cases a high note (usually E) tends to sound immediately. When this occurs, examine his occlusion and try to determine if the natural jaw position is offset (forward or back) and to what extent. It may be that his natural occlusion is perfectly normal, but he simply starts with the lower jaw in a forward position. The next step involves doing the interval exercise in reverse order: Have the student begin with the high E and slowly draw his chin back until the low A sounds a twelfth below.

On rare occasions some music students in training will find it virtually impossible to execute the head-joint interval exercise due to an extreme malocclusion. In such a case the only thing that can or should be done is to ensure that the future teacher understands the technique and can explain it accurately.

1. What is the primary aim of this text?
2. List the secondary objectives of this text.
3. Instrumental music teachers draw upon what primary source references?
4. List those points which you believe best substantiate the class instruction approach for minor instrument study.
5. List those points which you believe best substantiate the private lesson approach for minor instrument study.
6. What are the primary factors that must be taken into account in the study of tone production?
7. What are the secondary factors which must be considered in the study of tone production?
8. How does the author define the term *embouchure*?
9. What is the biggest problem instrumental teachers may be confronted with when they begin teaching recommended embouchure formats?
10. Complete this sentence: "Considering first things first, a woodwind performer may be observed to do the following: _____."
11. Embouchure can be studied visually to a large extent, but breath support remains covered or hidden. Can aural acuteness help in the mastering of effective breath support? Explain.
12. How does the author characterize a "full tone"?
13. How can you help a student to determine how much breath pressure should be used to attain a full resonant tone?
14. What is meant by "continuity of air flow"?
15. What does the author advise single-reed students concerning continuity of air flow?
16. Does the author allow for any exceptions in his discussion of continuity of air flow in single-reed instruments?
17. What are the key aspects that characterize the "3-and-3" exercise?
18. List those teaching techniques that you could use for remedial work in breath support.

Study Questions: Chapters 1 and 2

General Aspects of Woodwind Study/Part I

19. Can imagery and visual aids be of any help in the study of tone production? If so, explain.
20. Should the bassoonist use the same general rule for continuity of air flow as the single-reed student? Explain.
21. What is the significance of Professor James Thornton's quote; "Less fingers means more air"?
22. What does the author state about lip tensions and breath support concerning bassoonists?
23. Discuss the "three-octave" exercise.
24. What is the last control center for air flow into the lip plate opening on the flute?
25. Explain how the lack of a register key, octave vents, or breaker keys would have a bearing on the flutist's study of tone production.
26. Does the aperture of the flutist's embouchure change sizes with each register of the instrument? Explain.
27. Describe the flute's natural tonal line.
28. What is the purpose of the head-joint interval exercise?
29. Explain the four steps involved in executing the head-joint interval exercise.
30. What else can a flutist study (in addition to the head-joint interval exercise) to develop flexibility?
31. What are the key points to be remembered under the topic "Exceptions"?

Fundamental Techniques and Supplemental Aids — PART II

Part II of this text consists of five chapters. A chapter has been assigned to each of the following woodwinds: flute, oboe, clarinet, bassoon, and saxophone. Additionally, subsections covering lower clarinets and saxophones respectively have been included in Chapters 5 and 7.

In keeping with the primary intent and scope of this text, basic information and fundamental techniques are emphasized. Each chapter will include a presentation of the following topics, all of which are essential to the study of woodwinds:

1. Instrument assembly and care
2. Instrument angle and hand position
3. Tone production
    a. embouchure
    b. breath support
    c. tonguing
4. Fingering
    a. standard fingering chart
    b. trills
    c. standard trill chart
    d. frequently used special fingerings
5. Study questions
6. A problem chart
7. Teaching aids
8. Literature
    a. graded solos
    b. class methods
    c. individual methods and supplemental studies
    d. recordings

To teach effectively one must search for truth. To search for truth in any endeavor is indeed the most noble of all man's pursuits, but to share truths found—that is God-like!

The Flute

3

FIGURE 4.
(left) An open-ring flute (French model)

FIGURE 5.
(right) A closed-ring flute (plateau model)

Photographs courtesy of The Selmer Company, Elkhart, Indiana.

Flute Assembly

FIGURE 6.
(left) Foot joint and middle joint

FIGURE 7.
(right) Head joint and middle joint

FIGURE 8.
Complete assembly and approximate alignment

Ch. 3/The Flute

Instrument Assembly and Care

Careful instrument assembly can prevent much frustration, loss of time, and financial expense. Ideally, the assembling of a delicate musical instrument would be demonstrated by the instructor. Be that as it may, the following key points can be of value to the reader:

1. When assembling the flute, place one hand near the end of the foot joint and the other near the top of the main body so as to avoid hand pressure on the key mechanism. (See Figure 6.)

2. Never force joints together. If a tenon will not fit into its socket, check to see if an end is bent, damaged, or dirty.

3. It is always best to assemble the foot and head joints to the main body of the flute with a slight turning motion.

4. With a new instrument it is sometimes necessary to wet the tenon surface with a light oil. Be sure to wipe the oil off before assembling, allowing only the residue to remain in order to eliminate friction.

5. The stopper in the head joint is preset at the factory. The adjustment of this stopper affects the intonation of the flute, and through years of experience the manufacturer has been able to determine the best setting for his particular instrument design. The wisest thing a student can do with a new instrument is to have his instructor take the cleaning rod—which is also a meter rod—and determine where the stopper was preset. Thus, if the stopper cap is ever turned for any reason, it can be reset at its original position if careful note has been made regarding it.

check all stoppers for correct length

Generally speaking, the scored line on the meter rod will fall in the

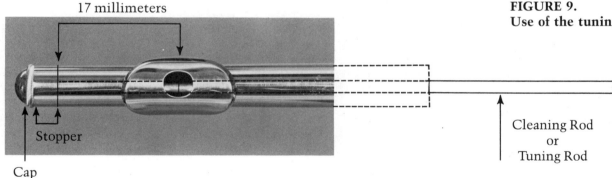

FIGURE 9. Use of the tuning rod

center of the tone hole as illustrated in Figure 9. If the presetting from the factory deviates slightly either to the left or right of center, this can be so noted for future reference. (To be perfectly exact in determining the original setting, the instructor can make a short, scored line on the tuning rod where the open end of the head joint lies [Figure 9].)

6. By adjusting the stopper it is possible to set the pitch for a favorable balance between the low, middle, and upper registers of the flute. As a student gains proficiency, it may become necessary to check his three Ds for correct pitch relationship. This should be done, however, by a flute teacher who can ascertain whether the instrument needs adjusting or if the student is at fault and playing the octaves out of tune. The reason for such caution is that an experienced flutist knows that the upper and lower registers must be tem-

pered by the player—"*played* in tune"—and that the stopper adjustment done at the factory represents an educated compromise which works well for most players. It is therefore recommended that students not tamper with the stopper for purposes of improving intonation; leave this to the guidance of a professional.

7. The bore of the flute should be wiped clean after playing. This can be done with a soft cloth and the cleaning rod. The cloth should fold around the rod to prevent metal scraping metal.

8. The key mechanism should be oiled at the pivotal locations at least three times a year.

9. The adjustment screws should be changed only by someone qualified to do so.

10. If the pads become sticky—as many do—a lubricant powder is recommended, and can be obtained at most music stores.

11. As a final note of precaution, the cork used to stop the end of the head joint can be ruined if forced out of the wrong end. Since the head joint is conical in shape, the cork stopper should always be removed from the end of the joint fitting into the main body of the flute.

FIGURE 10. Instrument angle—parallel

FIGURE 11. (left) Tilted angle

FIGURE 12. (right) Tilted angle

Ch. 3/The Flute

Instrument Angle and Hand Position

As for the angle at which the flute is held in relation to the body, there are two points which should be considered: first, practical convenience; second, the individual need. As a matter of practicality and convenience, most flutists tilt their heads slightly to the right and play with the foot joint somewhat lower than the head joint. Occasionally one may see a flutist with the instrument at an angle almost parallel to the floor. While this parallel position is not used generally, it certainly should be when it fits the needs of a particular individual. (See Figures 10, 11, and 12.)

For the beginning student, the head joint may be aligned so that the mouthpiece tone hole falls directly in line with the first-finger key of the left hand. (See Figure 13.) As the student gains proficiency the position may vary from this original starting point. The professional flutist will ultimately align the head joint from memory, through sensitivity to touch, and may at times vary the position in order to make fine pitch adjustments.

FIGURE 13. Initial alignment

It should also be noted that some student-line flutes have scored markings where the sleeve end of the head joint is inserted into the main body of the flute. These scored lines allow for clear and easy alignment by the student. For those young beginners whose flutes are not score-marked at the factory, it is recommended that the instructor align the flute as depicted in Figure 13, and then with a pen knife place a similar, tiny but visible scored line on the flute. Only one short line need be drawn, from the sleeve of the head joint to the main body of the instrument. Adjustments using this center line can then be made with accuracy and ease by the student. This will also help him develop consistency in learning to "feel" instrument alignment.

As for the alignment of the foot joint, it may simply be set at that point most convenient for the length of the individual's right-hand little finger.

An additional item of importance is the manner in which the flute is held with the hands. (See Figures 14, 15, and 16.) When playing the

**FIGURE 14.
Right hand with thumb under flute**

**FIGURE 15.
Right hand with thumb against flute**

**FIGURE 16.
Left-hand position**

Ch. 3/The Flute 33

flute, there are three points of body contact; where (1) the lip plate rests slightly below the lower lip, (2) the upper main section of the flute rests on the index finger of the left hand, and (3) the right-hand thumb rests either *underneath* the lower side of the flute or *against* the side (pushing the flute slightly against the left-hand point of contact, which is then made to serve as a brace or fulcrum). It is the third point that warrants consideration: Should the right-hand thumb rest against or under the flute? In E. C. Moore's *The Flute and Its Daily Routine,* Moore takes a firm stand for placing the thumb against the side of the flute rather than underneath it (Figure 15). The line of reasoning behind this approach has considerable merit; however, one key point must be considered by each teacher before attempting to resolve this question; namely, that individual hand sizes vary, and for anyone with thumbs longer than average or forefingers proportionately shorter than the thumb it would be wise and practical to rest the thumb underneath the flute. Actually, both positions may be used with great effectiveness. We may conclude that in the final analysis such decisions must be made in the light of individual needs.

EMBOUCHURE

Tone Production

It was pointed out in Part I that the flute is unique among woodwinds. As indicated there, one reason for this is that the flutist must develop and control the aperture (the small opening between the lips through which air flows), whereas a single- or double-reed student must learn to grip a preset aperture that may be viewed as constant in its dimensions. Additionally, the size of the flutist's aperture can —and should—vary depending on the particular circumstance.

The object of an effective flute embouchure is to control, regulate, and focus a stream of air across an open tone hole in such a manner as to achieve with maximum efficiency the production of a tone. Simply stated, the flutist is obligated to harness and control the air flow across the tone hole so as not to misdirect and waste it (hissing). Speaking by way of analogy, we know that a water hydrant is of little help in watering a yard if there is no water pressure or no hose, nozzle, or sprinkler. And light from a light bulb may be diffused or focused as a concentrated beam of light. Just as each analogous situation has certain physical requirements in order to accomplish an end, so does a flutist's harnessing a stream of air demand specific physical requirements of his embouchure. The important questions now center on these physical requirements. First of all it is obvious that flutists do not "in-mouth" the lip plate, in contrast to clarinetists and oboists inserting the mouthpiece or double reed into the mouth. With flutists the concept "out-mouth" is of key importance in the matter of embouchure.

The recommended embouchure format, shown in various perspectives in Figures 17–19, should be of considerable assistance in developing one's own flute embouchure.

FIGURE 18

FIGURE 17.
Perspectives of embouchure format (See also Figs. 18, 19)

FIGURE 19

Figures 20 and 21 show that the lip muscles are flexed, but only enough to produce a lower tone. In Figures 22 and 23 the lips are stretched by increasing muscular tension at the corners of the mouth and at the center of the aperture.

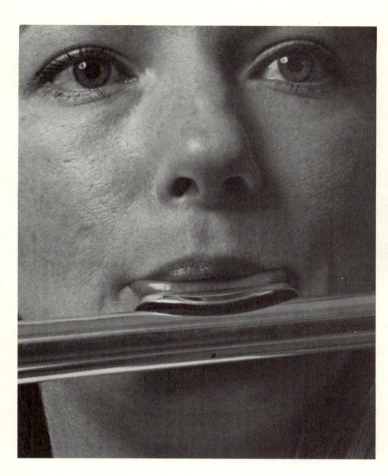

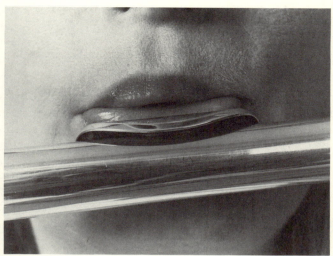

FIGURE 21.
Aperture size for low F

FIGURE 20.
Amount of lip flex for low F

FIGURE 22.
Amount of lip flex for high F

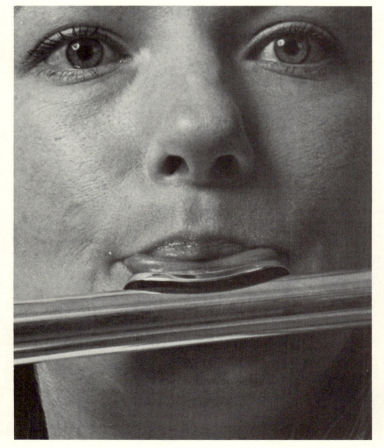

FIGURE 23.
Aperture size for high F

Additionally, the following points can serve as important teaching aids.

1. Always begin with the aid of a mirror when doing embouchure exercises in the initial stage.
2. Beginning students should be given preliminary exercises to relax the lips as well as focus them outward. For example, many teachers traditionally advocate pursing the lips to form a "sardonic smile." (When using this approach, one should inform the student that a slight increase in muscular flex should be felt near the corners of the mouth.) Prior to this, it is recommended that the student relax his lips and blow air through them so they bounce together and turn outward; a funny noise will result. This first routine—however humorous—will set the initial stage for relaxing the lips—and the student—and turning them outward.
3. Have the student spit an imaginary seed out of his mouth. At this point a degree of muscular flex should occur at the corners of the mouth. Some teachers have students flex their lips and expel the air as though cooling a spoon of hot soup.
4. Provide the student with adequate visual aids. Also, encourage student attendance at clinics, recitals, and televised concerts.
5. To further increase lip control and aperture position, have the student expel a stream of air and then *gradually* close both lips until the flow is completely stopped. This should be done in front of a mirror, without the flute.

These five teaching aids are primarily preparatory in nature, and do not require the use of instruments. A mirror, pictures of the recommended embouchure, and an instructor are all the student needs to cover this preliminary work. The purpose of these aids is to establish first concepts and percepts of embouchure. Subsequent work on applied tasks with the instrument can be achieved with greater ease and speed when such preparatory efforts are done effectively.

The following is a recommended sequence of beginning applied assignments for the junior high school grade-level.

1. Before the student reads any music, have him work first with the head joint alone (its open end may be closed with the right hand). Next, have the student, imitating the picture of the recommended flute embouchure, strive to produce a tone as clear as possible (c. A = 440 v.p.s.).
2. After the student can manage a fairly clear tone with the head joint, have him assemble the flute and begin work on the 3-and-3 tone production exercise for flute (see page 19).
3. After some proficiency has been gained with the 3-and-3 routine, *then* begin the initial task of reading music symbols.
4. When the student progresses and his reading level warrants work in the upper register, introduce him to the head-joint interval exercise and the initial octave studies (see pp. 19–22).

As the student progresses, gradually introduce him to the following

Ch. 3/The Flute   37

performance practices. Allow him ample time to memorize and sub-sequently demonstrate each applied technique.

1. Try to play with moist lips.
2. Play on the inner lining of the lips, i.e., turn the lips outward enough to allow the air to pass over the delicate inner lip tissue, rather than the outer portion (which is sometimes chapped).
3. Some teachers advise hooking the lower lip over the tone hole so that about one-fourth of the opening is covered. Although this will vary with the individual, it should be pointed out that *all professional flutists do cover a portion of the tone hole with the lower lip.*
4. Beginning students should be allowed to slow the air flow when first producing the lowest tones.
5. The lowest tones on flute are produced with greater ease if the lower jaw is back; conversely, the higher tones can be produced without overblowing by extending the jaw forward. This is because the movement of the jaw affects the direction of the air stream: When the jaw is back, the air column tends to go slightly downward into the tone hole, while a forward position tends to focus it upward across the hole.

Embouchure Exceptions and Deviations

It was stated earlier that there is a basic embouchure format for each woodwind instrument. Knowing *when* and *how* to deviate from the basic format poses a true challenge for the instructor. The teacher who knows when deviations from the accepted norm are warranted and valid; can correctly analyze the exception in light of his given circumstances; takes the time and has the patience and energy to verify, to assimilate, and then to form a conclusion and make logical and effective recommendations—this is the teacher who has met and conquered the most challenging aspects of competent instruction! Flexibility, imagination, and initiative are essential when dealing with exceptions to the rule.

For work on the fundamental level, there are a few points regarding deviations and exceptions which should be mentioned. First of all, if a recommendation is to be offered to a beginning student concerning his suitability to a particular instrument—flute, in this instance—the instructor should determine first if the prospective flutist has a normal occlusion or a malocclusion.[1] If the lower jaw either protrudes or recedes radically, the student should be advised to pursue an instrument other than flute.

Second, the size of the student's lips could be a factor to consider.

---

1. A normal occlusion may be said to occur when the mouth is closed and the lower teeth rest behind, but immediately adjacent to, the upper teeth. When the mouth is in a closed position and the lower teeth are parallel with the upper teeth, we may say that a minor deviation from normal occurs. When the mouth is in a closed position and the lower teeth rest *in front of* the upper teeth, the occlusion may be said to be radical. On the other hand, if the lower teeth fall *extremely behind* rather than immediately adjacent to the upper teeth, a malocclusion may again be in evidence. Whether such alignment of the teeth is caused by the natural setting of one's jaws, or by the vertical misalignment of the teeth, the problem remains the same for the prospective woodwind student.

Again it would be a matter of extremes—very thin or very thick lips. Fortunately, this aspect does not appear to occur with great frequency. A hard and fast ruling regarding lip size and its problems may be viewed as a difficult variable. The best recommendation might be to allow a trial period before drawing a final conclusion.

A third point centers on the shape and alignment of the aperture. To a large extent, the horizontal alignment (left to right) of the aperture over the tone hole is self-adjusting. If it is not centered over the tone hole, the resulting sound should elicit an immediate response from the flutist, due to its inferior tone quality. In the matter of vertical alignment of the aperture over the tone hole, automatic self-adjustment does not seem to be as frequent as with the horizontal alignment. In this instance, the student more often must practice regularly to learn to hook a portion of the lower lip over the back edge of the tone hole.

Generally speaking, most flutists' natural aperture falls in the center of the mouth (looking again from left to right) (Figure 24). Occasionally one may encounter a flutist whose aperture does not appear to be centered, but is slightly to left or right of center (Figures 25, 26). Although the causes for this vary, the important point to remember is that there are permissible exceptions to the rule; as long as the aperture is not radical *in its shape* there is no major problem regarding the matter of alignment. Almost invariably, the flutist whose aperture is slightly offset will automatically adjust it to the center of the tone hole.

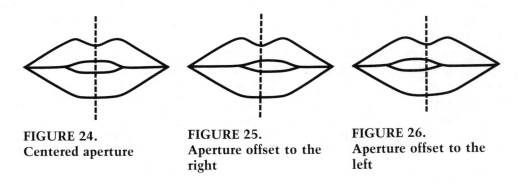

FIGURE 24.
Centered aperture

FIGURE 25.
Aperture offset to the right

FIGURE 26.
Aperture offset to the left

The subject of a "Cupid's bow" is sometimes brought up in the consideration of flute study. Just what a "Cupid's bow" is, whether there is more than one kind, and of what importance this is to teacher and student are questions which to the best of the author's knowledge are rarely, if ever, discussed in books on woodwind study. Although the point need not be labored, some comment is warranted, since *the type* and *extent* of a "Cupid's bow" can affect embouchure and, ultimately, tone production.

The term "Cupid's bow" refers to the shape of the line formed by the upper and lower lips when the mouth is closed. When the shape of this line appears as illustrated in Figure 27, the person may be said to have an "accommodating Cupid's bow." Note that the upper lip has a dip or tab at the center, and the lower lip a slight indentation that accommodates the dip. Figure 28 depicts an "unaccommodating Cupid's bow."

Ch. 3/The Flute

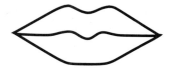  

FIGURE 27.
"Accommodating Cupid's bow"

FIGURE 28.
"Unaccommodating Cupid's bow"

FIGURE 29.
No "Cupid's bow"

Note that for the dip in the center of the upper lip there is no corresponding indentation in the lower lip. Figure 29 illustrates the absence of a "Cupid's bow." From a teacher's standpoint it is the *unaccommodating* "Cupid's bow" that stands as a definite physical handicap to the prospective flutist. The reason for this is that the aperture is obstructed —possibly even divided into two sections—and the flutist's flow of air is thus curtailed adversely.

BREATH SUPPORT

The subsequent points should be explained—and demonstrated where applicable—to beginning flutists. Note that, as these items show, it is indeed difficult, if not altogether unwise, to discuss breath support for the flute without relating it to embouchure.

1. Breath support is as essential to a beautiful tone and tonal line as an electrical current (supported by a generator) is to a light bulb.
2. Breath support must be regulated and controlled. An excessive amount of electrical current can burn out a bulb and an insufficient amount will cause it to burn dimly. Similarly, a flute tone can be *overblown* or *underblown* through poor breath support.
3. In addition to taking in an appropriate amount of air to be expelled, the flutist must harness the flow of air with his embouchure so that it is truly focused across the tone hole.
4. There are two preliminary exercises which a beginning flutist may practice to achieve both effective breath support and aperture control at the initial stage.

   1. He should make a pencil mark in the center of his palm, flex his lips in the recommended position, and then try to focus a steady stream of air on the pencil mark. Immediately he will note that the air strikes the entire area of the palm, not just the penciled dot. Perfection, of course, is not expected in this practice routine. The object is simply to draw the student's attention in a very vivid manner to the fact that the air stream should be harnessed through his aperture to cross the tone hole in a focused manner. If it is not so focused, then air is wasted and the resulting tone will be thin and breathy. Additionally, the student should take note of how long it takes him to expel the air he has taken in. With practice he should be able to gradually increase his time span.
   2. Some students may respond more rapidly by working at first with the head joint only. After they have practiced the various begin-

ning embouchure exercises, have them strive to produce a sustained tone (c. A = 440 v.p.s.) with the head joint closed. Use the graphic illustration below to emphasize the character and description of the sound desired.

Sustained tone

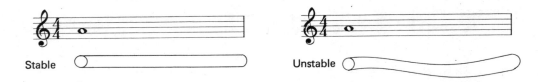

5. Inform the student as soon as it is feasible that a series of tones played on the flute becomes a *tonal line* in the mind of a serious and accomplished musician. This tonal line may be depicted using graphic illustrations.

For example, if the basic pattern shown above is executed with consistent breath support and a controlled embouchure, the tonal line may be said to sound or appear as follows:

The dark line might be placed below the staff to further illustrate the point.

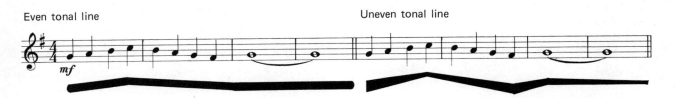

Also, the notes on the staff—if the line is performed unevenly—might be altered in size to show the *lack* of a consistent tonal line.

These grapic illustrations can be very valuable for all students, especially those whose technical advancement exceeds their musical development in the area of sensitive perception of tone quality and tonal line.

6. With younger students it should be emphasized that *at this stage* breath support be for the most part constant and even. An exception at this stage would be the lower register. (Generally speaking, beginning flute students must let up considerably on their breath pressure when first producing the lowest tones. With practice and experience they can learn to use the exact amount that would be considered maximum for the lowest tones. To be able to sense that degree of breath pressure which stops short of overblowing a low D or C requires much practice and experience.)

7. The principle of contrast remains one of the best teaching aids. With most beginners it will help greatly to hear a tone that is deliberately overblown or underblown followed by one that is properly supported so that it sounds "centered" or "placed." To tell any student that his tone is too dark, thin, weak, or too harsh will not in itself remedy the problem. If he can have the concept demonstrated aurally, he will then have one sound to compare with another. It is really a matter of establishing guidelines where heretofore none existed.

The use of graphic charts will again enhance his perception and accelerate cognition (see Figures 30 and 31).

A centered tone will reflect definition and character in one's ear.

FIGURE 30

A breathy tone lacks character (resonance) and aural definition.

FIGURE 31

8. Exercises based on simple, slurred, scale-like, conjunct lines are best for work on breath support for the beginner. Disjunct musical lines should be avoided until after conjunct lines can be executed with proficiency.

9. Good posture is essential to all wind performers. The writer strongly recommends that all woodwind students spend some of their time standing when practicing (except of course for those playing the large lower wind instruments).

TONGUING

Initial Stage

For the first few lessons it is best to allow the beginner to slur as much as possible. Allow him to simply use a breath attack upon beginning a tone. After the student has gained a reasonable degree of control over breath support and aperture—that is, when he can maintain a fairly stable tone, execute the beginning 3-and-3 routine, and find his first tones with at least 80 percent accuracy—tonguing may then be introduced. The time involved prior to introducing tonguing will of course vary with the individual student.

In allowing the student to make breath attacks for the first few lessons, advise him to leave the tongue resting in the lower part of the interior of the mouth. Usually the tongue will lay against the lower teeth in an almost natural manner.

When tonguing is introduced, the initial stroke is best produced by saying the syllable "too" or "doo." Either syllable will compel one's tongue to strike the roof of the mouth slightly above the upper teeth. It is best for beginners to avoid tonguing between the teeth. Although there are several types of tonguing and each should be studied, the single-tongue placement attained with the "too" or "doo" syllable is the one used with the greatest frequency and should be cultivated first.

Double and Triple Tonguing

After the basic single tongue stroke is developed, double tonguing and triple tonguing should be introduced in a progressive, step-by-step manner. Both of these methods may be considered fundamental performance techniques of the flutist. (Although flutter tonguing and other advanced tonguing strokes should be considered by the advanced flutist, they do not fall within the scope of this text, and thus will not be discussed.)

These multiple tonguing strokes should be introduced on the intermediate level of study. A standard method such as the Rubank *Intermediate Method for Flute* is recommended; in that particular series of flute studies the initial presentation is clear and easy to grasp, and it is highly structured, allowing the student to develop in a gradual manner.

Double tonguing is used in rapid staccato passages where duple rhythmic patterns are predominant. By using the syllables "too-coo" or "te-ke" the technique may be developed.

Double tonguing

Triple tonguing is generally executed with the syllables "te-ke-te," and is most practical in playing rapid triplet rhythmic patterns.

Triple tonguing

Ch. 3/The Flute

Among the more important points to remember regarding tonguing methods are:

1. The elements of time and sequence are of key importance. The order of presentation and study should be: single tonguing, double tonguing, and then triple tonguing.
2. Multiple tongue strokes should be practiced in a slow, gradual, and methodical manner using a recommended method.
3. The choice of syllables should be left to the discretion of the instructor. Depending on the individual and the music, the syllables "too-coo," "ti-ki" (or te-ke), "doo-goo," or "di-ki" may be used for multiple tongue strokes. The author has found the syllable "loo" very effective for single tonguing in a legato manner; and the syllable "toe" is very helpful when tonguing in the lowest register of the flute.

(Flute reference chart is on page 44; Standard Fingering Chart starts on page 45.)

Fingering

FIGURE 32.
Flute reference chart

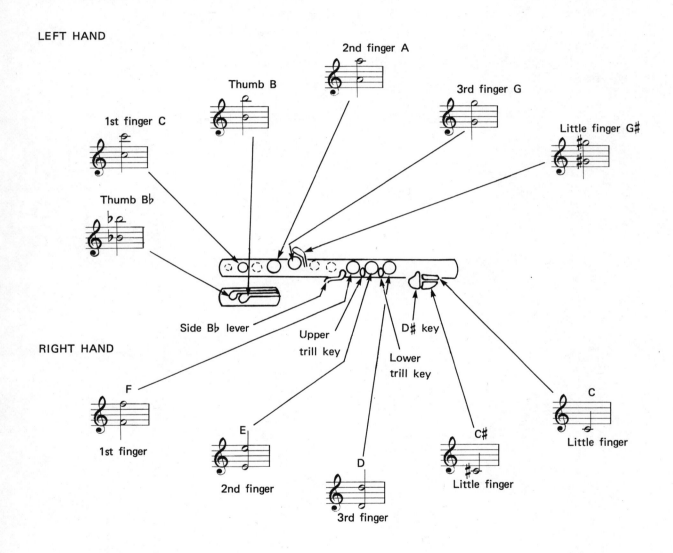

Standard Fingering Chart

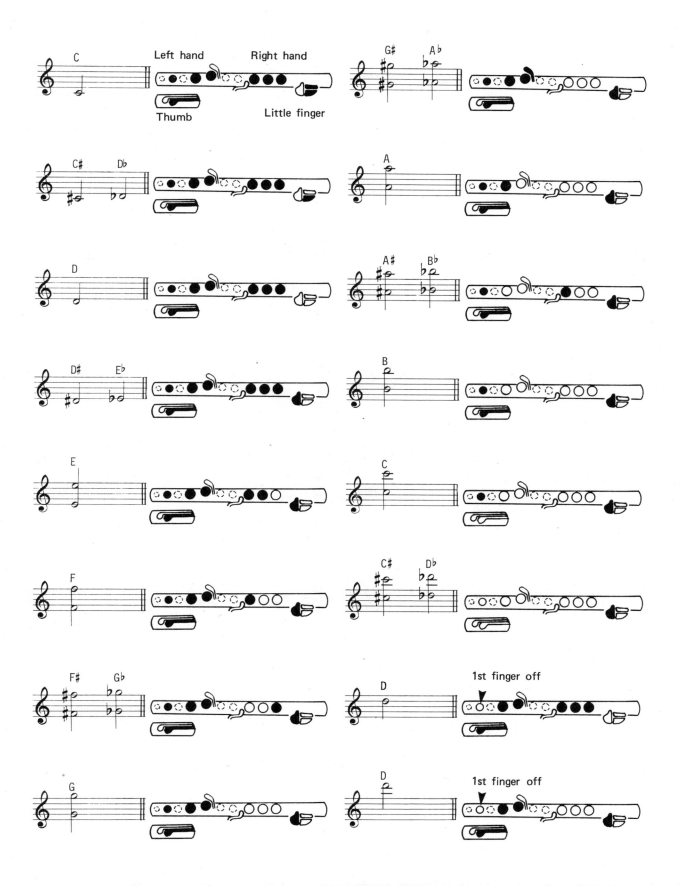

Fundamental Techniques and Supplemental Aids/Part II

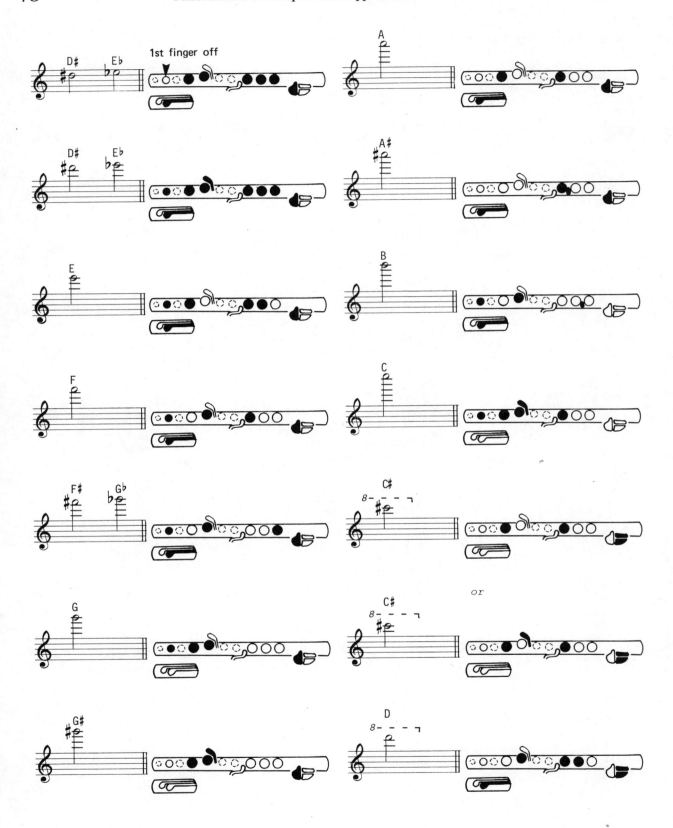

Ch. 3/The Flute

(Flute reference chart is on page 48; Standard Trill Chart starts on page 49.)

TRILLS

The flute, oboe, and bassoon are the oldest members of the orchestra among the woodwind instruments. The single reeds—in the form of the clarinet—were introduced into the orchestra only after a wealth of Baroque and Rococo instrumental literature had been written; thus for all practical purposes single-reed literature may be said to begin with the early Classic style—allowing, of course, for the clarinet's introductory period into the orchestra. The point of the matter is that there is considerably more older music literature for flute and double reeds.

Additionally, the music of these earlier music styles utilized ornaments (trills, grace notes, etc.) to a much larger extent than did subsequent style periods. Although the trill in its various forms was only one of the many musical ornaments which composers (and performers) added to their music, it is the ordinary trill that has remained as probably the most popular of all the ornaments.

A trill consists of the rapid alternation of two notes. Generally speaking, the trill notes form either half-step or whole-step intervals. However, in some instances trills may involve intervals larger (or even smaller) than these. Composers use trills as colorful ornaments to enhance their music. The following table of trills consists of the standard trills, which may be introduced on the elementary and intermediate levels of study.

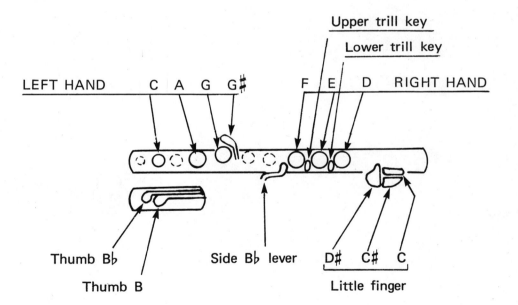

FIGURE 33. Flute reference chart

Standard Trill Chart

Arrows denote the keys to be trilled; shaded circles denote closed tone holes; unshaded, open tone holes. When more than one fingering is listed for a trill, they are listed in order of preference. * denotes trill may begin with index finger (left hand) open, but should be closed after E is sounded; ** denotes that on some flutes it may be easier to begin the high G-A trill with the *regular* high G fingering and then use either of the trills indicated.

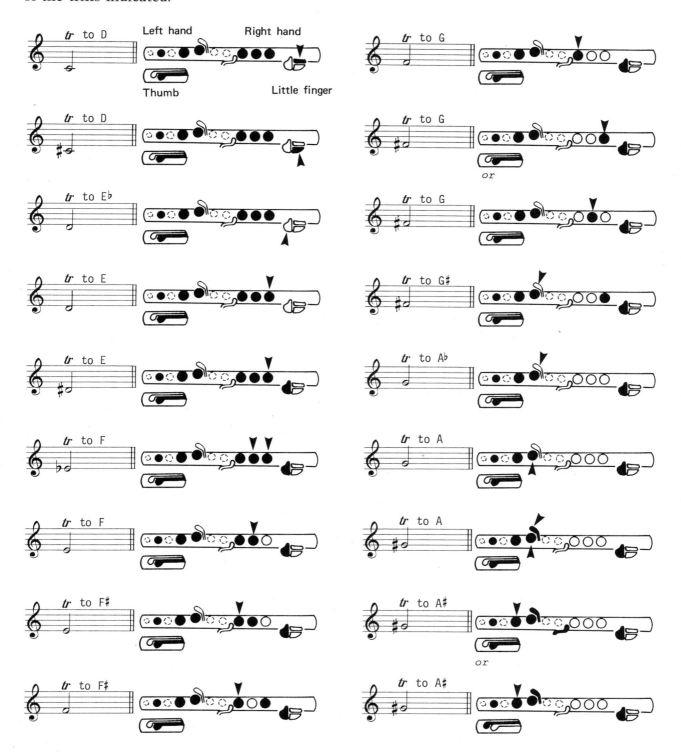

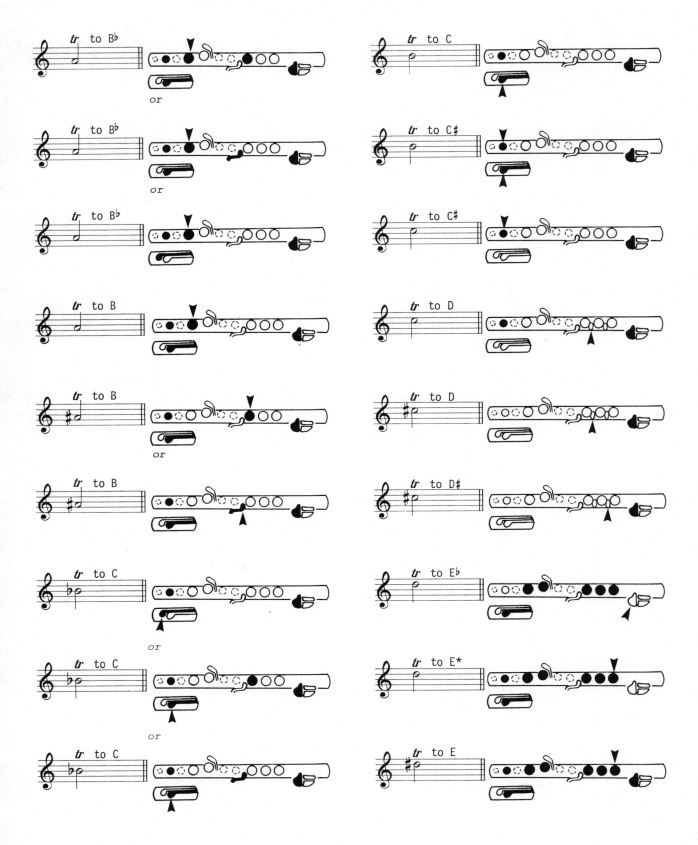

Ch. 3/The Flute

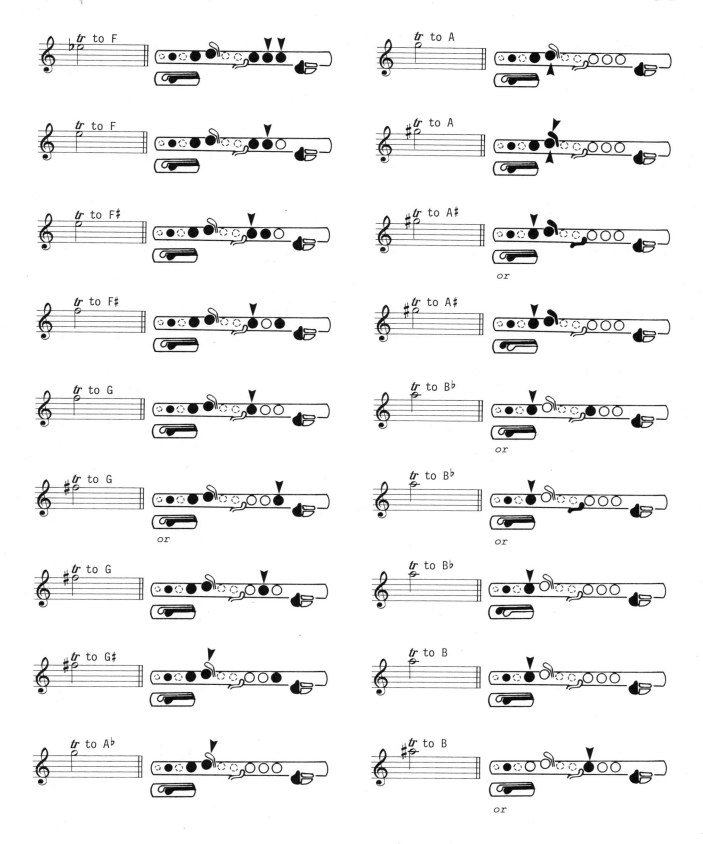

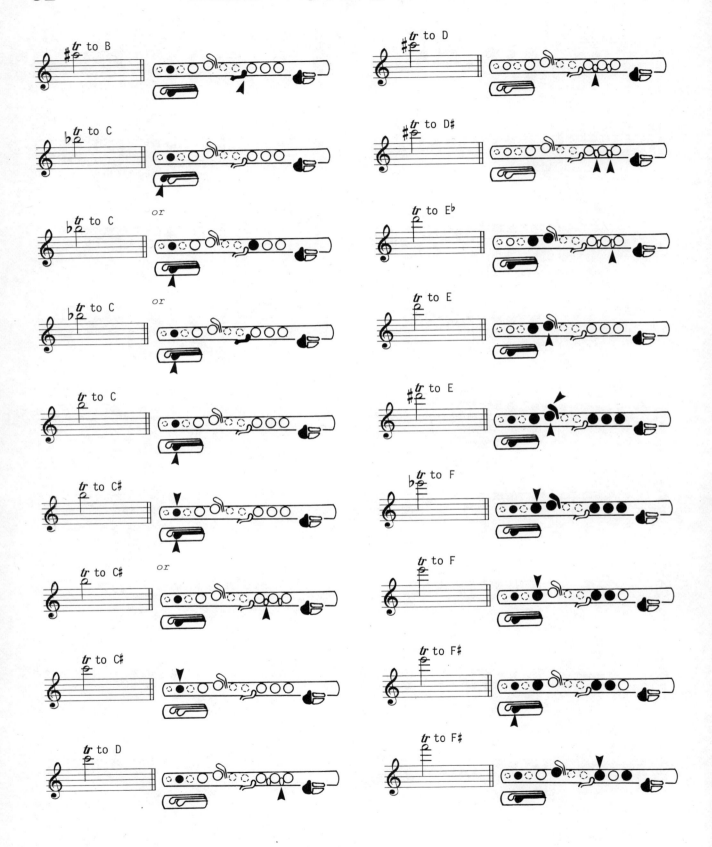

Ch. 3/The Flute

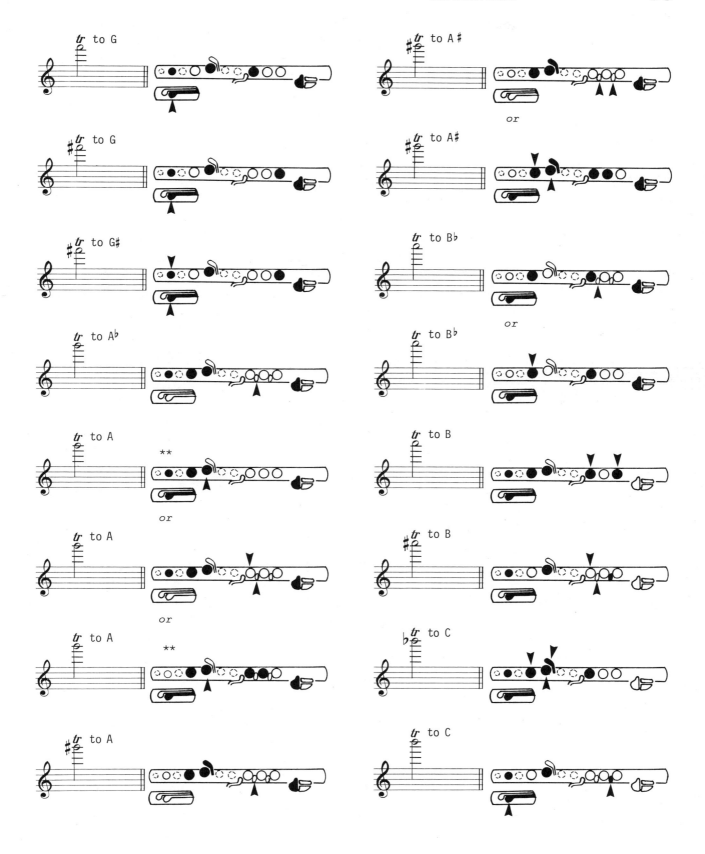

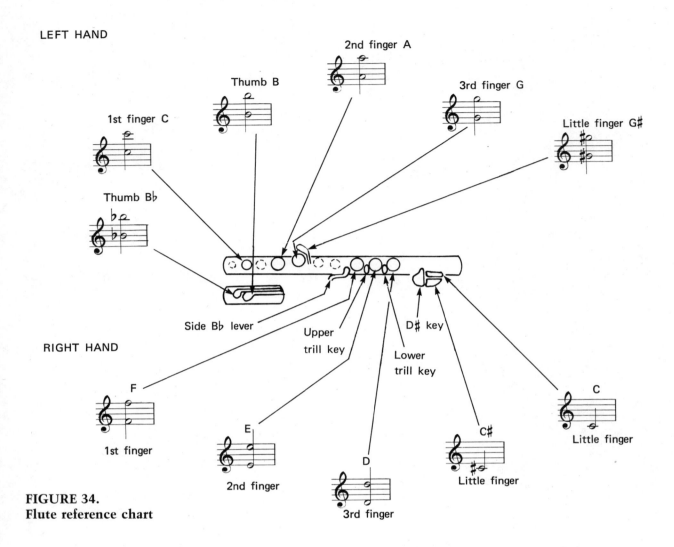

FIGURE 34.
Flute reference chart

FREQUENTLY USED SPECIAL FINGERINGS

EXAMPLE 1. The trill fingering for F-sharp is recommended in rapid passages where the regular F-sharp would be impractical. The little finger D-sharp key may also be omitted in such an extremely fast passage as the following:

EXAMPLE 2. Generally speaking, the three fingerings for B-flat are best used as follows:

1. The most frequently used B-flat fingering employs the B thumb key, the two index fingers, and the low D-sharp key (little finger). This fingering is recommended as the first for beginners; the remaining B-flat

fingerings should only be introduced *after* the elementary stage of study. This is to avoid indiscriminate sliding of the thumb during early stages.

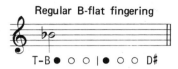

2. The side B-flat fingering is primarily a trill fingering, but may also be used in trill-like passages. In example b below the side B-flat lever is used beginning with the first B-flat and *should remain depressed throughout the passage.*

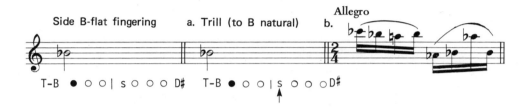

3. The third fingering for B-flat (B-flat thumb key, left index finger, and low D-sharp key) is used only in those instances when it is more practical to do so. An example is listed below.

The most important points to remember concerning the use of the three B-flat fingerings are that the regular fingering (1) is the most widely used, the second fingering is for trills or trill-like passages, and the third is employed only when it is more practical.

EXAMPLE 3. The high E and second A above the staff are two of the more difficult notes to manage on flute. When playing the high E as indicated in bar one, omit the use of the D-sharp key and roll out slightly to maintain the correct pitch. In bar two, the interval A to E (ascending or descending) will break with greater ease and accuracy *with* the use of the D-sharp key on A and *without* the use of the D-sharp key on E. Again it will be necessary to roll out on the E in order to maintain the correct pitch.

EXAMPLE 4. In slow, sustained passages or at phrase endings high A and high F-sharp can be played with greater control by using the low C-sharp key (rather than the D-sharp key) with the regular fingering.

EXAMPLE 5. When trilling from D to E in the staff, the left-hand index finger may remain closed after the E is sounded.

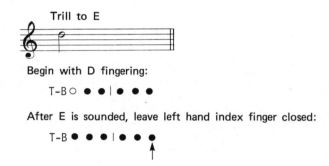

Harmonic Fingerings

Harmonic fingerings involve the use of a single fingering pattern to produce different pitches. Flutists make more use of harmonic fingerings than do any other woodwind instrumentalists. To notate harmonics, a small circle is placed above the note. However, flutists use harmonic fingerings at their own discretion, depending on the musical circumstance. Generally speaking, harmonics are used in pianissimo passages to facilitate control. And in certain fast technical passages they may be used as a matter of practicality.

Harmonics on flute are produced by advancing the lower jaw slightly forward, flexing the lips slightly so as to decrease the size of the aperture, and increasing the breath pressure as needed. The following examples are designed to serve as an introduction to flute harmonic fingerings.

EXAMPLE 1. The B harmonic uses the same fingering as the regular E note.

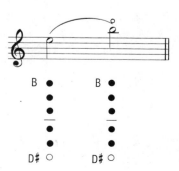

EXAMPLE 2. Additional harmonic fingerings are shown below.

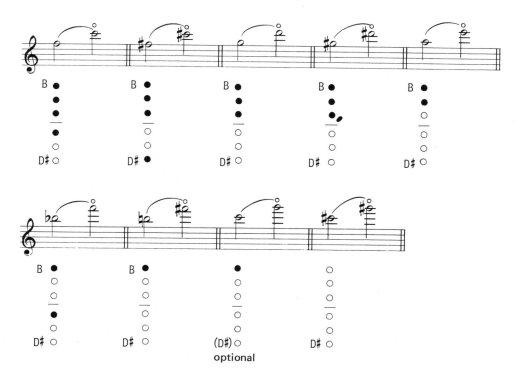

1. List those key points which should be cited in assembling the flute.
2. Discuss the purpose and care of the stopper in the head joint of the flute.
3. If it ever becomes necessary to remove the head joint stopper, what precautions and care must be taken?
4. Discuss the angles at which the flute may be held in relation to the body.
5. Considering beginning students who own student-line flutes that were not "pre-scored" at the factory, what recommendation would you make to them?
6. What does E. C. Moore recommend regarding right-hand thumb placement?
7. What does the author recommend regarding right-hand thumb placement?
8. Is the flute truly unique when compared to the other woodwinds?
9. If your answer to Question 8 is "Yes," explain how this is so. (See Part One, p. 17, and also Chapter 3, pp. 33–39.)
10. "The object of an effective flute embouchure is to _____."
11. Why does the author use such terms as "in-mouth" or "out-mouth"?
12. Cite a current definition of the term *embouchure*.
13. List five teaching aids which may help in the development of flute embouchure.
14. List five "performance practices" which may aid in the development of embouchure and tone production.
15. When an instructor is faced with exceptions to the rule concerning embouchure, what is the obligation which the author proposes?
16. How does the author distinguish between a normal occlusion and a malocclusion?
17. What significance does the author attach to the natural shape and alignment of an individual's aperture?
18. What is a "Cupid's bow"?
19. Cite three types of flute aperture.
20. Cite two preliminary exercises which a beginning flutist may practice to achieve effective breath support *and* aperture control at the initial stage of study.

Study Questions

Fundamental Techniques and Supplemental Aids/Part II

21. How does the author use the principal of contrast as a teaching aid?
22. Should the beginning flute student *tongue* or *slur* the 3-and-3 routine?
23. What syllables does the author recommend when the initial single-tongue stroke is introduced?
24. What syllables are recommended for double tonguing?
25. What syllables are recommended for triple tonguing?
26. Does the author recommend the use of any other syllables for multiple tonguing? Explain.

A Problem Chart

Problem	*Probable Cause*	*Suggestions for Improvement*
A. Breathy tone overall.	1. Aperture is too open. 2. Lower lip placement may be at fault.	1. With the aid of a mirror, have the student practice closing the aperture while blowing a steady stream of air. 2. Have student study the pictures of the recommended flute embouchure. 3. Have student strive to create the "sardonic smile" by flexing the corners of the mouth slightly. 4. Experiment with lower-lip placement until tone reaches its clearest point. (One-quarter to one-third of the lower lip should be over the tone hole.)
B. Lower tones are weak and breathy.	1. Aperture is too open. 2. The chin may not be drawn back far enough. 3. Corners of mouth may not be flexed enough.	1. Same as suggestions 1, 2, and 3 above. 2. Have student practice moving chin forward and back—leaving it back for lower tones. 3. The student should practice flexing the corners of the mouth with the aid of a mirror.
C. Upper tones are harsh and too breathy.	1. Student may be literally overblowing. 2. Lips may be too tense. 3. The chin may not be extended forward enough.	1. With the aid of a mirror, have student practice moving chin forward and back using only the head joint. (A slight forward movement of the chin and/or lips is required in progressing up the flute scale line.) 2. Introduce the "head-joint interval" exercise. 3. Remind student that higher tones should not be produced by blowing excessively harder, but through embouchure, chin movement, and adequate breath support.
D. Tone lacks resonance and support.	1. Lack of breath support and control of embouchure. 2. Lower-lip placement may be at fault.	1. Student should increase breath support *and* strive to play with a wider aperture (horizontal). 2. Try the "sardonic smile" approach in order to increase aperture's horizontal width and at the same time decrease its vertical height. 3. Check lower-lip placement. Some of the lower lip should cover the tone hole.
E. Student plays consistently sharp.	1. Lower-lip placement may be at fault. 2. The head joint alignment may be at fault.	1. Same as suggestion 3, immediately above. 2. The head joint may be pulled out slightly. 3. Student should turn the flute in toward lower lip.

Ch. 3/The Flute   59

A Problem Chart (*continued*)

Problem	Probable Cause	Suggestions for Improvement
F. Student plays consistently flat.	1. Lower-lip placement may be at fault. 2. The head joint alignment may be at fault.	1. Don't allow too much lower lip to cover the tone hole. 2. The head joint should be pushed in. 3. Flute should be turned outward from lower lip.
G. Student plays sharp in high register and flat in low register.	1. Student does not understand internal pitch behavior of flutes. 2. Student is not listening to his intonation carefully.	1. Remind student that flutes tend to go sharp in high register and flat in lowest register. 2. Head joint should be rolled in slightly for higher tones. 3. Head joint should be rolled out slightly for lower tones. 4. Have student practice octave exercises with a well-tuned piano or electronic tuner.
H. Student frequently misses intervals by over- or under-shooting desired pitch.	Lack of embouchure control and lip flexibility.	1. Have student study flexibility exercises such as those for thirds, sixths, etc., and then follow up with appropriate work on the head-joint interval exercise. 2. Intermediate students may be advised to play "Taps" *using only* the low-C fingering throughout the exercise. The exercise begins on the twelfth above low C (G).
I. Student lacks endurance and often complains of embouchure fatigue.	Student is using lips as *sole means* to achieve flexibility in overall range.	1. Advise the student to study and master the head-joint interval exercise. 2. The student should be informed *not to rely solely* on flexing of the lips to facilitate changes in pitch. In the median range on flute a slight movement of the jaw may be all that is required to break larger intervals (forward for ascending and back for descending intervals). Using only the lips to facilitate playing intervals causes fatigue by placing the entire burden of physical movement on lip muscles. However, *in the extreme ranges* both lip (aperture) flexing and jaw movement are necessary for accurate and controlled tone production; (*in the extreme upper range,* air pressure must also be increased). But this is not the case in the median or practical range of the flute.
J. Tonguing sounds labored and often with unwanted extraneous sounds.	Wrong tongue placement.	1. Check to see if student is tonguing between the teeth or lips or at a point just above or behind the front incisors. 2. Recommend the use of the syllables "too" or "doo" to achieve best tongue placement. 3. Make certain that students hold their heads upright and erect so as not to cramp throat and tongue muscles.

Teaching Aids

1. In aligning flute, have the tone hole (located in the head joint) in a straight line with the keys. Later this alignment may be adjusted slightly to suit individual needs.
2. The flute should be held parallel with the lips. If it is tilted downward, then the player's head should be tilted slightly to the right so that the lip alignment remains parallel.
3. Have the student practice the 3-and-3 finger exercise (without actually playing) in order to seat the fingers evenly over the tone holes.
4. Demonstrate the recommended embouchure format using visual aids, and then have the student do the following:

   a) Try the "sardonic smile" with a slight flex in the corners of the mouth.
   b) Turn lips outward.
   c) Try to hook one-fourth to one-third of the lower lip over the tone hole.
   d) Strive to play on the *inner lining* of the lips.
   e) In other words "out-mouth."
   f) Strive to produce an A (440 v.p.s.) that is even and clear, using only the head joint.
   g) Refer to a mirror frequently and use visual aids such as pictures.
   h) Experiment by moving the head joint (a) in and out; (b) up and down, and (c) to the left and right.
   i) Assemble the flute, practice the 3-and-3 routine, and heed E. C. Moore's advice to "use no music" in the initial stage.
   j) As he progresses, have him practice head-joint interval exercises.

Chin forward, then back.

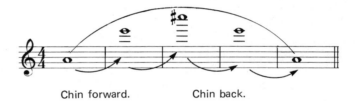
Chin forward.   Chin back.

First, using the head joint only (closed), play the A (440 v.p.s.) and then extend the jaw forward to produce high E and back again for A. (The second exercise—calling for the high C-sharp—should be introduced later at the instructor's discretion.)

   k) Use the above technique in playing octaves. (Listen to see if the student is using sufficient breath support.)

Flute Literature

SELECTED LIST OF GRADED SOLOS

The following list has been compiled as a convenient source reference for the instrumental music teacher. It is by no means complete, and readers are encouraged to study publisher catalog listings for their additional needs. This listing is intended to serve as a primer offering; although it has been carefully graded, some overlapping should of course be expected.

Considering the solos' technical difficulty, they have been ranked according to the following scale:

Grades 1–2: very easy to easy

Grades 3–4: moderate to moderately difficult

Grades 5–6: difficult to very difficult

Grades 1–2

Composer	Title	Publisher
Albéniz	Berceuse	Leduc
Alwyn	Three Easy Pieces	Mills
Aubert	Air	G. Schirmer

Ch. 3/The Flute

Grades 1–2 (continued)

Composer	Title	Publisher
Bach	Arioso	G. Schirmer
Bartók	Evening in the Country	Ludwig
Beeson	Song	Hargail
Bizet	Minuet	Carl Fischer
Bove	Praeludium	Carl Fischer
Bozza	Aria	Leduc
Cavally	Solos for the Debutant Flutist	Southern
Cui	Bagatelle	Mills
Fleury	"Greensleeves"	Leduc
Gee	Ballade	Pro-Art
Gluck	Air [concert album]	Edition Musicus
Gossec	Gavotte	Rubank
Gretchaninoff	Two Miniatures	Leduc
Handel (arr. Voxman)	Bourée and Minuet	Rubank
Haydn	Minuetto in C major	Belwin
Haydn	Serenade	Rubank
Hindemith	"Echo"	AMP
Koechlin	Fourteen Pieces for Flute	Salabert
Labate	Venetian Serenade	Carl Fischer
Lewallen	Nocturne	Belwin
	Country Dance	Belwin
Moyse (ed.)	Forty Little Pieces	G. Schirmer
	Music for the Flute Player	G. Schirmer
Mozart	Seven Salzburg Minuets	Presto
Saint-Saëns	Pavane	G. Schirmer
	"The Swan"	G. Shirmer
Weber	"Autumn Leaves"	Belwin

Grades 3–4

Composer	Title	Publisher
Alain	Three Movements	Leduc
Andersen	Scherzino	Belwin
Bach, C.P.E.	Sonata in A Minor [unaccompanied]	Schott
Bach, J. S.	Polonaise and Badinage	Carl Fischer
Barber	Cazone	Southern, Texas
Batiste	"Lament of Pan" [unacc.]	Mills
Bloch	Suite Modale	Broude
Bozza	Aria	Baron
Brun	Romance	Rubank
Caplet	Rêverie and Petite Valse	Southern, Texas
Cavally (ed.)	Twenty-Four Short Concert Pieces	Southern, Texas
Cowell, H.	"Two-Bits"	Carl Fischer
Debussy	"En Bateau"	Elkan-Vogel
DeFrumerie	Pastoral Suite	G. Schirmer
Dohnányi	Aria, Op. 48, No. 1	Associated Music Publishers
Fauré	Fantaisie	Belwin
	Pièce	Leduc
Gaubert	Romance	Baron
	Ballade	Century
Gillis	Three Short Pieces	Mills
Goldman	Two Monochromes	Shawnee

Fundamental Techniques and Supplemental Aids/Part II

Grades 3–4 (continued)

Composer	Title	Publisher
Handel	Ten Sonatas	International
Haydn (arr. Taylor)	Gypsy Rondo	Mills
Ibert	Aria	Baron
	"The Little White Donkey"	Elkan-Vogel
Jacob	The Spell, from The Pied Piper [unacc.]	Oxford
Kubik	Nocturne	G. Schirmer
Labate	Rondino	Carl Fischer
Mozart	Andante in C, K. 315	Associated Music Publishers
Nielsen	"The Children are Playing" [unacc.]	Associated Music Publishers
Pares	Fantaisie Caprice	Alfred
Pessard	Rêverie	Baron
Purcell	Two Pieces	Boosey and Hawkes
Ravel	Pièce en Forme de Habanera	Leduc
Roussel	Andante et Scherzo	Elkan-Vogel
Saucier	"Image" [unacc.]	Kendor
	"An Impression"	Kendor
Spinks	"Pebmarsh Fancy"	Oxford
Voxman (ed.)	Concert and Contest Collection	Rubank

Grades 5–6

Composer	Title	Publisher
Adler	Flauting [unacc.]	Theodore Presser
Alwyn	Divertimento [unacc.]	Boosey & Hawkes
Bach, C.P.E.	Concerto in A Major	International
Bach, J. S.	Partita in A Minor [unacc.]	International
Bach, J. S.	Six Sonatas	International
Barrère	Nocturne	G. Schirmer
Beethoven	Sonata	C. F. Peters
Berio	Sequenza [unacc.]	Associated Music Publishers
Bloch	Two Last Poems	Broude
Bozza	"Image" [unacc.]	Leduc
Bozza	Three Impressions	Baron
Chaminade	Concertino	Carl Fischer
Debussy	"Syrinx"	Elkan-Vogel
Dutilleux	Sonatine	Elkan-Vogel
Gaubert	Fantaisie	Salabert
	Nocturne and Allegro Scherzando	Baron
Giannini	Sonata	Franco Colombo
Goosens	Three Pictures	G. Schirmer
Griffes	"Poem"	G. Schirmer
Haydn	Sonata in G Major	Boosey & Hawkes
Hindemith	Eight Pieces for Flute Alone	Schott
Honegger	"Dance of the Goat" [unacc.]	Ricordi
Ibert	Concerto	Leduc
Ibert	Piece for Flute Alone	Leduc

Ch. 3/The Flute

Grades 5–6 (continued)

Composer	Title	Publisher
Kennan	"Night Soliloquy"	Carl Fischer
Krenek	Six Divertissements, Op. 68 [unacc.]	International
Martin	Ballade	Presser
Messiaen	Le Merle Noir	Leduc
Mozart	Concerto in G	International
	Concerto in D	G. Schirmer
Piston	Sonata	Boosey & Hawkes
Poulenc	Sonata	Baron
Prokofiev	Sonata, Op. 94	Leeds
Quantz	Concerto in E Minor	Franco Colombo
Reinecke	Sonata, Op. 167	International
Reynolds	Sonata for Flute and Piano	Carl Fischer
Schubert	Introduction, Theme, & Variations, Op. 160	Associated Music Publishers
Scott	"The Ecstatic Shepherd" [unacc.]	Andraud
Scott	Scotch Pastorale	Hansen
Saucier	Expansion 9 for One or More Flutes	Kendor
Stamitz	Concerto in D Major	Belwin-Mills
Tartini	Concerto in G Major	Belwin-Mills
Telemann	Suite in A Minor	Southern
Templar	"Sonnet"	Kendor
Tomasi	Concertino	Baron
Vivaldi	Concerto in D Major	International

CLASS METHODS FOR THE PUBLIC SCHOOL INSTRUMENTAL MUSIC PROGRAM

The Belwin Band Builder, Part I by Wayne Douglass; edited by Fred Weber. This is an "elementary band method" designed for "class instruction of mixed instruments or full band."[1] It is published by Belwin-Mills, Melville, N.Y.

The Belwin Band Builder, Part II by Wayne Douglass; edited by Fred Weber. This is a "continuation of *The Belwin Band Builder, Part I*." It is published by Belwin-Mills, Melville, N.Y.

Learning Unlimited Class Series by Art C. Jenson is a two-part work designed for class and home use. Part A is a "complete beginning band method." Part B is a "supplementary book/cassette package" designed to help the student structure and guide home practice. The materials in both parts have been correlated and include a "Coordination Chart" for student use. This series is published for two categories, Level One (beginning) and Level Two. It is published by Hal Leonard Publishing Corporation, Milwaukee, Wis.

Take One: Today's Method for the Contemporary Bandsman by Charles Peters and Matt Betton. This class method is for beginning bands and is designed to prepare the student for "future membership in either Symphonic Bands or Jazz Bands and Combos." It is distributed solely by the Neil A. Kjos Music Co., Park Ridge, Ill.

Take Two: Today's Method for the Contemporary Bandsman by Charles Peters and Matt Betton is a continuation of the beginning class method, *Take One.*

Silver Burdett Instrumental Series (2 vols.) by Harry I. Phillips. (Contributing

1. The quotations used to describe each applied method are direct quotations drawn from each published method that has been considered. All quotes have been reprinted with permission of the publishers.

64   Fundamental Techniques and Supplemental Aids/Part II

consultants include Saul Feldstein and Edgar Q. Rooker.) This series may be used for "individual, class, ensemble, or full band instruction." Published by the Silver Burdett Co., Morristown, N.J.

First Division Band Course (Parts 1–4). This collection is "a complete course in band instruction, in four parts," which correlates "Supplementary Band Books, Technic Books, Band Composition and Arrangements, Instrumental Solos and Ensembles to a basic band method by Fred Weber." In addition to Mr. Weber, twenty-four distinguished band and instrumental specialists were "called upon to compose or arrange the many publications—solos, ensembles, technic and program books, band selections —all correlated to the basic Method Book." Published by Belwin-Mills, Melville, N.Y.

INDIVIDUAL METHODS AND SUPPLEMENTAL STUDIES

Major Applied Methods

BELWIN SERIES FOR FLUTE

The Flute Student by F. Weber and D. Steensland is published for three graded levels of study: elementary, intermediate, and advanced intermediate. In addition to each basic method ("levels one, two, and three"), there is a separate series of supplementary studies correlated to each grade level. Published by Belwin-Mills, Melville, N.Y.

The Flute Student represents one part of Belwin-Mills's grand Student Instrumental Course series. Its publisher and authors view this multiple offering as "the first and only complete course for individual instruction of all band instruments." Like the Rubank publication series for individual flute study (see below), Belwin's Student Instrumental Course is widely used by American instrumental music teachers and is highly recommended. Although lacking in visual aids and pictures, this series is exceptionally well organized, diversified, and balanced, and it progresses logically from one grade level to the next. Additionally, it provides graded solos with piano accompaniment *for each level of study*.

RUBANK SERIES FOR FLUTE

Elementary Method for Flute by A. C. Petersen.

Intermediate Method for Flute by J. E. Skornicka and A. C. Petersen.

Advanced Method for Flute (2 vols.) by H. Voxman and W. Gower.

All published by Rubank, Inc., Miami, Fla.

The Rubank series is also one of the more widely used methods for private lessons among American junior and senior high school instrumental music teachers. Although lacking in visual aids, the Rubank offerings are exceptionally well-structured, balanced, and diversified, and progress logically from one grade level to the next.

Another key reason for the wide acceptance in America of both the Belwin and the Rubank series is that they are geared to native educational practices. In all fairness to the older and highly respected European methods, it should be pointed out that most of them were prepared in the light of European educational programs. In many cases this meant that the European music student was often required to study preparatory music fundamentals—such as *solfeggio* (Italian term; *solfège* in French) or keyboard study—prior to initial study of his chosen instrument. As a consequence, older European or European-influenced method books progress from elementary to intermediate levels at a much faster pace than do most American offerings—such as the Rubank or Belwin series, *which assume and require no prior musical study*.

It is with the above points in mind that this author recommends that the following major methods be introduced *after* the applied instrumental music student has completed a highly structured and carefully graded method of study such as the Belwin or Rubank series or a similar method of equivalent rank.

Method for the Boehm Flute by H. Altes. Published by A. Leduc, Paris, France.

Modern Method for Flute By A. Brooke. Published by Carl Fischer, New York, N.Y.

Complete Method for Flute by H. Soussmann (revision by W. Popp). Published by Carl Fischer, New York, N.Y.

Complete Method for Flute by P. Taffanel and P. Gaubert. Published by A. Leduc, Paris, France.

Foundation to Flute Playing by E. F. Wagner. Published by Carl Fischer, New York, N.Y.

Supplemental Studies

A highly recommended preliminary text:

The Flute and Its Daily Routine by E. C. Moore. Published by Leblanc Publications, Kenosha, Wis. This supplement might well be recommended as required reading for all future instrumental music teachers. Although a very short and concise offering, it contains many valuable teaching aids and includes an individualized, unique abstract concerning tone production drawn from Marcel Moyse's celebrated book, *The Art and Technique of Tone Production [De la sonorité: art et technique]*

A highly recommended reading for intermediate and advanced levels:

The Flutist's Guide by Fred Wilkins is published in cooperation with the Artley flute manufacturing company, Nogales, Ariz. This is a record-text combination which is strongly recommended to all flute enthusiasts. It is this author's assessment that this is the most significant pedagogical offering concerning flute that is available!

Other supplemental studies that are much recommended:

25 Etudes, Op. 15 by Andersen. Published by Southern Music Co., San Antonio, Texas.

The Flutist's Formulae by G. Barrère. Published by G. Schirmer, New York, N.Y.

Eighteen Exercises or Etudes for the Flute by T. Berbiguier with revision and editing by G. Barrère. Published by G. Schirmer, New York, N.Y.

Melodious and Progressive Studies for Flute by R. Cavally. Published by Southern Music Co., San Antonio, Texas.

Supplementary Studies for the Flute by R. Endresen. Published by Rubank, Miami, Fla.

The Art and Technique of Tone Production [De la sonorité: art et technique] by Marcel Moyse. Published by A. Leduc, Paris, France.

Modern Pares for Flute by G. Pares. Published by Rubank, Miami, Fla.

Studies in Time Division by L. Teal. Published by University Music Press, Ann Arbor, Mich.

12 Daily Exercises in All the Major and Minor Keys by J. Wummer. Published by Carl Fischer, New York, N.Y.

RECORDINGS OF FLUTE LITERATURE

Pedagogically Oriented Recordings

It is indeed encouraging to witness the increasing number of record-text publications that are being made available for both teacher and student use. Although this area of research remains virtually unexplored on the university level, the achievements of such pioneer publications as Fred Wilkins's *The Flutist's Guide* and Music Minus One's entire Laureate Series serve as ample testimony for what can be accomplished in the way of record-text offerings. While the content and design of each work in this category may differ, all are nonetheless pedagogically oriented.

The Music Minus One Series. Essentially, the Music Minus One Corporation makes professionally recorded backgrounds—minus a particular "solo" instrument—for all types of music, including the orchestral concerto, the sonata, chamber music, and various jazz forms. The original concept behind the MMO series was to afford the student performer a professional accompaniment against which to practice and perform a musical work in its original and complete context, that is, with full orchestra, string quartet, or jazz ensemble, as the case might be. The bulk of the recorded accompaniments made by MMO falls in this category. However, the Laureate Series of Contest Solos goes beyond the practical asset of offering a professional accompaniment. With the Laureate Series, the student or teacher is offered in one package a performance by a major performing artist, a copy of the printed music, a professional accompaniment, and interpretive suggestions for performance by the performing artist.

This series has within the past quarter century proved a valuable music education tool; it is highly recommended as a teaching aid. It is published by Music Minus One, 43 West 61 Street, New York, N.Y.

The Flutist's Guide by Fred Wilkins is published in cooperation with the Artley Manufacturing Company, Nogales, Ariz. (Fred Wilkins was a faculty member at the Juilliard School of Music, the Manhattan School of Music, and the Chautauqua School of Music; principal flutist for the "Voice of Firestone" radio and television program and for the Radio City Music Hall Orchestra; a clinician, virtuoso, and music educator extraordinaire.)

This record-text publication includes an analysis of recommended and proven performance practices for flute, with corresponding recorded demonstrations. Visual aids, although limited, are used with expertise. Also included are flute excerpts (written and recorded) from the works of such composers as Handel, Karg-Elert, Mendelssohn, Chaminade, Andersen, Doppler, and Bona, and the complete recording of Platti's Sonata in D Major. Although Wilkins's achievement in this offering represents a pedagogical tour de force, its ultimate influence is yet to be realized.

Flute Contest Music (2 vols.) is distributed under the name of Lanier Records; it may be ordered from the H. and A. Selmer Corporation, Elkhart, Indiana. Professor Charles DeLaney of the University of Florida is the flute performer. *Flute Contest Music* was produced for the purpose of serving as an aural guide for flute students. No text or analysis is provided; however, the album cover includes a brief descriptive comment about each selection listed. It may be of special interest to flutists to note that on sides A of both volumes Professor DeLaney uses a student-line flute (Bundy) while on sides B of both he uses a professional model flute (Selmer). An additional note of importance is that each selection has been graded on a scale of 1 (easy) to 7 (difficult). Both flute and piano parts are graded separately.

The first volume of this two-part collection consists of twelve flute pieces which most would agree have become part of the standard flute repertoire. Professor DeLaney is here accompanied by pianist Edwin Thayer, staff accompanist at the University of Illinois. (Selections are listed here in recorded order.)

Handel: Larghetto and Allegro from Sonata No. 4

J. S. Bach: Polonaise and "Badinerie"

Émile Pessard: Andalouse

Ernesto Kohler: "Butterfly (Etude de Concert)"

Benjamin Godard: Allegretto

J. Andersen: Scherzino

J. Lewallen: Three Pieces for Flute and Piano

G. Enesco: Cantabile and Presto

W. A. Mozart: Allegro aperto from Concerto in D Major

H. Busser: Prelude and Scherzo

F. Martin: Ballade

A. Honegger: "The Dance of the Goat" [*unacc.*]

In Volume 2 Professor DeLaney is accompanied by Professor George Reeves of the University of Illinois. Selections here include the following works:

G. P. Telemann: Cantabile and Allegro from Sonata in G

G. F. Handel: Siciliana and Giga from Sonata No. 5

J. Andersen: Two Pieces for Flute and Piano

J. J. Quantz: Allegro from Concerto in G

A. Bournonville: "Danse pour Katia"

G. Hue: Two Pieces for Flute and Piano

L. Ganne: Andante and Scherzo

C. M. Widor: Romance and Scherzo

J. Ibert: "Jeux"

P. Gaubert: Nocturne et Allegro Scherzando

The Flute Family is a collection of flute solos demonstrating the sounds of six members of the flute family. It may be obtained from Mark Records, 4249 Cameron Dr., Buffalo, N.Y. 14221.

Harry Moskovitz, the soloist, performs unaccompanied on the following flutes: piccolo, sopranino flute in A-flat, soprano flute in E-flat, concert flute in C, alto flute in G, and bass flute in C. The album includes descriptive notes about the instruments, the composers, and the music. Selections included in this album are listed in the order of recorded performance.

C.P.E. Bach: Sonata in A Minor [*concert flute*]

J. Andersen: Etude in E Minor, Op. 33, No. 6 [alto]

J. Donjon: "Will-o'-the-Wisp" [piccolo]

F. Couperin: Gigue [sopranino in A-flat]

J. Donjon: "Le Tambour" [piccolo]

P. O. Ferroud: "Jade" [soprano in E-flat]

G. F. Handel: Allegro from Sinfonietta in G Minor [soprano in E-flat]

J. Donjon: "Song of the Wind" [concert flute]

J. S. Bach: Sarabande from Partita No. 2 [bass]

J. Donjon: Elegie-Etude [concert flute]

F. Kuhlau: Adagio from Grand Solo, Op. 57, No. 2 [concert flute]

F. Doppler: "Hungarian Pastoral Fantasy" [alto]

C. Debussy: "Syrinx" [concert flute]

C. Debussy: "Syrinx" [soprano in E-flat]

Concert Pieces for the Flute is a collection of frequently performed flute solos. It may be obtained from Golden Crest Records, Inc., 220 Broadway, Huntington Station, N.Y.

The performers here are Mark Thomas (flute) and Russell Woollen (keyboard). Although the textual comment is limited to the type of programmatic notes customarily appended to record album covers, this publication offers the listener the advantage of the collection album devoted exclusively to flute solos, which, additionally, are performed by professional artists.

G. F. Handel: Sonata in A Minor, Op. 1, No. 4

J. S. Bach: Siciliano from Sonata in E-flat Major

G. Platti: Adagio and Allegro from Sonata in G Major

Gluck: Minuet and Dance of the Blessed Spirits from *Orpheus.*

Debussy: "Syrinx"

J. Andersen: Scherzino

A. Caplet: Rêverie et Petite Valse

M. Shinohara: Kassouga

E. Pessard: Andalouse

A. Jolivet: Fantaisie-Caprice

The aforementioned recorded publications tend more or less to embrace a wide educational format, in that each was designed in some way to offer more than just an artistic performance of a musical work. It is of special interest to note that the flute manufacturer W. T. Armstrong Co. has taken this line of thought and further developed it by producing a twenty-four

minute sound-and-color movie entitled *Flute Playing: A Study with Mark Thomas.* It is to be hoped that it will be only a matter of time before the talents of other major artists are utilized similarly.

Traditional Recordings

The remaining partial list of long-playing recordings can well serve as a beginning repertoire source for student flutists.

C.P.E. Bach: Concerto in A Minor. Jean-Pierre Rampal. Oiseau 50121

———: Six Sonatas. Jean-Pierre Rampal. Nonesuch 71034

J. S. Bach: Eight Sonatas. Jean-Pierre Rampal. Telefunken 9402/3

Beethoven: Serenade for Flute, Violin, and Viola. Julius Baker (flute), J. and L. Fuchs (strings). Decca 9574

L. Berio: "Differences." Jacques Castagner. Time 8002

A. Caplet: Rêverie et Petite Valse. William Kincaid. Columbia ML4339

Debussy: "Syrinx." Julius Baker. Decca DL9777

———: "Syrinx." William Kincaid. Columbia ML4339

———: "Syrinx." Jean-Pierre Rampal. Educo 4001

C. Griffes: "Poem." Julius Baker. Decca DL4013

Handel: Ten Flute Sonatas. Jean-Pierre Rampal. Epic HSC153

Hindemith: Sonata for Flute and Piano. William Kincaid. Columbia ML4339

Honegger: "Dance of the Goat." Jean-Pierre Rampal. Mercury MG10061

———: "Dance of the Goat." Charles DeLaney. Lanier. (H&A Selmer, Inc.)

K. Kennan: "Night Soliloquy." William Kincaid. Award Artists 33-706

F. Martin: Ballade. Charles DeLaney. Lanier

Mozart: Andante in C. Camillo Wanausek. Vox 8550

———: Andante in C. Julius Baker. Vanguard VSD-71153

———: Concerto No. 1 in G Major. William Kincaid. Columbia ML5851

———: Concerto No. 1 in G Major. Julius Baker. Vanguard VSD-71153

W. Piston: Sonata for Flute and Piano. Doriot A. Dwyer. Claremont 1205

J. Quantz: Concerto in G: Allegro. Charles DeLaney. Lanier Records

A. Vivaldi: Flute Concerto ("The Bullfinch"). Julius Baker. Vanguard VSD-71153

The Oboe

4

FIGURE 35.
Oboe (Signet model, plateau system)

Photograph courtesy of The Selmer Company, Elkhart, Indiana.

Oboe Assembly

FIGURE 37.
Bell and lower joint

FIGURE 36.
Gripping the bell

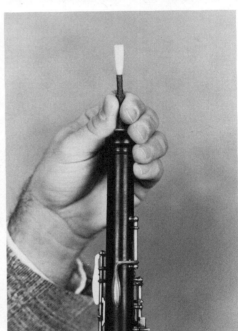

FIGURE 38.
(left) Top and lower joints

FIGURE 39.
(right) Reed and top joint

Instrument Assembly and Care

It should be noted that the oboe has a very complicated key system which is completely exposed and very delicate, and thus subject to greater possible damage than are the other winds. The upper and lower joints have bridge keys which must be joined together without damaging the ends that are fitted with cork or plastic sleeves. The most expensive damage, however, occurs from bending the long metal rods, which serve multiple uses.

1. It is recommended that the middle joint and bell be assembled first. Guide the lower, connecting bridge keys carefully so as not to tear

Ch. 4/The Oboe 71

the cork off the key ends. The bell may be gripped easily enough; however, the middle joint should be handled with care: Strive to exert your strongest finger pressure on the top of this joint, thus avoiding any possible damage to its main body. The cork on the tenons should be wiped with cork grease before inserting. If it appears that too much cork is on the tenon, *never* force the joints together. Ask your instructor or a repairman to sand the excess cork off.

2. After the middle and bell joints are assembled, the top joint may be added. Holding the bell in the right hand, carefully connect the top and middle joints. You must guide the two connecting bridge keys so that you do not damage the cork on the ends; the keys extending out and over the tenon may be raised slightly, if necessary.

Without question a visual demonstration of all this is superior to any written description. (See Illustrations on p. 70)

3. Cork grease should be used sparingly on the tube of the double reed. When inserting the reed, a slight twisting motion will aid immensely in keeping the cork-end of the tube from becoming frayed.

4. After each playing period the oboe should be swabbed with a small turkey feather. Due to the small bore size, most oboists simply spread the moisture that has collected inside the bore with the small, delicate feather. It will dry faster as a result; the soft edges of the feather pose no danger of scraping the bore.

5. There are no factual, statistically valid rules regarding how often— or even whether it is absolutely necessary—to oil the bore of a wooden musical instrument. It is recommended that the oboist follow the advice of the manufacturer on this point. Since plastic instruments are generally recommended for beginners, this matter may be held in abeyance until a more advanced level is reached.

6. The pivotal positions of the key mechanism should be oiled at least three times a year. Be careful not to drop any oil on the oboe's pad or cork areas.

7. Should you own a wooden oboe, make certain that you do not expose it to sudden temperature changes or extreme heat or cold. It is a known fact that even the finest grenadilla wood will crack under extreme temperature conditions.

8. Never leave the oboe lying on a chair or propped on a music stand. It is safer to keep the instrument in one's hands or return it to its case when finished performing.

Instrument Angle and Hand Position

There appears to be much less unanimity among oboists or clarinetists regarding instrument angle than among flutists, and perhaps rightly so. Some teachers recommend a high position, with the oboe up and away from the body. On the other hand, many excellent performers play with the instrument in close to the body. The author has found, in teaching woodwind instruments over many years, that instrument angle with student performers—especially among the more gifted—is a self-adjusting matter. This, however, is not the case with older students doing minor instrument study; this group must be observed carefully and made to experiment to find the best position. It has been the author's experience that with this group a higher angle—away from the body—

FIGURE 40.
Instrument
angle—profile

FIGURE 41.
Front view

usually works best for most students. Be that as it may, the determining factor regarding instrument angle rests upon the individual's particular occlusion. If the lower jaw noticeably recedes, the tendency is to bring the oboe closer to the body; if the lower jaw protrudes outward, the tendency is to lift the oboe up and away from the body. The experienced teacher will make his recommendations according to the individual's needs—not another's.

Some teachers recommend that the oboe reed be aligned so that its aperture is *not* perfectly parallel with the lips but at a slight angle (Figure 42). One reason offered for this angle of reed placement is that it may prolong the life of the reed.

FIGURE 42.
Position of oboe tip
opening

Parallel

Angled

While the above point may be controversial, the preference for placing the same blade of the double-reed on the upper lip each time it is used is both valid and noteworthy. The rank beginner may be insensitive to "top" and "bottom" sides of a double reed; however, after the elementary stage some students may be observed making a half turn with the tube of the reed to change the position of the blades; the reason for this is that the students seem to have instinctively discovered that no two reed blades are identical. One blade will inevitably be stronger than the other, due to the way the reed is made, and the reed may respond more favorably when the stronger blade is placed against the upper lip—or vice versa. Through exposure and experience the young player will develop sensitivity to top and bottom blade placement.

Hand position on the oboe will tend to be self-adjusting. Although the older open-ring oboes have largely been replaced by instruments with "plateau" systems (whereby the tone hole is covered by a cork or pad

Ch. 4/The Oboe

rather than the finger), the distance between consecutive tone holes on an oboe is still larger than with the flute or clarinet. Thus the finger spread on oboe is wider and less natural. The young oboist should be so informed, and advised that his best hand position is one with fingers arched and spread slightly apart. The right-hand thumb should be placed so as not to cramp the hand.

FIGURE 43.
Hand position—Left thumb placement

FIGURE 44.
Right-hand thumb placement

FIGURE 45.
Left and right hand placement

Tone Production

EMBOUCHURE

How one grips a double reed with the lips is indeed a crucial aspect of effective performance. Double-reed instruments should always be gripped with both lips turned inward, resting against the top and bottom reed blades. The teeth are never permitted to touch the reed.

An effective approach for beginners is to advise them to lay the reed on the lower lip and fold or roll it into the mouth. Next, seal the opening of the mouth by raising the lower jaw until the reed is surrounded by both lips. The amount of reed to be inserted into the mouth must be sufficient to allow the blade ends to vibrate freely. If too much reed is taken into the mouth, the resulting tone may be described as large, open, raucous, and dull in character; if too little, small, pinched, bright and narrow. It is advisable to have the student experiment with the amount of reed to be inserted into the mouth. Deliberately allow him to insert only a small amount of reed into the mouth and then have him listen to the resulting sound. Next, have him take an excessive amount of reed into the mouth, and then, have him compromise and use a medium grip, in both cases noting the resulting sound. The aural experience of sharply contrasting sounds can be the first step in ear training for timbre and "tone placement."

Ideally the oboist's embouchure (grip) should encircle the reed so as to maintain a consistent muscular flex—neither too loose nor too tight—throughout the general playing range of the instrument. While the clarinetist may grip with the lower jaw offset in a forward manner, and the bassoonist's chin is more often offset with the lower jaw back, the oboist's grip usually represents the middle of the road between these two extremes.

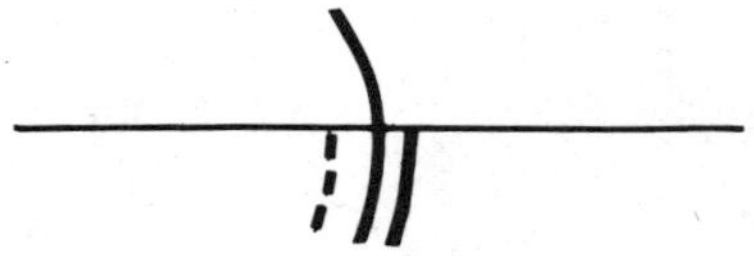

The lower jaw should "feel" forward of the upper teeth.

FIGURE 46.
Clarinetist's lower-jaw placement

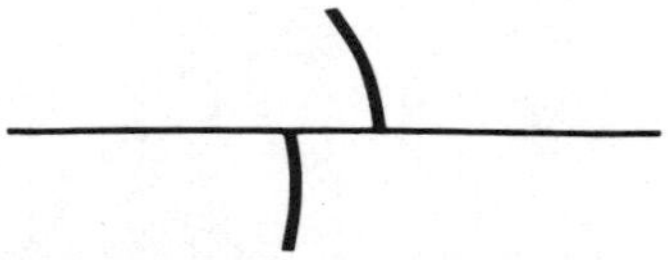

The lower jaw should be pulled back so that the lower teeth are behind the upper teeth

FIGURE 47.
Bassoonist's lower-jaw placement

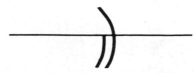

The lower teeth may appear even with the upper teeth, but usually are slightly back of the upper teeth

FIGURE 48.
Oboist's lower-jaw placement

Ch. 4/The Oboe   75

Whether an oboist uses a parallel grip or a modification of this is determined largely by the occlusion of upper and lower teeth. In an extreme case where it is visible that the lower jaw protrudes or recedes excessively, the prospective student should be informed of the malocclusion and the problems this can pose.

Young oboists often tend to overgrip and use a vice-like embouchure. For best results a circular grip is recommended. While the vice-like grip emphasizes muscular tensions that may be depicted as largely vertical, the circular grip emphasizes equal muscular flex from all parts of the mouth—the sides as well as the upper and lower portions.

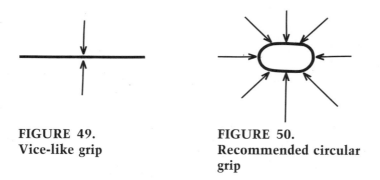

FIGURE 49.
Vice-like grip

FIGURE 50.
Recommended circular grip

Figures 51, 52, and 53 show a basic procedure for forming the recommended embouchure for oboe.

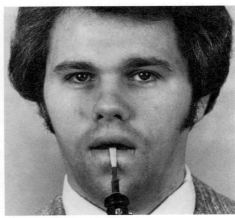

FIGURE 51.
(left) Step 1: Place oboe reed on lower lip.

FIGURE 52.
(right) Step 2: Fold or roll lower lip and reed into mouth

FIGURE 53.
Step 3: Close mouth, encircling reed with lips

FIGURE 54.
Profile view of the
recommended oboe
embouchure

FIGURE 55.
Profile view of an
incorrect oboe
embouchure

A close examination of the recommended embouchure format will reveal the following key points:

1. The lip muscles surrounding the reed are flexed.
2. The cheeks are not puffed.
3. The lips—especially the lower lip—are turned *into* the mouth so that little if any of the red tissue of the lips is visible.

It is of major importance to understand that lower-lip placement on oboe is quite different from lower-lip placement on clarinet. More lower lip is turned inward on oboe, whereas on clarinet the dark red part of the lip is allowed to rest on the lower teeth, showing at least half of the red tissue (see Figures 56, 57, and 58).

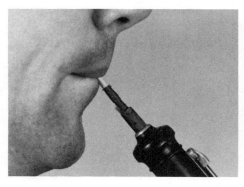

FIGURE 56.
Lower-lip placement
for oboe

FIGURE 57.
Lower-lip placement
for clarinet

Ch. 4/The Oboe

Many single-reed and trombone students studying music education on the college level tend to "carry over" certain physical habits associated with their major instruments into their study of oboe. This often results in the student using a clarinet or trombone embouchure on the oboe. A similar problem may occur with young single-reed students on the secondary level of study who switch to or double on oboe. Note in Figure 58 that a clarinet embouchure is being used to grip the oboe reed. The lower lip is flexed, smooth, and *turned outward.* This embouchure form is not recommended for oboe. A close study of Figures 51–58 can help immensely in the problem of the "carry-over" habits often encountered in minor instrument study.

FIGURE 58. Oboist using a clarinetist's embouchure (note that the lower lip is turned outward; compare this with Figure 56)

Probably the most difficult task confronting both student and teacher regarding oboe embouchure is trying to put into words the *how much, where,* and *why* of muscular flex in the lips. The *why* aspect may be dismissed with a quick demonstration; for the *where* aspect mirror and picture demonstrations are sufficient. *How much* lip tension to use is the real enigma that looms as formidable. The author has found that the following analogous demonstration has helped numerous oboe students gain a quicker understanding of and feeling for effective lip tension: Simply grip the student's wrist with the thumb and middle finger; the amount of pressure may be very firm, but should not squeeze upon the wrist. Then ask the student to gently pull his wrist away. He will quickly observe that although the teacher is not actually squeezing his wrist he is nonetheless using enough muscular flex to restrain it. Next, increase the finger tension to the maximum—still without really squeezing the student's wrist—and then ask the student to pull his wrist away, this time using greater effort. The object of this demonstration is to show that muscular tension exerted in a circular manner can be controlled and suspended so as not to bind the wrist—or, in the case of embouchure, the double reed. If the double reed is gripped in a similar manner, consistent stability of control is attained without curtailing reed vibration.

The following list of points can serve as excellent teaching aids:

1. Have the student soak the reed in water before playing.
2. Have the student practice with the reed only and make it "crow" or "cackle." The reed can be made to crow by inserting a little more of it into the mouth than is usually needed, and using less lip tension around it. If the reed produces a harmonic sound consisting of two pitches—one high and one low, with both tending to be bal-

anced in volume—then it is an indication that both reed blades are vibrating freely and in a homogeneous manner. Many advanced oboists who make their own reeds will test a reed in this way.

This exercise can aid in determining how much reed is to be taken into the mouth and how much lip tension used. Primarily, it can help the developing student to cultivate aural and physical sensitivity. At a later date when the student begins his study of reed making, he may then use this technique of making the reed crow to check for proper balance between the reed blades.

3. Beginning oboe students should be advised to practice only for short periods of time, since it is impossible for most beginners to play with proper lip tension in the initial stages for more than a few minutes at a time.
4. The use of photographic illustrations and a mirror are indispensable for developing embouchure.
5. When working on sustained tones for embouchure development, use graphic illustrations. For example:

Even and consistent tone   Wavering tone

6. Encourage the student to avoid bunching the lower lip around the reed.
7. Generally speaking, the muscular tension (flex) in the embouchure should remain constant; it should not tighten or loosen with register changes. An exception for beginners to this recommendation is to drop the lower jaw slightly for the lowest tones. (Some teachers advise the student to "point the chin down" to accomplish this.)
8. Introduce the three-octave exercise on D as soon as possible (see pp. 15–16 and 81).

BREATH SUPPORT

The dimensions of the oboe reed aperture are the smallest for the major reed instruments. While a flutist must labor over an extended period of time to develop a controlled, effective, and thus functional aperture, the oboe aperture is preset; its given stability is inherent in the makeup of the finished reed.

FIGURE 59. Approximate woodwind aperture dimensions

Because of the small size of the oboe reed aperture, oboists from the very beginning play with considerably more "back air pressure" than other woodwind players. Whereas the young flutist is constantly allowing too much air to escape—and experiencing a dizzy, lightheaded feeling quite often—the young oboist is faced with the opposite problem: often feeling that he cannot get rid of the air fast enough. Thus while the flutist may spend years developing his aperture to help achieve appropriate "back air pressure," the oboist will spend an enormous amount of time concentrating on those factors which will help relieve him of excessive "back air pressure," for example; reed making, proper phrasing, and determining the amount of air to be inhaled.

Although the key statement "Less fingers means more air" is a more acute matter for bassoonists, it is nonetheless applicable to oboists. The bassoonist applies this principle literally in executing the 3-and-3 routine, whereas the oboist will find it indispensable when playing octaves, in particular in the top octave.

After elementary work on embouchure (grip) and tonal line (see the 3-and-3 routine below), it is highly advisable to begin work on octave exercises. Subsequently—as soon as is feasible—the three-octave exercise should be introduced. It is imperative that the oboe student learn through experience as early as possible that the top register tones are achieved with increased breath pressure—*not* through an acute increase in lip tension.

Generally speaking, many beginning oboists overgrip the tones in the top octave—causing them to go sharp—rather than maintain consistent lip tension. It should be remembered that the small vibratory source of the oboe's sound—the reed—is very sensitive to touch. Any fluctuation in lip tension will immediately affect its vibration and thus raise or lower pitch. It is important to guide the student to increased breath pressure for higher tones rather than a "biting" or vice-like grip.

The following exercises can be of immense help to the oboist in developing a concept of consistent breath support and tonal line and in negotiating upper-register tones.

1. 3-and-3 Routine: Basic Pattern

For the beginner no music is needed; this routine is simply a matter of lifting and depressing fingers consecutively. It thus allows concentration to be centered on a few tasks rather than many. Note that the 3-and-3 routine is always slurred.

2. Basic Pattern Graphically Depicted

Note that the series of notes actually forms a melodic line. This tonal line can be depicted with two parallel lines as shown here. Breath pressure in this range should be even and stable.

As the student progresses, this basic pattern can be modified to fit the particular level of assignment. For example, when reading music notation is attained, patterns such as the following may be used effectively:

3. Basic Pattern Modified

In executing the above exercise have the student imagine that he is sustaining a whole note while moving his fingers. This is a marvelous approach to use in achieving an even tonal line, and one that reflects discipline in all aspects.

The instructor may sketch other variations of the 3-and-3 routine or hand-pick similar excerpts from a beginning text to fit the student's needs. As soon as possible the student should be introduced to octave studies and the three-D's octave exercise.

4. Octave Exercises

Although there must be a slight increase in air pressure when the second octave is rendered, it is in playing the third octave that the student will become very cognizant of the need for increased air pressure.

5. The Three-D's Octave Exercise

Another advantage in playing the three-D's octave exercise as early as possible is that the student will then be less apt to develop fear of high notes. It simply is not necessary to wait until the student can vote before introducing him to the third octave range. It is, however, necessary to guide the student carefully here, so that he renders these high tones with added breath pressure rather than by overgripping with his embouchure.

Ch. 4/The Oboe

TONGUING

Once the elementary student has acquired some degree of fluency over the 3-and-3 routine and its slurred variations, tonguing may be introduced at the discretion of the instructor.

With all single- and double-reed students, the best advice to give for *initial work* in single-stroke tonguing is: Strive to always place the tip of the tongue at the tip of the reed. The important thing to remember at this stage is that a basic physical habit is to be cultivated first; development and refinement of tone comes gradually. The polished *breath attack,* the more complicated *Selmer release attack,* and other advanced tonguing techniques should be introduced only after the basic tongue stroke is well developed. By placing emphasis on placement of the tip of the tongue and the reed tip in this initial stage, a clean and articulate single tongue stroke can be developed without difficulty.

Syllables which may be used on the beginning level are "tu" (for general tonguing), "tee" (staccato tonguing), and "doo" (legato). The lighter the tongue stroke used in making the "doo" syllable, the more legato the sound will be. A slightly heavier tongue stroke may be used in detached staccato passages ("tee") to create a more crisp effect.

(Oboe reference chart is on page 82; Standard Fingering Chart starts on page 83.)

Fingering

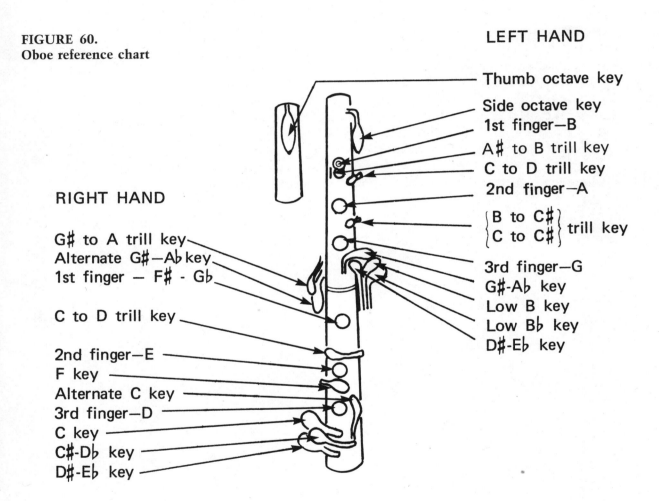

FIGURE 60.
Oboe reference chart

Ch. 4/The Oboe

Standard Fingering Chart

Where drawing is marked (*) omit E-flat key on oboes with F automatic resonator key.

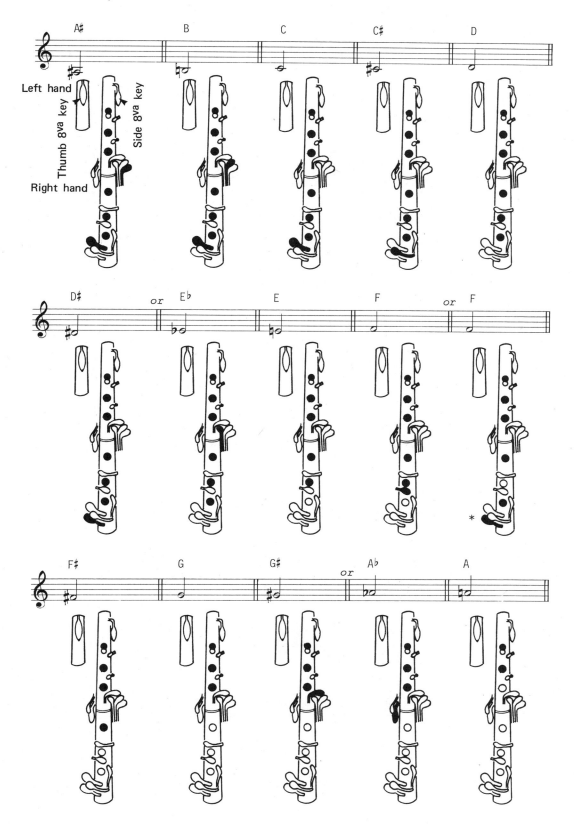

84 Fundamental Techniques and Supplemental Aids/Part II

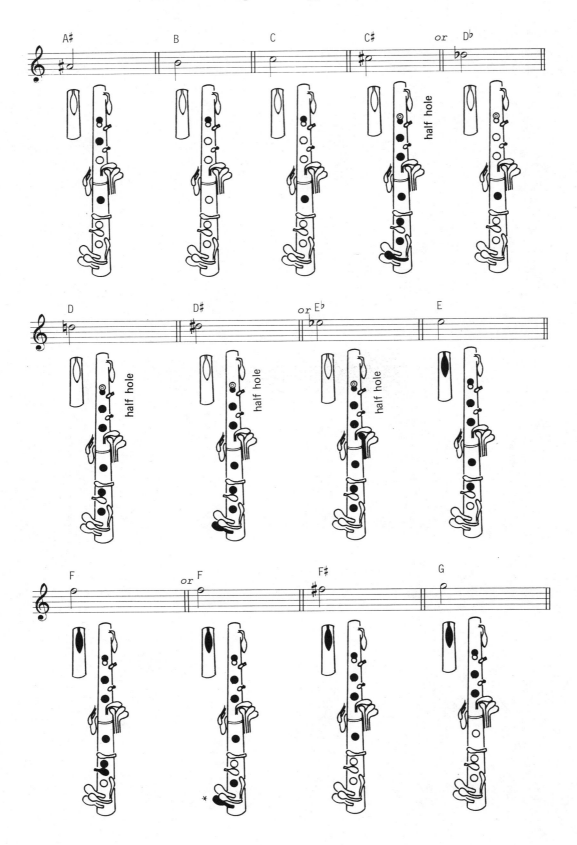

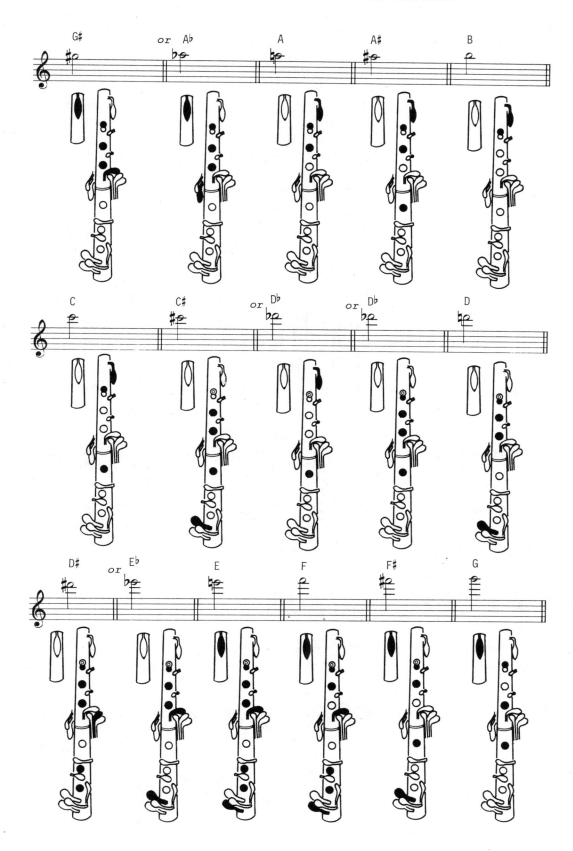

TRILLS

It is imperative that all oboists achieve a thorough working knowledge of the standard trills. (A trill consists of the rapid alternation of two notes.) The following trill chart is devoted to the more common trills, which involve half steps and whole steps. On the elementary level trills may be considered only as needed; however, systematic study of standard trills should begin at the intermediate level.

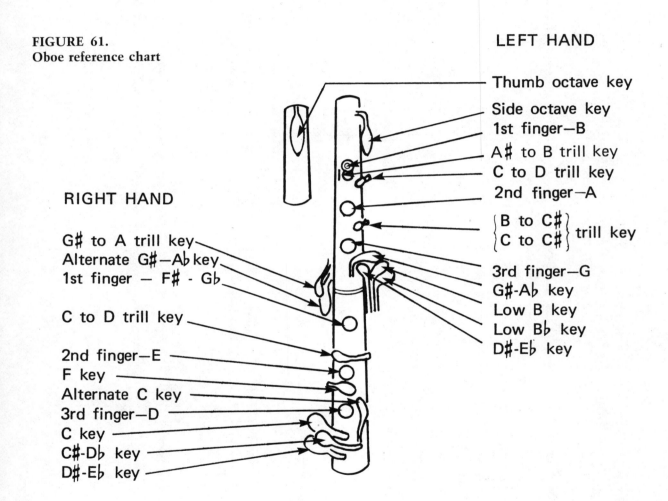

FIGURE 61.
Oboe reference chart

Standard Trill Chart

Arrows denote the key or keys to be manipulated. The symbols (1) and (2) denote additional trill possibilities. This chart is primarily for the standard student-line oboe which does not include the F automatic resonator key; with oboes having this key, omit the E-flat key where drawing is marked: *. * * denotes plateau model only; * * * denotes open-hole model only.

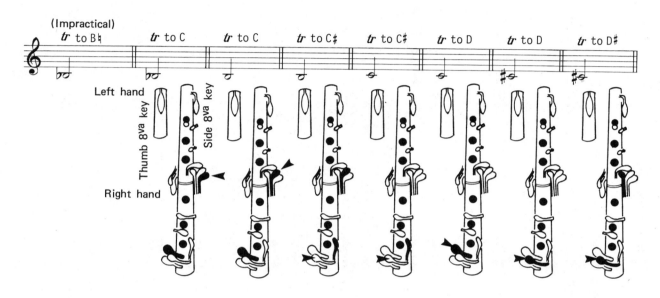

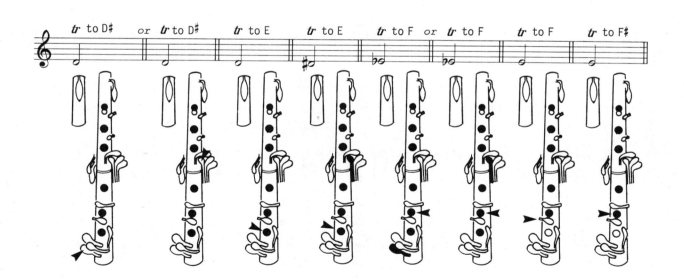

88 Fundamental Techniques and Supplemental Aids/Part II

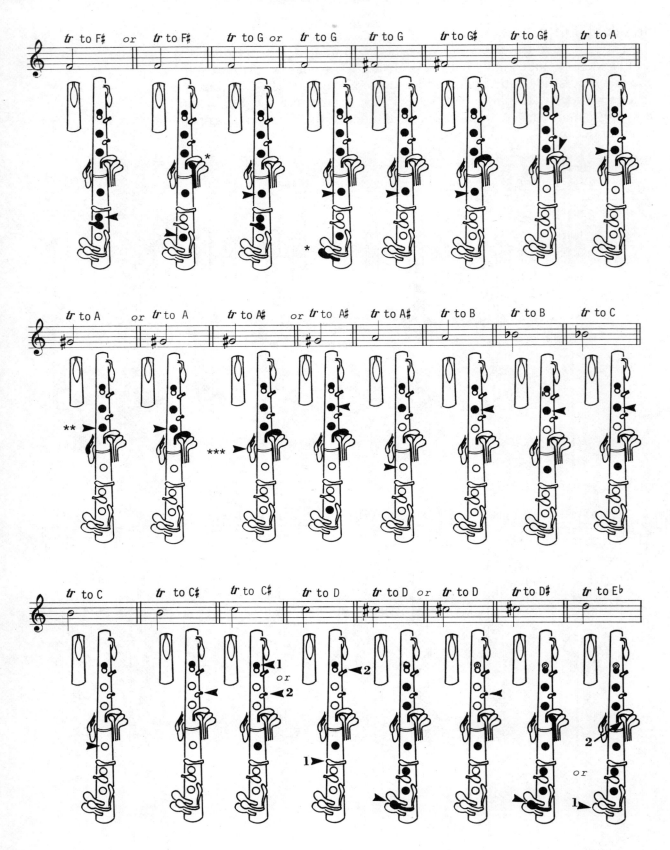

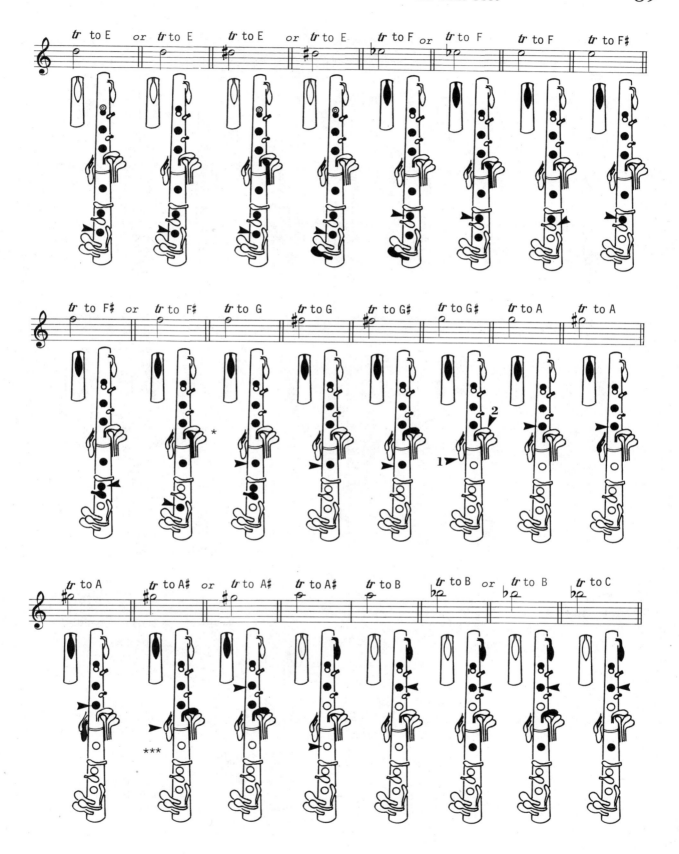

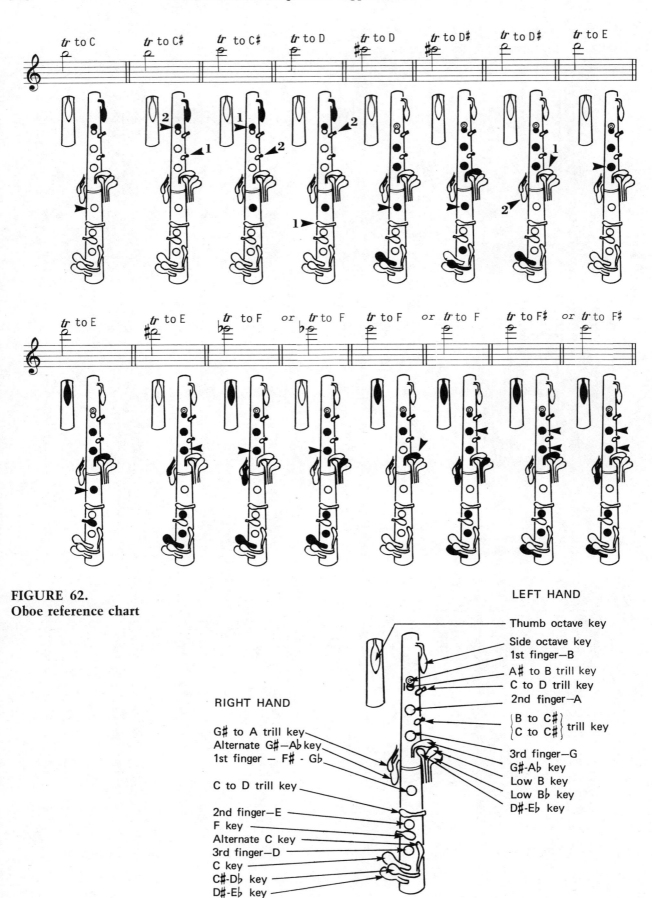

FIGURE 62.
Oboe reference chart

Ch. 4/The Oboe

FREQUENTLY USED SPECIAL FINGERINGS

EXAMPLE 1. There are two fingerings for F, the diatonic and the arpeggio; it is essential that the oboist know how and when to use each pattern. Note that on oboes without an F automatic resonator mechanism the E-flat key (left or right—marked *) must be depressed when using the arpeggio F fingering.

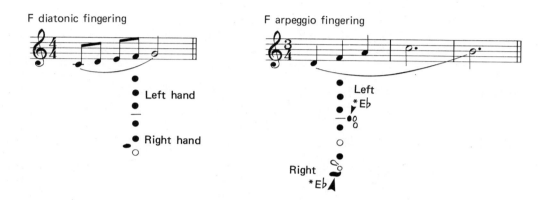

EXAMPLE 2. When E-flat is preceded or followed by F in the following manner, use the F arpeggio fingering:

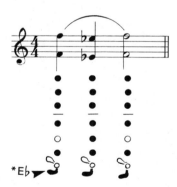

EXAMPLE 3. When E-flat is preceded or followed by D-flat, alternate right-hand and left-hand little fingers rather than sliding the little finger of one hand to execute both notes.

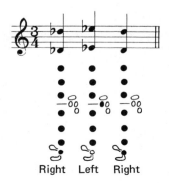

EXAMPLE 4. The C to D trill fingering may also be used (where marked *) in rapid passages such as the following:

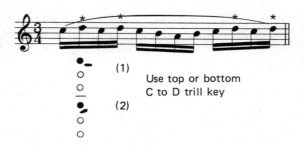

EXAMPLE 5. The C to C-sharp trill fingering may also be used in rapid passages such as the following:

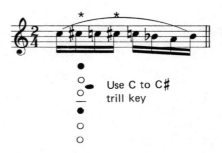

EXAMPLE 6. All woodwinds utilize octave vents at one time or another. The oboe customarily uses three octave vents, as follows:
  1. The half-hole octave vent is used regularly for the notes below.

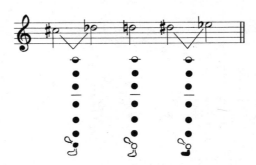

Roll the index finger (left hand) down and allow the air to be vented from the *top* half of the tone hole key.
  2. The following notes call for the use of the thumb octave key.

  3. These notes call for the use of the side octave key.

EXAMPLE 7. It can be advantageous to use the little finger of the left hand to depress *both* the E-flat and G-sharp keys simultaneously in passages such as the following:

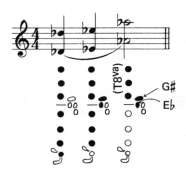

EXAMPLE 8. In certain passages the G-sharp key may remain depressed (marked *) throughout the entire sequence.

EXAMPLE 9. Contemporary music of the twentieth century gives evidence of an increasing demand for the use of harmonics on all woodwind instruments. The following harmonics are among the more practical ones for oboe. They are often used in preference to regular fingerings in soft, delicate passages to achieve greater control and improve pitch. While some teachers feel that harmonics are best left to advanced students, they may in fact be effectively introduced at the intermediate level of study.

To produce a harmonic on oboe, use the finger pattern of the lower note shown—with correct octave key—and then increase the lip tension in the embouchure until the twelfth above sounds (upper note in example). A slight increase in breath support may sometimes be necessary; covering more of the reed with the lips ("rolling in") on the harmonic may also help. Since harmonic fingerings generally require the use of several fingers, they are often referred to as "long fingerings."

Fundamental Techniques and Supplemental Aids/Part II

Study Questions

1. Upon assembling an oboe, there are certain key areas which can be damaged if not handled with care. What are these areas?
2. What is the best advice you can offer a student regarding the oiling of an oboe with a wooden bore?
3. What is the determining factor for oboists regarding instrument angle?
4. Explain "top" and "bottom" as applied to the sides of an oboe reed.
5. Cite a short effective approach that beginners can use in correctly gripping the oboe reed with the lips.
6. What are the purposes in having a beginning oboist experiment with the amount of reed to be inserted into the mouth?
7. Write a concise comparison of lower-jaw placement for the oboe, clarinet, and bassoon.
8. Does your author recommend the "vice-like grip" or the "circular grip" for beginning oboe students?
9. What is the major difference between lower-lip placement on oboe and on clarinet?
10. Cite an analogy that you might use to help "oboe students gain a quicker understanding and feeling of effective lip tension."
11. List the eight "teaching aids" which your author recommends.
12. What does the author mean by "back air pressure"?
13. How does the key statement, "Less fingers means more air," apply to oboe students?
14. Explain the purpose of the three-D's octave exercise.
15. What is the best advice you can offer the oboe student when he attempts to play the higher tones?
16. Explain the purpose and method of the 3-and-3 routine.
17. What is the best advice—according to the author—that one can offer for initial work on single-stroke tonguing?
18. Distinguish between "open ring–" and "plateau-system" oboes.
19. What are "harmonic fingerings" on oboe?
20. What is the purpose in using "long fingerings"?

A Problem Chart

Each woodwind instrument may be said to pose its own unique problems, and the oboe is certainly no exception to this rule. Without question, the matter of a double-reed source of quality is of the utmost importance to the instrumental music teacher whose personal major instrument may be neither oboe nor bassoon. Even the most competent teacher using the most effective teaching techniques will be severely handicapped if unable to provide serviceable reed source of quality for his students. This problem is by no means insurmountable; however, it does require effort and perseverance. Many music instructors have solved it by acting in one of three ways: (1) Assuming the initiative in bearing the trial and expense of finding the best commercial reed source currently available, (2) seeking out an individual professional oboist willing to supply reeds as needed, or (3) doing as some instrumental music teachers do—learning to make one's own oboe reeds.

Regardless of the course you choose, how your double-reed student sounds will inevitably depend equally on effective teaching techniques, the student himself, and *a good serviceable reed.* Since an inferior reed is often the cause of many tone production problems encountered by young students, the instrumental teacher should view the problems, probable causes, and suggestions listed below with extra caution when advising double-reed students.

Problem	Probable Cause	Suggestions for Improvement
A. The student cannot produce the lowest tones.	1. The embouchure or grip is too intense or tight. 2. Pads on the instrument may be leaking.	1. Advise the student to drop the jaw slightly for the lowest tones. 2. Check for leaks. Should service be needed, see a qualified repairman.
B. The student produces a tone that sounds small, narrow, and pinched.	1. There may not be enough reed in the mouth. 2. He may be overgripping or biting the reed excessively. 3. Lower-lip placement may be at fault.	1. Student should take more reed into the mouth. 2. Advise the student to imagine that he is gripping the reed in a circular manner with his lips, avoiding the vice-like grip, where tension comes only from the lower jaw at an upward angle. 3. Have the student regrip the reed in the following manner: Lay the reed on the lower lip and "roll" or "fold" it into the mouth.
C. The student produces a tone that sounds forced, harsh, and not *placed* or *centered* correctly.	1. There may be too much reed in the mouth. 2. The reed may be too stiff. 3. The student may be overblowing.	1. Student should take a little less reed into the mouth. 2. Have student adjust the reed by scraping its tip and/or sides—not the center unless it is excessively stiff. 3. Have him try less breath pressure.
D. The student plays his instrument consistently flat or consistently sharp.	1. Usually this is caused by the reed; however, some older oboes were built at a higher pitch level. 2. If flat, the student may not have the reed inserted completely into the top joint.	1. First, check the overall length of the reed (from tip to end of tube). (A standard reed length is 70 mm. and this measurement equates closely to A = 440 v.p.s.) Second, determine if the instrument is at fault by switching and testing the student on other oboes. 2. Mark the reed tube, after it is completely inserted, as a guide or reminder for the student.
E. The student plays sharp in the upper register of the oboe.	The student is "biting" in the upper register by using excessive pressure from the jaw.	Advise student to study the three-D's octave exercise, striving to produce the highest D with *increased breath support*—not with increased lip tensions or increased pressure from the jaw.
F. The student's reed shows evidence of mildew.	The reed case may be airtight or nearly airtight.	Remind him that his reed case *must* have an air vent.
G. The student's attacks on notes sound harsh or rough.	1. His tongue stroke may be too heavy. 2. Tongue placement for the attack may be incorrect.	1. Advise the student to try for a light, quick tongue stroke. 2. Have the student experiment with tongue placement. Recommend placing *the tip of the tongue at the tip of the reed.*

Fundamental Techniques and Supplemental Aids/Part II

A Problem Chart (continued)

Problem	Probable Cause	Suggestions for Improvement
H. Internal intonation within the instrument appears poor and is consistently evident in the student's performance.	Although no musical instrument is perfectly in tune within itself, the appearance of poor internal intonation is usually the fault of the player or the reed or a combination of both.	First, recheck the student's embouchure and determine if his lip tensions fluctuate as he plays. If so, advise him to use a stable grip whereby lip tensions remain constant *for the most part*. Second, check to see if the reed has a sufficient center "heart" line. The best way to check this is to play it. Another check which experienced oboists use effectively is to examine the reed against a bright light. Held against a light, a "W-cut" reed would appear as follows:  **FIGURE 63**
I. The student complains of lightheadedness.	The student is not aware that the oboe aperture is the smallest of all the woodwinds', and he must at times release the reed to expel all of the air he has taken in.	Have the student mark those places in his music assignment where he can appropriately expel air that he has held in reserve.

Teaching Aids

1. Show the student how to assemble the instrument so that the extension keys at the joints are not damaged.
2. Alignment may vary with the individual; however, try it up and away from the body, and then adjust inward toward the body as needed.
3. Have the student use all available visual aids—for example, pictures of a recommended embouchure format. Also, have the student use a mirror frequently to check his embouchure formation.
4. The reed should be placed along the lower lip and then folded (rolled) in over the lower teeth. Both lips cover the teeth.
5. Explain how to make the reed *crow* and why this is done.

6. A slight overbite is used by most oboists. The lower jaw is pulled slightly behind the upper jaw.
7. Begin playing with the 3-and-3 routine. Use no music.
8. Master the three-D's octave exercise as soon as is feasible.

The object here is to execute each D above the low D with an increase in breath support—especially the highest D. *Do not* use an increase in lower jaw pressure to produce the highest D.

9. Remind the student that the upper register tones should be reinforced with breath support: *"Don't bite* to produce high tones."
10. Stress circular lip tensions.
11. Experiment: (a) Take more or less reed into the mouth, (b) flex more, then less, (c) find the best grip.
12. In the initial elementary stage it may be necessary to advise the beginner to drop the jaw slightly in order to produce the very lowest tones. Consistency in lip tension requires time and practice.
13. Have the student try several reeds of different strength to find the amount of reed resistance that best suits him.
14. Stress the importance of taking short rest periods in the initial stage of embouchure development.

A SELECTED LIST OF GRADED SOLOS

Oboe Literature

The following list has been compiled as a convenient source reference for the instrumental music teacher. It is by no means complete, and readers are encouraged to study publisher catalog listings for their additional needs. This listing is intended to serve as a primer offering; although it has been carefully graded, some overlapping should of course be expected.

Considering the solos' technical difficulty, they have been ranked according to the following scale:

Grades 1–2: very easy to easy
Grades 3–4: moderate to moderately difficult
Grades 5–6: difficult to very difficult

Grades 1–2

Composer	Title	Publisher
Bizet	Aragonaise	Carl Fischer
Bizet	Barcarole, from "The Pearl Fishers"	Rubank
Cohen	Arioso	Carl Fischer
Dvořák	Slavonic Dance	Carl Fischer
Fauré	"En Prière"	Edition Musicus
Franck (arr. Doney)	Piece No. 5	Leduc
Handel (arr. Rothwell)	Air and Rondo	Chester
Head	Gavotte	Boosey & Hawkes
Labate	Barcarolle	Carl Fischer
	Oboist's Repertoire Album	Carl Fischer
	"Strolling"	Carl Fischer
Mendelssohn	"On Wings of Song"	Belwin-Mills

Fundamental Techniques and Supplemental Aids/Part II

Grades 1–2 (continued)

Composer	Title	Publisher
Nave	Serenade	Carl Fischer
Nicholas	Melody	Chester
	Rhapsody	Chester
Rimsky-Korsakov	"Song of India"	Rubank
Saint-Saëns	"The Swan"	Belwin-Mills
Stravinsky	Berceuse	Carl Fischer
Warren	Meditation	Ludwig
Weber	"Evening Shadows"	Belwin-Mills

Grades 3–4

Composer	Title	Publisher
Bach (arr. Johnson)	Andante	Boosey & Hawkes
Bach	Arioso	Carl Fischer
Bakaleinikoff	Elegy	Belwin-Mills
Bakaleinikoff	Pastorale	Belwin-Mills
Dunhill	Three Short Pieces	Boosey & Hawkes
Handel	Concerto No. 1	Boosey & Hawkes
Hanson	Pastorale	Carl Fischer
Haydn	Serenade	Carl Fischer
Labate	Serenata	Alfred
	Villanella	Carl Fischer
Niverd	Elegy	Alfred
Purcell	Two Pieces	Boosey & Hawkes
Richardson	Roundelay	Oxford University Press
Schumann	Three Romances	G. Schirmer
Sibelius	"Swan of Tuonela"	Belwin-Mills
Tcherepnin	"Pièce Calme"	G. Schirmer
Wagner	Three Pastorales	Boosey & Hawkes

Grades 5–6

Composer	Title	Publisher
Albinoni	Concerto No. 3, Op. 7	Boosey & Hawkes
Bach	Air from *St. Matthew Passion*	Alfred
Bozza	Fantaisie Pastorale	Ricordi
Delmas	"Complainte" et Air de Ballet	Alfred
D'Indy	Fantaisie, Op. 31	Durand
Goosens	Concerto	Curwen
Guihaud	Concertino	Rubank
Handel	Sonata in C Minor	Carl Fischer
	Concerto in G Minor	Ricordi
Haydn	Concerto in C Major	Breitkopf and Hartel
Hindemith	Sonata	AMP
Mozart	Concerto in C Major	Boosey & Hawkes
Poulenc	Sonata	Chester
Saint-Saëns	Sonata, Op. 166	Durand
Telemann	Concerto in F Minor	Southern
Vaughan Williams	Concerto	Oxford University Press
Vivaldi	Concerto in A Minor	Boosey & Hawkes
Voxman (ed.)	Concert and Contest Collection	Rubank

Ch. 4/The Oboe

CLASS METHODS

See "Class Methods for the Public School Instrumental Music Program," pp. 63–64.

INDIVIDUAL METHODS AND SUPPLEMENTAL STUDIES

Major Applied Methods

RUBANK SERIES FOR OBOE

Elementary Method For Oboe by N. W. Hovey.
Intermediate Method For Oboe by J. E. Skornicka and R. Koebner.
Advanced Method For Oboe by H. Voxman and W. Gower.
All Published by Rubank, Inc., Miami, Fla.

BELWIN SERIES FOR OBOE

Oboe Method by K. Gekeler. This is a three-volume work which begins on the elementary level and continues through the advanced intermediate stage.
Oboe Student by F. Weber and B. Edlefsen is another three-volume series beginning with the elementary level and continuing through the advanced intermediate stage. Additionally, this work is correlated with four other volumes of solos, études, and studies.
The Belwin series is published by Belwin-Mills, Inc., Melville, N.Y.

In Chapter 3 several key points were cited regarding the use of American or European applied method books at the initial level of instrumental music study. The single most important point made in that discussion centered on a crucial difference between certain American and European method books: On the one hand, many if not most of the American books *assume no prior musical study*; on the other hand, most of the celebrated European (or European-influenced) method books *assume prior musical study* and tend to progress from elementary to intermediate levels at a rate that becomes impractical for students without preparatory music backgrounds. Consequently, music methods such as H. Klosé's *Celebrated Method for the Clarinet* or Julius Weissenborn's *Practical Method for the Bassoon* are never used by American instrumental music teachers on the initial level of study. These same books are, however, widely used by American teachers *after* the stu-

dent has completed the basic foundation work.

The above-mentioned situation is by no means limited to just the clarinet and bassoon; rather, it is the case with many wind-instrument method books. In consequence of this fact, each section of this text devoted to the applied method literature will always begin with a listing of standard American method books and follow up with appropriate recommendations suitable for subsequent work.

The following oboe methods are recommended for study *after* the student has completed his basic foundation work with a standard method such as the Belwin or Rubank series.

Practical and Progressive Oboe Method by Albert Andraud. Published by Southern Music Co., San Antonio, Tex.
Vade-Mecum of the Oboist by A. Andraud. Published by Southern Music, San Antonio, Tex.
Complete Method for Oboe by A.M. Barret. Published by A. Leduc, Paris, France.
The Methodical Study of the Oboe by J. Marx. This work is published in four volumes by McGinnis and Marx, New York, N.Y.
Method for Oboe by T. Niemann. This is an excellent text for older transfer students. It is published by Carl Fischer, New York, N.Y.

Supplemental Studies

La technique du hautbois by L. Bleuzet. This three-volume work is published by A. Leduc, Paris, France.
18 Études by E. Bozza. Published by A. Leduc, Paris, France.
48 Famous Studies for Oboe, Op. 31 by W. Ferling. Published by Southern Music Co.
Practical Studies for Oboe by K. Gekeler. Published by Belwin-Mills, Melville, N.Y.
Progressive Method by A. Giampieri. Published by Ricordi, Milan, Italy.

Études and Scales for Advanced Oboists by B. Labate. Published by Carl Fischer, New York, N.Y.

Daily Technical Exercises for Oboe by G. Pares. Published by Carl Fischer, New York, N.Y.

A Book of Scales for Oboe by E. Rothwell. Published by Oxford University Press, New York, N.Y.

24 Melodic Studies, Op. 65 by S. Verroust. Published by Ricordi, Milan, Italy.

Selected Studies for Oboe by H. Voxman. Published by Rubank, Inc., Miami, Fla.

RECORDINGS OF OBOE LITERATURE

Pedagogically Oriented Recordings

The Music Minus One Series. Essentially, the Music Minus One Corporation makes professionally recorded backgrounds—minus a particular "solo" instrument—for all types of music, including the orchestral concerto, the sonata, chamber music, and various jazz forms. The original concept behind the MMO series was to afford the student performer a professional accompaniment against which to practice and perform a musical work in its original and complete context, that is, with full orchestra, string quartet, or jazz ensemble, as the case might be. The bulk of the recorded accompaniments made by MMO falls in this category. Recently MMO began a new Laureate Series which embraces a wider spectrum and is even more pedagogically oriented than the aforementioned recordings. Unfortunately, this new series is not yet available for oboe, but the older, still-available offerings are certainly recommended. Both series are published by Music Minus One, 43 West 61 Street, New York, N.Y.

Special Collections

The following recorded collections will be of special interest to the oboist. Each album is devoted exclusively to the oboe, and features various performing artists of our time.

The Art of Harold Gomberg
Britten: Fantasy Quartet for Oboe and Strings, Op. 2
Six Metamorphoses after Ovid for Solo Oboe, Op. 49
Mozart: Quartet in F Major for Oboe and Strings, K.370. Harold Gomberg (solo oboist, New York Philharmonic Orchestra). Vanguard VCS 10064

The Baroque Oboe
Handel: Sonata in G Minor for Oboe and Continuo, Op. 1, No. 6
Telemann: Concerto in D Minor for Oboe, Strings, and Continuo
Telemann: Sonata in C Minor for Oboe and Continuo
Vivaldi: Concerto in F Major for Oboe, Strings and Continuo. Harold Gomberg. Columbia MS 6832

Music from France for Oboe and Orchestra
Françaix: "L'Horloge de Flore" ["The Flower Clock"]
Ibert: Symphonie Concertante for Oboe and String Orchestra
Satie (Debussy): *Gymnopédies I* and *Gymnop*édies II. John de Lancie (principal oboe, Philadelphia Orchestra). RCA Victor LSC-2945

An Oboe Recital
Sammartini: Sonata in G
Poulenc: Sonata for Oboe and Piano
Schumann: Drei Romanzen
Saint-Saëns: Sonata pour Hautbois
Head: Three Pieces for Oboe
Monti: Csardas. Patricia Stenberg (principal oboe, Tampa Philharmonic). Golden Crest Recital Series RE 7022

The Virtuoso Oboe
Cimarosa: Concerto for Oboe and Strings
Handel: Concerto in G Minor for Oboe and Orchestra
Haydn: Concerto in C Major for Oboe and Orchestra
Albinoni: Concerto in B-flat Major for Oboe and Strings, Op. 7, No. 3. André Lardrot (principal oboe, Chamber Orchestra of the Vienna State Opera). Vanguard VRS 1025

Traditional Recordings

Albinoni: Concerto in B-flat for Oboe and Orchestra. Andre Lardrot. Vanguard 2030

Ch. 4/The Oboe

————: Concerto in C Major for Oboe and Orchestra. Helmut Winschermann. Nonesuch H71148

Cimarosa: Concerto for Oboe. Heinz Hollinger. Deutsche Grammophon LPM 39152

Foss: Concerto for Oboe. Bert Grassman. Crystal S851

Ginastera: Duo for Flute and Oboe. Peter Christ (oboe) and Gretel Shanley (flute). Crystal S812

Handel: Concerto in G Minor. Robert Casier. Nonesuch 71013

————: Concerto in G Minor. Marcel Tabuteau. Columbia ML4629

Marcello: Concerto in C Minor for Oboe and Orchestra. John de Lancie. Columbia MS6977

Martinu: Concerto for Oboe. F. Hantak. Parliament 5606

Mozart: Concerto for Oboe in C Major, K.314. John de Lancie. Columbia MS6452

————: Quartet for Oboe. Alfred Sous. Turnabout TV34035S

Poulenc: Sonata for Oboe and Piano. Pierre Pierlot. Nonesuch H71033

Telemann: Concerto for Oboe in F Minor. Theodora Schulze. Amphion CL2139

Vivaldi: Concerto for Oboe in D Minor. Egon Parolari. Musical Masterpiece Society MMS84

The Clarinet

5

Photograph courtesy of the Selmer Company, Elkhart, Indiana.

Photograph courtesy of the G. Leblanc Corporation, Kenosha, Wisconsin.

FIGURE 64.
(left) B-flat clarinet (Selmer Mazzeo model)

FIGURE 65.
(right) B-flat clarinet (Leblanc Noblet model)

Clarinet Assembly

FIGURE 66. (left) Bell and lower joint

FIGURE 67. (right) Lower and upper joints

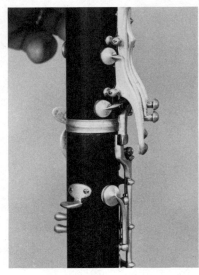
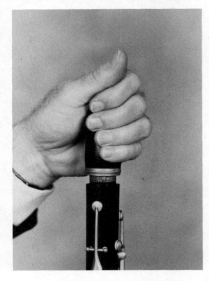

FIGURE 68. (left) Side view of main joints

FIGURE 69. (right) Barrel and top joint

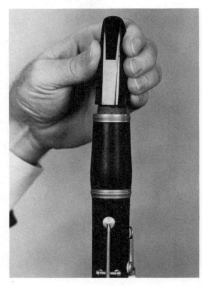
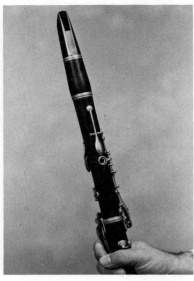

FIGURE 70. (left) Mouthpiece and barrel

FIGURE 71. (right) Alignment of mouthpiece with register key

Ch. 5/The Clarinet

Instrument Assembly and Care

The clarinet, like the oboe, is often damaged by students while being assembled. Most woodwinds have bridge keys at one or more of the joints, and it is these sections that should be assembled with care. First, the bell of the clarinet should be joined to the lower joint. Then the bell and lower joint may be gripped together without touching the lower joint, and subsequent assembly of the two main joints can be made with relative ease. Care should be taken not to tear the cork off the bridge keys that connect the upper and lower joints. Next the barrel and mouthpiece may be assembled.

Cork grease should be used on all joints; none should ever be forced together. If there is too much cork on a tenon, it should be removed by the instructor or a repairman. *Never* put a ring joint together if the ring is loose; the ring should be shrunk by a repairman. As a temporary measure, the instructor may remove the ring and wrap the ring groove with a thin piece of paper, and then replace it.

Before handling any woodwind instrument it is a good habit to wash one's hands. Since the reed and mouthpiece come in direct contact with the mouth, such a habit amounts to a simple common-sense health matter. After wetting the single reed, it is best to place and adjust it on the facing of the mouthpiece *without touching its vamp*. After washing hands many people show signs of perspiration within a matter of moments. Any foreign matter rubbed into the grain of the reed vamp is undesirable, and over a period of time can choke the open pores of the wood. Moisture and residue from the mouth is expected to collect on the reed; however, grime and perspiration from the hands is unwanted. Figures 72 and 73 show how a single reed can be affixed to the mouthpiece with no touching of the reed vamp.

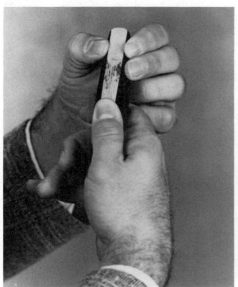

FIGURE 72 FIGURE 73

When the clarinet is not in use, the mouthpiece cover should be placed over the mouthpiece. It is best to return the instrument to the case or hold it. *Never* leave it lying on a chair or propped on a music stand. Countless instruments have been damaged because of careless handling.

The key mechanism of a clarinet should be oiled at least three times a year. Wooden clarinets should always be swabbed after playing, but the matter of oiling a wooden bore is debatable. While this author's Cabart oboe has never been oiled, his Buffet clarinet has been oiled regularly; neither instrument has ever cracked over twenty-four and sixteen years of respective usage. As a practical matter of insurance, one should follow the advice of the manufacturer's warranty with regard to oiling the bore. Occasionally the clarinet mouthpiece should be washed with *luke-warm* water and soap.

FIGURE 74.
Instrument angle—profile view

FIGURE 75.
Front view

Instrument Angle and Hand Position

The matter of instrument angle and alignment is self-adjusting for many performers. For others, however, this is not the case. But there is one rule in this matter that applies to everyone: Effective instrument angle should be determined by the individual's occlusion. Occasionally some students will need guidance in this area. When this occurs the instructor can experiment by raising or lowering the instrument angle until the best sound is achieved.

With regard to the mouthpiece setting, the table of the mouthpiece can be aligned parallel to the register key in the beginning (see Figure 71). Subsequently the student will invariably adjust it slightly to the right or left to suit his own needs. This adjustment will tend to vary according to the shape of the upper teeth (incisors).

A practical hand position should be cultivated as early as possible.

The author has found the following approach to be very effective: Have the student sit or stand with hands and arms in a natural and relaxed position adjacent to the body; then have him raise his right hand—always with the same relaxed feeling—and place it in its approximate position on the lower joint. If this is done in as relaxed a manner as possible, the appropriate amount of arch in the fingers will inevitably result. The first—and only—muscular tension the player should feel is the weight of the clarinet on the end of the thumb (see Figure 80.)

FIGURE 76.
Right hand in relaxed, natural position

FIGURE 77.
Right hand in playing position

Left-hand placement should be approached in the same relaxed manner; however, the structure of the upper joint will require a slightly wrap-around position, particularly with the index finger. Fortunately, the left-hand position tends to be self-adjusting; in three decades of teaching and performing, the author has yet to find it necessary to advise clarinet students to alter their left-hand position. However, it is often necessary for them to alter their right-hand position. Many place the right thumb too far beyond the thumb rest; this results in excessive arching of the fingers, and students then find themselves unconsciously leaning the right-hand index finger against the side B-flat key.

108 Fundamental Techniques and Supplemental Aids/Part II

FIGURE 78.
Left-hand wrap-around position

FIGURE 79.
Left thumb position

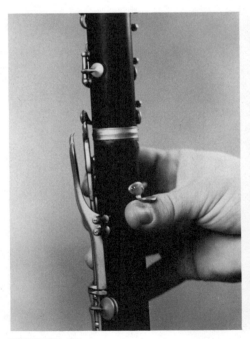

FIGURE 80.
Right thumb position

FIGURE 81.
Both hands in playing position

If the woodwind student will practice the following exercise, the matter of hand position will rarely if ever pose any difficulty: First, have the student practice the 3-and-3 routine (see p. 12) *without actually playing the instrument.* Next, have him slide each finger of one hand forward over the tone hole, around it and back, and then finally center it evenly over the hole. By doing this several times with each hand before practicing, he will quickly learn to seat each finger so that air does not escape when playing the 3-and-3 routine where consecutive finger movement is used. Although this is a very simple exercise and requires very little effort, it is very effective.

EMBOUCHURE

Although there is considerably greater unanimity among clarinetists regarding a basic embouchure format today than ever before, it should be mentioned again that there are always valid exceptions to a general rule. Knowing when these exceptions are justified and how to accommodate them is the real challenge for the dedicated teacher.

By and large, most clarinet teachers in the United States and abroad now advocate an embouchure that requires a reasonable degree of muscular flexing of the lips. This type of grip stresses an oval-shaped flexing of the lip muscles. Here the lower lip is turned only partially inward, allowing for maximum single-reed vibration. The upper teeth are placed against the top of the mouthpiece. The lower lip is not allowed to double or bunch upward around the reed nor are the cheeks permitted to puff outward.

Tone Production

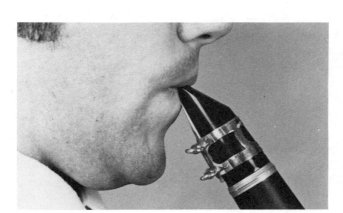

FIGURE 82.
Recommended embouchure

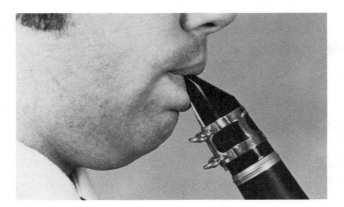

FIGURE 83.
Incorrect embouchure

This type of embouchure has been used by many of the foremost clarinetists the world has known. Its advantages are numerous, well worth any effort required to develop it. It is not an embouchure that follows the road of least resistance. Most clarinetists will have to spend a reasonable amount of time and energy to develop it. The following exercises and comments can aid immensely in developing this recommended embouchure:

1. Have the student flex his lips in a circular manner, as illustrated in the Figure 84. He should use a mirror at first, practicing several times a day.

FIGURE 84.
Embouchure exercise

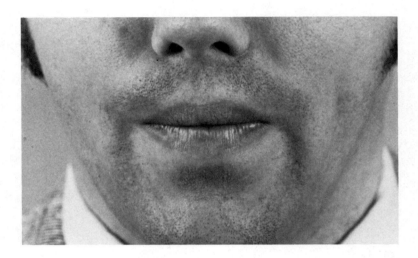

The repetition of this flexing of the lips will strengthen the muscles. The absence of the mouthpiece simplifies the matter. Within a short period of time the student will be able to insert the mouthpiece and maintain the desired flexed position with it. Eventually this flexed grip will become a habit and require no conscious thought.

2. Have the student practice turning the lower lip inward and then withdrawing it until the red part of the lip is about halfway over the lower teeth. Next, he should draw the corners of the lips together slightly so as to form an oval-shaped position.

3. When the lips become tired in the initial stage of development, the student should *stop* and *rest*. It is best to practice for short intervals several times a day if possible.

4. No one should expect to develop this type of embouchure overnight. As individuals vary, so will the time-span of development, from one lesson (rare) to several (more common).

5. By and large, most "natural" clarinetists play with the lower jaw in an offset forward position (Figure 85).

FIGURE 85.
Lower-jaw placement

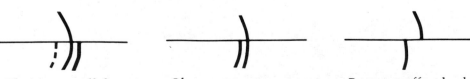

Clarinet: parallel or offset, forward

Oboe: may appear parallel, but is usually slightly offset back

Bassoon: offset back

Ch. 5/The Clarinet

The extent to which each clarinetist will use an offset grip will of course vary. Whether the clarinetist's lower teeth are in fact parallel with his upper teeth or slightly forward of them will vary according to the individual. The important point to remember is that a clarinetist cannot successfully employ a lower-jaw position that is decidedly offset and back (a position associated with many bassoonists). The prospective student whose lower chin recedes to an extreme degree or whose upper teeth turn inward excessively should be advised of the serious problems these physical factors pose.

6. Perhaps one of the most valuable teaching aids a teacher can utilize to help a student develop a stable embouchure is the "mouthpiece exercise." This exercise, if mastered, helps stabilize pitch fluctuation, and is essential to the development of a consistent tonal line and beautiful tone quality. It may be introduced as soon as the instructor deems it appropriate.

THE MOUTHPIECE EXERCISE

Have the student take his mouthpiece (with the reed) and "buzz" it. If he is using a well-formed grip the resulting pitch will fall between high C and C-sharp (concert pitch). This can be depicted graphically as follows:

The sound should be straight, even, and consistent in its pitch level. It should not appear as uneven, wave-like, or with deviations, as shown here:

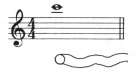

If the resulting pitch is lower than high C or produced with a concomitant quiver, the individual's embouchure is weak and inconsistent. The objective of producing an even, straight sound with no waves can only be attained with lip muscles that are flexed, controlled, and well developed. If the student will practice the lip-flexing exercise (p. 110) prior to working on the mouthpiece exercise, building and strengthening the lip muscles, he can then achieve the desired control more quickly and with greater ease.

The mouthpiece exercise can be included in the daily practice routine (for two or three minutes of each period), and mastered within a relatively short time. The use of a mirror can aid in the initial stages.

Finally, it should be mentioned that the flexed embouchure format can serve as a cornerstone for such advanced performing techniques as flutter tonguing, extended portamento (such as the opening of Gershwin's *Rhapsody in Blue*), the delayed tongue release, the Selmer release attack, and others. The value of developing such an embouchure is truly manifold in nature.

BREATH SUPPORT

Many students go through public-school music programs without ever actually using effective breath support to produce a full tone. Effective breath support is not an enigma, a mystery, or an abstract phenomenon inaccessible to all but a select few. Effective breath support is simply a matter of using breath pressure in a *consistent* and *measured* manner.

With single-reed instruments the degree of air pressure and the rate of air flow make the best effect when maintained at a constant level. Ultimately the student must *experience* these concepts, or he may never achieve the desired goal.

If teachers of beginning clarinetists do the following, their students can acquire effective breath support in a surprisingly short time:

1. Permit the student to slur as much as possible during his initial stage of study.

2. Have him execute the 3-and-3 routine from memory or by rote, and continue this exercise concurrently with reading materials as they are introduced.

3. Above all, encourage the student to experiment with his breath pressure. Have him deliberately overblow a sustained tone—or the 3-and-3 pattern—and observe the resulting sound; then have him underblow a tone and observe it. Finally, have him strive for a compromise between these two extremes, stopping when the tone sounds best. (The principle of contrast—one of the most effective tools in teaching—if used as outlined here, can be of immense value to both teacher and student.)

4. As much as is possible, avoid presenting multiple task assignments. Although this may be impossible to do totally, the challenge of multiple tasks can be greatly reduced through the manner of presentation. For example, the use of long tones with no music allows for maximum concentration on breath pressure; the 3-and-3 routine—with no music at first—eliminates eye training, allowing for greater concentration on listening.

5. After reading materials are presented, use graphic illustrations to depict such intangibles as tone quality or tonal line (examples are for B-flat clarinet).

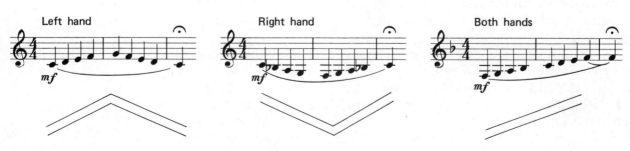

Note that in the drawing the parallel lines—depicting the tonal line—are even and consistent in appearance.

Sustained tones may be depicted as follows:

The lines depicting a controlled sustained tone are straight, even, and consistent.

6. Always explain musical terminology as simply as possible to the young student. The use of synonyms and antonyms can be very helpful for many in the learning process. For example, to tell a beginning student that he is sharp or flat may be totally meaningless if your criticism rests solely on the use of those two words. Ideally, using additional adjectives *plus* a demonstration based on the principle of contrast can aid most students in the matter of pitch perception. Explain to the student that a tone which is flat in pitch has a dark, dull, large, and very heavy character. If it is sharp, its character may appear thin, bright, metallic, or light. If this word description is followed by a live illustration, the results can be most effective. Have the student play the offensive tone which, for convenience's sake, we will say is flat relative to the tuning source. Describe the sound and have him play it again, but this time overgrip or "lip" it so that its pitch level rises. With repetition of practice the student can cultivate pitch perception very rapidly using this method.

In conclusion it should be remembered that although embouchure and breath support have been discussed here under separate sections, they are (as presented in other sections of this text) the primary factors in tone production, inseparable in the sense that each must compliment the other if beautiful tone is to be rendered.

TONGUING

Single-reed students should avoid tonguing during their first few lesson assignments. The teacher should try to avoid confronting the beginner with multiple tasks in the initial stage of study, stressing matters with priority. After preliminary work on such basics as grip, breath support, and general control, a beginning tongue stroke may be introduced: Simply advise the student to place the tip of the tongue at the tip of the reed as lightly as possible. The experienced teacher knows that the initial tongue stroke is usually rough and unpolished; it must be cultivated. This is normal and to be expected. The object at this point is simply to start developing a basic action. It should be noted that not all students will use the exact tip of the tongue. Some will strike the end of the reed at a point on the top side of the tongue perhaps a quarter-inch behind the tip.

How the student is executing the beginning tongue stroke is often evident in the resulting sound. Those students blessed with a natural flair for tonguing will of course progress more rapidly, and produce a lighter, more incisive attack. On the other hand, some students may go through stages where they give an audible impression of "licking," "slapping," or "striking" the reed.

The important point to remember is that, although articulate and refined tonguing must be cultivated by *all* wind performers, overexpectation in the elementary and even intermediate stage should be avoided. Once the student has developed the concept and habit of placing the tip of the tongue at the tip of the reed, he is well on his way toward the goal of polished refinement.

The instructor who can correlate the sound of an attack with its respective tongue placement is truly a teacher who will be sought out by those needing help in this area. More often such a person will be an applied teacher attuned to the subtleties of his major instrument. The following points can be of considerable help to the teacher in training and the instructor in the field:

1. Generally speaking, it is the accompanying audible sounds preceding or following an attack that indicate the type of tongue placement used, although again there are exceptions to this general rule. For example, most beginning students produce a hissing sound just before starting a tone with the tongue; actually, a tone should begin without this hiss. When students first discover the concept of breath attack, it may be noted that again the first few attempts reveal a hiss just prior to the actual sound of tone. The time span of this hiss in beginning breath attacks is usually longer than in the first case. All this is perfectly normal, for in both cases the students are actually using the breath—not the tongue—to start the tone. It would be an overexpectation to expect these subtleties to be mastered in the elementary or even intermediate stage. It is, however, essential that the instructor learn to distinguish between the sounds of different attacks so that he may make constructive criticism.

2. When the beginning of a tone is devoid of all extraneous sounds and gives the impression of having commenced with pure tone, the action of the tongue will inevitably have been delicate, light, and fast.

3. When the tongue is placed low under the tip of the reed, the pure tone will always be accompanied by a nonmusical sound that can be approximated by the syllables "thugh" or "thut."

FIGURE 86.
Recommended tongue placement: Tip of the tongue is at the tip of the reed

FIGURE 87.
Low tongue placement is not recommended

Ch. 5/The Clarinet   *115*

4. Some students unknowingly stop *all* tones with the tongue. This usually occurs in class work and may go unnoticed until the instructor hears the students individually. Private instruction for young beginners is, of course, recommended, but when this is not possible always advise both single- and double-reed students to stop the tone with the breath. It is only in staccato passages that the tongue is used to both begin and stop a tone; this type of articulation should not be introduced in the elementary stage.

5. For legato tonguing "da" is an effective syllable to use. If a more pronounced tongue stroke is desired, use the syllable "tah."

6. When staccato tonguing is introduced, many students find the syllable "tuh" (or "tut") to be very effective.

7. Occasionally some students will fall into the habit of using a separate burst of air with each individual attack. They automatically stop this unnecessary habit as soon as the music changes and rapid tonguing is demanded, but revert to the use of separate bursts of air when slower passages recur. Caution them that the tonal line is completely disrupted when this happens, and advise them to leave the matter of articulation to the tongue—not the respiratory system.

(B-flat clarinet reference chart is on page 116; Standard Fingering Chart starts on page 117.)

Fingering

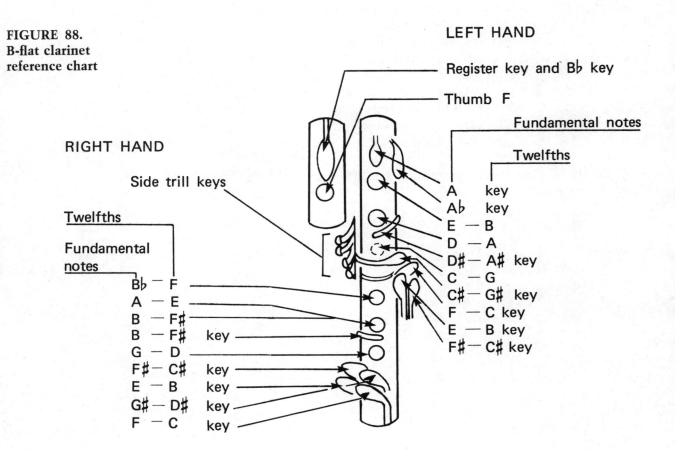

FIGURE 88.
B-flat clarinet
reference chart

Note that the clarinet, unlike all other woodwinds—which overblow at the octave—overblows at the interval of a twelfth when the register key is depressed.

Ch. 5/The Clarinet

117

Standard Fingering Chart

Asterisk denotes recommended sequence for beginners.

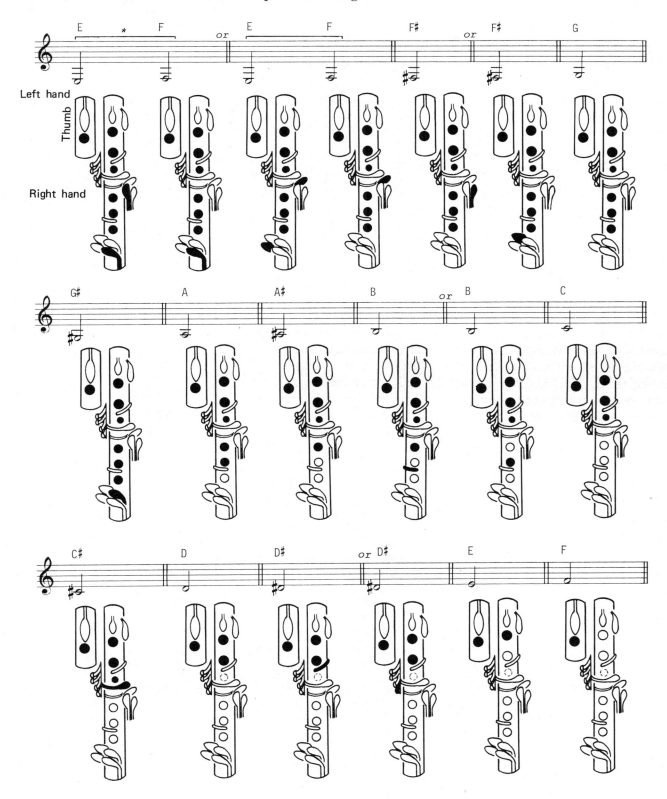

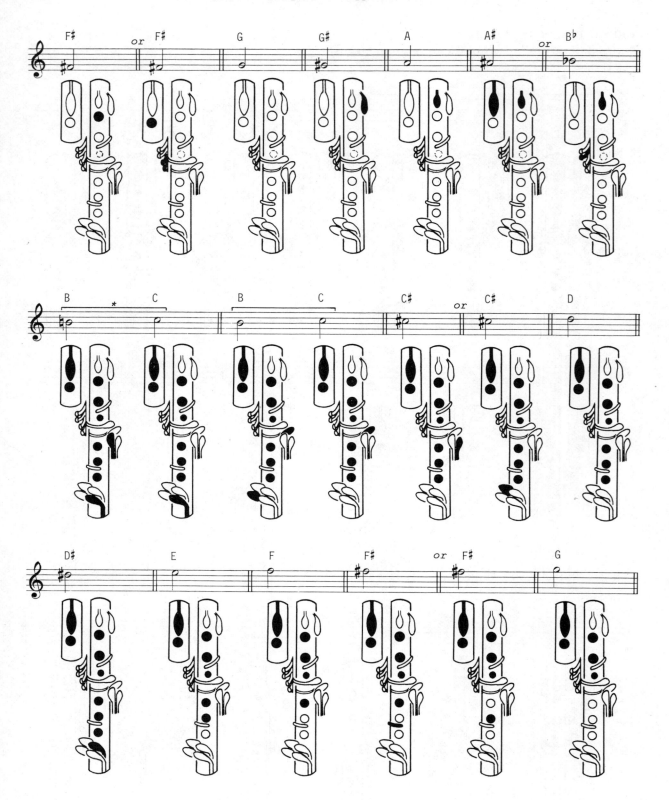

Ch. 5/The Clarinet
119

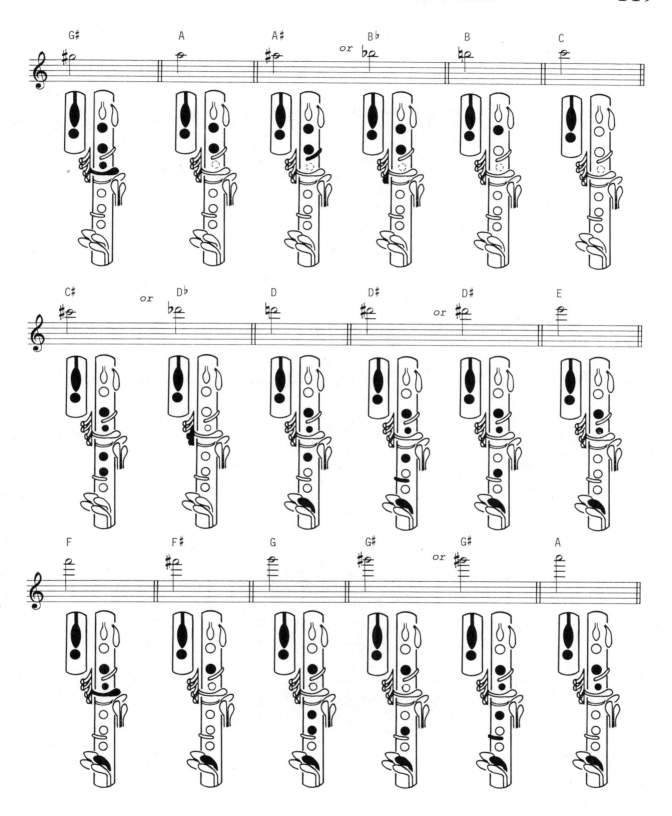

TRILLS

Even though clarinetists are not generally called upon to perform music from the Baroque and Rococo style periods—when the use of ornaments was at its peak, and the instrument had only just been invented (1690)—the music literature of subsequent style periods makes it imperative that they acquire a thorough knowledge of the standard trills. Of all the musical ornaments that have been used down through the ages, it is the trill—the rapid alternation of two notes—that has remained the most popular among composers.

The following trill chart is devoted to the more common trills, which involve half steps and whole steps.

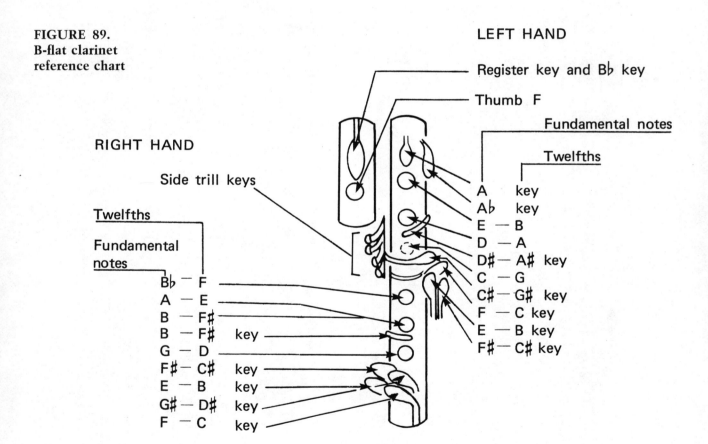

FIGURE 89.
B-flat clarinet reference chart

Ch. 5/The Clarinet
121

Standard Trill Chart

This chart is primarily for the standard six-ring clarinet. Note that in the drawings the arrows denote the key or keys to be manipulated; the numerals (1) and (2) denote alternate trill possibilities; * indicates use of right-hand index or middle finger; ** indicates that, when possible, depress the A-flat key with index finger of *right hand* and trill with *left-hand* index finger and thumb (clarinet must be braced on knees), otherwise use left hand entirely.

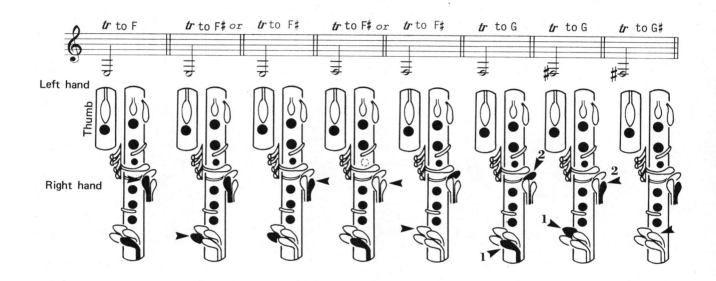

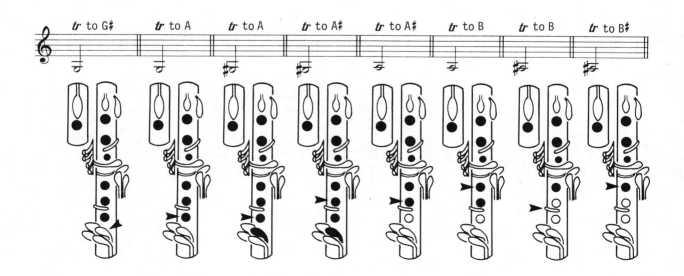

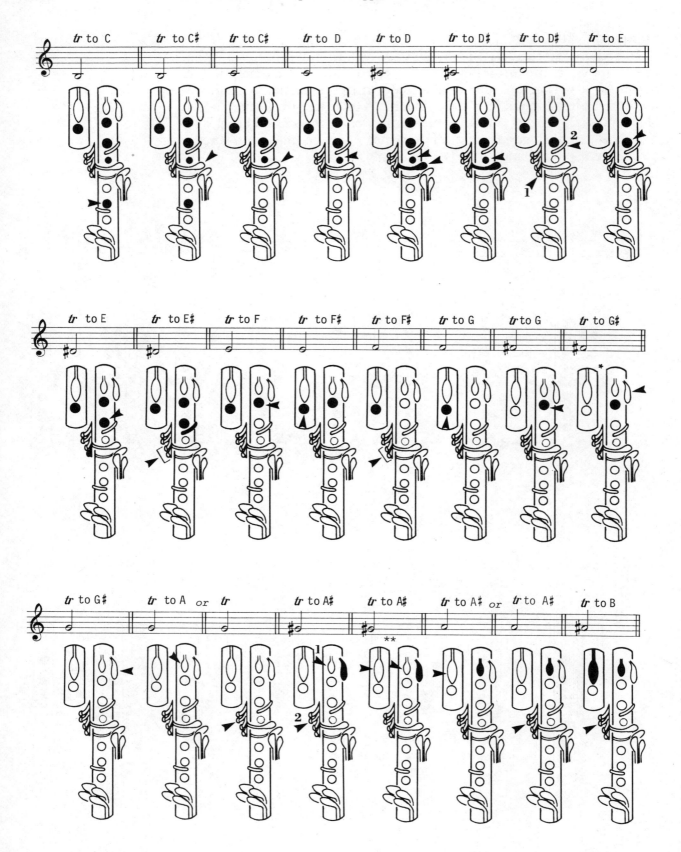

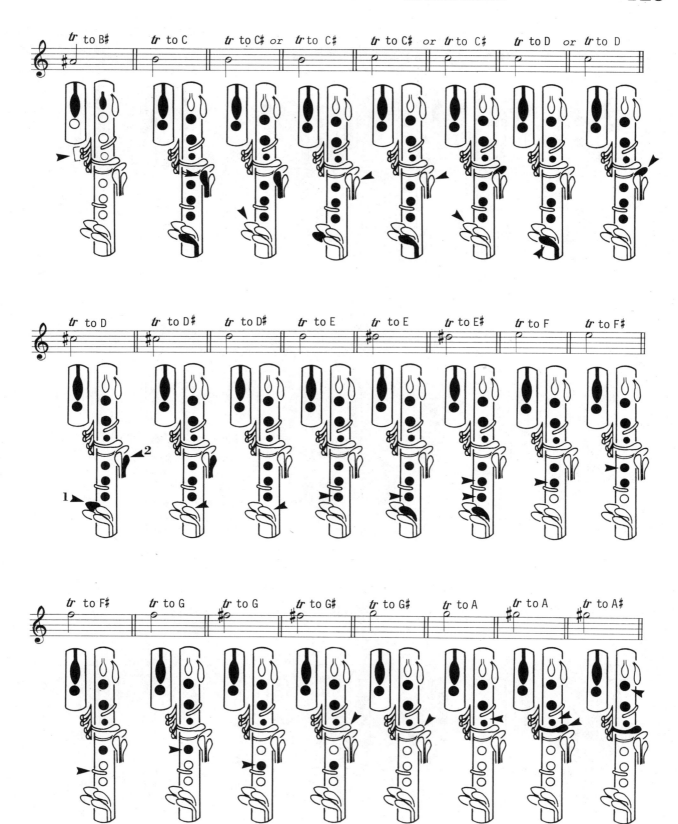

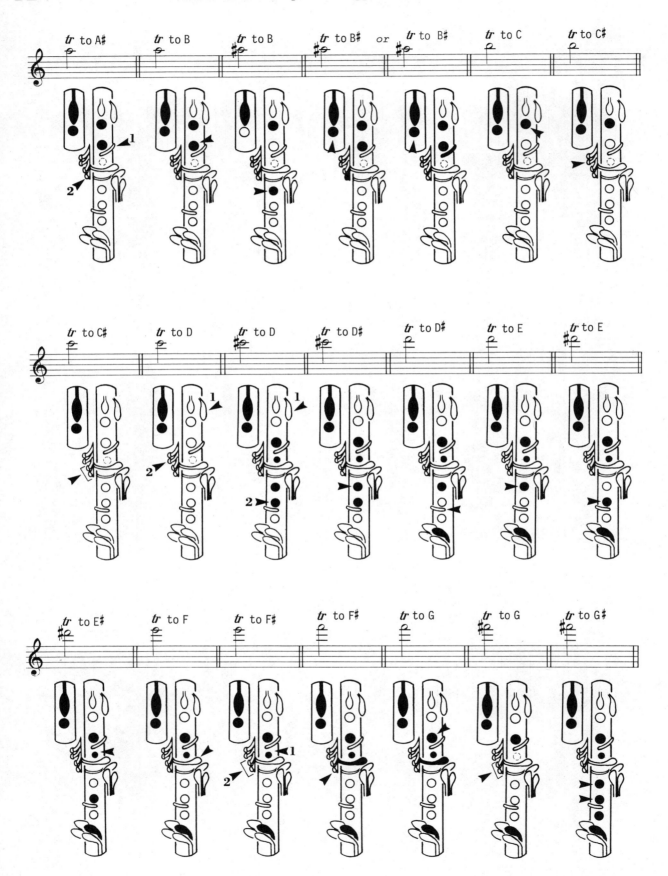

Ch. 5/The Clarinet

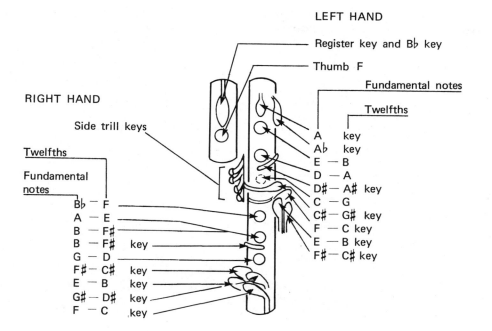

FIGURE 90.
B-flat clarinet
reference chart

FREQUENTLY USED SPECIAL FINGERINGS

EXAMPLE 1.   There are two fingerings for the following B natural, one for chromatic passages and the other for arpeggio and diatonic passages.

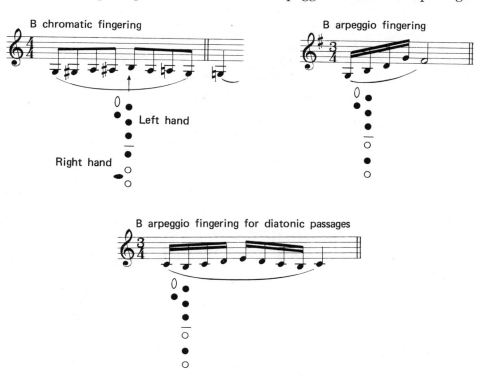

With the addition of the register key, the same fingering pattern used for B natural may also be used for F sharp (a twelfth above B).

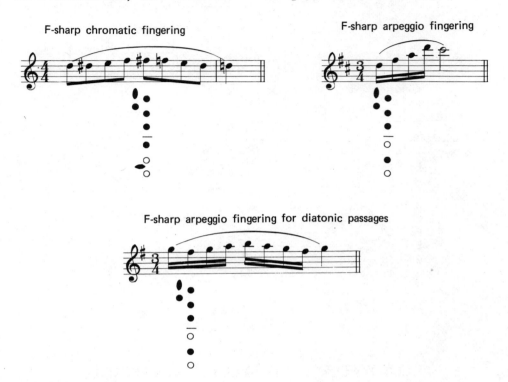

EXAMPLE 2. There are four different fingerings for the E-flat just above middle C. Listed below are examples showing the recommended use of each E-flat fingering.

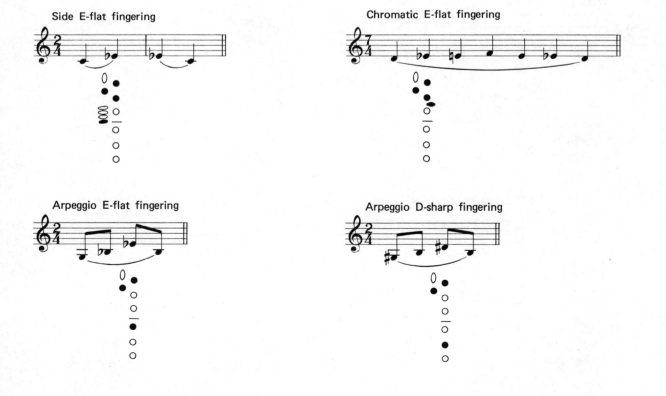

Ch. 5/The Clarinet 127

With the addition of the register key, the same finger pattern used for E-flat in Example 2 may be used for B-flat (a twelfth above E-flat).

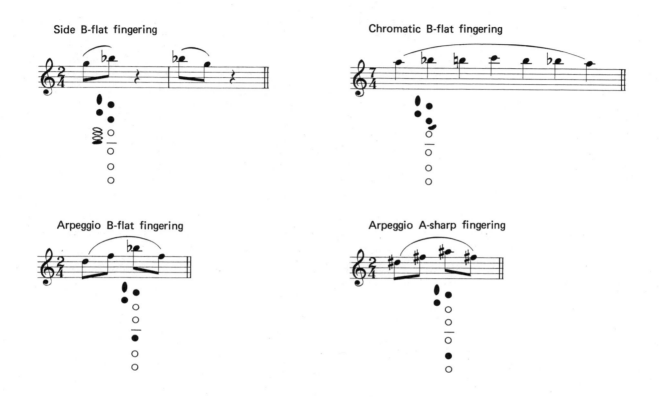

EXAMPLE 3. Since the second E-flat above middle C has only one fingering, it is necessary to use the left-hand duplicate fingerings in passages such as the one shown.

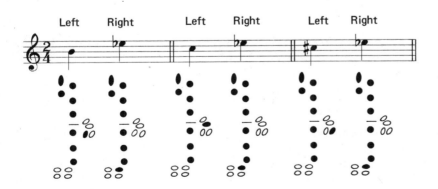

Generally speaking, the B, C, and C-sharp should always be played with the left hand so that the right hand may be free to manipulate the E-flat key *without sliding the little finger*. (See examples 5 and 6, pp. 129–30 for exceptions to this general rule.)

The same applies to those notes that are exactly a twelfth below the B, C, and C-sharp: low E, F, and F-sharp. For example:

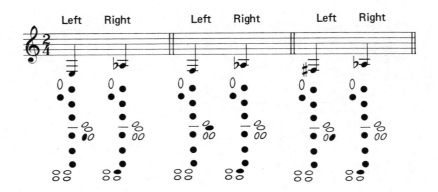

EXAMPLE 4. The following notes have duplicate fingerings and may be played with either the left or right hand. The important point to remember is that it is best to alternate from left to right (or vice versa) when possible, in order to avoid sliding with either little finger.

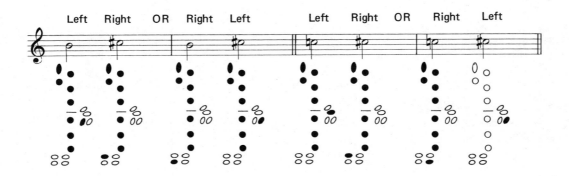

Since the same keys are used by the little fingers for the notes a twelfth below, the same rules would apply.

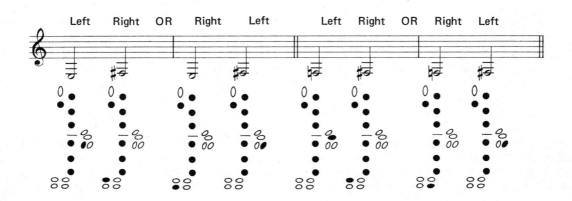

Ch. 5/The Clarinet

EXAMPLE 5. Occasionally it is necessary to slide one of the little fingers. In the accompanying excerpt the right-hand little finger slides from D-sharp to C-sharp.

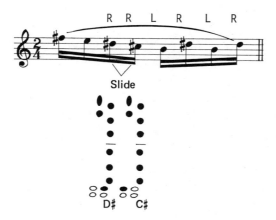

If this example is played a twelfth below, the finger pattern would be essentially the same; the right-hand little finger slides from G-sharp to F-sharp.

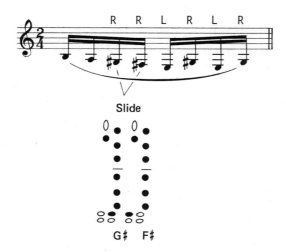

Figure 91 gives an instance of sliding the right-hand little finger from E-flat to C.

FIGURE 91.
Sonata for Clarinet and Piano, Op. 120, No. 2—Brahms

Published 1939 by Carl Fischer, Inc., New York, N.Y. Reprinted by permission.

If these same notes are played a twelfth below, it becomes necessary to slide the right-hand little finger from A-flat to F. (The sliding finger movement is identical for both examples.)

EXAMPLE 6. Occasionally it may be necessary to change from the left to the right little finger on the same note (a practice common among organists).

**FIGURE 92.
Sonata for Clarinet and Piano, Op. 120, No. 1—Brahms**

Published 1939 by Carl Fischer, Inc., New York, N.Y. Reprinted by permission.

It should be noted that the twelfths below E-flat, D-flat, and C would call for the same type of finger movement.

Study Questions

1. Which sections of the clarinet should be assembled with extreme care?
2. "*Never* put a ring joint together if the ring is loose." Why?
3. What is the best advice you can offer a student concerning oiling a wooden bore?
4. Effective instrument angle should be determined by what factor?
5. What exercises can the beginning clarinetist utilize to quickly attain effective hand position?
6. Describe the author's recommended approach to clarinet embouchure.
7. What exercises can the beginning clarinetist practice in order to develop the "flexed, offset" embouchure?
8. Describe the lower-chin placement for the clarinet, oboe, and bassoon.
9. What is the purpose of the "mouthpiece exercise"?
10. What does the author recommend regarding rate of air flow for clarinetists?
11. List the points that your author recommends for achieving effective breath support on the clarinet.
12. How does the author use the following terms to help establish aural guidelines for young beginners: "the principal of contrast" and "experiment"?
13. Why does the author recommend avoiding use of the tongue in the initial stages of clarinet study?
14. When should you introduce tonguing to the elementary student?
15. What kind of tongue stroke is advocated for beginners when single tonguing is introduced?
16. List as concisely as possible seven points the author presents concerning the development of single-reed tonguing.

A Problem Chart

Problem	Probable Cause	Suggestions for Improvement
A. The overall tone quality is too dark and sounds breathy.	The reed is too stiff for the mouthpiece.	Have the student try an assortment of softer reeds.
B. The overall tone quality is too bright, and sounds either thin or too resonant.	The reed is too soft for the mouthpiece.	Have the student try an assortment of stiffer reeds.
C. The clarinet squeaks; student gives evidence of a control problem.	1. The reed may be too soft. 2. The student's embouchure may be at fault. 3. The instrument may need repair.	1. Advise the student to try an assortment of harder reeds. 2. Refer the pupil to visual aids depicting the flexed offset clarinet embouchure, and have him imitate this format. 3. Check for leaks, bent keys, or damaged corks at the bridge keys.
D. The student tends to play flat as he progresses into the higher register.	1. Embouchure alignment may be at fault. 2. The reed may be too soft.	1. It is impossible to play the clarinet in tune in the higher register if the chin is drawn back behind the upper teeth. Have the student extend the lower jaw forward and up (see page 109 for pictures of clarinet embouchure). 2. Have the student try a slightly stiffer reed.
E. The student's overall pitch level is flat.	The amount of mouthpiece taken into the mouth can create this problem.	Have the student take less mouthpiece into the mouth. Too much creates a large flat sound; too little mouthpiece insertion creates a small pinched sound which tends to be sharp overall.
F. The student's overall pitch level is sharp.	Either the mouthpiece or the student can be at fault.	1. Some student-line mouthpieces tend to be built on the sharp side. Have the student try two or three reputable mouthpiece brands. 2. Student may be taking in too little mouthpiece.
G. The instrument's internal intonation appears generally poor.	1. This is most often caused by an unstable embouchure. 2. The student's sensitivity to pitch may be below par.	1. Check the student's pitch stability by having him try the mouthpiece exercise. If he produces a pitch lower than high C his embouchure is at fault. He should strive to master this exercise (see page 111). He should also study the picture of the flexed, offset clarinet embouchure and try to imitate that format. 2. A regular portion of his lesson time should be devoted to duos where he must play unisons, octaves, thirds, etc., with his instructor.
H. The student produces a small, narrow, weak tone.	1. There is not enough mouthpiece in the mouth; or 2. he may not be using enough breath support; or 3. both of these may be the cause of the problem.	1. Student should take more mouthpiece into the mouth and allow for maximum reed vibration. 2. Have the student deliberately overblow a tone, then underblow it. By hearing the results of these two extremes, he can quickly establish aural guidelines and learn to calibrate his breath support in order to make a well-placed, centered tone.

A Problem Chart (continued)

Problem	Probable Cause	Suggestions for Improvement
I. The student produces a tone that sounds overblown and too large in volume.	There is too much mouthpiece inserted into the mouth.	Have the student take less mouthpiece into the mouth. (Allow him to experiment in order to find the amount that is best for him.)
J. The student produces extraneous sounds when tonguing.	1. The method of placement of tongue against reed can cause this problem. 2. He may be moving his chin as he tongues. 3. He may be adding a burst of breath with each tongue stroke in slower passages.	1. Advise the student to place the tip of the tongue at the tip of the reed as lightly as possible (see Figure 86, p. 114). 2 and 3. Noticeable visual movement of the chin, lips, throat, or the entire chest area is usually an indication that the student does not understand single-reed tonguing. Advise him to use the syllable "dah" for legato tonguing, and to blow continually against the mouthpiece—even when the tongue is on the reed. He should use the syllable "tut" or "tuh" for staccato notes, and again should blow against the mouthpiece even while the the tongue is against the reed.
K. When reading music the student stops and starts excessively.	The student is using improper reading habits when he practices.	Fluency in reading music in the *initial stage* is dependent on work that is graduated and systematic. Have student read exercises slowly at first, and gradually increase the speed over a period of several days.

Teaching Aids

1. Show the student how to assemble the clarinet so as to avoid damaging the extension keys at the middle joint.
2. Instrument angle will vary according to the individual's particular occlusion. Generally speaking, the clarinet should be held slightly away from the body.
3. Show the student examples of the recommended embouchure format.
4. Have the student practice flexing the lips in the appropriate position daily.
5. Have student place the upper teeth on top of the mouthpiece.
6. Have the student master the mouthpiece exercise: Take the mouthpiece and, using the recommended grip, try to produce a steady, straight tone pitched at about high C. The pitch should sound straight and even.

Not every student will be able to perfect this immediately, nor should he. The exercise serves mainly as a guide to perfect embouchure stability, the desired goal.

7. Begin the 3-and-3 routine; have student use no music and slur.
8. As reminders, have the student (1) flex the chin muscles so they are flat and smooth and (2) experiment with mouthpiece insertion: Take a large "bite", then a small one; finally, compromise between these two extremes until you find the best position for control and a clear tone.
9. Have the student deliberately overblow a tone, contrast that sound with a tone that is underblown, and then strive for a centered, well-placed tone that lies between the two extremes.
10. Have the student refer to a mirror frequently.

Ch. 5/The Clarinet 133

11. Recommend frequent rest periods.
12. Stress using a minimum amount of lower lip over the lower teeth.
13. Have the student play twelfths as soon as feasible. In the initial stage, have someone else depress the register (or "twelfth") key.
14. For students who are prone to bunch the lower lip against the reed, have them play long tones with a double-reed (oboe) embouchure for a *few* minutes daily—but not continually.

A SELECTED LIST OF GRADED SOLOS

Clarinet Literature

The following list has been compiled as a convenient source reference for the instrumental music teacher. It is by no means complete, and readers are encouraged to study publisher catalog listings for their additional needs. This listing is intended to serve as a primer offering; although it has been carefully graded, some overlapping should of course be expected.

Considering the solos' technical difficulty, they have been ranked according to the following scale:

Grades 1–2: very easy to easy
Grades 3–4: moderate to moderately difficult
Grades 5–6: difficult to very difficult

Grades 1–2

Composer	Title	Publisher
Buchtel	"Novelette"	Kjos
	Serenade	Kjos
Edmunds	"Highland Croon"	AMP
	"Lament"	AMP
Gretchaninoff	Suite Miniature, Op. 145	Rubank
Hovey and Leonard (arrs.)	Theme and Variation	Belwin
Humperdinck (arr. Lowry)	Song and Prayer from "Hansel and Gretel"	Belwin
Klauss	"Moonlight Melody"	Kendor
Langenus	"Donkey Ride"	Carl Fischer
	Scale Waltz	Carl Fischer
Phillips	Air	AMP
	Eight Bel Canto Songs	Shawnee
Purcell (arr. Worley)	Little Serenade	Spratt
Swain	"Derry Down"	Mills
Warren	Sonatina	Ludwig
Weber	"Bluebird Waltz"	Belwin

Grades 3–4

Composer	Title	Publisher
Aubert (ed. Waln)	Aria and Presto	Kjos
Barat	Berceuse	Rubank
Barlow	Lyrical Piece	Carl Fischer
Bassi	"Lamento"	Rubank
Bergson (ed. H. Voxman)	Scene and Air, Op. 82	Rubank
Bozza	Aria	Leduc
Christmann (ed.)	Solos for the Clarinet Player	G. Schirmer
Conley	Summer Nocturne	Kendor
Delmas	Promenade	Carl Fischer
Dunhill	Phantasy Suite	Boosey & Hawkes

Grades 3–4 (continued)

Composer	Title	Publisher
Endresen	Rhapsody in G Minor	Belwin
Frangkiser	"Elegance"	Belwin
Frank	Evening Piece	Carl Fischer
Guilhaud	First Concertino	Rubank
Handel	Concerto in G Minor	Kjos
Kell	"Moods"	Boosey & Hawkes
Langenus	"Chrysalis"	Carl Fischer
Leclair	Musette and Scherzo	Kjos
Mozart	Adagio from Concerto in B-flat Major, K. 622	Carl Fischer
Pierné	Piece in G Minor	Southern
Ravel	Pièce en Forme de Habanera	Leduc
Saucier	"An Impression"	Kendor
Schumann	Fantasy Pieces, Op. 73	G. Schirmer
Tuthill	"Chip's Piece"	Southern
	"Chip's Fast Piece"	Southern
Vaughan Williams	Six Studies in English Folk Song	Galaxy
Voxman (ed.)	Concert and Contest Collection	Rubank
Wanhal	Sonata	McGinnis and Marx

Grades 5–6

Composer	Title	Publisher
Barat	Fantaisie Romantique	Leduc
Bozza	Fantaisie Italienne	Costallat
Brahms	Sonata in F Minor, Op. 120, No. 1	Carl Fischer
	Sonata in E-flat Major, Op. 120, No. 2	Carl Fischer
Debussy	Première Rhapsodie	Durand
Delmas	Fantaisie Italienne	Alfred
Hindemith	Concerto	Schott
	Sonata	AMP
Mozart	Concerto in B-flat Major, K. 622	G. Shirmer
Piston	Concerto	Associated Music Publishers
Poulenc	Sonata	Chester
Saucier	Fantasy (MS)	Opus 2
	Three Pieces for Clarinet	G. Schirmer
Stamitz	Concerto in B-flat Major	Leeds
Stravinsky	Three Pieces for Clarinet	Chester
Tomasi	Introduction and Danse	Leduc
Weber	Concertino, Op. 26	Carl Fischer
	Concerto No. 1	Carl Fischer
	Concerto No. 2	Carl Fischer
	Grand Duo Concertant	Carl Fischer

CLASS METHODS

See "Class Methods for the Public School Instrumental Music Program," pp. 63–64.

INDIVIDUAL METHODS AND SUPPLEMENTAL STUDIES

Major Applied Methods

BELWIN SERIES FOR CLARINET

Belwin Clarinet Method by K. Gekeler and N. Hovey. This is a three-volume study beginning at the elementary level and continuing through the advanced intermediate stage.

Student Instrumental Course for Clarinet by F. Weber and B. Lowry is a three-volume series designed to cover elementary through advanced intermediate study. This work is correlated with supplementary studies of solos, duos, and technical exercises.

These series are published by Belwin-Mills, Melville, N.Y.

RUBANK SERIES FOR CLARINET

Rubank Elementary Method for Clarinet by N. Hovey.

Rubank Intermediate Method for Clarinet by J. E. Skornicka.

Rubank Advanced Method for Clarinet (2 vols.) by H. Voxman and W. Gower.

All published by Rubank, Inc., Miami, Fla.

In Chapter 3 several key points were cited regarding the use of American and European applied method books at the initial level of instrumental study. The single most important point made in that discussion centered on the differences between certain American and European music method books: On the one hand, many American method books *assume no prior musical study*; on the other, most of the celebrated European or European-influenced books *assume prior musical study* and tend to progress from elementary to intermediate levels at a rate that becomes impractical for students lacking preparatory music backgrounds. Consequently, such music methods as Taffanel and Gaubert's *Complete Method for Flute* or A. M. R. Barret's *Complete Method for Oboe* are never used by American instrumental music teachers at the initial level of study. These same books are, however, widely used by American instrumental music teachers after their students have completed basic foundation work.

This situation is by no means limited to the flute and oboe. It is in fact the case with many method books written for woodwinds, including the clarinet. The following method books are recommended for study *after* the clarinet student has completed his basic foundation work with a standard American method such as those published by Belwin or Rubank.

Complete Method for Clarinet by Carl Baermann. The five-volume edition of this work is published by Carl Fischer, New York, N.Y.

Celebrated Method For Clarinet by H. Klosé is published by Carl Fischer, New York, N.Y.

Complete Method for the Clarinet by G. Langenus is published by Carl Fischer, New York, N.Y.

Complete Method for Clarinet by H. Lazarus is published by Carl Fischer, New York, N.Y.

Supplemental Studies

Scales and Chords by S. Bellison. Published by Carl Fischer, New York, N.Y.

Sixteen Phrasing Studies by D. Bonade. Published by Leblanc Publications, Kenosha, Wis.

30 Caprices by E. Cavallini. Published by Carl Fischer, New York, N.Y.

416 Progressive Studies by F. Kroepsch. Published by Carl Fischer, New York, N.Y.

Clarinet Cadenzas: How to Phrase Them by G. Langenus. Published by Carl Fischer, New York, N.Y.

Daily Technical Exercises by G. Pares. Published by Carl Fischer, New York, N.Y.

40 Studies for Clarinet by C. Rose. Published by Carl Fischer, New York, N.Y.

48 Etudes for Clarinet (2 vols.). by A. Uhl. Published by Schott, Germany.

Selected Studies for Clarinet by H. Voxman. Published by Rubank, Miami, Fla.

RECORDINGS OF CLARINET LITERATURE

Pedagogically Oriented Recordings

The Music Minus One Series. Essentially, the Music Minus One Corporation makes professionally recorded backgrounds—minus a particular solo instrument—for all types of music, including the orchestral concerto, the sonata, chamber music, and various jazz forms. The original concept behind the MMO series was to afford the student performer a professional accompaniment against which to practice and perform a musical work in its original and complete context, that is, with full orchestra, string quartet, or jazz ensemble, as the case might be. The bulk of the recorded accompaniments made by MMO falls in this category. However, the Laureate Series of Contest Solos goes beyond the practical asset of offering a professional accompaniment. With the Laureate Series, the student or teacher is offered in one package a performance by a major performing artist, a copy of the printed music, a professional accompaniment, and interpretive suggestions for performance written by the performing artist.

This series has within the past quarter century proved a valuable music education tool; and is highly recommended as a teaching aid. The MMO regular series and the Laureate Series are published by Music Minus One, 43 West 61 Street, New York, N.Y.

Three Pieces for Clarinet: Composition, Performance and Analysis by Gene Saucier is a contemporary, virtuoso display piece for unaccompanied clarinet written for and dedicated to the twentieth-century clarinet virtuoso, Benny Goodman. Although the music is published separately, the recorded package includes (1) a performance by the composer, (2) the composer's interpretive analysis of advanced performance techniques used in the recordings (e.g., quarter tones, flutter tonguing, delayed tongue releases, and vibrato, as well as the exercise of musical taste), and (3) a provocative list of "pro and con" critiques by distinguished American artists. Additionally, there is ample background data relating to the music, the performer, and those who have performed or evaluated this work. This record-analysis is published by University Press Releases and may be obtained from Opus 2, Box 727, University, Mississippi, or Opus 1, Box 1164, Decatur, Ga.

Special Collections

The following recorded collections will be of special interest to the clarinetist. Each album is devoted exclusively to selected clarinet literature and features various performing artists of our time. This listing is by no means complete; however, it is more than adequate as an aural source-reference for the beginning student of clarinet.

Donald McGinnis Plays Clarinet
Bozza: Fantaisie Italienne
Mazellier: Fantasy Ballet
Quet: Petite Pièce
Schumann: Three Romances
Spohr: Concerto No. 1
Telemann: Sonata in C Minor. Donald McGinnis (clarinet) and Rosemary Platt (piano). Coronet LPS 1705

Music for Clarinet and Piano
Bernstein: Sonata for Clarinet and Piano
Milhaud: Sonatine pour Clarinette
Debussy: Petite Pièce pour Clarinette
Honegger: Sonatine pour Clarinette et Piano
Bax: Sonata for Clarinet and Piano. Stanley Drucker (clarinet) and Leonid Hambro (piano). Odyssey Y 30492

Meeting at the Summit: Benny Goodman
Bernstein: Prelude, Fugue, and Riffs
Copland: Clarinet Concerto
Gould: Derivations for Clarinet and Band
Stravinsky: Ebony Concerto. Benny Goodman. Columbia ML 6205

New Virtuoso Music for Clarinet
M. Doran: Sonata for Clarinet and Piano
F. Campo: "Kinesis"
B. Phillin: Sonata for Clarinet and Piano
W. Schmidt: Rhapsody No. 1. David Atkins (clarinet) and Sharon Davis (piano). WIM Records (2859 Holt Avenue, Los Angeles, Calif.)

Rolf Legbandt Plays Clarinet
Bozza: Concerto for Clarinet and Piano
JeanJean: "Au clair de la lune"
Poulenc: Sonata for Clarinet and Piano

Widor: Introduction and Rondo Op. 72. Rolf Legbandt (clarinet) and Michel Bourgeot (piano). Coronet LPS 3027

Reginald Kell, Clarinet
Debussy: Première Rhapsodie
Schumann: Phantasiestücke, Op. 73
Weber: Grand Duo Concertant, Op. 48. Reginald Kell (clarinet) and Joel Rosen (piano). Decca DL 9744

The Los Angeles Clarinet Society
F. Campo: Concertino for E-flat, B-flat, and Bass Clarinets and Piano
G. Heussenstamm: "Tetralogue"
D. Michalsky: Divertimento for Three Clarinets
H. Owen: Chamber Music for Four B-flat Clarinets. Roy D'Antonio, David Atkins, Hugo Raimondi, Julian Spear (clarinets), Sharon Davis (piano), and Karen Ervin (percussion). WIM Records.

Three Sonatas for Clarinet and Piano
Reger: Sonata No. 1
Sonata No. 2
Sonata in B-flat Major, Op. 107. Frederic Lubrani (clarinet), and Edwin La-Bounty (piano). L.M.R. (Available from Viking Union Co-op Bookstore, 511 High street, Bellingham, Wash.)

Traditional Recordings

Brahms: Sonata No. 1 in F Minor; Sonata No. 2 in E-flat Major. Reginald Kell (clarinet), Joel Rosen (piano). Decca 9638

————: Sonata No. 1 in F Minor; Sonata No. 2 in E-flat Major. Harold Wright. Musical Heritage Society MHS 1496
Debussy: Première Rhapsodie. Stanley Drucker. Columbia ML 6059
————: Première Rhapsodie. Anthony Gigliotti. Columbia MS 6977
————: Première Rhapsodie. Reginald Kell. Decca DL 9744
Hindemith: Sonata for Clarinet and Piano. Sidney Forrest. Lyrichord 15
A. Manevich: Concerto for Clarinet and Orchestra. Isaac Roginsky. Monitor MC 2030
Mozart: Concerto for Clarinet, K. 622. Anthony Gigliotti. Columbia MS 6452
————: Concerto for Clarinet, K. 622. Reginald Kell. Decca DL 9732
————: Concerto for Clarinet, K. 622. Karl Leister. Deutsche Grammophon 136550
————: Concerto for Clarinet, K. 622. Robert Marcellus. Columbia ML 6368
Nielsen: Concerto for Clarinet. Benny Goodman. RCA Victor R66-3363
Poulenc: Sonata for Clarinet and Piano. Andre Boutard (clarinet), J. Fevrier (piano). Nonesuch H-71033
Reger: Sonata No. 1; Sonata No. 2. Dieter Klöcker (clarinet), Werner Genuit, (piano). Musical Heritage Society MHS 1521

138   Fundamental Techniques and Supplemental Aids/Part II

FIGURE 93.
E-flat alto clarinet

FIGURE 94.
B-flat bass clarinet

FIGURE 95.
E-flat contrabass
clarinet

Photographs courtesy of the Selmer Company, Elkhart, Indiana.

The Lower Clarinets

The lower clarinets include the E-flat alto clarinet, B-flat bass clarinet, E-flat contrabass clarinet, and B-flat contrabass clarinet.

In view of the size of the lower clarinets—especially the bass and contrabass clarinets—many instrumental music teachers do not start young beginners on these instruments. And many teachers prefer to introduce students to one of the lower clarinets only after they have developed a reasonable degree of proficiency on the B-flat clarinet or possibly one of the saxophones. On the other hand, some teachers will start a student on one of the lower clarinets if his or her physical size permits, thus eliminating the "transfer step." While there may be advantages or disadvantages to either approach, there are certain critical points one should consider. These include (1) individual suitability, (2) embouchure modifications appropriate to the lower single reeds, and (3) suitable study materials.

Individual Suitability

The student's physical size is an obvious criterion; a quick assessment can be made by simply having him "finger" the instrument. Less obvious, however, is the matter of the natural oral occlusion.

In transferring an upper single-reed student to one of the lower instruments, it would be best to transfer that student whose upper front teeth tend to slant inward. While students whose upper front teeth appear even, smooth, and perpendicular can progress on upper single-reed instruments into the high register with ease and control, those students whose upper front teeth tend to turn noticeably inward will be inclined to take more of the B-flat clarinet mouthpiece into the mouth than is practical, and consequently will be faced with a serious control problem. If, however, they switch to a lower clarinet—which requires a slightly larger amount of mouthpiece in the mouth—then this aspect of suitability of occlusion can be effectively resolved.

Additionally, it may be observed that some students appear to have lower jaws that recede or protrude. Students with receding lower jaws will inevitably have more success on the lower single-reed instruments or bassoon than on the upper single-reed instruments, which require that the lower jaw be in a position that is forward and up. If it is pulled back—as is so often the case with bassoonists—it is impossible to play the upper register of a B-flat clarinet (or B-flat soprano saxophone) in tune. Playing with the lower jaw in a forward and raised position is an essential requirement for control among *all* upper single-reed instruments. Consequently the student with a naturally receding lower jaw

139

140 Fundamental Techniques and Supplemental Aids/Part II

Embouchure Modifications

will inevitably have difficulty with upper single-reed instruments. It would be best to switch him to a lower single-reed instrument or bassoon.

While the basic embouchure formats for the instruments of the clarinet family may appear similar, there are marked differences between the upper and lower clarinets. The most practical dividing line would fall between the alto and the bass clarinet. The reasons for this are: First, the angle that the mouthpiece makes with the mouth is considerably wider with bass and contrabass clarinets than with the other instruments; the mouthpiece enters the mouth in a line almost parallel to the floor. For the other clarinets—beginning with the alto—the mouthpiece enters the mouth at a sharp angle. Second, the mouthpiece size of the bass and contrabass clarinets demands that more of the mouthpiece be taken into the mouth. As a consequence of these acute physical differences, certain modifications of the basic clarinet embouchure become imperative for the bass and contrabass player.

E-FLAT ALTO CLARINET

1. The flexed, offset embouchure format may be used here just as with the upper single-reed instruments. No changes or modifications are necessary.
2. Determining the correct *amount* of mouthpiece to be inserted into the mouth is absolutely essential with *any* clarinet mouthpiece. This may be determined on an individual basis by playing middle C or open G and experimenting with the mouthpiece. If one undergrips or takes too little mouthpiece into the mouth, the tone will sound pinched, thin, and small. If too much is taken into the mouth, there is an acute tendency to squeak, and the tone will sound large, flat, and too open. Through experiment one can find the point that best suits the individual.

BASS AND CONTRABASS CLARINETS

Flexed Approach

The distinguished concert artist and woodwind doubler, Alfred Gallodoro, gave the appearance of using the same embouchure for B-flat clarinet, E-flat alto saxophone, and B-flat bass clarinet. However, this was deceptive; while certain professional doublers may appear to use the same grip, the amount of muscular intensification applied in the embouchure is an aspect that cannot be seen. The flexed-grip approach *can* be used on bass clarinet; however, here the lower jaw is dropped and held in suspension so that pinching or overgripping is avoided. The flexed-grip format requires considerable stability of control when used on bass or contrabass clarinet.

Ch. 5/The Clarinet *141*

Relaxed Approach

The main point of difference between the flexed and relaxed grips for the lower clarinets centers on the choice of either flexing the muscles in the lip area or allowing them to relax. Many bass clarinetists—especially contrabass clarinetists—use the relaxed embouchure approach. In this instance the lower lip is allowed to cushion against the reed; in some cases it will even appear to be bunched up around the reed. The key to control in this type of embouchure centers on (1) controlled jaw pressure, (2) the appropriate amount of mouthpiece insertion, and (3) a balanced mouthpiece-reed combination.

Although either the flexed or relaxed approach may be used effectively, the final choice in deciding which method to use should remain with the individual under the guidance of his instructor.

In determining the right amount of mouthpiece to be taken into the mouth the method outlined above for the E-flat alto clarinet may be used for all clarinets. After the individual degree of mouthpiece insertion is determined, the next step is to discover the amount of lower-jaw pressure that works best for the general tessitura of the instrument. This can be ascertained by experimenting: While sustaining a long tone, the student should simply overgrip (bite) and observe the aural results. Then he should repeat the same sustained tone, this time relaxing the lower-jaw pressure to an extreme degree and observing the results. The object here is to reach a compromise whereby the controlled amount of lower-jaw pressure becomes effective—not detrimental.

Of the three critical points one should consider in starting a student on one of the lower clarinets, two have been considered above; the third point, *suitable study material,* is of equal importance.

For the developing instrumentalist, suitable study material is understandably a major and essential factor if meaningful progress and ultimate excellence are to be achieved. While the volume of original study material and solo literature for the lower single-reed instruments is much smaller than that of upper single-reeds, there are nonetheless noteworthy publications of quality available for them. The following list of study material has been divided into three categories: (1) material for beginning students, (2) material for transfer students, and (3) supplements. Its express object is to call to the reader's attention the most highly used and widely recommended study material currently available.

Recommended Study Material

BEGINNING STUDENTS

The Belwin-Mills Student Instrumental Course series—designed for American public school music programs—is the most complete offering of study material currently available to lower single-reed students today. This series may be used for the rank beginner or the transfer student. It consists of three levels of graded study material: level one, elementary; level two, intermediate; and level three, advanced intermediate. Additionally, each basic method (level 1, 2, or 3) is correlated with supplementary publications devoted to etudes, technique, and solos with piano accompaniment. In view of the importance of this educational series of studies, two descriptive excerpts for alto and bass clarinets have been reproduced in Figures 96 and 97.

FIGURE 96

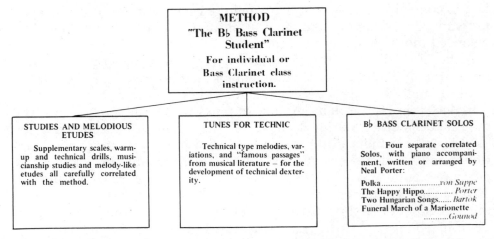

Copyright © 1970 by Belwin-Mills Publishing Corp., Melville, N.Y. International copyright secured. Made in U.S.A. All rights reserved. Used by permission.

FIGURE 97

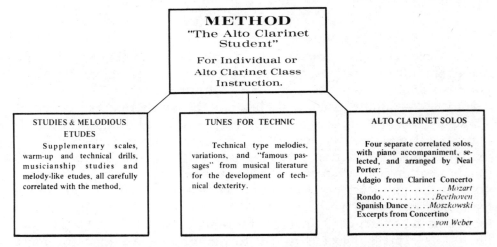

Copyright © 1971 by Belwin-Mills Publishing Corp., Melville, N.Y. International copyright secured. Made in U.S.A. All rights reserved. Used by permission.

TRANSFER STUDENTS

For those who prefer to transfer students with previous instrumental experience to one of the lower single-reed instruments, Rubank has published a highly recommended transfer method widely used by instrumental music educators: *Introducing the Alto or Bass Clarinet*, by H. Voxman, a transfer method for intermediate instruction. The basic design of this method is primarily one for individual study. While its content is limited, the material is presented in a thorough and struc-

Ch. 5/The Clarinet   143

tured manner. This work also contains "Special Notes on Fingerings" (including special pitch problems), and key performance practices imperative for the lower single-reed instrumentalist. The accompanying informative excerpt (Figure 98) is representative.

FIGURE 98

	Page		Page
Introducing the Alto or Bass Clarinet	2	Additional Chromatic Fingerings	22
Dynamic Development	5	Grace Notes	23
The Register Change	6	Recapitulation Studies	24
Dynamic Gradations	7	Studies in D Major	26
Register Change With B♭	8	Studies in B Minor	27
The Accent (Sforzando)	9	Table of Trills for the Boehm Clarinet	28
The Half-Staccato (Portamento)	10	The Trill (Shake)	30
Studies in Articulation	11	The Turn (Gruppetto)	31
Studies in C Major	12	Studies in E♭ Major	32
Studies in A Minor	13	Studies in C Minor	33
Studies in F Major	14	Studies in A Major	34
Studies in D Minor	15	Studies in F♯ Minor	35
Studies in G Major	16	Studies in A♭ Major	36
Studies in E Minor	17	Studies in F Minor	37
Developing Chromatic Fingerings	18	Additional Recapitulation Studies	38
Technical Studies	19	Studies in E Major	40
Studies in B♭ Major	20	Studies in C♯ Minor	41
Studies in G Minor	21	Pastorale and Bourrée	42
		Advanced Studies	44

Copyright © 1952 by Rubank, Inc., Chicago, Ill. International copyright secured. Used by permission.

ADDITIONAL SUPPLEMENTS FOR ALTO AND BASS CLARINETS

Baermann for Alto And Bass Clarinet by C. Baermann (ed. W. Rhoads). Published by Southern Music Co., San Antonio, Tex.

Playing and Teaching the Clarinet Family by D. McCathren. Published by Southern Music Co., San Antonio, Tex.

Method for Alto and Bass Clarinets by P. Mimart. Published by Carl Fischer, New York, N.Y.

Method for Bass Clarinet and Alto Clarinet by Orsi (ed. Giamperi). Published by Ricordi, Milan, Italy.

35 Technical Studies by W. Rhoads. Published by Southern Music Co. San Antonio, Tex.

21 Foundation Studies by W. Rhoads. Published by Southern Music Co. San Antonio, Tex.

The Bassoon

**FIGURE 99.
Bassoon (Heckel system)**

Photograph courtesy of the Selmer Company, Elkhart, Indiana.

Bassoon Assembly

FIGURE 100. (left) Boot and long joint

FIGURE 101. (right) Boot, long joint, and tenor joint

FIGURE 102. (left) Bell and long joint

FIGURE 103. (right) The hand rest

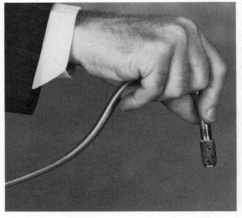

FIGURE 104. (left) Gripping the bocal

FIGURE 105. (right) Inserting the bocal

FIGURE 106. The boot strap

Ch. 6/The Bassoon

Instrument Assembly and Care

Like the other woodwinds, the bassoon should be carefully assembled so as not to damage the bridge keys at the joints or the long key rods which are subject to bending. Apply cork grease to the tenon joints first; remember that with the bassoon the boot and upper joints must appear to fit slightly tighter than do the joints of the clarinet. Again, one should never force joints together. Due to its size and the fact that two tenons are to be inserted into the boot joint, it is best to rest the boot joint in one's lap, inserting the upper joints very gradually, applying finger pressure on the key posts—not on the key rods. The bell joint may be attached next; care should be used to avoid damaging the bridge key at this joint. The bocal should always be inserted with a twisting motion, gripped just above the cork in order to avoid bending. The reed too should be attached with a twisting motion, after it has been soaked in water for a few minutes. Failure to use a twisting motion in either case can result in bending the bocal!

The use of the hand rest and type of strap used may vary, depending on the teacher and student. Be that as it may, if one elects to use the seat strap rather than the neck strap, one must remember to either hold the bassoon or rest it on the floor before rising.

It is best to follow the manufacturer's advice concerning the oiling of the bassoon bore. Generally speaking, most makers are in agreement on the following points: Oil directly only the wood sections of the bore. Those sections that are rubber-lined—the tenor joint and the small side of the boot joint—should not be oiled; the remaining sections may be oiled lightly with a bassoon swab. If an excessive amount of oil is used, it may seep through some of the tone holes and collect on the pads. After each playing session the bassoon should be swabbed out. Although the bell and bass joint collect little water, the remaining joints and various tone holes tend to collect water. The tone holes that do absorb water may be blotted with thin paper. Remember, water left in any wooden instrument can have a serious adverse effect on wood and pads!

FIGURE 107. (left) Instrument angle—profile view

FIGURE 108. (right) Front view

Instrument Angle and Hand Position

The most important factor in instrument angle and position is practicality. Generally speaking, the bell of the bassoon leans to the front of the player, and the boot joint falls to the right side and slightly back. The height of the bassoon should be adjusted with the seat or neck strap to allow the player to sit comfortably and without strain.

The bocal may be adjusted slightly to the right or left, but there is a limit here. The pad covering the whisper-key vent will not "seat" if this adjustment is excessive. Reed alignment poses no problem in that it is usually a self-adjusting matter. (As mentioned above, it is most important to twist or screw the reed on—do *not* push it into place.) Eventually most students will develop a feel for the "top" and "bottom" sides of the double reed. Although the appearance of a bassoon reed may not reveal the difference between the two blades, no two are ever exactly alike in their finished form. Consequently, the reed's responsiveness and amenability to control may be (and usually is) more favorable if a particular blade is placed against the upper lip. As the double-reed student acquires greater intimacy with the physical feel of reeds, he will invariably turn the reed blades to his favored position and thus establish a "top" and "bottom" to every reed he plays.

It is best to use discretion in starting students out on woodwinds. Many instrumental teachers consider the following criteria before recommending a student to study bassoon: (1) overall size, (2) oral occlusion, and (3) prior musical background (training in piano or other instrument). Hand size is a key factor; holding the instrument can indeed be a problem for the person with small hands. For the student with small or medium hands, removal of the right hand rest can help immensely. Since the tone holes on bassoon are spaced much more widely than on the smaller woodwinds, be sure that the student can adequately spread the fingers.

FIGURE 109.
Left-hand position

FIGURE 110.
Right-hand position

FIGURE 111.
Both hands in playing position

Tone Production

EMBOUCHURE

The recommended embouchure format illustrated in Figure 112 is a basic approach that is widely accepted, one that seems to work the best for most bassoonists.

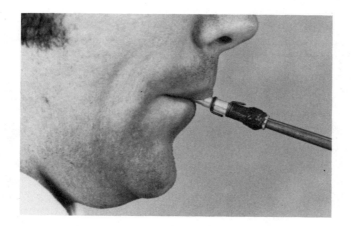

FIGURE 112. Recommended embouchure format for bassoon: the flexed offset grip

Note that here the lip muscles are flexed and the lower jaw is offset and back. This type of embouchure may be described as the flexed offset grip. Also note that the lip muscles—particularly those of the lower lip—are flat and smooth, not relaxed and bunched up around the reed.

Compare this format with Figure 113, which depicts an embouchure type characteristic among beginners.

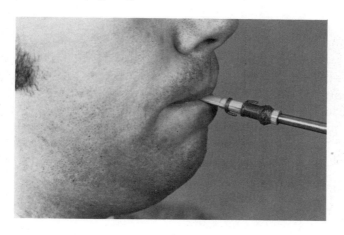

FIGURE 113. Incorrect embouchure: loose, unflexed, with parallel jaw position

Note the parallel position of the lower jaw here and the amount of lower lip bunched up around the reed. This type of embouchure is what young students tend to use in the first stage of study.

Although it does not fall within the scope of this text to prove in an exhaustive manner the advantages of a particular performance practice, a simple test to determine the potential of the flexed offset grip may be found below under the heading "Remedial Work" (p. 150).

In developing any recommended embouchure format, the element of timing and the method of approach are key factors. Always begin with a visual aid, such as a picture of the recommended embouchure. After the visual concept is established, use preliminary exercises that can make embouchure development relatively easy. One of the main problems that faces beginners is that they have no guidelines to fall back upon. The concept acquired through pictures is only a beginning.

Present the simple "Pencil Exercise" (Figure 114) to the student so that he can develop a sense of direction in the movement of his lower jaw. After studying the picture of the recommended embouchure, have the student, with the aid of a mirror, take a pencil and rest his upper

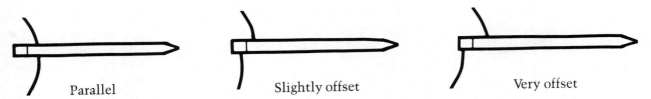

FIGURE 114.
Pencil exercise

teeth (covered by the lip) at the end of the metal sleeve holding the eraser. Next, have him place his lower lip against the bottom side of the metal sleeve in a parallel manner with the top lip. Leaving the top lip in stationary position, have him practice placing the lower lip back slightly, then back as far as possible, by allowing the lower jaw to recede. He should also try similarly extending the lower jaw forward beyond the upper lip.

It is through the repetition of different lower-lip placements that the student acquires a sense of direction and is enabled to determine the degree of offset angle that he can use effectively and comfortably.

After the "Pencil Exercise" is mastered, have the student practice with the reed. As with the pencil, the upper lip should rest in a stationary manner near the end of the reed blade, almost touching the wire; the lower jaw should be drawn back as far as is comfortably possible and placed against the reed so as to create the appearance of an offset grip. If too little reed is inserted in the mouth, reed vibration will be dampened and quality will thus be affected; if too much reed is inserted, it will be difficult to control the reed. The exernal factors which can affect reed vibration are (1) the amount of reed taken into the mouth, (2) the amount of lower-lip pressure on the reed, (3) breath support, and (4) the kind of grip used. It is the homogeneous functioning of these external factors that accounts for effective tone production. When the bassoonist can exercise control over these four factors, he will then be able to make the reed vibrate with maximum efficiency.

Remedial Work

Briefly, if one has a student who uses the embouchure depicted in Figure 113 (p. 149) and gives evidence of difficulty in controlling pitch, attaining a consistent tonal line, or producing a resonant centered tone, have him try the following simple test: First, allow him to study both types of embouchure grip. Then have him play the F major scale one octave in a slurred manner at a moderate tempo, using the flexed offset grip. He should follow this by playing the same pattern with the loose parallel grip. The object here is to allow the student to hear the difference in sound—specifically, in pitch and quality—and experience the additional ease of control that the flexed offset grip affords. It has been this author's experience to find those remedial students approaching the test with an open and unbiased attitude inevitably changing their embouchure to the flexed offset grip.

The main reasons for change will vary according to the individual. The student who may be more sensitive to pitch and control immediately senses the increase in control and pitch stability that the flexed offset grip affords; these advantages alone can convince him of the need for change. On the other hand, a student more acutely sensitive to tonal line and quality will respond instantly to the even and resonant tonal line that is characteristic of the flexed offset grip. Occasionally, though, an older student may voice an objection to the brighter, more resonant sound that the flexed offset grip produces. He will have cultivated, in all probability, a taste for a darker tone, and the change may appear radical to him. If such a student still needs to improve his control, pitch, or tonal line, remind him that he can attain a darker or brighter quality through the choice of reed.

In developing a woodwind player's embouchure the following points should be remembered:

1. Use effective preliminary exercises prior to any playing of the instrument. In the case of the bassoon the Pencil Exercise is indispensable.
2. Always encourage the student to use a mirror and to study recommended picture illustrations.
3. Allow the student to rest frequently, so that his lip muscles can develop gradually and systematically.
4. Avoid the use of written music with rank beginners for the first lesson or two, concentrating on consecutive finger movement as outlined in the 3-and-3 routine.
5. With the bassoon—where changes in the muscular intensification of the embouchure occur simultaneously with changes in breath pressure (as with flute and, occasionally, clarinet)—the interaction between embouchure and breath should be spelled out as simply as possible. For example, embouchure intensification and breath pressure *increase* in the upper register and *decrease* in the lower register on bassoon.

BREATH SUPPORT

The acoustical design of the bassoon is such that it naturally produces a tonal line that appears to gradually taper from "large" (low register) to "small" (upper register). This may be evidenced aurally by playing the F major scale one octave *with the same amount of breath pressure*. But if the performer will play the same scale and remember that "Less fingers means more air," he will then tend to produce a line that sounds even throughout.

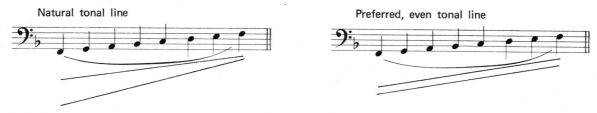

This simple exercise attests to the fact that although the factor of breath support is definitely a common denominator among wind players, how it is used is indeed another matter.

Since change in breath pressure tends to be a more acute matter with bassoon (and, to a lesser extent, saxophone), the 3-and-3 routine takes on added importance to the prospective bassoonist. The principle, "Less fingers means more air," should be applied to the 3-and-3 routine as early as is feasible. Bassoon tends to be among the more challenging of the woodwinds to finger; and it is suggested that the 3-and-3 routine be presented as shown here, in sections. No music need be used at first; the line should be slurred. The simplicity of consecutive finger movement (except for B-flat) aids facility and allows for greater concentration on tonal line and quality.

3-and-3 routine for elementary bassoonists

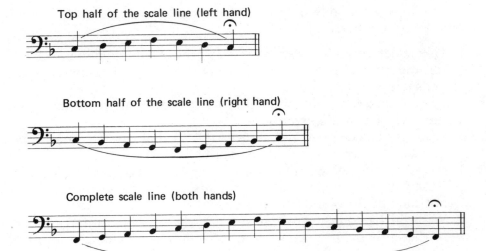

When the instructor deems it appropriate, the concept "Less fingers means more air" should be applied to the *complete* F scale line. Through increased air pressure at the top of the tonal line, the overall line can be made to sound even and very consistent.

It should be pointed out that while one may understand and employ breath-support habits appropriate to the bassoon, such adequate use of breath pressure will not be sufficient in itself in producing tones in the *extreme registers.* For example, as the bassoonist increases his playing range, muscular tension in the embouchure and air pressure must be developed to function homogeneously. In the lowest range of the bassoon, the embouchure will require less tension: The lower jaw will be dropped slightly. (This does not mean the lips will become loose, flabby, or bunched up.) If any tonguing is required in the very low register, it can be facilitated by dropping the jaw with each attack and keeping the throat open by thinking the syllable "ah" or "yah." In the higher range of the bassoon, increased breath support must be accompanied by a slight lifting of the lower jaw and a slight increase in overall lip tensions. Although the "vice-like" grip is something which practically all single- and double-reed teachers shun, the successful bassoonist will actually use vertical pressure changes (through raising or lowering the jaw) in the extreme ranges of the instrument. Such intensification of jaw pressure, however, is not used indiscriminately, and is never allowed to choke the reed or cause one-reed vibration. The offset grip allows very effectively for deviation in lower-jaw pressure and proves a real boon in realizing the pitch of certain tones.

The reader should note that no woodwind instrument is built perfectly in tune; even the finest instruments must ultimately be *played* in tune. The flexed offset grip utilizes the principle of the fulcrum in rais-

Ch. 6/The Bassoon *153*

ing or lowering pitch; the response is immediate. The parallel grip does not offer this immediate response in pitch control.

Finally it should be remembered that it takes *time* and *effort* to develop good breath-support habits. Do not expect overnight results. Much can be accomplished in this area by allowing the student to experiment in the early stages. For example, after the 3-and-3 routine is "in the student's fingers," so to speak, have him play the top half of the scale line using different levels of air pressure. Let him play this fractional line with minimum breath pressure, then with maximum breath pressure, and finally with pressure that falls between these extremes. Such experimentation can be of immense help in learning; it provides aural guidelines where none previously existed for the student!

TONGUING

After preliminary work on embouchure and breath support, initial attempts at tonguing can be introduced. The bassoonist should be advised in developing the single-tongue stroke to place the tip of the tongue at the tip of the reed. Whether or not the exact tip of the tongue touches the reed tip will be determined by the physical makeup of the individual. Some students may use that part of the tongue one-eighth to one-quarter inch from its exact end. Since physical makeup cannot be altered, the important thing is simply to have the student cultivate the habit of striving to use the area of the tongue as close to the tip as possible.

Other helpful aids in tonguing on the bassoon involve the use of syllables and lower-lip pressure. (As stated previously, while on the clarinet it is possible to play a low D and a high F [concert pitches] with the same feeling of intensification in the embouchure muscles, such is not the case with the bassoon.) As the bassoonist extends his range downward, he should be advised to drop his lower jaw, relaxing the pressure, and think the syllable "ah" or "yah" in attempting the lower tones. As he extends his range upward there will be a need to increase the lower-jaw pressure. Tonguing in the extreme top register can also be facilitated with the use of a syllable—"ee" rather than "ah." In order to facilitate tonguing in the lowest register of bassoon, some teachers advocate a slight vertical movement of the lower jaw with each attack. It should be remembered, though, that this is recommended only in the very lowest register of the bassoon.

THE BASSOON KEY SYSTEM   *Fingering*

Of all the woodwind instruments, the bassoon appears to many as having the most complicated and awkward fingering system. The essential reasons for this center on the following points:

1. The effect of the instrument's basic acoustical design on the fingering system.

2. The wide margin of difference that exists among bassoons of different manufacturers creates a need for a great number of alternate fingerings. In addition, there are related aspects that contribute to the notion of complexity but lie outside the realm of the instrument itself.
3. The failure, more often than not, of many teachers and writers to achieve simplicity and clarity in their presentations on bassoon.
4. The individual's attitude and frame of mind.

Since each of these points can have a direct bearing on the student's progress, they warrant consideration. The first two points are aspects over which we as musicians have little or no control. They are challenges to the craftsmen of the instrument trade. As stated earlier, each woodwind instrument poses its own unique problems, and the bassoon is no exception. While the bassoon imposes more work on the thumbs, the saxophone imposes a similar burden on the little fingers and *the sides of each index finger*. As a matter of fact, point 2 above demands considerably more of the teacher than of the student, for he or she is obligated to learn and teach the fingerings that work best for the particular student and his instrument. The best approach toward these factors is to just accept them and proceed positively to master the fingering system just as you would strive to conquer the awkward problems posed by any other instrument.

As for point 3, writers and teachers both can make the study of *any* instrument less complicated by stressing organization, simplicity, and clarity in their presentations. For example, it is best to use reference, fingering, and trill charts that are easy to read and use a minimum of symbols. The reference chart on p. 156, for example, uses no numerals; only the actual letter-name of each key is presented. Thus, the potential complexity is reduced by half; this type of chart is the best to use with beginners in their initial work. Additionally, if fingering and trill charts *show the fingering on the instrument*, the aspect of complexity is again reduced.

When presenting the bassoon key system to a student, have him, with the instrument in hand, consult the reference chart. Establish the four separate sections of the bassoon key system and which groupings of keys are assigned to which fingers. The author has found that, by beginning with the 3-and-3 routine and using no music, any music education student can learn to execute the F major scale within the time frame of the first class period of study.[1]

Point 4, attitude or frame of mind, should not be overlooked, for it can be a critical matter. It has long been established among psychologists that if one *believes* something to be difficult or complex—whether or not the difficulty is real or imagined—it in fact becomes more difficult as the intensity of one's belief increases. Some rare individuals are challenged by difficulty, but generally speaking more people are intimidated by it. Because of this, try to avoid telling beginners that something is

---

1. In using the 3-and-3 routine for bassoon, allow the beginner to play—and experience—a B-*natural* in the scale pattern at first. Then introduce the B-flat, with initial comments about key and tonality. This moment can be a valuable first experience with ear training for the youthful beginner.

Ch. 6/The Bassoon *155*

difficult or complicated. Use a different phrase, for example, "Playing over the *break* may challenge you, but with the correct approach you can do it very easily," or, "These finger patterns may appear unusual, but once you familiarize yourself with them they will become like old friends."

(Bassoon reference chart is on page 156; Standard Fingering Chart starts on page 157.)

FIGURE 115.
Bassoon reference chart

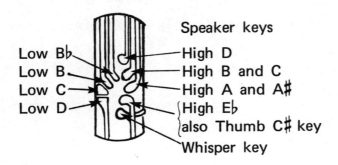
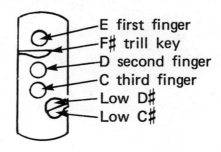
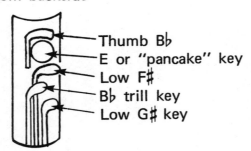
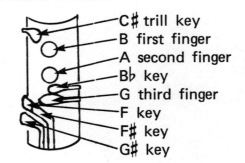

Ch. 6/The Bassoon

Standard Fingering Chart
Where marked *, place thumb on adjacent keys as needed.

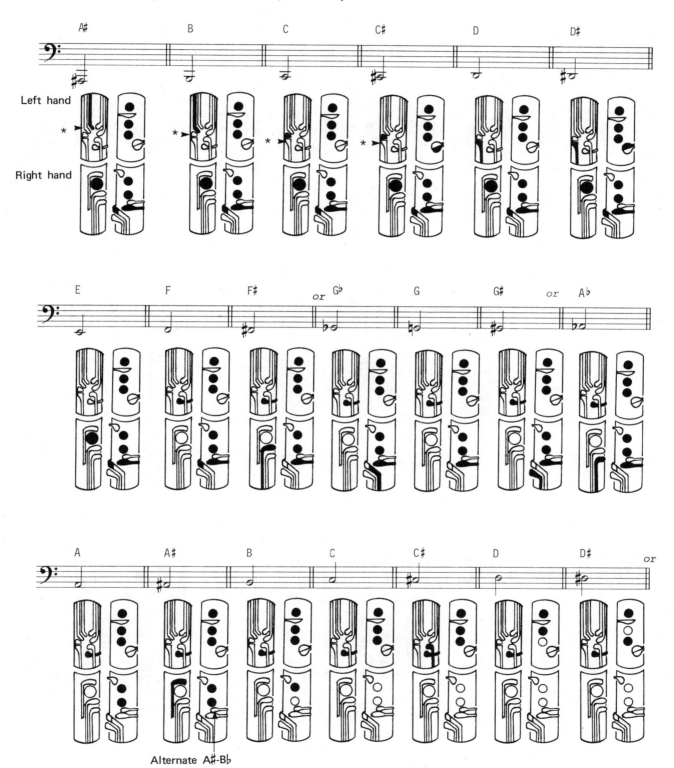

Alternate A#-B♭

158   Fundamental Techniques and Supplemental Aids/Part II

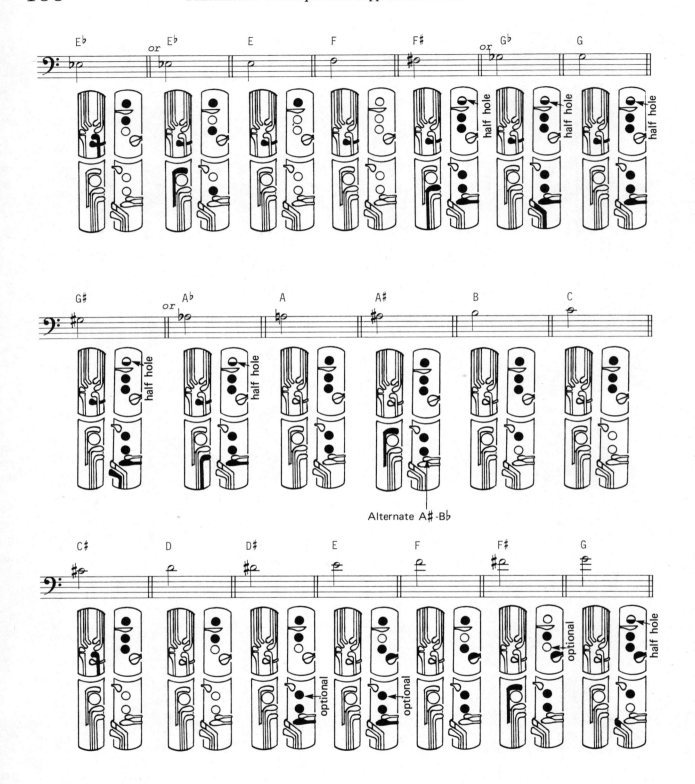

Ch. 6/The Bassoon

159

(Bassoon reference chart is on page 160; Standard Trill Chart starts on page 161.)

TRILLS

It is imperative that all bassoonists achieve a thorough working knowledge of the standard trills—the rapid alternation of two notes. Trills may be considered only as needed, at the elementary level; however, at the intermediate level a systematic study of the standard trills should begin. The following trill chart is devoted to the more common trills, which involve half steps and whole steps.

FIGURE 116.
Bassoon reference chart

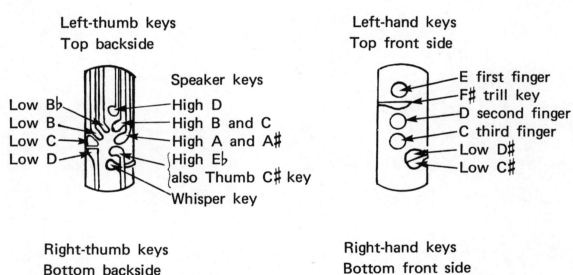
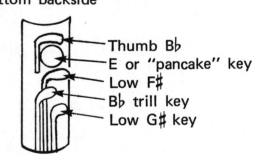
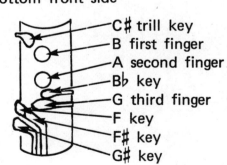

Ch. 6/The Bassoon

Standard Trill Chart

An arrow denotes the key or keys to be manipulated; the numerals (1) and (2) denote alternate trill possibilities; alternate marked * is for bassoons with the lower B-flat trill key; trills requiring impractical sliding of the fingers are not listed.

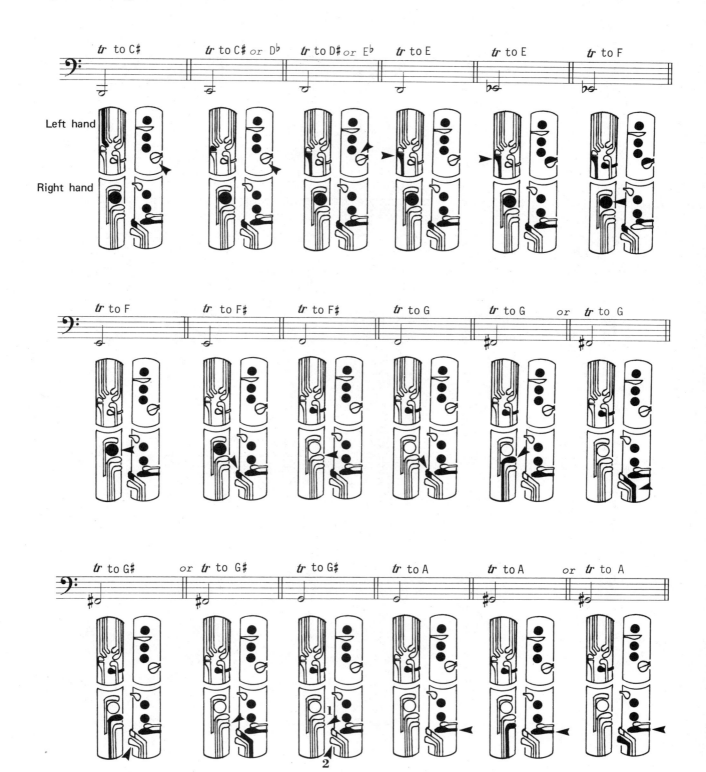

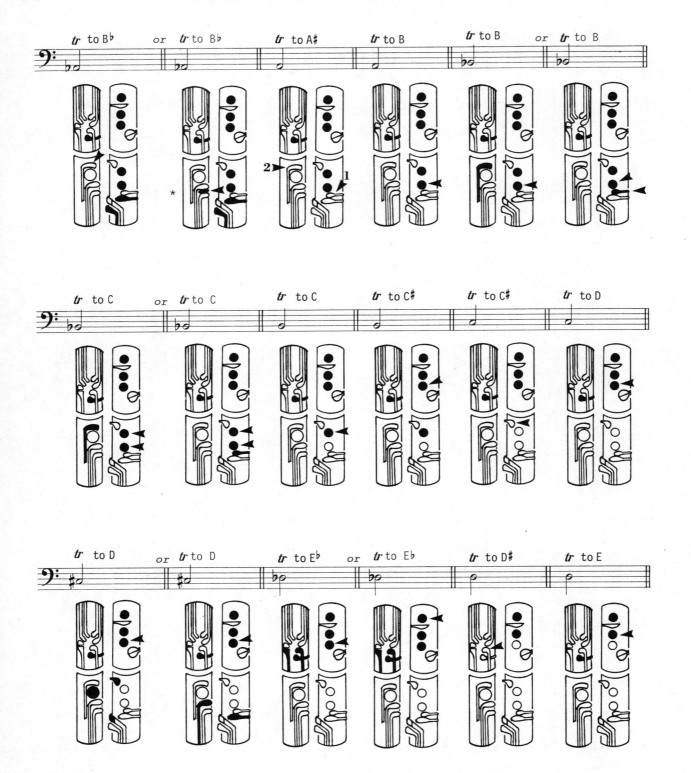

Ch. 6/The Bassoon

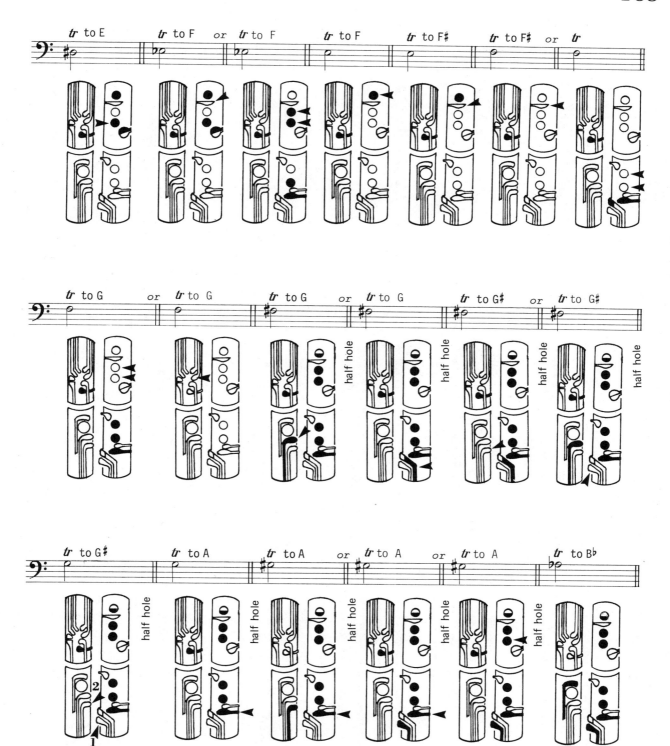

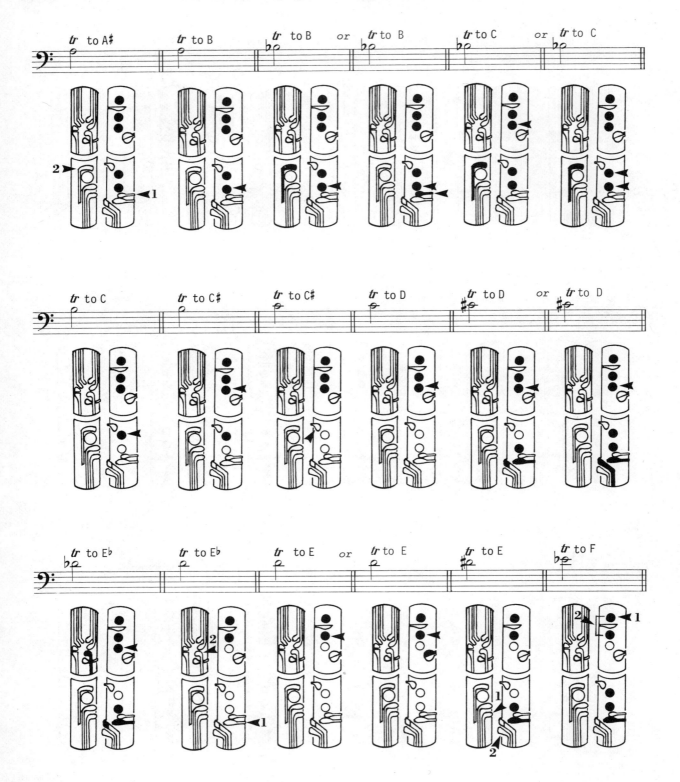

Ch. 6/The Bassoon

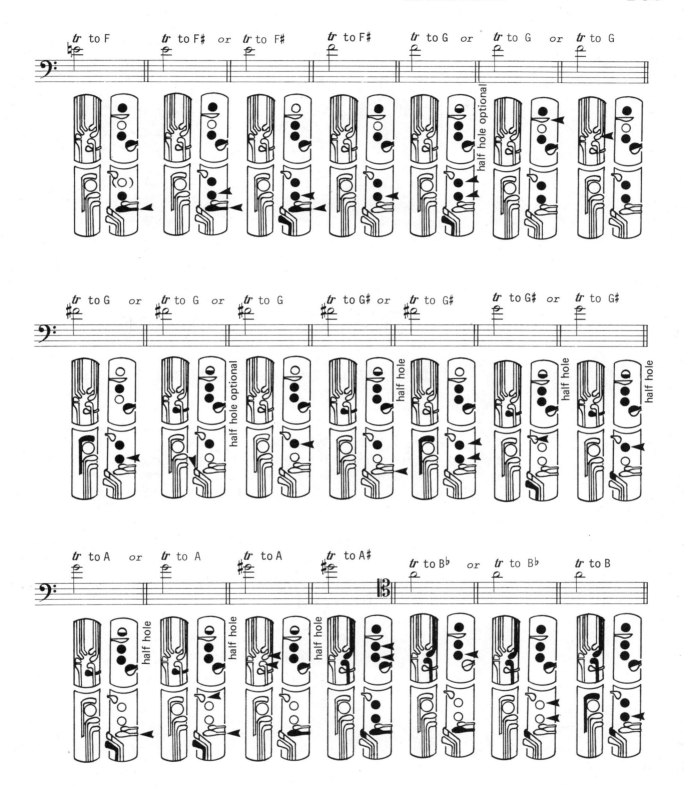

FIGURE 117.
Bassoon reference chart

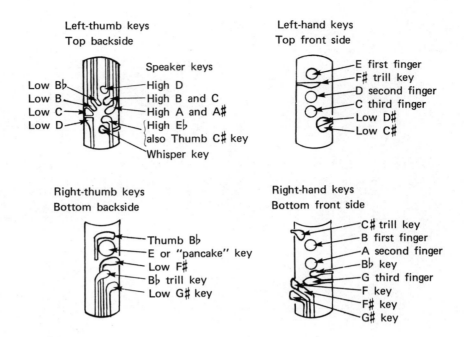

FREQUENTLY USED SPECIAL FINGERINGS

The Whisper Key

The "whisper" key was added to the bassoon near the turn of the century by Wilhelm Heckel. When open, this tiny speaker vent (see above) helps to produce a clearer tone quality in the upper register of the instrument. In the middle and lower registers, however, the whisper key should be closed. When it is closed in these registers, it becomes much easier to play soft passages. In certain technical passages, however, the whisper key is simply left open.

The following diagrams show the general use of the whisper key.
In this range depress the whisper key manually.

In this range the whisper key is automatically closed by the low E key.

In the high register the use of the whisper key is optional on certain notes; advanced students should experiment—with the aid of an instructor—to determine its best usage on a particular brand of instrument.

The Half-Hole Fingerings

The standard fingerings for these notes below require only half of the index fingertip to cover the tone hole. Other uses for the half-hole fin-

Ch. 6/The Bassoon

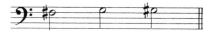

gering technique may be found in the bassoon trill chart (pp. 163–165) for tones in this range:

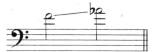

The Alternate Keys

With the exception of the E "pancake" key, all of the keys operated by the right thumb serve as alternate keys. In other words, B-flat, F-sharp, and G-sharp may be played with either the right thumb or one of the right fingers.

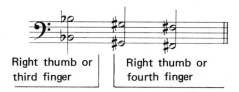

Clarinetists have the advantage of alternate keys for both little fingers.

The bassoonist is offered a similar advantage, but here the alternation occurs between the right-hand thumb and either of the last two fingers of that hand.

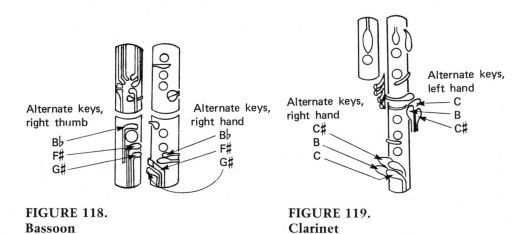

FIGURE 118.
Bassoon

FIGURE 119.
Clarinet

ALTERNATE F-SHARP (G-FLAT) FINGERINGS. F-sharp can be played either with the thumb or little finger of the right hand. In passages with other notes also playable with either the thumb or little finger, always try to alternate the right thumb with the little finger whenever possible in order to avoid sliding. See examples shown.

ALTERNATE G-SHARP (A-FLAT) FINGERINGS. G-sharp too can be played with either the right-hand thumb or little finger. Again, to avoid sliding try to alternate thumb with little finger.

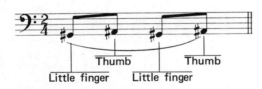

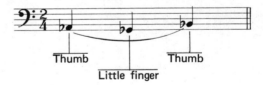

EXCEPTIONS. Occasionally it may be necessary to change fingerings *on the same note* (a practice common among organists).

In other instances it may be necessary to slide the thumb or little finger of the right hand. The choice between sliding the thumb or one of the fingers is often simply a matter of individual preference.

ALTERNATE B-FLAT FINGERINGS. The thumb B-flat is generally regarded as the basic fingering for this note. The right-hand third-finger B-flat fingering proves best for trills and chromatic passages.

The Speaker Keys

The speaker keys are used to help facilitate octave slurs and other large intervals on the bassoon. While the clarinet has one speaker key (the register key), the bassoon employs three speaker keys regularly and a fourth occasionally. These keys have two main purposes: First, they aid in "breaking" large ascending intervals. Second, they make it possible to slur certain ascending intervals without having intervening sounds occur between the two tones. It should be pointed out that the speaker keys—like the whisper key—can only be used when technically feasible.

In example *a* the slur can be made smoothly by flicking the A speaker key quickly. A light touch and immediate release of the key with the thumb is all that is required to "break" the interval. The same principle holds true for examples *b* and *c* where the D and B speaker keys respectively are used.

The following examples indicate the general function of specific speaker keys (see Figure 120) with regard to slurring:

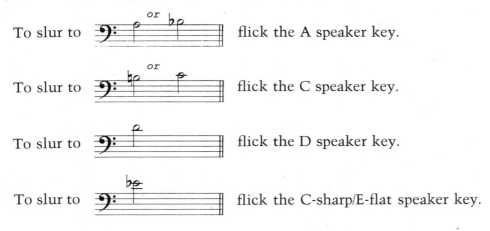

It should be noted that the E-flat speaker key serves more than one function. Consequently this same key is often identified as the C-sharp key which is used in the standard fingering for C-sharp (see Figure 115, p. 156).

FIGURE 120.
The speaker keys

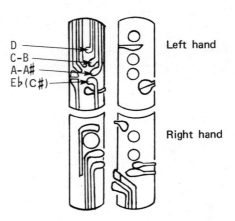

Study Questions

1. In assembling the bassoon, what sections of the instrument must be handled with particular care?
2. What would you advise the beginning bassoon student when he attempts to attach the bocal to the main body of the instrument?
3. What advice would you offer when he attempts to attach the reed to the bocal?
4. What is the key to determining instrument angle for a bassoonist?
5. Discuss bocal alignment and reed alignment for bassoonists.
6. Explain the author's use of the terms "top" and "bottom" for the sides of a bassoon reed.
7. What criteria should be considered before recommending that a student study bassoon?
8. Briefly describe the most widely recommended embouchure format for bassoonists.
9. Name a preliminary exercise that can help the beginning bassoon student establish definite guidelines for lower-jaw placement on the reed.
10. What are the external factors that can affect reed vibration?
11. Single out and list those key points about embouchure discussed under the heading "Remedial Work."
12. Name five points which can help all woodwind students in the initial development of embouchure.
13. How does the author describe the natural tonal line inherent in the acoustical design of the bassoon?
14. Describe the preferred tonal line which the author discusses.
15. Why does the author relate these teaching aids to each other: the 3-and-3 routine and "Less fingers means more air"?
16. How does the author relate breath support ("Less fingers means more air") to embouchure in his discussion of the extreme registers of the bassoon?
17. Initial attempts at tonguing should involve what areas of the tongue and reed?
18. How does the intensification of embouchure muscles differ with clarinetists and bassoonists?
19. What can you recommend to a bassoonist regarding tonguing in the lowest register?
20. What is the purpose and function of the "speaker keys" on bassoon?
21. Discuss the purpose and use of the bassoon's "whisper key."

A Problem Chart

Each woodwind instrument may be said to pose its own unique problems, and the bassoon is certainly no exception to this rule. Without question, the matter of a double-reed source of quality is of the utmost importance to the instrumental music teacher whose personal major instrument may be neither bassoon nor oboe. Even the most competent teacher using the most effective teaching techniques will be severely handicapped if unable to provide a serviceable reed source of quality for his students. This problem is by no means insurmountable; however, it does require effort and perseverance. Many music instructors have solved it in one of three ways: (1) assuming the initiative in bearing the trial and expense of finding the best commercial reed source currently available, (2) seeking out an individual professional bassoonist willing to supply reeds as needed, or (3) doing as some instrumental music teachers do—learning to make one's own bassoon reeds.

Regardless of the course you choose, how your double-reed student sounds will inevitably depend equally on effective teaching techniques, the student himself, and *a good serviceable reed.* Since an inferior reed is often the cause of many tone production problems encountered by young double-reed students, the instrumental music teacher should view the problems, probable causes, and suggestions listed below with extra caution when advising double-reed students.

Problem	Probable Cause	Suggestions for Improvement
A. The student complains of discoloration in the reed.	The reed case is not ventilated sufficiently; this can cause mildew to appear.	Plastic reed cases may be vented with a small pen knife. If a permanent reed case appears to be improperly vented, have someone drill a small hole in it.
B. The student produces a small, narrow tone.	1. More often than not, the student will not have enough reed inserted in the mouth. 2. The student may be biting and pinching the reed excessively. 3. Ocasionally the reed may be at fault.	1. Advise the student to use the wire on the reed as a guideline. That is, place enough reed into the mouth for the upper lip to touch or almost touch the wire. 2 and 3. Biting can be caused by a reed that is too soft, too stiff, or worn out. Have the student keep several reeds and date them. Also caution him about applying excessive pressure with the lower jaw.
C. When playing scales, the student's tonal line appears unusually out of proportion. That is, his sound is too large at the lower end and noticeably smaller at the upper end of the scale.	1. The student does not understand the bassoon's natural tonal line. 2. The student is not listening attentively or using his breath support correctly.	1 and 2. Use a diagram to illustrate the bassoon's natural tonal line, e.g., Natural tonal line Recommended tonal line The lines may be made "parallel" in sound by using more breath support as one plays an ascending scale line. The student should strive to produce a balanced line that is even in volume throughout the tessitura of the bassoon. (See p. 151.)

A Problem Chart (*continued*)

Problem	Probable Cause	Suggestions for Improvement
D. The student's overall pitch level is sharp or flat.	1. The reed could cause the overall pitch level to be high or low. 2. The student may need an alternate bocal. 3. The instrument may be at fault.	1. By trying different reed sources, one can then select reeds that fit one's particular needs regarding pitch. 2. Bassoons customarily are equipped with two bocals; however, in some cases a third bocal may be needed. Some companies make as many as four bocals. 3. Before making a judgment about the instrument, have it checked by a professional bassoonist. The professional may recommend a different bocal, a change in reed sizes, or having the instrument checked at the factory.
E. The internal intonation within the instrument appears generally poor.	1. The student may not be listening attentively. 2. A poor embouchure can cause these internal pitch problems. 3. The reed may be at fault. 4. Insufficient knowledge of alternate fingerings can be the fault. 5. The instrument may be at fault.	1. By assigning duos which have plenty of unisons, octaves, perfect fifths and fourths, the student can be greatly helped in training his ear. 2. Advise the student to do remedial work on embouchure and remind him that bassoonists do not play with a "stationary" or "fixed" embouchure. Lip and lower-jaw tension must vary as needed from the low to the high register. 3. Advise the student to keep several reeds on hand, and encourage him to study reed making and adjusting. 4. Alternate fingerings should be included as as a project in the student's lesson assignment. 5. Again, reserve judgment about the instrument until it is checked by a professional bassoonist. (See problem D, suggestion 3 above.)
F. The beginning student has difficulty producing the lowest tones.	1. The embouchure is usually at fault. 2. The instrument may have leaking pads.	1. Bassoonists must relax lip and lower-jaw pressure in the lowest register. Have the student use the syllable "yah" and drop the jaw slightly for the lowest tones. 2. If leaks are suspected, have a repairman examine the instrument with a leak light.
G. The student's tone lacks resonance and sounds dull overall.	1. The type of embouchure used can affect resonance and the ability to project tone. 2. The reed may be at fault.	1. A loose embouchure—where the lower lip bunches up around the reed and the lips appear parallel or even—inevitably tends to produce a darker quality that may in most cases be dull. Advise the student to try the flexed, offset embouchure grip and listen to the brighter, resonant quality this type of grip produces. Remind him that it is resonance that makes a tone project out into the audience—not just volume. 2. Have the student check with his reed source regarding the availability of brighter reeds.

A Problem Chart (*continued*)

Problem	Probable Cause	Suggestions for Improvement
H. The overall tone quality is thin and reedy.	The reed is too soft for the student.	The reed may be made stiffer by adjusting it; it may however be necessary to obtain harder reeds.
I. The overall tone quality is dark and breathy.	The reed is too stiff for the student.	The reed may be adjusted to make it softer, or it may be necessary to obtain softer reeds.
J. The student complains of difficulty in tonguing in the low register.	1. Improper use of the embouchure is usually the cause of this problem.	1. Professional bassoonists may be observed moving the lower jaw as they tongue in the lowest register. By loosening the embouchure grip on each attack, pressure is taken off the reed; this action helps to facilitate tonguing in the lowest register.
	2. The reed can be at fault.	2. If the reed is suspected, it may need to be adjusted. If it cannot be adjusted, remind the student of the need for keeping several reeds on hand.
K. When reading a lesson preparation, the student stops and starts excessively.	The student is using improper reading habits when he practices.	Fluency in reading is achieved through gradualism in the initial stage of study. Advise the student to practice at slow tempos in the beginning, gradually increasing his speed over several days.

Teaching Aids

1. Show the student how to assemble the bassoon so as to avoid damaging the extension levers and the bocal.
2. The choice between using a neck strap or a seat belt is the individual's.
3. The use of the hand rest will depend on the size of the individual's hand.
4. Have the student master the "Pencil Exercise."
5. Next, have the student demonstrate the recommended embouchure, using only the reed. Then have him make the reed "crow."
6. *Twist* the reed on the bocal—do not push it on!
7. Have the student begin with the 3-and-3 fingering routine to just *seat* or *cover* the tone holes. He should not play the instrument.
8. Next, have him use the 3-and-3 routine and play the instrument.
9. As the student develops more facility, introduce the "Less fingers means more air" concept.
10. Additional points for embouchure are: (1) both lips should cover the teeth; (2) recommend the offset grip, that is, with the lower jaw pulled back and the upper lip placed near the wire on the reed; and (3) strive to keep the lower lip smooth and flexed—not loose and bunched-up around the reed.
11. Explain the correct use of the whisper key, and introduce the speaker keys as needed.
12. Have student use syllable "yah" to achieve an open throat when playing in the lowest register.
13. He should experiment with lip tension to find the "correct placement" of the tone.
14. Have student use a mirror so that he may see his embouchure.
15. The embouchure should relax in the lowest register and gradually intensify from the middle to the highest register.

FIGURE 121.
Visual reminders: approximate lower-jaw position

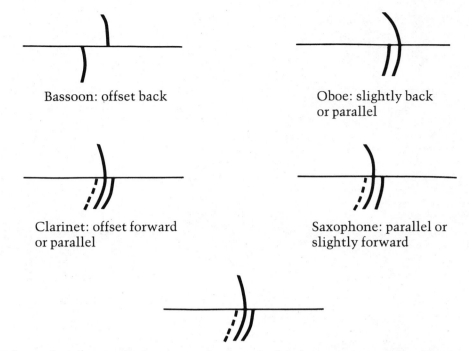

Bassoon Literature

SELECTED LIST OF GRADED SOLOS

The following list has been compiled as a convenient source reference for the instrumental music teacher. It is by no means complete, and readers are encouraged to study publisher catalog listings for their additional needs. This listing is intended to serve as a primer offering; although it has been carefully graded, some overlapping should of course be expected.

Considering the solos' technical difficulty, they have been ranked according to the following scale:

Grades 1–2: very easy to easy
Grades 3–4: moderate to moderately difficult
Grades 5–6: difficult to very difficult

Grades 1–2

Composer	Title	Publisher
Bach (arr. Stouffer)	Minuet	Kendor
Beethoven	Adagio Cantabile	Southern
Buchtel	"Neptune"	Kjos
	"The Reluctant Clown"	Mills
	Valse Romantique	Volkwein
Dearnley	Eight Easy Pieces	Chester
DeLamarter	Folk Song	Witmark
Koepke	Rondo	Rubank
Merle	"Mummers"	Carl Fischer
Mozart	*Mozart Solo Album*	Oxford
Schubert (arr. Isaac)	Three Themes	Carl Fischer
Schumann	"Traumerei" and "Romanze"	Carl Fischer

Grades 1–2 (continued)

Composer	Title	Publisher
Weber	*Three Favorites*	Belwin
Weinberger	Sonatine	Carl Fischer
Weissenborn	"Romance"	International
Willner	*Classical Album*	Boosey & Hawkes

Grades 3–4

Composer	Title	Publisher
Baines	Introduction and Hornpipe	AMP
Bakaleinikoff	Three Pieces for Bassoon	Belwin
Bratton	"The Teddy Bears' Picnic"	Witmark
Bates	Barcarolle	Alfred
Barret	Cantilene	Boosey & Hawkes
DeLamarter	Arietta	Witmark
Dunhill	Lyric Suite	Boosey & Hawkes
Galliard	Six Sonatas	McGinnis and Marx
Glière	Impromptu	International
Handel (arr. Gee)	Andante and Allegro	Southern
Jancourt	"Rêverie"	Carl Fischer
Labate	Humoresque in B-flat	Alfred
Marcello (arr. Oubradous)	Allegretto	Alfred
Mozart (ed. Pezzi)	Adagio	Southern
Pares	"Crepuscule"	Carl Fischer
Tcherepnin	Variations Simples	G. Schirmer
Weber	Hungarian Fantasy	Carl Fischer
Weissenborn	Capriccioso	International
	Romance	Rubank
(ed. H. Voxman)	"Song Without Words"	Rubank

Grades 5–6

Composer	Title	Publisher
Bach, J. C.	Concerto in E-flat	Sikorski
Bourdeau (ed. H. Voxman)	Premier Solo	Rubank
Bozza	Recitative, Sicilienne et Rondo	Leduc
Busser	Concertino, Op. 80	Leduc
Cohn	Declamation and Toccata	Elkan-Vogel
Decruck	Scherzo Fantasque	Baron
Handel	Concerto in C Minor	Baron
Hindemith	Sonata	AMP
Hummel	Concerto	Rubank
Mozart	Concerto in B-flat, K. 191	Edition Musicus
Pierné	Solo de Concert	Rubank
Saint-Saëns	Sonata, Op. 168	Durand
Telemann	Sonata in F Major	International
Vivaldi	Concerto in E Minor	International

CLASS METHODS

See "Class Methods for the Public School Instrumental Music Program," pp. 63–64.

INDIVIDUAL METHODS AND SUPPLEMENTAL STUDIES

Major Applied Methods

BELWIN SERIES FOR BASSOON

Bassoon Method (3 vols.) by K. Gekeler and N. Hovey.

Method For Bassoon (2 vols.) by D. Lentz.

Bassoon Student by F. Weber and H. T. Paine is a three-volume method so designed to be correlated with four additional volumes of solos, études, and technical exercises.

Published by Belwin-Mills, Melville, N.Y.

RUBANK SERIES FOR BASSOON

Elementary Method for Bassoon by J. E. Skornicka.

Intermediate Method for Bassoon by H. Voxman.

Advanced Method for Bassoon (2 vols.) by H. Voxman and W. Gower.

Published by Rubank, Inc., Miami, Fla. In Chapter 3 several key points were cited regarding the use of both American and European applied method books at the initial level of instrumental study. The most important point made in that discussion centered on the major difference between certain American and European music method books: On the one hand, many American method books *assume no prior musical study;* on the other, most of the celebrated European or European-influenced method books *assume prior musical study,* and tend to progress from elementary to intermediate levels at a rate that becomes impractical for students having no preparatory music background. Consequently, music methods such as H. Klosé's *Celebrated Method for the Clarinet* or Julius Weissenborn's *Practical Method for the Bassoon* are never used by American instrumental music teachers at the initial level of study. These books are, however, widely used by American instru-

mental music teachers after the student has completed the basic foundation work.

This situation is by no means limited to the abovementioned two instruments; it is in fact the case with many method books written for all woodwinds. In consequence of this fact, the following method books are recommended for study only after the bassoon student has completed his basic foundation work with a standard American method book.

Complete Bassoon Method by E. Jancourt. Published by Boosey & Hawkes, Oceanside, N.Y.

Tutor for Bassoon by Langey. Published by Carl Fischer, New York, N.Y.

Enseignement Complet du Basson (3 vols.) by F. Oubradous. Published by Baron, Long Island, N.Y.

Practical Method for Bassoon by J. Weissenborn. Published by Carl Fischer, New York, N.Y.

Bassoon Studies, Op. 8, 2 vols. by J. Weissenborn. Published by Carl Fischer, New York, N.Y.

Supplemental Studies

Twenty Studies for Bassoon by M. Bitsch. Published by Leduc, Paris, France.

Eighteen Studies by J. B. Gambaro. Published by International, New York, N.Y.

Le Debutant Bassoniste by J. Haultier. Published by Leduc, Paris, France.

Six Caprices by C. Jacobi. Published by International, New York, N.Y.

25 Studies in Scales and Chords by L. Milde. Published by International, New York, N.Y.

Scales and Daily Exercises for Bassoon by G. Pares. Published by Carl Fischer, New York, N.Y.

Twenty Studies for Bassoon by A. Vaulet, ed. H. Voxman. Published by Rubank.

RECORDINGS OF BASSOON LITERATURE

Pedagogically Oriented Recordings

The Music Minus One Series. Essentially, the Music Minus One Corporation makes professionally recorded back-

grounds—minus a particular "solo" instrument—for all types of music, including the orchestral concerto, the sonata, chamber music, and various jazz forms. The original concept behind the

MMO series was to afford the student performer a professional accompaniment against which to practice and perform a musical work in its original and complete context, that is, with full orchestra, string quartet, or jazz ensemble, as the case might be. The bulk of the recorded accompaniments made by MMO falls in this category.

Recently, MMO began a new "Laureate Series," which embraces a wider spectrum and is even more pedagogically oriented than the aforementioned recordings. Unfortunately, this new series is not yet available for bassoon. Among the older offerings—all of which are certainly recommended—the MMO 144 *Solos for the Bassoon Player* will be of particular interest to the student bassoonist. This series includes works by J. S. Bach, Beethoven, Bizet, Donizetti, Moussorgsky, Prokofiev, Stravinsky, and Tchaikovsky. This series is published by Music Minus One, 43 West 61 Street, New York, N.Y.

Special Collections

The following recorded collections will be of special interest to the bassoonist. Each album is devoted primarily to selected bassoon literature and includes performances by distinguished twentieth-century bassoonists. The list is by no means complete; it is intended to serve only as a beginning source-reference for the student.

Arthur Grossman Plays Bassoon
Saint-Saëns: Sonata for Bassoon and Piano
Tansman: Sonatine for Bassoon and Piano
Persichetti: "Parable IV" for Solo Bassoon
Perle: Three Inventions for Solo Bassoon
Cascarino: Sonata for Bassoon and Piano. Arthur Grossman (bassoon) and Randolph Hokanson (piano). Coronet LPS 2741
Four Bassoon Concertos
Vivaldi: Concerto No. 1 in C Major
Concerto in B-flat Major, "La Notte"
Concerto No. 3 in A Minor
Concerto No. 4 in C Major
Virginio Bianchi. Vox STPL 510.740
Leonard Sharrow, Bassoon
Luke: Concerto for Bassoon and Orchestra
Welcher: Concerto da Camera. Leonard Sharrow. Crystal S852
Music for Bassoon and Cello

Arma: "Three Evolutions" for Bassoon Alone
Arnold: Fantasy for Bassoon Alone
Bizet: Little Duet for Bassoon and Cello
Hindemith: Four Pieces for Bassoon and Cello
Jacob: Partita for Solo Bassoon
Mozart: Sonata in B-flat, K.292
Otto Eifert (bassoon), and Roy Christensen (cellist). Gasparo GS103 (Box 90574, Nashville, Tenn.)
Oboes, English Horns, Bassoons, and Contrabassoon: Music for Double-Reed Ensemble
Bach, J. S.: Ricercar [from *The Musical Offering*]
Handel: Two Pieces for Oboes, English Horns, and Bassoon
Heussenstamm: Set for Double-Reeds
Pillin: Three Pieces for Double-Reed Septet. Bert Gassman, Barbara Winters (oboes); Donald Muggeridge, Peter Christ (english horns); David Breidenthal, Walter Ritchie (bassoons); and Frederick Dutton, (contrabassoon). Crystal S871

Traditional Recordings

Bach, J. C.: Concerto in B. F. Henker. Deutsche Grammophon Gesellschaft ARC 3199
_____: Concerto in E-flat. G. Zukerman. Turnabout 34278
Boismortier: Concerto in D. M. Allard. Nonesuch 71080
_____: Concerto in D. G. Zukerman. Turnabout 34304
Beethoven: Octet For Winds, Op. 103. The New York Wind Ensemble (A. Weisberg, bassoon). Everest CPT 567-52405-5559
Bozza: Sonatine for Flute and Bassoon. Felix Skowronek (flute); and Arthur Grossman (bassoon). Crystal 351
Cascarino: Sonata. Sol Schoenbach. Columbia MS6421
Mozart: Concerto for Bassoon, K.191. Bernard Garfield. Columbia MS 6451
_____: Concerto for Bassoon, K.191. Leonard Sharrow. RCA LM 1030
_____: Divertimento No. 2 in B-flat Major, K.ANH.229 for Two Clarinets and Bassoon. L. Wlach, R. Bartosek (clarinets); and Karl Oehlberger (bassoon). Westminster WL 50-22
Persichetti: "Parable IV" for Solo Bassoon. A. Grossman. Coronet 2741
Poulenc: Sonata for Clarinet and Bassoon. A. Gigliotti (clarinet) and B. Garfield (bassoon). Golden Crest 4115

————: Trio for Piano, Oboe, and Bassoon. J. Fevrier (piano), R. Casier (oboe), and Gérard Faisandrier (bassoon). Angel S36261

Saint-Saëns: Sonata for Bassoon and Piano. A. Grossman (bassoon) and R. Hokanson (piano). Coronet 2741

Smith: "Straws" for Flute and Bassoon. F. Skowronek (flute) and A. Grossman (bassoon). Crystal 351

Stamitz: Concerto in F for Bassoon and Orchestra. G. Zukerman. Turnabout 34093

Weber: Andante and Rondo in C. B. Garfield. Columbia MS 6977

————: Andante and Rondo in C. G. Zukerman. Turnabout 4039

————: Hungarian Fantasy for Bassoon. B. Garfield. Columbia MS 6977

The Saxophone

7

FIGURE 122.
E-flat alto saxophone

Photograph courtesy of The Selmer Company, Elkhart, Indiana.

Saxophone Assembly

FIGURE 123.

FIGURE 124.

Instrument Assembly and Care

Although the saxophone has the advantage of a completely metal body, and assembly involves only the mouthpiece, neck, and main body, the instrument nonetheless poses its own unique problems regarding assembly and care. Like the bassoon, it has long external metal rods that can be bent if mishandled. Additionally, the entire key network is based on the "plateau system"; it is here that most problems occur.

The terms "plateau system" and "open-ring system" are used to denote the design of the network of keys on woodwind instruments. The older open-ring system allows for many of the fingers to seal and close certain tone holes on the instrument. The newer plateau system, on the other hand, does not require that the fingers directly touch and close the open tone holes. Instead, the fingers touch the top of a metal key that has a soft pad affixed beneath it which closes and seals the tone holes. Today most woodwind instruments utilize a combination of these two systems. Because of the unusually large tone hole openings found on saxophones, these instruments are built entirely on the plateau system of design.

Probably the most harm is done to saxophones through improper care and handling. In joining the neck to the body of the instrument, care should be taken not to damage the cork or plastic covered end of the octave key-extension lever. The tenon of the neck should be cleaned regularly; a moderate amount of cork grease may be applied infrequently. However, the cork end of the neck should be greased as often as needed. The mouthpiece may be washed with soap in lukewarm water every six to eight weeks. It is also best to swab the saxophone with a soft cloth after use.

The key mechanism should be oiled at the pivotal posts at least three times a year. The design of the saxophone is such that in playing, the tone holes are covered by pads rather than one's fingers. These "skin pads" wear out with age—which is normal—and eventually cease to seat properly. Quite often though, the pad key may have been knocked out of alignment, causing pad leakage. Additionally, if certain keys on the main body of the instrument become bent, this can affect one or more related keys in a chain-reaction pattern. Consequently, what may on the surface appear as one bent key may in fact be much more involved. Since the plateau key alignment on saxophones is such a sensitive matter, it is best that the instruments be returned to the case when not in use.

In closing, there are two important recommendations that warrant consideration:

1. It is wise to invest in only the best neck strap made, for inferior straps can break; this could lead to serious repair problems.

2. The instrumental teacher and older saxophonists should buy a leak light in order to check minor pad leaks. In many cases a small leak can be corrected by simply tying the key closed with soft string, and letting it sit overnight. One may also use a cork wedge to depress the key, leaving it in that position overnight.

Instrument Angle and Hand Position

The design of the alto saxophone is such that it is generally held at an angle, as pictured in Figures 125 and 126. By and large, most saxophonists grip the instrument so that the left hand rests near the center of the person's body, with the right hand placed downward and angled slightly to the right. This basic position applies for all saxophones except the straight soprano models (which are held like B-flat clarinets at a medium angle away from the body). Note, however, that the larger baritone and bass saxophones are often used with stands, and this results in a minor angle adjustment of the basic position pictured. The primary reason for these positions is one of practicality. Minor adjustments in angle and alignment are usually dictated by individual need and preference. It may be noted that where any extreme position is employed there is a corresponding extreme root cause—usually malocclusion.

FIGURE 125. (left) Instrument angle—standing position

FIGURE 126. (right) Sitting position

The alignment of the neckpiece has some leeway; however, like the bocal on a bassoon it too has its limitations. On curved saxophones this leeway is imperative to attaining comfort and an effective grip. If the neckpiece is turned excessively, however, the octave mechanism will not work properly. (See Figure 127.)

FIGURE 127. Alignment of the neck may be adjusted *slightly* to left or right of center to accommodate individual need

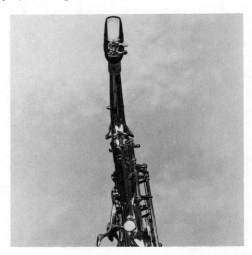

It is recommended that the student grip the saxophone with the hands relaxed, using the natural arch that occurs. The left-hand grip is generally self-adjusting; it requires a "wraparound" hand position due to the high D, D-sharp, E, and F keys. The right hand poses no special problems, although occasionally some students may extend the thumb too far past the thumb rest.

It would be wise to caution those students who may eventually double on clarinet or flute to place their fingers evenly over the pearl buttons. It is very easy to cultivate a lackadaisical finger placement where the fingers touch only as little as half the pearl buttons. Open-ring clarinets and flutes require exact finger placement, or else air will escape from the tone holes. Thus, the habit of even and centered finger placement is imperative to the prospective doubler on woodwinds (see Figure 128).

FIGURE 128. Center the fingers evenly over the pearl buttons

EMBOUCHURE

The preferred embouchure for saxophone is shown in Figure 129; an incorrect but commonly used embouchure is shown in Figure 130.

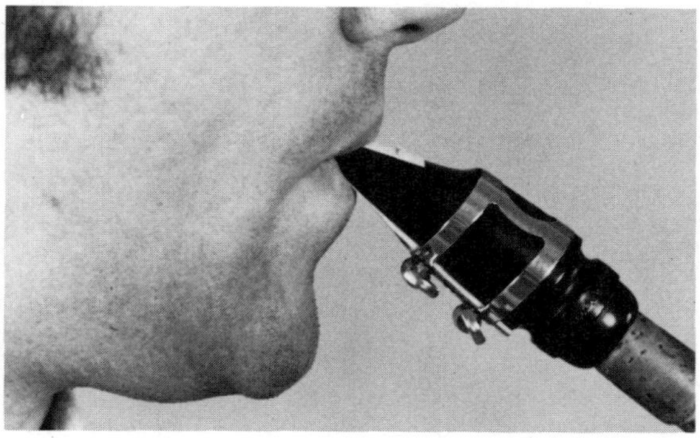

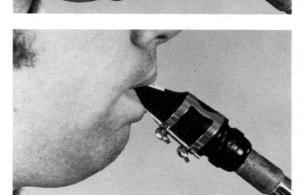

Tone Production

FIGURE 129. Recommended embouchure

FIGURE 130. Ineffective embouchure

The recommended embouchure format may be used for the entire saxophone family (with an optional minor modification for the baritone and bass members). Just as with the lower bass and contrabass clarinets, the baritone and bass saxophones may require a more open, less pronounced offset grip.

An examination of Figure 129 shows the lip muscles flexed, the lower lip and chin area smooth, and the occlusion slightly offset. Although the flexed, offset grip may appear to some as a tightly flexed, vice-like grip, it should be remembered that this is not in fact the case. To the contrary, the pressure of the lower teeth against the lip is held poised at a point that insures stability of control and pitch while allowing for complete freedom of single-reed vibration. By using flexed lips, the amount of lip surface placed on the vibrating reed is reduced to a minimum, thus allowing for greater reed vibration.

There are several teaching aids that can prove most beneficial in developing the flexed offset embouchure for saxophone. First, of course, the student should study the pictures above in order to establish a visual concept of the recommended embouchure. Second, he should practice flexing the lips without the mouthpiece periodically during the day. This will strengthen the lip muscles that have lain dormant and facilitate progress in other exercises, such as those used with the mouthpiece and a mirror. Third, the benefits of the clarinetists' mouthpiece exercise can be realized by student saxophonists also.

THE MOUTHPIECE EXERCISE

This is shown below for E-flat alto saxophone at concert pitch. With

mouthpiece and neck attached, the student should strive to produce the even tone shown. The tone should be full, straight, and consistent. (He should use a mirror to check lip muscles.) If the tone wavers, it is an indication of weak lip muscles or poor breath support. It is best that this exercise be practiced prior to each practice session for only a few minutes. It can serve to develop the lip muscles, and provides an excellent check on such matters as lower-jaw pressure, consistency in muscular flex of the lip muscles, and amount of mouthpiece insertion.

With regular practice and applied initiative, the student can develop the endurance that the flexed offset grip requires and subsequently use this embouchure without conscious effort. By all means remember that it takes time to develop an effective embouchure, and advise beginning students to *rest when their lips become tired*. Three ten-minute practice sessions are by far more profitable than one forty-five minute session, for most single-reed students working on embouchure development.

Thus far, four key teaching aids in developing saxophone embouchure have been cited: (1) visual aids such as pictures, live demonstrations, and the use of a mirror, (2) lip exercises without the mouthpiece, (3) the mouthpiece exercise, and (4) short practice sessions of five to ten minutes. Additionally, the following points can also be of help:

1. Substituting a pencil for the mouthpiece, have the student extend the lower jaw forward and up (the upper teeth remain stationary). Repetition of this exercise can help cultivate the "feel" of the offset grip, and save wear and tear on reeds and mouthpieces for younger players. (See Figure 131.)

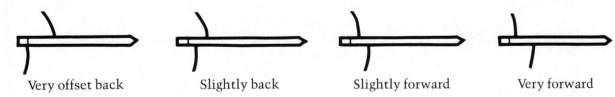

FIGURE 131.
Pencil exercise

Although this exercise involves extreme positions (forward and back), remember that its object is simply *to gain a sense of direction* in lower-jaw placement. The exact amount of lower-jaw extension to be used when playing the mouthpiece may vary for each person. As stated earlier, a slightly offset lower jaw position is recommended for saxophone.

2. Remind the student that the upper teeth rest on top of the mouthpiece, with the lower lip turned in slightly over the teeth.

3. Caution the student against bunching the lower lip around the reed or turning too much lip inward.

4. Explain that for each effect there is always a cause. For example, if

the tendency is to squeak often and produce a tone too large, open, and flat in character, then too much mouthpiece has been inserted into the mouth. If the sound of the tone is pinched, stuffy, and small, it is likely that too little mouthpiece is in the mouth.

5. Advise the student to experiment with the amount of mouthpiece inserted into the mouth and then strive to maintain that position giving the best sound and most control. If the sound remains choked in character—or too open—then have him experiment with the amount of pressure exerted from the lower teeth against the lower lip. These two simple experiments can prove invaluable in producing a centered, well-placed tone.

6. When referring to the muscular tension of the lips, use the phrase "circular grip." The object here is to achieve an oval-shaped flex of the lips, with appropriate pressure from the lower teeth.

7. If the student's lower lip persists in bunching around the reed, take a pencil and, placing it under the reed against the lip, slide it downward so as to smooth or flatten these muscles. Also, the student can be advised to use the "double lip" embouchure for a *few minutes* each day: Generally, when a student tries the double-lip embouchure, he will usually flex the lower lip muscles in a flat and smooth manner. Once he experiences the feel of a flexed and smooth lower lip position, he can then apply this new muscular control to the recommended single-lip embouchure.

BREATH SUPPORT

The acoustical design of the saxophone is such that its natural tonal line may sound uneven, as depicted in Figure 132.

FIGURE 132. Natural tonal line

By and large, it is safe to say that most artistically minded musical performers prefer a tonal line with consistency in its basic size and color. "Basic size" in this instance refers to a consistent *mezzo-forte* volume level, and "basic color" to the overall character of timbre (not the specific low, middle, or high registers which reflect shadings of the basic timbre). For example, it may be observed that one clarinetist has an overall brighter or darker tone quality than another. Ideally the tonal line for saxophone should appear as in Figure 133. It should be noted that this illustration depicts consistency in both contour and color.

FIGURE 133. Recommended tonal line

In order to achieve an even tonal line on saxophone, the following points should be kept in mind:

1. The teaching aid, "Less fingers means more air," may be applied to saxophones as well as other winds. More often than not most student saxophonists will play the first octave of the C major scale as depicted in Figure 132. In the initial stage of study this is, of course, expected. However, as the student gains control over the lowest tones (C, B-natural, and B-flat), he can do two things to improve this uneven tonal line: First, he should be on guard against excessive dropping of the jaw—which makes the lower tones sound larger and louder—remembering to begin the lower tones with a *mezzo-forte* volume level, not a *forte* level. (Many students continue to play loud in the low register out of habit.) Second, he can increase breath pressure as he ascends to the top of the C scale. The net result will be a tonal line that sounds even in character.

When playing from high C to high F, many students tend to produce a pinched and narrow tonal line. In this register an increase in breath pressure is definitely needed in order to balance the tonal line.

2. There are two key words that can play a decisive role in teaching this matter of breath support and beautiful tone: (1) "experiment" and (2) "contrast."

To illustrate, have the student sustain a tone and deliberately overblow and then underblow it. Next, have him strive for a compromise pressure that lies between these two extremes. In executing these simple tasks, the student begins his earliest ear training, and creates his own guidelines where previously none existed. These sounds resulting from too much or too little breath pressure stand in *diametric contrast* to each other, and highlight the well-placed, centered tone produced by a correctly measured amount of air pressure.

3. The 3-and-3 routine is recommended for all woodwind students. It should be noted that: (1) no music is needed with beginning students, (2) the music should be slurred, and (3) the student should try to maintain a constant mezzo-forte volume level throughout each exercise. With some students the low C may have to be omitted at first, then added later at the instructor's discretion.

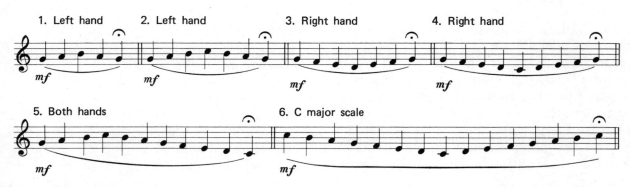

The 3-and-3 routine for saxophone

4. The principle of the 3-and-3 routine should be applied to subsequent studies of scales and to all little-finger exercises.

Ch. 7/The Saxophone *187*

TONGUING

With all single-reed students it is best to begin tonguing only after preliminary work has been accomplished with embouchure, breath support, and general control. When tonguing is presented, the student should be advised to simply place the tip of the tongue at the tip of the reed, using the syllable "dah." The important point to remember in developing the basic single-tongue stroke is initial tongue placement. If the habit of tonguing low on the reed is allowed to become inveterate, it can be difficult if not impossible to correct.

A visual demonstration can be of immense help. If the instructor does not play saxophone, he can select a capable advanced student to demonstrate approximate tongue placement. The demonstrator should leave the tip of the tongue against the tip of the reed and withdraw the instrument from the mouth slightly, extending the tongue forward slightly. Although there may be prettier sights than this demonstration, the main point will be very effectively made. (See Figures 86 and 87, p. 114.)

It was pointed out earlier that not all single-reed students may use the exact tip of the tongue for the single tongue stroke. It may be that an area one-eighth or even one-quarter of an inch from the tongue tip will strike the reed. Some leeway must be expected in this matter. The main objective of recommending "tip-to-tip" placement is to get the single-reed student to make an incisive, clean, sharp attack. Such attacks are best produced when the points of contact display *immediate response* to touch. Such is the nature of the relationship between the tongue tip and the vibrating tip of the reed.

Many young students may use various physical motions other than tongue movement in executing a tongued passage. The teacher should remember that tonguing requires only the movement of the tongue. Any extraneous movement of the body should be discouraged.

(Saxophone reference chart is on page 188; Standard Fingering Chart starts on page 189.)

Fingering

FIGURE 134.
Saxophone reference chart

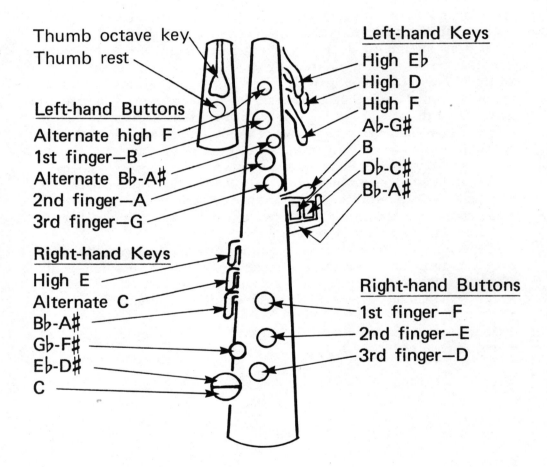

Standard Fingering Chart
Arpeggio fingering denoted by

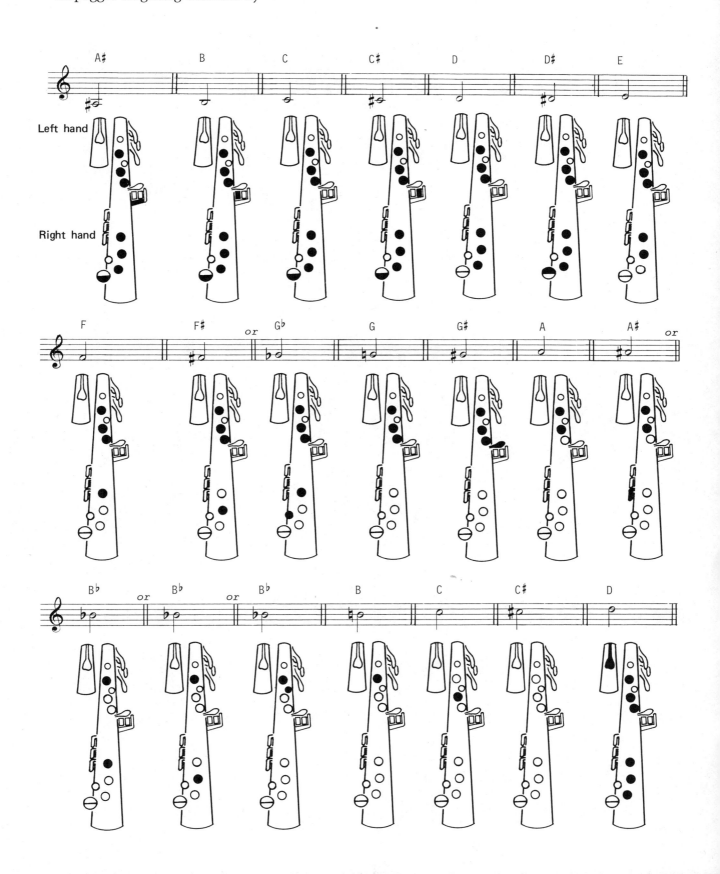

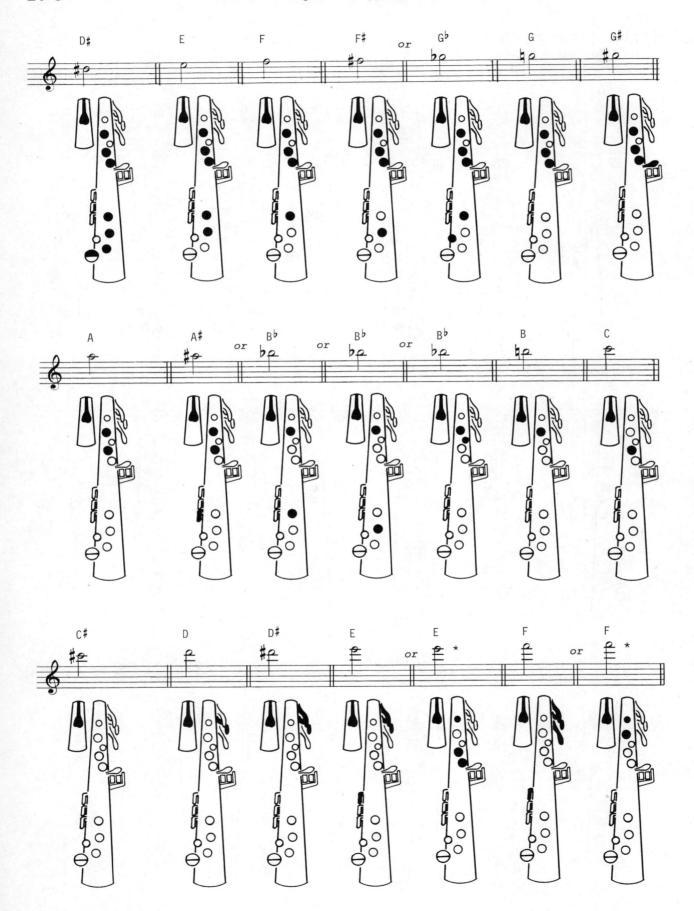

Ch. 7/The Saxophone

(Saxophone reference chart is on page 192; Standard Trill Chart starts on page 193.)

TRILLS

The saxophone—patented in 1846 by Adolphe Sax—is the newest member of the woodwind family. Consequently, the main body of music literature for saxophone consists of transcribed older music and original music composed since expressly for saxophone. The earlier styles of music utilized ornaments (trills, grace notes, etc.) to a much larger extent than did subsequent periods. Of all the musical ornaments used down through the ages, it is the trill—the rapid alternation of two notes—that has remained the most consistently popular among composers. It follows then that saxophonists must acquire a thorough knowledge of trills.

The following trill chart is devoted to the more common trills, which involve half steps and whole steps.

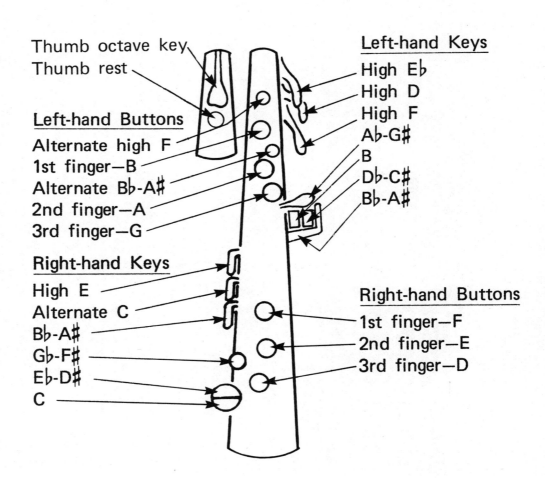

FIGURE 135. Saxophone reference chart

Standard Trill Chart

An arrow denotes the key or keys to be manipulated; an asterisk indicates cross fingers by alternating between F and F-sharp.

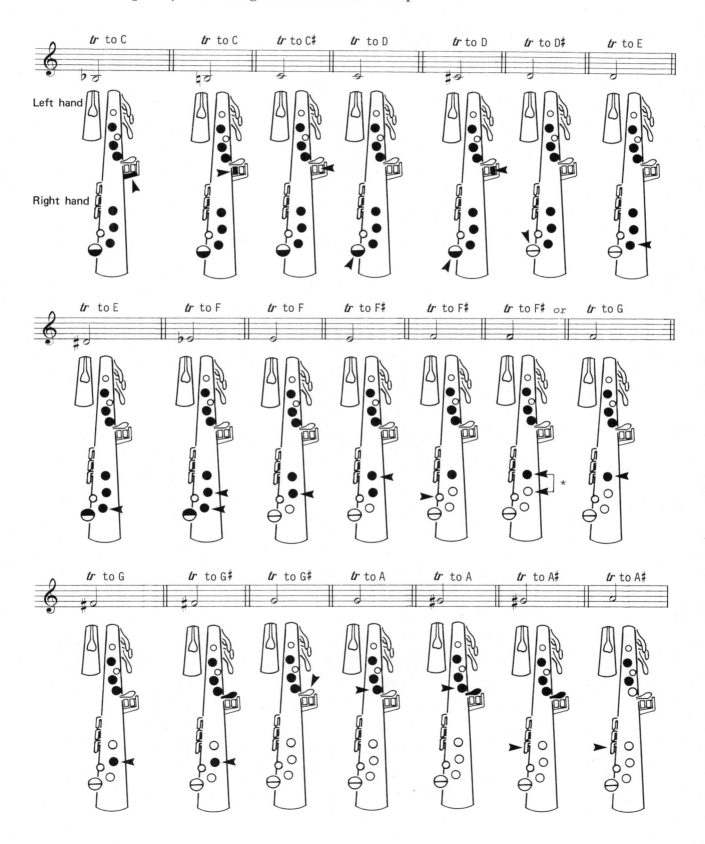

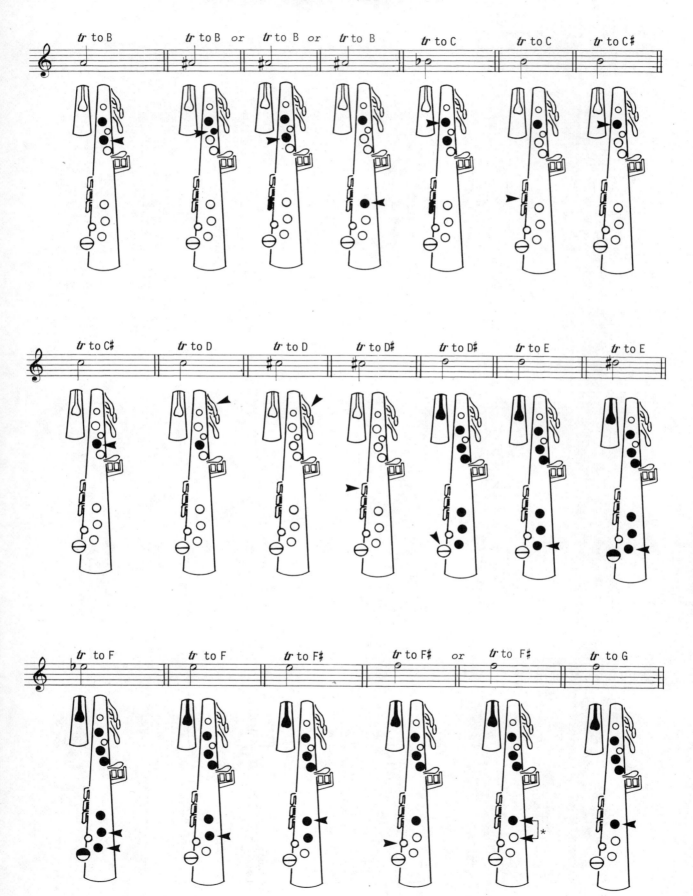

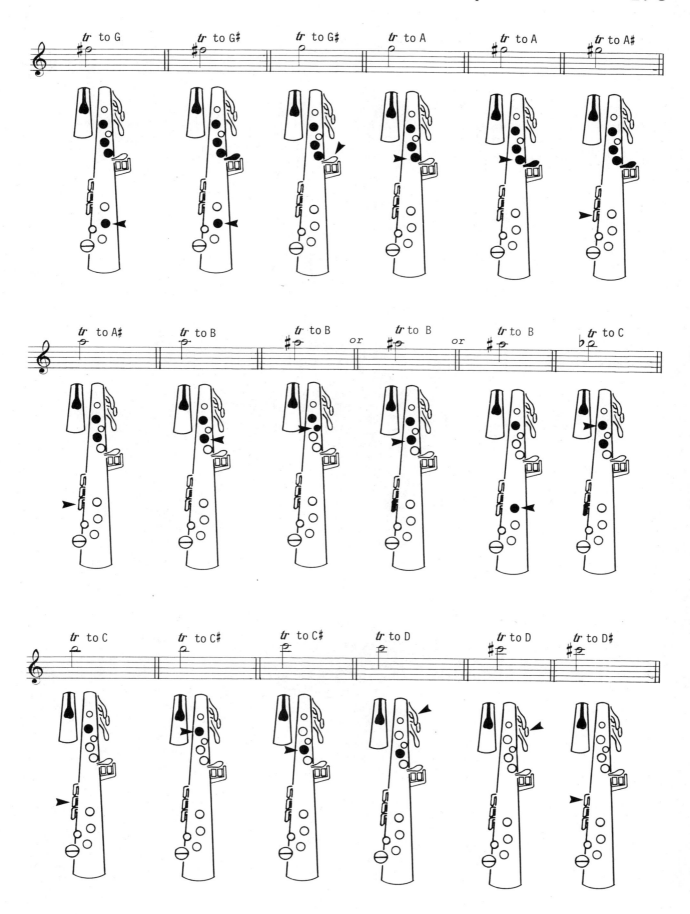

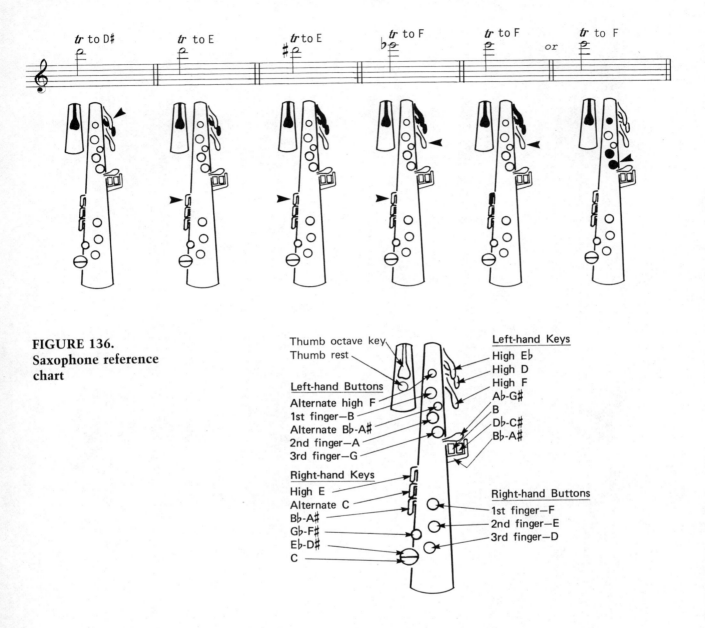

FIGURE 136.
Saxophone reference chart

FREQUENTLY USED SPECIAL FINGERINGS

EXAMPLE 1. There are two fingerings for F-sharp. The first fingering may be used in diatonic and arpeggio passages or for trilling.

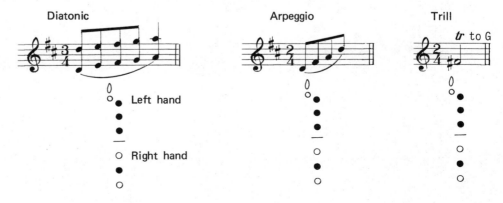

EXAMPLE 2. The second F-sharp fingering can be used for chromatic passages and as a trill fingering.

EXAMPLE 3. There are four fingerings for B-flat. The first fingering is regularly used for diatonic and chromatic passages.

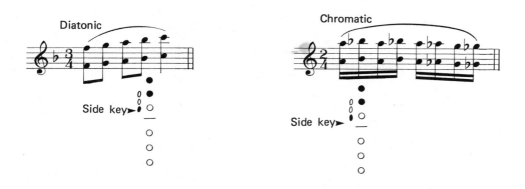

EXAMPLE 4. The second B-flat fingering is used primarily as an arpeggio fingering.

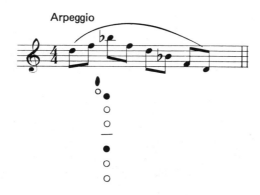

EXAMPLE 5. The third B-flat (or A-sharp) fingering may be best used in a passage such as the following.

EXAMPLE 6. Of the B-flat fingerings the fourth is perhaps the least used. It may be used as a trill fingering and in arpeggio passages.

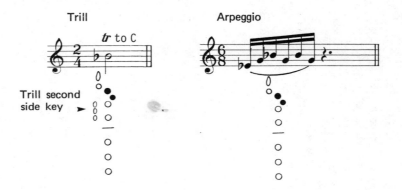

EXAMPLE 7. The E-flat and A-flat keys (marked *) may both remain depressed throughout the following passage:

EXAMPLE 8. The G-sharp key may remain depressed throughout this passage.

Ch. 7/The Saxophone

EXAMPLE 9. In passages such as the following, it is best to use the high E arpeggio fingering rather than the regular E fingering:

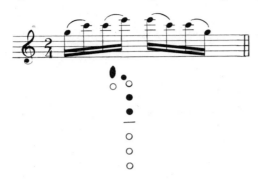

EXAMPLE 10. When playing an F arpeggio in the high register, use the high F arpeggio fingering.

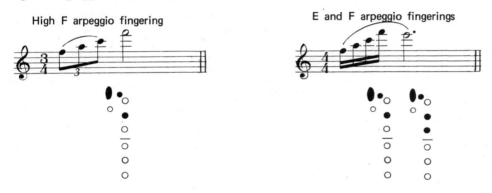

Study Questions

1. The entire key network of the saxophone is based on the "plateau system." How does this fact relate to the care of the instrument?
2. What are the "two important recommendations" which the author offers concerning the care of the saxophone?
3. Discuss instrument angles and hand position for the saxophone family.
4. What is meant by "wraparound" hand position on the saxophone?
5. Why should beginning saxophonists be cautioned to place their fingers evenly over the pearl buttons on each key?
6. Describe the recommended embouchure format for saxophone.
7. Are there any exceptions to the aforementioned embouchure format for saxophone?
8. List those teaching aids which can be most beneficial in developing the flexed offset embouchure for saxophonists in the initial stage of study.
9. Are there any additional points that can be of help in developing a saxophonist's embouchure? If so, list each point.
10. Describe the natural tonal line that is inherent to each member of the saxophone family.
11. Describe the recommended tonal line for the saxophone family.
12. Can the teaching aid "Less fingers means more air" be applied to saxophones as well as other winds?
13. How does the author relate the terms *"experiment"* and *"contrast"* to the matter of breath support and beautiful tone?
14. Would you recommend the 3-and-3 routine for all beginning woodwind students? Why?
15. When should one introduce single-stroke tonguing to beginning students?
16. Is there a visual demonstration that can be presented to the student so that he can *see* tongue placement? Explain.
17. A perceptive instructor may observe extra physical motions—other than tongue movement—when a student executes a tongued passage. What does the author advise in such a case?

A Problem Chart

Problem	Probable Cause	Suggestions for Improvement
A. The student produces a small, narrow tone.	1. There may not be enough mouthpiece in the mouth.	1. Have student experiment with the amount of mouthpiece taken into the mouth, and strive for a median grip with the embouchure.
	2. Excessive biting can be the cause.	2. For a few minutes each day, have him try playing a sustained A-flat (above middle C) using the mouthpiece and neck only. *Do not let the pitch or volume waver.*
	3. The reed may be too soft.	3. Try a harder reed.
B. The overall tone is dark and breathy.	1. The reed is too stiff.	1. Have the student try several different reed strengths so that he can experience the *feel* and *sound* of a reed that behaves as median on *his* mouthpiece.
	2. The embouchure may be at fault.	2. Check the amount of mouthpiece taken into the mouth and the amount of lower lip allowed to cushion against the reed. Too much mouthpiece taken in will darken the tone and too much lower lip against the reed may dampen the tone.
C. The overall tone quality is thin, nasal, and bright.	The reed is probably too soft.	Have the student try several different reed strengths so that he can experience the variations in resistance and tone quality. The objective is to find a reed that behaves as median on his mouthpiece.
D. The student's tone is too loud and sounds overblown.	There is probably too much mouthpiece in the mouth.	See suggestion 1, problem A, above.
E. The instrument's internal intonation appears generally poor.	1. This is usually caused by poor listening habits and an unstable embouchure.	1. Playing unisons and octaves can help most students improve intonation. If the embouchure is unstable, have the student practice suggestion 1, problem 1 above and also a few long tones each day.
	2. The instrument can also be at fault.	2. Some saxophones are notoriously out of tune. Have the instrument checked by a professional to determine if it should be replaced.
F. The student tends to play sharp in the high register of the alto saxophone.	1. He may not be listening attentively. Many are not aware of the almost natural tendency to play sharp on alto saxophones in the very high register.	1. Caution the student about attentive listening and remind him of the need to maintain a consistent grip on the mouthpiece.
	2. Biting excessively can cause one to play sharp in the upper register.	2. Again the mouthpiece and neck exercise outlined in suggestion 2, problem A is recommended.
	3. The high D, D-sharp, E, and F corks may need adjusting.	3 and 4. A competent saxophone instructor can ascertain very quickly if the instrument needs adjustment or if the mouthpiece is at fault.
	4. The mouthpiece may be at fault.	

Ch. 7/The Saxophone   *201*

A Problem Chart (*continued*)

Problem	Probable Cause	Suggestions for Improvement
G. The student tends to play sharp in the lowest register of the saxophone.	1. The student may not be listening and probably doesn't understand the pitch characteristics of his instrument. 2. Embouchure control may be at fault. 3. The mouthpiece could be the cause.	1 and 2. Remind the student that many saxophones tend to be sharp on the lowest tones. He must listen and adjust these tones by relaxing lower jaw pressure slightly. 3. If the problem continues after items 1 and 2 above have been tried, try a different mouthpiece.
H. The student has difficulty in producing the lowest tones.	1. The instrument may be the root of the problem. 2. The mouthpiece-reed combination may be the fault. 3. The embouchure is often the cause of this problem.	1. Use a leak light and check the pads. Minor leaks can be sealed by tying the pads closed over night. Major leaks require a repairman's expertise. 2. Although medium-faced mouthpieces and medium-strength reeds are the first recommendation, one's occlusion may warrant a facing considerably to the left or right of medium. Reed selection must then be matched to the desired facing of the mouthpiece. 3. Remind younger students that a slight decrease in lower-jaw pressure may be needed for the lowest tones on saxophone.
I. Unwanted sounds occur as the student tongues.	1. Tongue placement can be at fault. 2. Unnecessary movement in the chin area could be detrimental. 3. The student may be using breath and tongue movement simultaneously in slow passages.	1. Have student strive to place the tip of the tongue at the tip of the reed. 2. If movement in the lower-lip area is evident, remedial embouchure exercises are needed (long tones, octaves, the mouthpiece exercise, etc.). 3. Exercises in legato tonguing can be of immense help in correcting this bad habit.
J. When reading a lesson preparation, the student stops and starts excessively.	The student is using improper reading habits when he practices.	Fluency in reading music in the initial stage is dependent on graduated and systematic work. Have him read his exercises slowly at first, and gradually increase the speed over a period of several days.

1. Show the student how to assemble and align the neck so that the octave mechanism functions properly.
2. Instrument angle will vary according to the individual's occlusion; often it is self-adjusting.
3. Show the student pictures of the recommended embouchure format.
4. Have the student use a mirror and practice daily flexing his lips.

Teaching
Aids

5. Have him place the upper teeth on top of the mouthpiece.
6. Advise the student to try and master the mouthpiece exercise. Using only the mouthpiece with the neck he should try to produce a sustained tone that is straight and even with no waver in pitch or volume. (See p. 184.)

   Not every student will be able to perfect this exercise immediately, nor should he be expected to. The exercise serves mainly as a guide to perfect embouchure stability, the desired goal.
7. Begin with the 3-and-3 routine. Use no music and slur.
8. As reminders, have the student

   1. flex the chin muscles so they are flat and smooth, and
   2. experiment with mouthpiece insertion, taking a large "bite," then a small "bite," finally, compromising between these two extremes until he finds the best position for control and a clear tone.

9. Have the student deliberately overblow a tone, and then contrast that sound with a tone that is underblown. Then have him strive for a centered, well-placed tone that lies between the two extremes.
10. Have the student refer to a mirror frequently.
11. Recommend frequent rest periods of short duration.
12. Stress using a minimum amount of lower lip over the lower teeth.
13. Have the student play octaves as soon as is feasible. In the initial stage have someone else depress the octave key for the first few attempts.
14. For students prone to bunching the lower lip against the reed, have them play long tones with a double-reed (oboe) embouchure for a few minutes daily—but not continually.

Saxophone Literature

SELECTED LIST OF GRADED SOLOS

The following list has been compiled as a convenient source reference for the instrumental music teacher. It is by no means complete, and readers are encouraged to study publisher catalog listings for their additional needs. This listing is intended to serve as a primer offering; although it has been carefully graded, some overlapping should of course be expected.

Considering the solos' technical difficulty, they have been ranked according to the following scale:

Grades 1–2: very easy to easy
Grades 3–4: moderate to moderately difficult
Grades 5–6: difficult to very difficult

Grades 1–2

Composer	Title	Publisher
Bachmann	Dance Bretonne	Carl Fischer
Barnes	"The Young Artist"	Boosey & Hawkes
Corelli (ed. Mule)	Adagio	Leduc
Frangkiser	"Melody Perchance"	Belwin
Gretchaninoff (trans. Voxman)	Evening Waltz	Rubank
Handel (ed. Buchtel)	Cantilena	Kjos
Mozart (ed. Voxman)	Minuet	Rubank
Ravel (arr. Walters)	Pavane	Rubank
Schumann	"Einsame Blumen"	Spratt
Sibelius	"Swan of Tuonela"	Belwin
Tomasi	Chant Corse	Alfred
Weber	"Evening Shadows"	Belwin

Ch. 7/The Saxophone

Grades 3–4

Composer	Title	Publisher
Bach (ed. Mule)	Bourrée	Leduc
Beethoven (ed. Lefebvre)	Romance	Carl Fischer
Bozza	Aria	Leduc
Chailleux	Andante and Allegro	Rubank
D'Ambrosio (arr. Hummel)	Canzonetta	Rubank
Damico	Avilion (solo with string quartet)	Camara
Handel (ed. Rousseau)	Adagio and Allegro	Wingert-Jones
Handel (ed. Mule)	Bourrée	Leduc
Ostransky	Introduction and Rondo	Rubank
Paladilhe (ed. Voxman)	Concertante	Rubank
Saint-Saëns	"Rêverie Du Soir"	Durand
Saucier	An Impression	Kendor
Vivier	"Enchantress"	Carl Fischer

Grades 5–6

Composer	Title	Publisher
Bonneau	Caprice en Forme de Valse [unacc.]	Leduc
Bozza	Improvisation and Caprice [unacc.]	Southern
Creston	Concerto	G. Schirmer
	Sonata, Op. 19	Axelrod
Debussy	Rhapsodie	Durand
Glazounov	Concerto	Leduc
Heiden	Sonata	AMP
Ibert	Concertino da Camera	Leduc
Lecail	Fantaisie Concertante	Rubank
Moritz	Sonata, Op. 96	Southern
Platti	Sonata in G Major	Etoile
Reed	Ballade	Southern
Rimsky-Korsakov (trans. Davis)	"Flight of the Bumble Bee"	Rubank
Saucier	"2–7": For Tape Recorder and Improvisor (ms)	Opus 2
Tuthill	Sonata, Op. 20	Southern
Ward	"An Abstract"	Southern

CLASS METHODS

See "Class Methods for the Public School Instrumental Music Program," pp. 63–64.

INDIVIDUAL METHODS AND SUPPLEMENTAL STUDIES

Major Applied Methods

BELWIN SERIES FOR SAXOPHONE

Method for Saxophone (2 vols.) by Lucien Calliet is a beginners' method.

Saxophone Method (3 vols.) by K. Gekeler and N. Hovey is a beginning method.

Saxophone Student (3 vols.) by F. Weber and W. Coggins is part of Belwin's student instrumental course series.

Published by Belwin-Mills, Melville, N.Y.

RUBANK SERIES FOR SAXOPHONE

Elementary Method for Saxophone by N. Hovey.
Intermediate Method for Saxophone by J. E. Skornicka.
Advanced Method for Saxophone (2 vols.) by H. Voxman and W. Gower. Published by Rubank, Inc., Miami, Fla.

In Chapter 3 several key points were cited regarding the use of both American and European applied method books at the initial level of instrumental study. The most important point made in that discussion centered on the major difference between certain American and European music books: On the one hand, many American method books *assume no prior musical study;* on the other, most of the celebrated European or European-influenced method books *assume prior musical study,* and tend to progress at a rate that becomes impractical for students having no preparatory music background. It is for this reason that the following method books are recommended for use only after the saxophone student has completed his basic foundation work with one of the standard American methods.

Conservatory Method for the Saxophone (4 vols.) by J. B. Cragun. Published by Rubank, Inc., Miami, Fla.
Modern Conservatory Method for Saxophone (2 vols.) by G. Iasilli. Published by Carl Fischer, New York, N.Y.
Universal Method for Saxophone by Paul de Ville. Published by Carl Fischer, New York, N.Y.

Supplemental Studies

15 Two-Part Inventions by J. S. Bach (arr. L. Teal). Published by Theodore Presser, Bryn Mawr, Pa.
Twenty-seven Virtuoso Studies by L. Bassi (G. Iasilli). Published by Carl Fischer, New York, N.Y.
12 Etudes-Caprices by E. Bozza. Published by Leduc, Paris, France.
Fifty-two Progressive Etudes by J. B. Cragun. Published by Rubank, Miami, Fla.
Eleven Cadenzas and Twenty-six Etudes by J. B. Cragun. Published by Rubank, Miami, Fla.
Supplementary Studies for Saxophone by R. Endresen. Published by Rubank, Miami, Fla.
Practical Studies for Saxophone (2 vols.) by N. Hovey. Published by Belwin-Mills, Melville, N.Y.
Beginning Studies in the Altissimo Register by R. Lang. Lang Publications, Indianapolis, Ind.
Scales and Arpeggios by M. Mule. Published by Leduc, Paris, France.
Scales and Daily Exercises for Saxophone by G. Pares. Published by Carl Fischer, New York, N.Y.
The Saxophonist's Workbook by L. Teal. Published by University Music Press, Ann Arbor, Mich.
Selected Studies for Saxophone by H. Voxman. Published by Rubank, Miami, Fla.

RECORDINGS OF SAXOPHONE LITERATURE

Pedagogically Oriented Recordings

The Music Minus One Series.
Essentially, the Music Minus One Corporation makes professionally recorded backgrounds—minus a particular "solo" instrument—for all types of music, including the orchestral concerto, the sonata, chamber music, and various jazz forms. The original concept behind the MMO series was to afford the student performer a professional accompaniment against which to practice and perform a musical work in its original and complete context, that is, with full orchestra, string quartet, or jazz ensemble, as the case might be. The bulk of the recorded accompaniments made by MMO fall in this category. However, the new MMO Laureate Series of Contest Solos goes beyond the practical asset of offering a professional accompaniment. With the Laureate Series,

Ch. 7/The Saxophone

the student is offered in one package a performance of the work by a major performing artist, a copy of the printed music, a professional accompaniment, and interpretive suggestions for performance by the performing artist. Among the distinguished woodwind artists who may be heard in the Laureate Series are saxophonists Vincent Abato and Paul Brodie. The MMO series is a highly recommended teaching aid for both students and teachers. It is published by Music Minus One, 43 West 61 Street, New York, N.Y.

Special Collections

The following recorded collections will be of special interest to the saxophonist. Each album is devoted primarily to selected saxophone literature, and features various celebrated performing artists of our time. This is by no means a complete listing; however, it is more than adequate as a beginning source reference for the student.

James Stoltie Plays Music for Saxophone Alone
Bach, C.P.E.: Sonata in A Minor
Debussy: "Syrinx"
Persichetti: "Parable" for Solo Alto Saxophone
Hartley: Petite Suite
Gates: "Incantation and Ritual"
Del Borgo: "Canto"
Noda: Improvisation 1. James Stoltie. Coronet LP 3036
Ibert, Glazounov, Villa-Lobos
Ibert: Concertino da Camera for Saxophone and Orchestra
Glazounov: Concerto for Saxophone and Orchestra. Vincent J. Abato. Nonesuch H-71030
The Indiana Saxophone Quartet
Haydn: Quartet, Op. 76, No. 3
Bach, C.P.E.: Rondo
Smith, Glenn: "Mood Music 1"
Zajac: Five Miniatures
Mistak: Quartet. Kenneth Fischer, David Branter, James Carroll, and Michael Di Clemente. Coronet LP 3028
The Saxophone, Volume I
Bonneau: Caprice en Forme de Valse
Bozza: Improvisation et Caprice
Decruck: Andante et Fileuse
Pascal: Sonatine
Tcherepnine: Sonatine Sportive
Tomasi: "Giration." Marcel Mule (saxophone) and Marthe Lemon (piano). London LS 986
The Saxophone, Volume II
Bozza: "Pulcinella"

Creston: Sonata for Saxophone and Piano
Eccles: Sonata
Fiocco: Allegro
Galliard: Sonata
Handel: Air Varié
Heiden: Sonata for Saxophone and Piano. Sigurd Rascher.
Available from J. W. Pepper & Son, Inc. (1423 Vine St., Philadelphia, Pa.)
The Virtuoso Saxophone
Bonneau: Caprice en Forme de Valse
Chopin (arr. Rousseau): Largo
Dubois: A l'Espagnole
Hindemith: Sonata (1943)
Platti (arr. Rousseau): Sonata in G Major
Ruggiero: Trois Pièces pour Deux Saxophones. Eugene Rousseau. Coronet 1601
Trent Kynaston: Saxophone
Bach, J. S.: Prelude, Bourée, and Gigue
Ibert: Concertino da Camera
Kynaston: "Dawn and Jubilation"
Diemente: "Diary, Part II." Trent Kynaston (alto and tenor saxophone). Coronet LPS 3035

Traditional Recordings

Badings: La Malinconia. Paul Brodie (saxophone) and Myriam Shechter (piano). Golden Crest RE 7037
Creston: Sonata, Op. 19. Paul Brodie (saxophone) and Myriam Shechter (piano). Golden Crest RE 7037
Debussy: Rhapsody for Saxophone and Orchestra. Jules De Vries. Lyrichord 38
————: Rhapsody for Saxophone and Orchestra. Sigurd Rascher. Columbia ML 6059
Handel (arr. Gee): Sonata No. 1. Vincent J. Abato (saxophone) and Harriet Wingreen (piano). MMO 8028
Maurice: Tableaux de Provence. Harvey Pittel. Crystal S 105
Rodby: Concerto for Saxophone and Orchestra. Harvey Pittel. Crystal S 500
Stevens: "Dittico" for Alto Saxophone and Piano. Harvey Pittel (saxophone) and Ralph Grierson (piano). Crystal S 105
Van Delden: Sonatina. Paul Brodie (saxophone) and Myriam Shechter (piano). Golden Crest, RE 7037
Vivaldi: Sonata in G Minor. Paul Brodie (saxophone) and Antonin Kubalek (piano). MMO 8027
Ward: "An Abstract." Paul Brodie (saxophone) and Antonin Kubalek (piano). MMO 8027

FIGURE 138.
E-flat baritone saxophone

FIGURE 137.
B-flat tenor saxophone

Photographs courtesy of The Selmer Company, Elkhart, Indiana.

The Lower Saxophones

For all practical purposes we may say that the upper saxophones include the B-flat soprano and E-flat alto and the lower the B-flat tenor, E-flat baritone, and the rarely used B-flat bass saxophone.

While there are some minor variations in fingerings within the clarinet family, all the members of the saxophone family employ the same basic fingerings. Like the clarinet family, there can be a decided difference in how the embouchure is used for upper and lower saxophones. However, when we consider embouchure and tone production, the dividing line between the upper and lower saxophones is not so easily drawn as in the clarinet family. Only the straight B-flat soprano saxophone enters the mouth at an angle basically identical to that of the B-flat clarinet. Beginning with the alto saxophone, the angle between the mouthpiece and one's body tends gradually to widen as we progress from the alto to the lowest saxophone. (Bear in mind that some saxophonists perform with the instrument held more to the front of the body while others hold it to their sides, and as a consequence the angle at which the mouthpiece enters the mouth can be adjusted to some extent by the individual.) Another physical aspect to consider is that the lower saxophones use much larger mouthpieces.

Taking all of these factors into consideration, the following observations and recommendations can be of immense help when starting students on or transferring them to one of the lower saxophones.

B-flat Tenor Saxophone

1. The flexed offset embouchure described in the material on alto saxophone is highly recommended for tenor saxophone; many excellent saxophonists employ this format.

2. To determine the appropriate amount of mouthpiece insertion for an individual, have him experiment using extreme amounts of grip. That is, have him try producing a sustained tone (e.g., low G) with a small amount of mouthpiece in the mouth, listen to the resulting sound, and then take a larger amount into the mouth and observe the marked change in sound that occurs. After these two steps, it is simply a matter of having the student compromise between the two extremes by striving for a medium grip that allows a clear, open sound *that can be controlled.*

3. Another point to be considered centers on lower-jaw pressure. For many students who play the lower saxophones, this can be a definite problem. But, just as the correct amount of mouthpiece insertion can be determined by experimentation with extremes, so can precise jaw pres-

sure be determined. The real problem is not so much in discovering the correct amount of jaw pressure, but in maintaining it.

Experimentation with lower-jaw pressure against the reed will show that (1) biting or pinching causes a small, narrow sound which is sharp in pitch and (2) insufficient pressure results in a flat, dull, coarse sound. After the student has learned to "center" his tone—that is, calibrate lower-jaw pressure with appropriate breath support—remind him that it is imperative to develop the ability to maintain consistent control over lower-jaw pressure.[1] The saxophonist who allows the muscular tension in the lower jaw to fluctuate indiscriminately creates problems of pitch and control for himself *and* can literally create havoc within an ensemble!

E-flat Baritone Saxophone

The three major points discussed above for the tenor saxophone are all applicable to the baritone and thus need not be repeated. However, baritone saxophone technique is much like that for the lower clarinets in that some students and professionals embrace the "relaxed" embouchure approach in gripping the mouthpiece. (In this case, "relaxed" refers to the lower lip which is allowed to cushion against the reed). While the relaxed approach is not recommended for the other saxophones, the large size of the baritone mouthpiece permits it to be used effectively. Regardless of which embouchure format is employed, the following key points should be kept in mind:

1. The appropriate amount of mouthpiece insertion must be determined on an individual basis.

2. Lower-jaw pressure must be consistent throughout the *general tessitura* of the instrument; indiscriminate biting must be avoided.

3. A suitable mouthpiece-reed combination is essential for all single-reed instruments.

4. All lower single-reed mouthpieces require a larger grip on the mouthpiece.

5. Baritone saxophonists—much like bassoonists—may consciously increase the muscular tension of the embouchure in the *highest* register and conversely relax it in the very *lowest* register of the instrument.

Recommended Study Material

See "Individual Methods and Supplemental Studies," pp. 203 ff., and "Class Methods for the Public Instrumental Music Program," pp. 63–64.

---

1. All lower single-reed mouthpieces have facings that are longer and more open than those of upper single-reed mouthpieces. Thus, indiscriminate biting against the reed will have an immediate effect on pitch, volume, and consistency in control.

Secondary Factors

Part III of this text consists of three chapters. Each deals with subjects that may be viewed as secondary and is in keeping with the aims stated in the Preface. Although these subjects are secondary in nature, they are nonetheless of key importance in that each can indirectly affect the matter of tone production.

Chapter 8 involves woodwind mouthpieces and reeds. One of its objectives is to provide a guide for the reader in the matters of care and selection. Chapter 9, on double reeds, follows a similar format and is also intended to serve as a practical guide. Chapter 10 concerns vibrato, a subject which has become increasingly important to music pedagogy through the influence of twentieth-century composers and performers who have continually expanded its usage. Vibrato is now considered a standard part of most woodwind performers' repertoire of performance practices. Since the aspect of timing is of major importance in developing woodwind vibrato, a detailed account has been presented covering types, choice, and methods of development.

Recital preparation involves self-discipline in numerous areas for all serious musicians. However, it is only in the area of reed instruments that such preparation is compounded by Arundo donax sativa, the cane used in making single and double reeds. In addition to all the other preparation required to achieve excellence in music performance, the reed performer must continually pursue the task of selecting or making reeds of quality!!

Mouthpieces and Single Reeds: Selection and Care

FIGURE 139

Photograph courtesy of the G. Leblanc Corporation, Kenosha, Wisconsin.

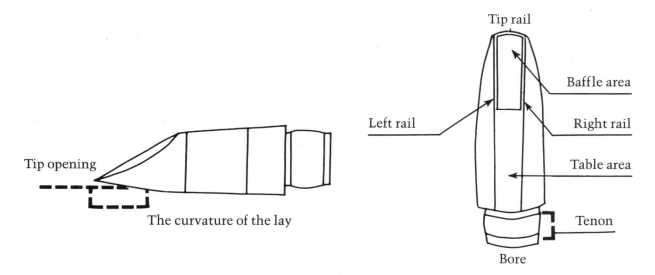

FIGURE 140.
A single-reed mouthpiece reference chart

Studying a musical instrument is for most lovers of music a thing of joy, and so it should be. However, such enjoyment can be lost and instrumental study become frustrating and disappointing if the learner must continually face problems caused by an unsuitable mouthpiece or reed. Although an exhaustive account of reed making or an in-depth analysis of mouthpieces does not fall within the intended scope of this text, some comment about the selection of mouthpieces and reeds is in order. Of equal importance is the matter of matching reed with mouthpiece, an aspect about which too little has been written.

211

Mouthpieces

SELECTION

Generally speaking, the mouthpiece included with a newly purchased woodwind instrument will be the most appropriate one for that instrument. The manufacturer has designed the mouthpiece as an integral part of the instrument, with specific dimensions that correlate with those of the rest of the instrument. When a mouthpiece of a different brand is substituted for the original, the effectiveness of the substitute will most often be determined by its degree of similarity to the original. If the original mouthpiece does not appear to fit the student, the first recommendation is to have the student try different *facings* of the original brand before selecting a completely different one. Each manufacturer produces a variety of mouthpiece facings for their stock mouthpieces in order to accommodate the varying needs of consumers. If this does not resolve the mouthpiece problem, then the next recourse is to try the different mouthpiece facings of another major manufacturer having an established reputation for producing products of quality.

A third consideration involves—and tends to reflect directly upon—the instrumental ensemble director. It concerns a major, often problematic, subject that all directors will encounter and must resolve effectively; namely, intonation within the ensemble. Pitch and intonation problems can be greatly minimized by outfitting an entire section of an instrumental ensemble with like mouthpieces and like instruments. Although such an achievement is not always feasible, it is certainly worth striving to attain. The use of like instrument brands within a section of an ensemble has become widespread among instrumental music directors. However, the same cannot be said about mouthpieces. If excellence in intonation, consistency in blend and balance, and uniformity of tonal quality and line are to be achieved within a single-reed section, then all contributing factors must be weighed, and reckoned with accordingly. Consequently, the use of like mouthpieces (allowing for variations in facings, of course) within a single-reed section is highly recommended.

The remaining aspects of mouthpiece selection to be considered involve (1) the material of which mouthpieces are made and (2) those mouthpiece facings that are extreme in length or in tip opening. Single-reed mouthpieces are made of rubber, plastic, glass, or metal. Many believe that the material of which mouthpieces are made can to a large extent affect the character of one's tone. However, while the material used may have a minute bearing on such matters, it is the *design* of a mouthpiece which is of paramount importance. For example, certain instrumental music directors are opposed to the indiscriminate use of rubber and glass mouthpieces within a clarinet section, for the reason that such combinations apparently nearly always create problems in intonation and overall blending. While what these sensitive directors hear is very real, the "why" of the matter is often attributed to the wrong cause. The root cause of these problems is to be found in the marked difference in design and dimension that exists among mouthpieces made of glass, rubber, metal, or plastic.

As stated earlier, instrument manufacturers produce a basic mouth-

Ch. 8/Mouthpieces and Single Reeds: Selection and Care

piece for each type of instrument and make it available in multiple facings. It is this facing—the tapered curve on the end of the mouthpiece—which is so critical to the effective fitting of the mouthpiece to one's particular occlusion. While some manufacturers produce as many as twelve different facings for a basic mouthpiece, it should be remembered that deviations on either side of an established norm should only be considered in light of actual individual need. Generally speaking, mouthpiece facings that tend to fall in the median range are the ones that should be recommended and tried first for fitting. Extreme facings are best used by those individuals where the natural occlusion warrants extreme dimensions in the curvature of the mouthpiece.

CARE

Mouthpieces should occasionally be washed in lukewarm water with a mild soap. Proper adjustment of the ligature—used to hold the reed securely on the mouthpiece—is of major importance. In order to avoid warping the table of rubber or plastic mouthpieces, never leave the ligature in a tightened position overnight. One leading manufacturer states that certain mouthpieces are subject to "coldflow," a trade term referring to the fact that if the mouthpiece is left under prolonged pressure—such as that caused by an excessively tight ligature over a period of time—it can become warped.

SELECTION

Single Reeds

While there are many factors that should be weighed in the matter of reed selection, first consideration should be given to correct reed strength. Correct reed strength is that which best fits the individual and his particular mouthpiece. It is best determined by the aural characteristics it can help produce. For example, the reed should be strong enough to enable the player to produce a full and controlled tone in the high register, but not so strong as to sound breathy in the middle and low registers.

The following is an example of the nomenclature used to classify single reeds. The listings used were taken from the advertising literature of three reed companies.

Nomenclature

Brand	Designated Strength		
	Soft	*Medium*	*Hard*
Rico	1, 1½, 2	2½, 3, 3½	4, 4½, 5
La Voz	Soft, Medium soft	Medium	Medium hard, Hard
Vandoren	1, 2	3, 4	5

FIGURE 141

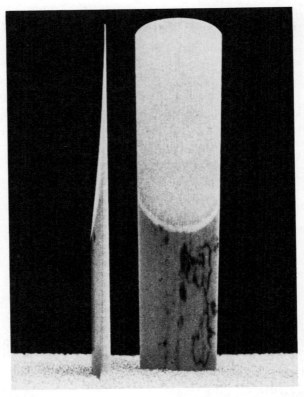

Photograph courtesy of the Rico Corporation, North Hollywood, California.

**FIGURE 142.
A single-reed reference chart**

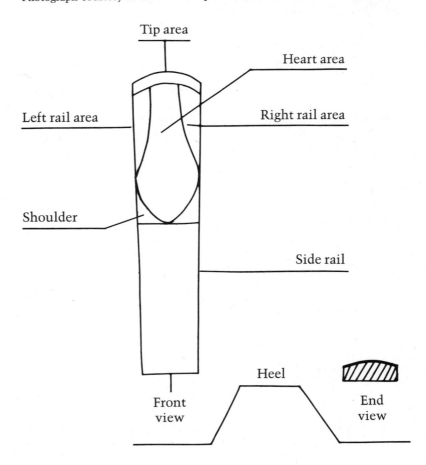

Ch. 8/Mouthpieces and Single Reeds: Selection and Care

While the nomenclature used by single-reed manufacturers to classify reed strengths gives the appearance of consensus, it should be pointed out that they are by no means in complete agreement on what specific strengths designated symbols (2½, 3, medium hard, etc.) will represent. Because of this variation in opinion as to what constitutes a designated grading, indiscriminate use of the reed nomenclature can be deceptive and expensive. Over the years the major producers of single reeds have continually improved the quality control of grading reeds (unfortunately, the same cannot be said about the use of quality cane per se). Even so, there is still this difference of opinion regarding uniform assignment of reed strengths. It will help the consumer to bear the following in mind when purchasing single reeds:

1. European reeds such as Vandoren (French) or Vic. Olivieri (Spanish) are made so that the center or "heart" area is left with more cane, rather than less, as is the case with most American-made single reeds. The net result is that European reeds tend to be about one grade strength stronger overall than those American reeds bearing the same grade indication.

2. There is one aspect of reed selection that is frequently—and understandably—overlooked. Reeds made in Europe tend to work more efficiently on European-made mouthpieces, as do American-made reeds with American mouthpieces. For example, those who play a Vandoren mouthpiece find that a Vandoren reed (or a similar European reed such as a Vic. Olivieri) usually gives the best results. This is not an absolute rule, but a general tendency worth considering in trying to find the best possible reed to meet individual need.

Since many students purchase reeds in small quantities, they should familiarize themselves with visual clues that can be of help in selecting well-seasoned cane of quality. The following check list can be of considerable help in this:

1. *Color.* Properly seasoned cane will have a whitish overall color. Cane with a green tint or streaks of green running through the grain on the vamp or backside of the reed should be avoided. Green cane is less stable and tends to become water-soaked almost immediately upon getting wet. Additionally, a reed that "water-soaks" tends to produce an unwanted buzz in the tone.

Occasionally some cane is processed which may have dark-brownish streaks running through the vamp area and backside of the reed. If this is excessive the reed will lack flexibility and prove unsatisfactory. The color of the bottom half of the reed—where the cane has not been cut or scraped—may vary considerably and in no way serves as an indicator for reed selection.

2. *Grain.* The pattern of the reed grain can be examined by holding the reed up against the light. Generally speaking, if the grain pattern has very fine lines that are close together and tend to "disappear" into the reed tip, the reed is prone to becoming water-soaked. (The water-soaked area of the reed will become noticeably darker than the original color of the reed.) Reeds that absorb too much moisture create an unwanted buzz in the tone. Reeds having a grain pattern with bolder, somewhat separated lines that tend to "flow" to the very tip

of the reed—and with one or two "windows"—often have excellent resilience and are not prone to water-soak.[1]

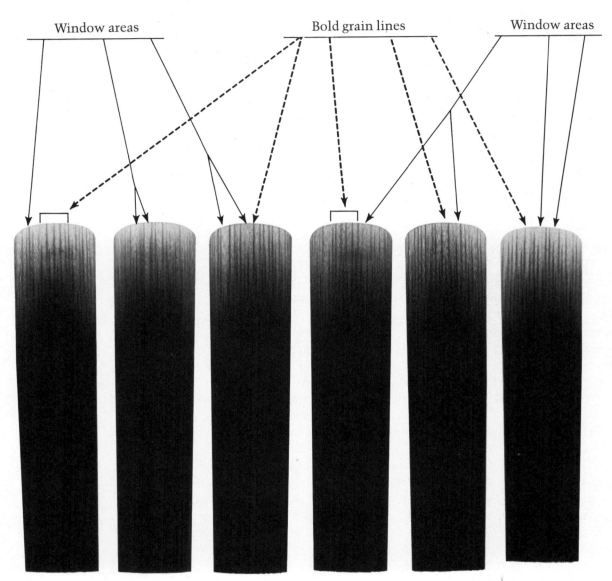

**FIGURE 143.
E-flat alto saxophone reeds, suitable for performance**

Figures 143–147 show the grain patterns of various single reeds. The reeds shown in Figure 143 were all used in recital or recording performances. The primary aural criteria used in selecting these recital reeds centered on: (1) sound, (2) response, (3) ease of control, (4) range, and (5) flexibility. Visual criteria which can be a time-saving aid prior to trying any reed involve: (1) color, (2) grain, and (3) the heel of the reed.

1. The term "window" is used by both double- and single-reed performers. With single reeds, it refers to an area of the reed that is light in color due to the absence of the bold grain line. With double reeds, the window areas result from purposely scraping the blades deeper at certain points.

Ch. 8/Mouthpieces and Single Reeds: Selection and Care   217

The B-flat clarinet reeds shown in Figure 144 were all used in recital or recording performances. (The same aural criteria used in selecting the E-flat saxophone reeds—see Figure 143—were used in selecting them; a close comparison of these two pictorial illustrations reveals a remarkable similarity and consistency in grain pattern.)

FIGURE 144. B-flat clarinet reeds, suitable for performance

The reeds in Figures 145 and 146 were *not* suitable for recital purposes. Careful examination of these reeds shows either (1) the absence of windows, (2) erratic spacing of windows, or (3) excessively bold lines.

FIGURE 145. B-flat clarinet reeds, unsuitable for performance

FIGURE 146.
E-flat alto saxophone reeds, unsuitable for performance

FIGURE 147.
B-flat clarinet and E-flat alto saxophone reeds

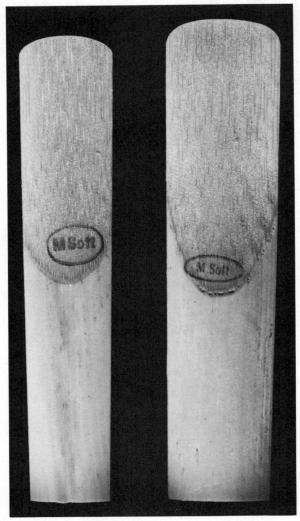

Although there are distinguishable characteristics associated with the reed grain patterns shown in Figure 147, we may say that for all practical purposes it is best to study grain patterns with reeds held up against the light. The figure readily shows the difficulty of trying to read grain patterns when viewed face down; without light against the backside of the reed, only the top surface area can be studied.

3. *Grade.* The heel or butt end of the reed may serve as an indicator of cane quality. It can be noted that at the top side of the heel there is a curved, eggshell-like rim which is actually the exterior surface of the cane. Beneath this thin top rim is the more porous second layer of cane. Those reeds which appear to have two distinct, clearly defined areas— the eggshell rim line and the more porous bottom section—contain the best cane. A reed with a rim line that is too thin or difficult to distinguish is generally from a poorer grade of cane.

In Figure 148 the rim line on the heel of the reed at the left of the picture is barely visible. The rim line on the heel of the reed at the right is clearly visible and well defined. (This reed was used for recital purposes.)

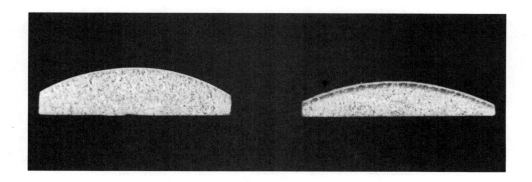

**FIGURE 148.
Single-reed heels and rim lines**

CARE

The life of any single reed can be prolonged by keeping it on a flat surface when not in use. Although commercial reed guards are available, many professionals prefer to use a small, flat piece of glass with ordinary rubber bands as a reed guard. If the reed is left on the mouthpiece overnight, it is common practice to slide the end of the reed down almost to the cork area. In this way the flat area of the mouthpiece table presses against the reed; the ligature is slipped into place to hold the reed in a snug, but not tight, position.

Many students inadvertently shorten the life-span of the reed in assembling mouthpiece, reed, and ligature. In order to align the reed on the mouthpiece, they will press the reed until it closes against the tip opening. This is almost the worst thing that can be done to it. By learning how to align the reed without pressing it closed, students can have reeds that last longer and function better in all registers. Additionally, the reed will have a cleaner appearance if the vamp area is not repeatedly touched by the fingers. It should also be mentioned that washing hands before handling an instrument is not only sanitary, but helps minimize the collection of dust and grime in open tone holes.

Double Reeds: Selection and Care

9

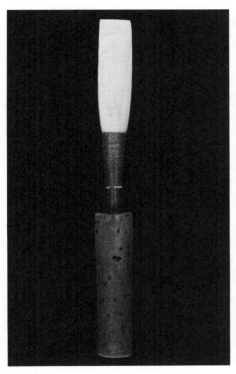

FIGURE 149.
A professionally made "W-cut" oboe reed

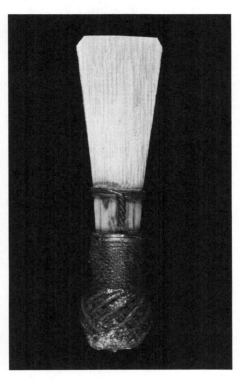

FIGURE 150.
A commercially made student-line bassoon reed

All beginning reed students are faced with the task and expense of obtaining good, serviceable reeds. The cost of commercial single reeds currently varies from sixty cents to two dollars and forty cents each; commercial double reeds range between three and six dollars. Obviously a double-reed student's difficulties in finding a reliable reed source may well be increased due to the economics of the matter. Since commercially made double reeds serve as the prime source for most elementary students, careful reed selection is of critical importance. The following points are intended to aid in selecting double reeds:

1. Reed *strength* is the first critical factor to consider in selecting a reed. While trial-and-error is ultimately the most valid test for determining the strength of any reed, it is best to begin with reeds with a "medium" rating for stiffness. Subsequent minor adjustments can then

Selection

be much easier. Manufacturers of commercial double reeds—unlike makers of single reeds—rarely use numerals to designate rank in grading. The common designations for reed strength in double reeds are soft, medium soft, medium, medium hard, and hard.

2. The *color* of the cane is a key aspect in reed selection, just as with single reeds. Cane of quality that is seasoned properly has a whitish tone throughout the scraped area of the reed. Any reed with tints of green showing in the scraped area should be avoided. (The likelihood of finding commercially produced double reeds with green cane is less than with single reeds.) A reddish-brown tint in the cane often indicates a lack of flexibility, especially if it is excessive.

3. Checking the *grain* of double reeds is not a practical matter for the untrained. For one thing, double reeds require a very bright light for examination, since it must pass through both reed blades.

4. By all means examine the *tip opening* of the reed before purchasing it. Extremes in the opening should be avoided. For example, an oboe reed with a tip opening that is completely closed when dry will usually turn out to be too soft to be usable. On the other hand, a reed with a tip opening that is excessively wide will open even further after it is wetted —as will all double reeds—and its stiffness will increase. Figures 151 and 152 depict approximate tip openings for oboe and bassoon.

FIGURE 151.
Tip openings, oboe

FIGURE 152.
Tip openings, bassoon

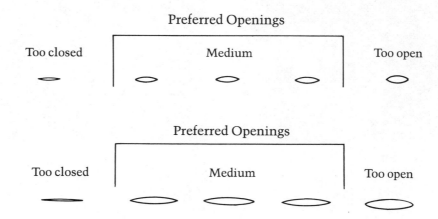

5. Another point to consider is *cracking* in the cane. If there is a split or crack in the scraped area of either reed blade, the reed will not function properly. However, many usable reeds will show evidence of a split in the unscraped area just above the tied nylon thread. Generally, if the crack has not already spread into the scraped facing of the reed, it will not do so. It must be said, however, that there is no way to predict with certainty about such reeds.

6. It is best that a double reed have both reed blades in perfect *alignment*, with flush edges throughout. Occasionally, though, a double-reed blade that has slipped slightly to the right or left will actually improve the behavior of the reed. The point here is not to buy reeds that are misaligned, but to take care before casting aside a reed that is already yours. Be sure to test any reed thoroughly before discarding it. (See Figures 153, 154, and 155; note that both the slipped and well-aligned bassoon reeds in Figure 155 are equally playable and have been used extensively.)

Ch. 9/Double Reeds: Selection and Care 223

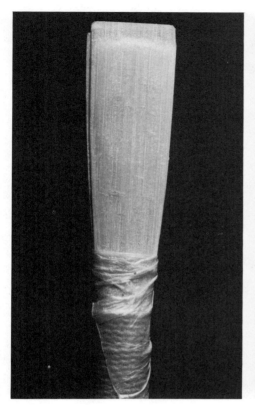

FIGURE 153.
Oboe reed-blades that have slipped

FIGURE 154.
Oboe reed-blades that are perfectly aligned

FIGURE 155.
Bassoon reed-blades, perfectly aligned (at left) and slipped (right).

Care

Double reeds should always be soaked in water for a few minutes before use. Bassoon reeds may be cleaned occasionally with water and a pipe cleaner: After the reed is thoroughly soaked, place the pipe cleaner in the round, bottom end and push it gently through the inside. (The tiny oboe reed would be destroyed by such procedure.)

One of the best small investments a double-reed student can make is in a commercial reed case. Double-reed cases not only protect reeds from external damage but are designed to allow them to dry properly after use. Students who elect to use the commercial containers in which reeds are sold should be advised to place a tiny air hole in the container. An airtight—or nearly airtight—container will cause the reed to mildew overnight.

Source References for Reed Making and Adjusting

Students who continue the study of double-reed instruments should be encouraged to pursue reed making and adjusting. All professional double-reed performers make their own reeds. Many students do not begin their study of reed making until the college level simply because they do not have access to a double-reed specialist. Actually, reed making and adjusting should begin at the senior high school level if a specialist is available.

The following source references are recommended for the study of double-reed making and adjusting:

OBOE

The Oboe and the English Horn by A. S. Best. Published by The Conn Corporation, Oak Brook, Ill.

Oboe Reeds: How to Make and Adjust Them by R. Mayer and T. Rohner. Published by The Instrumentalist, Glenn Ellyn, Ill.

Oboe Reed Making and Problems of the Oboe Player by Myron E. Russell. Published by Jack Spratt, Stamford, Conn.

The Art of Oboe Playing by R. Sprenkle and D. Ledet. Published by Summy-Birchard, Evanston, Ill.

BASSOON

The Bassoon by A. S. Best. Published by The Conn Corporation, Oak Brook, Ill.

Teacher's Guide to the Bassoon by Homer Pence. Published by H. and A. Selmer, Elkhart, Ind.

Bassoon Reeds by M. Popkin and L. Glickman. Published by The Instrumentalist, Evanston, Ill.

Bassoon Reed Making: A Basic Technique by C. Weait. Published by McGinnis and Marx, New York, N.Y.

Vibrato

10

Prior to the twentieth century, vibrato was employed mainly by singers, string players, some flutists, and those few double-reed performers who could execute this performance practice. It is only within this century that the use of vibrato has become an essential performance practice for *all* woodwinds. It is therefore imperative for today's instrumental music teacher to possess (1) a thorough understanding of the various types of vibrato, (2) sound, practical methods of approach that can be used to develop a beautiful vibrato, and (3) an understanding of when to introduce the subject to a woodwind student for study and development.

Seen from an instrumental point of view, vibrato is an *additive* to tone, used to enhance the instrumentalist's basic sound while adding expressiveness to a musical presentation. Vibrato added to a poor basic tone quality cannot be equated with a beautiful sound. The first prerequisite to studying vibrato, then, is the development of sound basic tone-production habits. The same primary factors that account for tone production are of key importance in developing a beautiful vibrato— namely, stability of embouchure control and effective breath support. When the student has developed a reasonable command of tone production he is then ready to study vibrato. Since individual development is such a variable matter, a more specific timetable is not practical; some students could begin the study of vibrato as early as the junior high school level, while others may not be ready until the senior high school level. It should also be noted that some students will from the beginning use a vibrato that appears totally involuntary—much like that of a vocalist.

The term "vibrato" denotes a regular pulsation which is added to a basic tone, and involves audible changes in pitch and volume and inaudible changes in timbre. It should be mentioned at this point that verbal definitions of applied musical terms can only represent partial meanings in the mind of the listener. They serve at best as starting points for the learner, and must be supplemented with live or recorded aural demonstrations. To convey the meaning of vibrato more completely one must use (1) concept (verbal definition) and (2) percept (aural perception). It should also be remembered that among the musically inclined, perceptual knowledge often precedes conceptual knowledge by a considerable margin. Thus, many students will ask an instructor, "How do you make that wave in your tone?" long before the instructor plans to introduce the subject of vibrato. The word "wave" serves as an informal definition of vibrato for the growing student at a particular time of development.

Defining Vibrato

To summarize then, vibrato—or any applied musical term—should be defined for the inquiring student with first, a simple verbal definition; second, ample live or recorded aural demonstrations; and third, appropriately related visual aids. This order of presentation is recommended. Descriptive visual aids such as those shown in Figure 156 should be utilized.

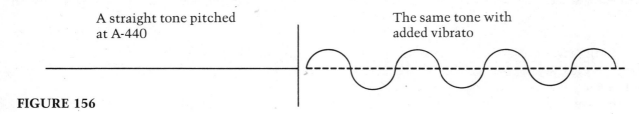

FIGURE 156

Note that
1. the waves are distributed equally above and below the established A-440 v.p.s. pitch level;
2. the height and width of each wave is consistent throughout; and
3. the basic format of any beautiful vibrato will reflect consistency in every aspect.

Deviations in consistency of the basic wave form such as those employed by mature professional performers are the result of conscious choice based on study and practice. For example, a tone may begin straight and pure and gradually be colored with vibrato (Figure 157).

FIGURE 157

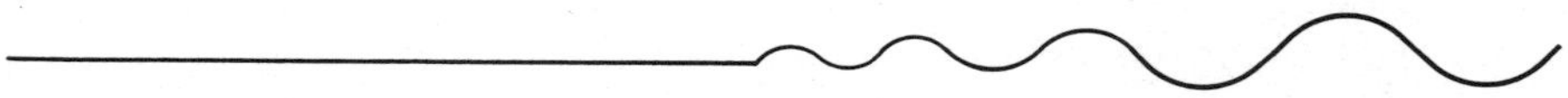

Or the opposite approach may be taken, with vibrato followed by a straight, pure tone (Figure 158).

FIGURE 158

Also, the dimension of the wave (pulsation) may be altered in a gradual manner (Figure 159).

FIGURE 159

Remember that these examples of variation in vibrato wave-form rightfully fall in the domain of the artistic professional. The learner must first master the basic technique of vibrato before proceeding to advanced variations.

After the basic characteristics of a beautiful vibrato have been fully examined, a specific method of approach that works best for a particular instrument or student can be introduced and developed.

Types of Vibrato

In a broad, general sense there are two basic categories in which the various methods of producing vibrato fall: (1) voluntary vibrato (in this instance vibrato can be developed and controlled at will) and (2) involuntary vibrato (in this case vibrato is natural, occurring without conscious effort or will). With regard to the latter, it is important to note that involuntary vibrato can be modified by some with subsequent conscious effort and practice. Others, however, appear to be "preset" at birth and can in no way change the speed and size of the pulsation of their given vibrato.

INVOLUNTARY VIBRATO

Involuntary vibrato is a natural vibrato most often associated with singers. This type of vibrato lends itself naturally to the human voice, for most singers appear to be endowed with it. For all practical purposes, it is not recommended for instrumentalists in general because there is no established method whereby it can be taught and developed effectively. While involuntary vibrato is impractical from a teaching standpoint, its use is not impractical for an instrumentalist endowed with the natural ability to produce it. The fact of the matter is that only rarely will a woodwind student endowed with a natural singer's vibrato be able to apply this type of vibrato to his instrument. Those rare individuals who can apply their given vocal vibrato to their musical instruments should be informed of the uniqueness of this gift and encouraged to use it. If modification of the natural vibrato is warranted, it is recommended that the student study privately and learn through practice to exercise control over it. The object would be to cultivate the natural vibrato and use it as good musical taste may require.

VOLUNTARY VIBRATO

The two most practical methods of producing vibrato at will are (1) jaw vibrato (recommended for all single-reed and some double-reed students) and (2) diaphragmatic vibrato (recommended for flutists and certain double-reed students).

Choice of Vibrato

The choice of vibrato type that an instrumentalist ultimately makes largely rests on practicality. Common sense dictates that it must be of a vibrato type capable of being put to use or account by the learner. It has long been common knowledge among woodwind teachers that single-reed instrumentalists by-and-large use jaw vibrato; recent surveys of the subject by Cecil Gold confirm this fact with overwhelming statistical figures.[1] From a teaching standpoint, diaphragmatic vibrato is the most

---

1. Cecil V. Gold, *Clarinet Performing Practices and Teaching in the United States and Canada* (Moscow, Idaho: University of Idaho School of Music, 1972); idem, *Saxophone Practices and Teaching in the United States and Canada* (Moscow, Idaho: University of Idaho School of Music, 1973).

practical type that can be recommended for flutists. Considering double reeds, diaphragmatic vibrato would be the first recommendation of most teachers, with jaw vibrato serving as an alternate choice. These recommendations of course are based on the student not possessing a natural vibrato that can be applied to his instrument and consideration of practical aspects as related to the individual.

While it is essential to know which type of vibrato lends itself best to a particular woodwind instrument, exceptions must be respected. The rare woodwind instrumentalist who can apply a natural vocal vibrato to his instrument without conscious effort may be considered a true exception to the general rule. If such a person can subsequently develop the ability to control his natural vibrato, then there is no valid reason why his natural vibrato should not be viewed as the most practical vibrato for him to use.

Considering the practical aspects of voluntary vibrato, it can be observed that some double-reed students simply cannot develop diaphragmatic vibrato, no matter how conscientious their efforts may be. In such cases the only recourse for vibrato to be achieved is to try to develop jaw vibrato. In this regard the application of jaw vibrato to bassoon is much more feasible than to oboe, due to the fact that the bassoonist's reed is considerably larger than that of the oboist. With serious study and practice, jaw vibrato can work very effectively on bassoon.

Applying jaw vibrato to oboe is generally viewed as impractical by many woodwind teachers; this is quite understandable. However, for those oboists who find diaphragmatic vibrato to be simply beyond their capacity, it is recommended that they at least try jaw vibrato before ruling it out. This recommendation is based on the author's personal experience, having personally listened to a highly successful symphony oboist who uses jaw vibrato. Upon first hearing this solo oboist in concert, the author assumed that a natural or diaphragmatic vibrato was being employed, due to its consummate beauty. In a subsequent discussion with the soloist, the author was delightedly surprised to learn that this assumption was wrong—jaw vibrato was being used by the soloist, and beautifully so. Since the oboe reed is the smallest and most sensitive of all the reeds, it takes considerable patience and effort to successfully apply jaw vibrato to it, but it can be done. While this may work for only a few, the learner who has reached an impasse with his attempts to develop diaphragmatic vibrato on oboe may be comforted to know that there is an alternative approach.

Developing Jaw Vibrato

Jaw vibrato is unquestionably the most widely used type of vibrato among single-reed instrumentalists. It is a practical and effective type of vibrato which any single-reed student can develop with practice in a relatively short period of time. While it is possible to master jaw vibrato within a week, many students will usually require several weeks of study and practice.

The key points to bear in mind in the development of both jaw and diaphragmatic vibrato center on these aspects: gradualism, exaggeration, and consistency. The author uses and recommends the following approach in teaching and developing jaw vibrato.

Jaw vibrato is produced through a biting motion of the lower jaw. Ideally, it is best to demonstrate this so that the student may see the slight movement in the lower jaw and hear the resulting sound. Understandably, a live demonstration may not always be possible, nor is it absolutely required; but it is highly desirable. Next, while the student is sustaining a full, straight tone have him increase the pressure (bite) from the lower jaw until he almost chokes the tone; this should be a *gradual* upward movement. Then have him relax the lower-jaw pressure, again gradually. The diagram in Figure 160 can be of immense help at this initial stage of development. It should be noted that the arrows indicate the movement of the lower jaw.

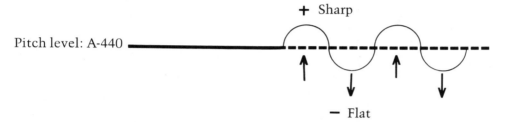

FIGURE 160

It is very important for students to realize that the waves or pulsations should be evenly divided above and below the fixed pitch level established by the sustained straight tone. The easiest thing to do wrong in the beginning is to make the waves lopsided or uneven by allowing the lower jaw to drop disproportionately to its upward movement. Such a vibrato form may be depicted as in Figure 161.

FIGURE 161

In this instance the performer would be playing on the low side of the established pitch level. Since the downward stroke of the jaw is the easiest to produce, the tendency is to elongate it. Consequently, it is best to have the student start with an *upward* movement of the lower jaw and then strive to match this movement on the downstroke.

In the initial stage of development the vibrato is supposed to sound exaggerated—which is in no way appealing to the ear—but very gradual and perfectly even. Silently pronouncing the syllable "ya" will help the student considerably in keeping the throat open and the tongue down. Remind him that as the speed of the waves is increased, there is a natural tendency for the exaggerated size of the pulsations to diminish. This is actually a self-adjusting matter, to a certain extent. But if the beginning jaw movement is too small, the subsequent pulsations will diminish excessively, making the waves lack sufficient breadth and depth to create a vibrato with clear definition *at a distance*. (Note that a well-defined vibrato may appear to have too much breadth and depth five feet in front of the performer; twenty-five to one hundred feet back in an auditorium is the more appropriate distance to judge the "finished" vibrato.)

Considering the broad stages in developing either jaw or diaphragmatic vibrato, the initial phase is literally a "crawling" stage where exaggerated pulsations, gradualness of speed, and consistent evenness are the key points on which to concentrate. In this stage one pulsation—or "ya"—would occur on each rhythmic beat (forty-four to fifty per minute). In the second stage, the "walking" stage, the pulsations should increase from two to four waves ("ya's") per rhythmic beat. In the final "running" stage the pulsations range from four to six per rhythmic beat. Of utmost importance is the fact that *one must not try to move from one broad stage to the other too soon*. Graduated changes in speed are absolutely essential to achieving evenness and consistency in the vibrato wave form.

There are two ways to apply meter to jaw vibrato in the developmental stage; it is imperative to use one of these basic approaches. However, after the vibrato is developed and refined, conscious thought of meter as stressed in the developing period is not needed, nor is it necessarily advisable.

The first approach may be handled as follows: First, have the student sustain a tone for two beats to establish the fixed pitch level and then alternately bite upward and relax the jaw on each of beats 1, 2, 3, and 4.

STAGE 1

(F above middle C is a good starting note for saxophones.) The object here is to begin stage 1 slowly and then *gradually increase* the speed. When the speed of the vibrato begins to approach that found in stage 2, subdivide the number of jaw movements (represented by arrows and the syllable "ya") over the basic rhythmic pulse. (See metronomic marking, stage 2.)

STAGE 2

In order to avoid confusion, an upward-pointing arrow is used for the *beginning upward* movement of the jaw *only in the initial stage* (see Figure 160). After one's initial strokes are balanced and even, conscious thought of starting vibrato on the up part of the beat is not needed or practical. Subsequent use of arrows is then best done to indicate the correlation between the pulsations of jaw and the basic quarter note beat which is used in each example (see stages 1, 2, and 3).

Eventually the speed can be increased, and four jaw movements may be placed on each rhythmic beat.

Ch. 10/Vibrato

STAGE 3

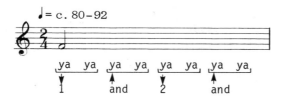

In the final stage, four to six pulsations of the jaw can be placed on each beat—depending, of course, on the tempo and the requirements of good musical taste. It must be pointed out that steps 1, 2, and 3 represent broad stages of development. There should be numerous gradations in vibrato speed between stage one and the final stage.

The second approach toward meter—which some students develop or discover on their own—involves *imitation*. Have the student think of how a train sounds when it begins to move. Then have him substitute the syllables "ya-ya" for the train's "shoo-shoo" as he alternately bites upward with the jaw and relaxes—always striving to keep the jaw movement even and perfectly controlled. The movement of the lower jaw should imitate the gradual increase in speed one associates with a train beginning to move.

The following points may well arise with students working on vibrato:

1. Often students want to proceed from the slow, exaggerated initial stage immediately to stage two. While exceptional students can do this, many more will require two to three weeks to make such an advance.

2. Advise the student that the moment his vibrato becomes uneven he has reached that point where he should stop increasing speed and should rework all lower speeds for several days. At the end of this brief remedial period most students can then proceed to a slightly faster rate of pulsation. When the rate increase reaches a new point where the vibrato becomes shaky and uneven, the same remedial process should be repeated; the student should simply retard the rate of pulsation for a few days and then strive for a new mark in speed. The development of jaw vibrato is physical and not unlike the physical discipline an athlete undertakes, as in pole-vaulting, where the bar is gradually raised over a period of time in developing skill at jumping heights.

3. Invariably, many students fail to realize that the exaggerated, wide pulsation in the initial stages of developing vibrato is necessary. Remind such students that this exaggerated phase is only temporary.

4. Occasionally a student may be observed moving the jaw forward rather than up, as in biting or chewing. Only the vertical movement of the jaw is needed or recommended.

Developing Diaphragmatic Vibrato

Many of the requirements necessary to developing diaphragmatic vibrato are identical to those for jaw vibrato. Self-imposed physical discipline, such key concepts as exaggeration, gradualism, balanced wave form, and consistency are essential aspects in teaching and developing either type of vibrato. The main point of divergence between the two types rests with the exciting agent—that part of the body which physically causes the pulsating wave form. While the movement of the lower jaw is the physical cause in jaw vibrato, it is the respiratory system that initiates movement in diaphragmatic vibrato.

The following approach is recommended for developing diaphragmatic vibrato. The author is indebted to Alfred Fenboque, former solo flutist with the Cincinnati Symphony and professor of flute at the Cincinnati Conservatory of Music, for the essential concept of this approach. The visual and verbal embellishments added by the author in no way alter the basic ideas of Professor Fenboque and have been included in the hope of enhancing this presentation.

Diaphragmatic vibrato is produced with one's breath and respiratory system. Ideally, a live demonstration of this should be presented, if at all possible. Have your student take a large breath, flex his lips to form a small aperture, and then gradually expel the air through it. The stream of air should be continuous and uninterrupted. Next, repeat this series of actions; this time have the student silently repeat the word "who" slowly while expelling the air. Thinking and saying the word "who" silently (or in a soft, audible manner) will activate the respiratory system in such a way that pulsations in the flow of air occur. At this beginning stage the object is to initiate movement or pulsations in the *continual* flow of air. There should be no stop in the flow of air—only continual pulsations with a high point and a low ebb in aural character should occur. Repeat this entire series of actions again; this time have the student hold his hand directly in front of his face in order to feel the highs and lows in the air flow.

The author has never encountered a student of music who could not execute this basic initial pulsation movement within one lesson meeting. With younger students it is recommended that they do these aforementioned steps for a few minutes daily as part of their lesson assignment. After the first week the matter of developing speed, form, consistency, and evenness should be handled in a gradual and structured manner using both *meter* and *imitation* as guides.

The second step is to take the instrument and repeat the basic steps executed in the first stage. Diaphragmatic vibrato is primarily used by flutists; a good starting tone on flute is the second D above middle C. First, the student should sustain the D in a straight tone (no pulsation) long enough to establish a fixed pitch level, and then play the series of silent "who's" in meter, very slowly at first (one pulsation per beat).

Remind the student that the pulsations should be even and consistent in size and speed. Use graphic illustrations such as Figure 162.

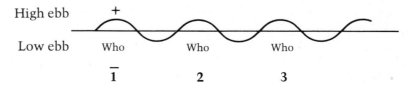

FIGURE 162

Fortunately, diaphragmatic vibrato tends to "divide itself" evenly above and below the established, fixed pitch level—quite unlike jaw vibrato, where the tendency is to make the low side of the pulsation greater than the top side. Still, occasionally a flute student will fail to listen attentively and will distort the balance and evenness that is desired. There is a way to check on this, and it can be shown to the student very simply. At the close of one or two measures of vibrato, have him cease using vibrato and continue with a straight tone. If there is a noticeable rise or fall in the pitch level of the original straight tone, then the waves were obviously uneven on one side or the other of the established, fixed pitch level.

After the student can manage quarter-note pulsations with balance, control, and evenness, proceed to subdivide the rhythmic beats as follows (arrows indicate pulsations):

When the student is ready to increase the speed of the pulsations and is approaching the second broad stage of development, the following pattern may be used:

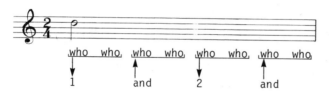

The development of speed in diaphragmatic vibrato should be governed by the same rules previously outlined for jaw vibrato. In the final phase of the third broad stage of development, the following rhythmic pattern may be used to achieve six pulsations per rhythmic beat:

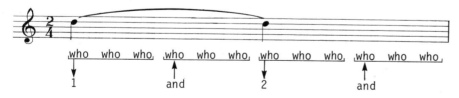

The aforementioned examples represent the broad stages of development. The learner must experience and practice the numerous gradations of speed that occur from stage one through the final stage. It should be pointed out that the use of meter in the study of vibrato is primarily for developmental purposes. After a working command of vibrato is achieved, the conscious use of a meter pattern to produce vibrato should be dismissed. A functional working command of vibrato permits the performer to slow or increase the rate of his vibrato according to the dictates of good musical taste without having to count a specific number of pulsations. Questions concerning how fast or slow the "finished" vibrato should be executed must be answered with appropri-

Secondary Factors/Part III

ate qualifications. For all practical purposes, a rate of four waves per rhythmic beat (with a tempo marking of eighty-two beats per minute) represents a speed that I as a performer use with considerable frequency. However, I also frequently use a much slower vibrato in the lowest register of my instrument, and, conversely, a faster vibrato in the highest register. The reasons for this variation in vibrato frequency are purely aesthetic in nature and represent the influence which both singers and violinists have had on my personal musical tastes. Unquestionably one of the best guides for the application of vibrato in a musical and artistic manner is the work of major artists, vocal and instrumental.

The subsequent points should be used as key reminders for the student studying diaphragmatic vibrato:

1. The exaggerated size and speed of pulsation in the initial stage is absolutely imperative if the final vibrato form is to have clear definition of breadth and depth.

2. As the rate of pulsation is increased, the size of the waves will generally diminish automatically. If not, conscious effort must be exerted to mold the form of the waves to become balanced.

3. During the development period, always stop when you reach that speed at which the pulsations become uneven. At that point slow the vibrato down, and do remedial work for a few days before trying to reach a new goal of increased speed.

4. Generally speaking, it takes much longer to develop a refined control over diaphragmatic vibrato than over jaw vibrato. Depending on the student, a working command of diaphragmatic vibrato can be achieved within several months of conscientious and structurally directed study.

Index

A

Air flow, continuity of, 9
  and flute, 17
  and double reeds, 14
  and single reeds, 11–12
Alto clarinet, E-flat, 138
  embouchure modifications for, 140
Alto saxophone, E-flat, 179
Aperture
  approximate dimensions for, 78
  angled oboe, 72
  openings for double reeds, 222
  preset, 10
Aperture, flute
  alignment, 38
  as a controlling point, 17
  for different registers, 18, 35
  flexibility exercises, 22, 59
  format, 34
  and harmonics, 56–57
  self-adjustment of, 18, 38
  types of, 38–39
Applied methods, major, 64; *see also* Bassoon literature; Clarinet literature; Flute literature; Oboe literature; Saxophone literature
Arundo donax sativa, 209
Assembly and care, instrument
  bassoon, 146–147
  clarinet, 104–105
  flute, 28–30
  oboe, 70–71
  saxophone, 180–182
Attitude and achievement, 154–155
Aural acuteness, 4, 9
Aural guidelines, establishing, 10, 41, 186

B

"Back air pressure," oboe, 79
Baritone saxophone, E-flat
  embouchure for, 207–208
  picture of, 206
  study material for, 208
Bass clarinet, B-flat
  embouchure for, 140
  picture of, 138
  study material for, 141–143
Bassoon, 145
Bassoon embouchure
  development of, 149–150
  format recommended for, 149
  lower-jaw placement for, 74, 110, 149
  parallel grip vs. offset grip, 149, 152–153
  "Pencil Exercise" for, 149–150
  remedial work for, 150–151
Bassoon key system
  attitude toward, 154–155
  discussion of, 153
  problems of, 154
Bassoon literature
  class methods, 63–64
  graded solos, 174–175
  individual methods, 176
  supplemental studies, 176
Bassoon recordings
  pedagogically oriented, 176–177
  special collections of, 177
  traditional, 177–178
Bassoon students, criteria for prospective, 148
Bell tones: *see* Tone, "bell"
Brahms, Johannes, 129–130
Breaker keys, 17; *see also* Speaker keys
Breath attacks, 42, 81
Breathing habits, 10
Breath support
  aural acuteness and, 9

235

Breath support *(continued)*
    and bassoon, 151–153
    and clarinet, 112–113
    as a common denominator, 17
    definition of, 9
    and double reeds, 14–17
    and flute, 17–23, 39–40
    and instrument angle, 8
    as a major determinant, 8–11
    and oboe, 78–80
    as a primary factor, 7
    and remedial work, 13, 17
    and saxophone, 185–186
    and single reeds, 11–14
Bridge keys
    on bassoon, 146–147
    on clarinet, 104–105

C

"Carry over" habits: *see* Oboe embouchure
Clarinet, 103
Clarinet embouchure
    exercise for, 110
    format recommended for, 109
    lower-jaw placement for, 74, 110
    lower-lip placement for, 76
    mouthpiece exercise for, 111–112
Clarinet literature
    class methods, 63–64
    graded solos, 133–134
    individual methods, 135
    supplemental studies, 135
Clarinet literature, lower
    for beginners, 141–142
    for transfer students, 142–143
    supplemental, 143
Clarinet Performance Practices and Teaching in the United States and Canada (Gold), 227n.
Clarinet recordings
    pedagogically oriented, 136
    special collections of, 136–137
    traditional, 137
Clarinets, lower: *see* Lower clarinets
Cleaning rod: *see* Tuning rod, flute
Closed-ring flute, 27–28

Contrabass clarinet, E-flat, 138
    embouchure modifications for, 140–141
"Crow," 77
"Cupid's bow"
    absence of, 39
    accommodating, 38–39
    unaccommodating, 4n., 38–39

D

Delayed tongue release: *see* Techniques, advanced performance
Delmas, Marc, 11
Diaphragmatic vibrato: *see* Vibrato, types of
Double reeds
    adjusting and making, reference for, 224
    with blades aligned, 223
    with blades slipped, 223
    care of, 224
    color of, 222
    cracking of, 222
    grain in, 222
    strength of, 221–222
    tip openings for, 222
    "top" and "bottom" sides of, 72
Double tonguing, 42–43

E

Embouchure: *see also* Bassoon; Clarinet; Flute; Oboe; Saxophone
    basic format of, 8
    definition of, 7
    exceptions, 7
    as a primary factor, 7
    types of, 7–8
Extended portamento: *see* Techniques, advanced performance

F

Fantaisie Italienne (Delmas), 11
Fenboque, Alfred, 232

Fingering chart, standard
for bassoon, 157–158
for clarinet, 117–119
for flute, 45–46
for oboe, 83–85
for saxophone, 189–190
Fingerings, frequently used special
for bassoon, 166–170
for clarinet, 125–130
for flute, 54–57
for oboe, 91–93
for saxophone, 196–199
Flexibility exercises, flute
and aperture size, 22
and breath pressure, 22–23
and jaw movement, 22
Flick keys: *see* Speaker keys, bassoon
Flute
closed-ring, 27
open-ring, 27
Flute and Its Daily Routine, The (Moore), 12, 33, 65
Flute embouchure
aperture alignment for, 38
aperture shape, 39
aperture size for, 17–18, 22, 33–35
exceptions and deviations, 37
format recommended for, 33–35
performance practices for, 37
purpose of, 33
and register changes, 17
and the "sardonic smile," 36
teaching aids for, 36
Flute literature
class methods, 63–64
graded solos, 60–63
individual methods, 64–65
supplemental studies, 65
Flute recordings
pedagogically oriented, 65–67
traditional, 67
Flutist's Guide, The (Wilkins), 65–66
Flutter tonguing: *see* Techniques, advanced performance
French model flute: *see* Flute, open-ring

G

Gallodora, Alfred, 140
Gold, Cecil V., 227

H

Half-hole fingerings
on bassoon, 166–167
on oboe, 92
Hand position
bassoon, 148
clarinet, 106–109
flute, 30, 32–33
oboe, 72–73
saxophone, 181–182
Harmonic fingerings
flute, 56–57
oboe, 93
Head-joint, flute
initial alignment of, 31–32
picture of, 29
Head-joint interval exercise
exceptions in execution of, 23
performance of, 20
purpose of, 19
as a teaching aid, 60
Heckel, Wilhelm, 166
Heckel system bassoon, 145

I

Imagery and visual aids
cognition, related to, 41
pitch perception, applied to, 113
timbre, applied to, 41
tone, applied to, 13
and principle of contrast, 41
Introducing the Alto or Bass Clarinet (Voxman), 142–143
Instrument angle
bassoon, 147
clarinet, 106
flute, 30–31
oboe, 71–72
saxophone, 181–182

L

"Less fingers means more air": *see also* Thorton, James
applied to bassoon, 151–152
applied to oboe, 79
applied to saxophone, 186

Literature: *see* Bassoon; Clarinet; Flute; Oboe; Saxophone
Long fingerings: *see* Harmonic fingerings
Lower clarinets
  embouchure modifications for, 140–141
  individual suitability for, 139–140
  literature for, 63–64, 141–143
  starting beginners on, 139–140
  transferring students to, 139–140
Lower saxophones
  embouchure for, 207–208
  recommended study material for, 63–64, 203–204
  starting students on, 207–208
  transferring students to, 207–208

M

Malocclusion, 37n.
Manual interval mechanism: *see* Head-joint interval exercise
Mazzeo model clarinet, Selmer, 103
Minor instrument study
  advantages of group, 4–5
  current practice in, 3–5
  group vs. individual, 3–5
Moore, E.C., 12–13, 65
Mouthpiece exercise
  for clarinet, 132
  for saxophone, 184
Mouthpieces, single-reed
  American-made, 215
  care of, 213
  European-made, 215
  reference chart for, 210
  selection of, 212–213

N

Noblet model clarinet, Leblanc, 103

O

Oboe, 69
Oboe embouchure
  and the "circular grip," 75

format recommended for, 76
  forming recommended, 75
  influence of "carry over" habits on, 77
  and lower-jaw placement, 74, 110
  and lower-lip placement, 75–76
  teaching aids for, 77–78
  and "tone placement," 74
  and the "vice-like" grip, 75, 79
Oboe literature
  class methods, 9
  graded solos, 97–98
  individual methods, 99
  supplemental studies, 99–100
Oboe recordings
  pedagogically oriented, 100
  special collections of, 100
  traditional, 100–101
Occlusion, normal, 37n.
Octave vent
  on flute, 17
  on oboe, 92
"Open-ring system," 180; *see also* Flute, open-ring
Open tones: *see* Tone, an open
Ornaments: *see* Trills

P

Pitch perception, 4, 113
Plateau model flute: *see* Flute, closed-ring
Principle of contrast
  aural guidelines, used to establish, 186
  and breath support, 186
  and class instruction, 3–4
  and Head-joint interval exercise, 20–21, 60
  and pitch perception (tuning), 113
  and timbre, 186
  and tone placement, 9–10, 41
Problem chart
  bassoon, 170–173
  clarinet, 131–132
  flute, 58–59
  oboe, 94–96
  saxophone, 200–201

R

Recordings: *see* Bassoon; Clarinet; Flute; Oboe; Saxophone
Record-text publications
   The Flutist's Guide (Wilkins), 65–66
   "Laureate Series of Contest Solos" (MMO), 65–66, 136, 204–205
   Three Pieces for Clarinet: Composition, Performance, and Analysis (Saucier), 136
Reed alignment
   for oboe, 72
   on clarinet, 105
Reed-blades, oboe, 221
   aligned, 222–223
   slipped, 223
Reed-blades, bassoon, 221
   aligned, 222–223
   slipped, 223
Reed cane: *see* Double reeds; Single reeds
Reed-making, double
   references for bassoon, 224
   references for oboe, 224
Reed, student-line bassoon, 221
Reference chart, fingering
   for bassoon, 156, 160, 166–167, 170
   for clarinet, 116, 120, 125, 167
   for flute, 44, 48, 54
   for oboe, 82, 86, 90
   for saxophone, 188, 192, 196
Register (twelfth) key, 116; *see also* Twelfth key
Remedial work
   in bassoon, 17, 171–173
   in clarinet, 13, 131–132
   in flute, 58–59
   in oboe, 17, 95–96
   in saxophone, 13, 200–201

S

"Sardonic smile"
   for initial work, 36
   for remedial work, 58
Saucier, Gene: *Three Pieces for Clarinet: Composition, Per-*
formance, and Analysis, 11, 136
   vibrato, and personal use of, 234
Sax, Adolphe, 192
Saxophone, 179
Saxophone embouchure
   and the "circular grip," 185
   and an ineffective grip, 183
   and the mouthpiece exercise, 184
   and the pencil exercise, 184
   recommended, 183–184
Saxophone literature
   class methods, 63–64
   graded solos, 202–203
   individual methods, 203–204
   supplementary studies, 204
Saxophone recordings
   pedagogically oriented, 204–205
   special collections, 205
   traditional, 205
Saxophones, lower: *see* Lower saxophones
Selmer release attack: *see* Techniques, advanced performance
Single reeds
   American-made, 215
   care of, 219
   color of, 215
   European-made, 215
   grade of, 219
   grain patterns in, 215–219
   heels and rim lines in, 219
   nomenclature for, 213–215
   reference chart for, 214
   selection of, 213–219
   suitable for recital work, 216–217
   unsuitable for recital work, 217–218
   "windows" in, 216
Sonata for Clarinet and Piano, Op. 120, No. 1 (Brahms), 130
Sonata for Clarinet and Piano, Op. 120, No. 2 (Brahms), 129–130
Speaker keys, bassoon, 156, 160, 166, 169–170
"Splitting tones," 18
Stopper cap, flute, 29
Student Instrumental Course series, Belwin-Mills, 141–142
Study questions
   Bassoon (Chapter 6), 173
   Clarinet (Chapter 5), 130
   Flute (Chapter 3), 57–58

Study questions (continued)
  General Aspects of Woodwind
    Study (Chapters 1 and 2), 23–24
  Oboe (Chapter 4), 94
  Saxophone (Chapter 7), 199
Swab, turkey feather, 71

T

"Taps," 59
Teaching aids
  bassoon, 173–174
  clarinet, 132–133
  flute, 60
  oboe, 96–97
  saxophone, 201–202
Teaching resources
  based on deductive observation, 3
  based on personal experience, 3
  utilization of, 3
Techniques, advanced performance
  extended portamento, 111
  delayed tongue release, 112
  flutter tonguing, 111
  Selmer release attack, 112
Tenor saxophone, B-flat, 206
Thornton, James, 14
"3-and-3 Exercise"
  for bassoonists, 151–152
  and breath support, 112
  and ear training, 154n.
  explanation of, 12–13
  for flute, 19
  and hand position, 108–109
  for oboe, 79–80
  for saxophonists, 186
  for single reeds, 12–13
Three-D's octave exercise, 16, 80, 97
Three Pieces for Clarinet (Saucier), 11, 136
Tonal line
  bassoon, 15, 151, 171
  clarinet, 14, 112–113
  definition of, 40
  flute, 17–19, 40
  oboe, 16, 78–80
  saxophone, 14, 185–186
Tone
  "bell," 9
  breathy, 41

centered, 41, 186
focused, 39
full, 9
open, 9
overblown, 39
pinched, 15–16
"placement," 41, 74, 186
"splitting" a, 18
throat, 9
underblown, 39
Tone perception, developing
  breath support, as related to, 9
  pitch, as related to, 4, 113
  timbre, as related to, 4, 40, 41
  tonal line, as related to, 13, 14, 40
Tone production
  and primary factors, 7
  and secondary factors, 7
Tonguing
  for bassoonists, 152–153
  for clarinetists, 113–115
  for flutists, 41–43
  for oboists, 81
  for saxophonists, 187
Transfer students, 142–143; *see also* Lower clarinets, transferring students to
Trill chart, standard
  bassoon, 161–165
  clarinet, 121–124
  flute, 49–53
  oboe, 87–90
  saxophone, 193–196
Trills, 48
Tuning rod, flute, 29
Turkey feather: *see* Swab, turkey feather
Twelfth (register) key, 17; *see also* Register key

V

Vamp, B-flat clarinet reed, 105
Vandoren
  mouthpiece, 211
  reeds, 213–215
Vibrato
  choice of, 227–228

definition of, 225–226
development of, 228–234
purpose of, 225
types of, 227
use of, esthetic, 225, 233–234
Visual reminders, 174
Voxman, Himie: *Introducing the Alto or Bass Clarinet*, 142–143

W

"W-cut" oboe read
   external view of, 221–223
   internal view of, 96
Whisper key, 166
"Window," 216*n.*
Wilkins, Fred: *The Flutist's Guide*, 65–66